THE
BICYCLE
MAN

A Novel by

BOB DEANS

EVENING POST
BOOKS

Published by
Evening Post Books
Charleston, South Carolina

Copyright © 2020 by Bob Deans
All rights reserved.
First edition

Editor: John M. Burbage
Designer: Gill Guerry
Cover Design: Karen Deans

First printing 2020
Printed in the United States of America

A CIP catalog record for this book has been applied for from the Library of Congress.

ISBN: 978-1-929647-50-7

For Conrad

 Prologue

Sandy Rivers stepped from the crowded elevator and into the Richmond Times-Daily newsroom, looked up and saw a gangly figure bounding from the managing editor's office and headed his way.

"I'm on it," Rivers called out. "Just spoke with …"

"That story can hold a day," his editor fired back, as Rivers tossed a dog-eared notebook onto his desk.

"Look Rivers, you haven't filed your expenses since June. I gave you a November deadline. Now it's December. Hell, it's got'ta be close to two hundred dollars."

It wasn't exactly news to Rivers, but it was painful to have to listen to it all the same.

"Now, you're not making a phone call today, you're not writing a sentence, not a word, 'til you've straightened this out with accounting. We're done."

Rivers looked at the greying newsroom relic, a crumbling pillar of ravaged potential, his bony chest heaving beneath a threadbare shirt.

"Yes, sir."

Rivers slumped into his chair and pushed away a nest of newspaper clips, business cards and press releases on his desk. In nearly a decade at the Times-Daily, he'd gone from writing about school board meetings and garden club awards to the paper's premier beat, covering the state legislature, making him, at 34, one of the most influential reporters in Virginia. That wasn't much what he felt like, though, as he turned over a dented coffee can to spill out the crumpled receipts, scraps of paper and other remnants of parking fees, lunch bills and dinner tabs he'd piled up in four months of statehouse reporting.

He leaned forward, dropped his head in his hands and caught a headline low on the Times-Daily front page: "Roy Orbison; Dead at 52."

"Can't be," he whispered, skimming the December 6, 1988 wire-service tribute to the Texas crooner with the warbling falsetto, as almost forgotten lyrics wandered into Rivers' mind like ghosts. "Too soon. Way too soon."

He turned the page to read the jump, but his paper had been gutted. He shot an accusatory glare at his rookie desk mate, stood up and headed across the newsroom to the obituary desk.

"No, no, get back man," said Timmy Toussaint, a veteran newsman with failing knees. "The idea is to stay off the obits desk, remember? Here lies death."

Here lies death, indeed, thought Rivers. Beside a hand-scrawled list of the city's cemeteries, funeral parlors, hospitals and morgues, Toussaint maintained a large spiral notebook, a log of those he eulogized on deadline each day. As he finished each obituary, Toussaint methodically tucked away a copy and struck through the name with blood-red ink in what he reverentially called "The Book of the Dead."

It was to that grim compendium Rivers quickly turned for clues to the full story on Roy Orbison when Toussaint admonished him once more, quoting Richmond's own patron saint of the macabre, Edgar Allan Poe: "Death man, cold and still. Get thee back into the tempest, and the night's Plutonian shore."

Something, though, caught Rivers' eye. Jutting from the pages of Toussaint's notebook was a faded photograph of an elderly man astride what appeared to be an equally aged bicycle. Sandy stared into the picture as if he'd lost something there, picked it up and tilted it against the glare of the fluorescent newsroom lights.

"Who's this guy," he asked, as Toussaint stepped behind him, took the picture from his hand and consulted the "Book of the Dead."

"Henry Clayton Woods. Died in his home out on Midsummer Night's Lane. Seventy-two. Coupl'a kids. Grandkids. Gon'na be buried this morning, I b'lieve."

"Wha'd you say?"

"Well, hell, read the damned thing yourself."

Rivers stared at the page like it was a stone.

"Time's the funeral?"

"'Leven this mornin', says here," Toussaint replied, turning toward a clock on the newsroom wall. "Started twenty minutes ago."

Rivers heard the soft ping of the elevator bell. A woman stepped out, the down arrow went green and Rivers bolted toward the empty chamber.

"Wait a second, let me tell you where the damned funeral service is," Toussaint said.

Rivers froze for a moment and felt an eternity blast through him. He stepped into the elevator and left the newsroom behind.

"Oh, I know where it is," he said, as much to himself as to the worn little man frantically leafing through his notes. The doors closed, the buzz of the newsroom melted away and Rivers felt himself free-falling through a cluttered corridor of years and into the distant reaches of his own boyhood.

"Yeah." He let out a deep breath. "I know where it is."

# Chapter 1

Starlight sifted through the canopy of pines beyond Sandy's open window and fell like the dust of silver across the bed where he lay sleeping. A tattered set of blinds chattered softly in the April breeze. The alarm clock sounded from his nightstand, Sandy threw his arm across his sheets and groped in the darkness.

"I win," he groaned, heaving out the first deep breath of the day and rolling his legs over the side of the bed. "If that's what you call winning."

He turned on the lamp and squinted: five a.m. He pulled on his jeans, tied his sneakers and scanned the room.

"There you are," he whispered, rising to grab a pair of wire cutters from atop his bookcase. He flicked off the lamp, stole quietly down the hallway and walked out of his family's house on a hill above a tarred-and-graveled lane. Morning air, cool and moist, washed over his face. Walking down the front steps, he saw the mist of his breath against the delicate points of a crescent moon slung low in the western sky. At the base of a broad fir tree, nestled in a bed of needles, his bicycle lay on its side.

It was red where it wasn't rusted, and a trace of moonlight shimmered off the large wire basket he'd bought at the Broad Street Pep Boys the Saturday before. He'd spent much of Sunday bolting it to his handlebars, adjusting its height and pitch, before taking over his newspaper route.

Sandy lifted his steed of spokes and steel, sat on the dew-covered seat and felt a chill move through his body. He coasted down the slope, onto the street and into the perfect emptiness the night left behind.

His world lay shuttered and sleeping. The soft whir of his wheels was all he heard as he glided past darkened lawns, somnolent Chevys, Buicks and Fords, and the silent suburban forms of ditches, driveways and shrubs. Rising onto his pedals to meet the grade of the road, Sandy began to sing to himself, "And when I see the sign, that points one wa-ay . . ."

He leaned right into a bend in the road and looked up toward a pale lamp on a creosoted pole at the top of the long hill ahead. He stood hard on his pedals and felt his chest open. "Just walk a-way Renee, you won't see me follow you back home . . ."

Breathing heavily at the crest, he wheeled left onto the rolling blacktop of Misty Hollow Road. He glanced over his shoulder toward a plank fence, its warped and wooden shoulders slouching along the thinly forested border of a broad field of wild grass and cane. He coasted past a vacant clapboard building that once housed a one-room sewing shop. He remembered standing there as a child, on dusty wooden floors, while his mother searched through bolts of brightly colored fabric, endless spools of thread and files of patterns printed on thin paper that crinkled like music when she unfolded them to see hairline sketches of summer shifts and pleated skirts.

The time-weathered little building held down a triangular lot wedged inside a yawning fork, where Misty Hollow merged into Ridgetop Road, a serpentine ribbon of asphalt skirting the gentle crest of a hill that rose from the north bank of the great river several miles away.

As he rolled through the quiet junction, Sandy felt the pavement flatten. Two lanes stretched out before him toward a distant traffic light then disappeared into the soft and frayed edges of darkness beyond.

To Sandy's right and just back from the road, three small brick houses lined a dirt driveway that crossed a narrow ditch. Large stones, half-buried and painted white, marked common ground connecting the cluster of homes lit by a single bulb that dangled bare from an ancient oak. Sandy instinctively wondered whether Old Blue was tied up to the tree so he couldn't sprint out after cars and paperboys. He didn't see the dog anywhere, a momentarily worrisome thought, even if folks had stopped calling him Big Blue since he slowed with age and picked up a slight limp.

Sandy veered left and felt his wheels drop onto the hardscrabble surface of the paper stop, a vacant lot with a large, wire-mesh trashcan under a telephone pole. A single street lamp cast a pale and faintly pulsing light upon the wood-strut carcass of a summer vegetable stand. A torn and faded sheet of canvas, gone the reddish-brown hue of the dirt, sagged over empty bins like the windless sail of some phantom ship adrift on a sea of clay.

It was on that patch of unwanted land, sandwiched between the First Methodist Church of Tuckahoe and the Sinclair gas station, where the papers arrived each morning. Sometime between four-thirty and five, a wrinkled but sturdy old man pulled up in a white step van with "Richmond Times-Daily" painted across it, slung open a wide door and heaved out bundles, each wrapped in brown kraft paper and bound with a single strand of silvery wire.

Sandy leaned his bike against the telephone pole and searched in the dim light for the bundle with an envelope that read F-45. He ran his thumb down the smooth, straight spines of freshly printed newspapers, counting softly to himself, one for each of the eighty-eight customers on his route.

In the soft lamplight he saw the front page, its crisp black letters chiseled into newsprint. "Richmond Times-Daily," it read in bold Cloister type. "Largest Morning Circulation in Virginia."

Sandy strained to read the dateline.

"Thursday, April 4, 1968."

And below it, in large block type stripped across the top of all eight news columns, was a two-deck headline: "Hanoi Agrees to Preliminary Talks, Dropping Demand All Raids End First."

Sandy shrugged, slipped his fingers beneath the wire to pick up the bundle and heard a vile and caustic laugh. A heavy bike veered off the roadway and skidded wildly before slamming into Sandy's bike, knocking it onto the hard-packed clay.

"Get your crap bike out'ta my way," the rider sputtered, as Sandy straightened up, startled, and tried to figure out how best to respond to the morning salutation of Wade Eckert.

"Ah, sorry Wade," was all that came out as Sandy picked up his bike.

"Sorry's right," Wade spat back. "That's my light pole."

Trailing along behind was Paul, Wade's younger brother, who pulled in and brought his bike to a halt.

"Morning Sandy," Paul said with an apologetic air.

"Are you his girlfriend or something," Wade snapped. "Get the papers."

At sixteen, Wade was nearly three years older than Sandy and a good eighty pounds heavier. The paper stop was Wade's turf, a sandlot fiefdom he ruled with a tyrant's fury. This was not a morning for trifling with him, thought Sandy, straddling his bike and hauling his bundle up into his basket.

There was a crash, as Wade let his bike fall onto the ground.

"Gim'me a paper," he sputtered, unsheathing a pair of wire cutters from his pocket and lunging toward Sandy's bundle.

"C'mon Wade," he protested, pulling back his bike, listing with the weight of the papers.

"Oh, C'mon Wade," the big guy mocked, raising the pitch of his voice.

He took hold of Sandy's basket with thick, chubby hands, pushed the bike backward and shook the handlebars as Sandy scrambled to keep it from falling over again.

"Wade, stop. Seriously, I don't have any extras."

"Ain't that a damned shame."

In the glow of the streetlamp, Wade's fleshy cheeks seemed about to burst. He took a deep breath, grabbed Sandy's basket and lifted his front wheel off the ground, jamming the steel frame between Sandy's legs.

"Oww, quit it," Sandy let out, as Wade dropped the bike, then shoved it toward Sandy again.

"Did you say somethin' to me?"

"Not really, no."

"Didn't think so."

Wade pressed his wire cutters against the wire holding Sandy's papers together and squeezed. There was a snapping sound and a dull pop as the papers sprang open to fill the basket.

"Get me a good one," Wade said. Sandy reached into the middle of the bundle, carefully grasped a paper and tugged.

"Too tight?" Wade taunted. "I can fix that."

He pressed his heavy hands into the center of the basket and spread the papers apart just enough for Sandy to slip it out.

"For me? Aw, you shouldn't have," said Wade, taking the paper and turning toward Paul.

"Get me two sticks," Wade commanded, yanking out the wire from Sandy's bundle.

"What for?" Paul asked with instantaneous regret, as Wade smacked him across the arm with the paper.

"Alright, alright."

Paul shuffled over to the vegetable stand, scrounged beneath the bins and broke off a splintery slat a couple feet long from the side of a tomato crate. He handed it to Wade, who held it lengthwise over the trash can.

"Get a long one," Wade demanded, as Paul headed toward the high grass, broken bottles, fallen limbs and ragweed at the edge of the lot.

Little good seemed to come of time spent with Wade, Sandy thought. It wasn't that Wade was an altogether bad guy. But he had a mean streak, and a way of bringing on bad luck. This was beginning to have an uneasy feel to it.

Sandy rose on his bike to pedal off, but Wade grabbed hold of his basket.

"Where you think you're going?"

"Deliverin' my route."

"You ain't deliverin' nothin' 'til I say so," Wade snapped, reaching his hand out to take a long, crooked branch Paul held out to him.

"Yeah," Wade clucked, wrapping the wire around the sticks where they joined. He held them up to admire his handiwork — a small wooden cross, about three feet high and a little shorter across. He laid it atop the trash can, began pulling apart Sandy's paper, sheet by sheet, and wrapped the struts of the cross in newsprint, held in place with more wire he culled from the waste bin.

"Load up the bikes," Wade ordered Paul. "Let's go."

The two younger boys walked behind him toward the Sinclair station.

"Hold this," Wade told Paul, handing him the cross. Wade lifted a nozzle from a pump marked "Regular Leaded" and stretched out the long rubber hose. Gasoline dribbled out and soaked into the paper like rain on parched dirt.

Sandy struggled to imagine how gasoline, a cross and Wade's single-minded devotion to malice might be combined for good. He watched him repeat the steps, until the cross was soaked and the smell of gasoline hung heavy in the morning air.

Wade pulled a pack of matches from his pocket and motioned toward the row of small houses across the street.

"Go put it in the middle of that yard," he ordered Paul.

"Then you light it," he said, handing the matches to Sandy.

"What the …?"

"Go on," Wade shot back. "Get goin'."

"Wade," said Paul. "What about the dog?"

"Go to the house on the far right, 'cross from the old store. He won't get you over there."

Paul looked out toward the street, then down at the cross. Sandy could see his hand was shaking.

"You 'fraid of the dog, you pussy?" Wade shot back, his fisted hand cocked. "Go on, 'fore somebody comes."

Paul raced across the street, jumped the ditch and ran up into the yard.

"You too," Wade snarled at Sandy, with a shove against his back.

Sandy bounded into the yard behind Paul, who was pushing the cross into the freshly tilled soil of a cantaloupe patch.

"Light it and let's get out of here," Paul said.

Sandy struck a match, smelled its sulfuric fumes. "Stand back," he warned then flicked it toward the cross.

There was a low, rushing sound, the roar of flame, and the cross was a blazing fountain of fire. It lit a circle of the common ground like daylight spreading out twenty feet or more. Flames flared a brilliant orange against the windows of the tidy, one-story brick house at the far end of the lot, singeing the young cantaloupe shoots, casting the rage of its undulating light against the white stones along the narrow driveway and stirring Old Blue from a fitful sleep. A low growl gurgled up from deep inside, and he lunged, teeth bared and barked like a devil possessed.

"Good God," Sandy sputtered, backing away from the flaming cross.

"Take off," shouted Paul, who was already halfway to the ditch, as Wade pedaled furiously down the flame-lit pavement.

Sandy heard the fierce barking of Old Blue, the sounds of his own panicked breathing and his feet slamming against the road. He slid across the paper stop and clambered onto his bike as Paul pedaled out of sight.

Sandy struggled to get his bike rolling across the loose dirt and onto the road. Smoke rose from the cross and flames lit the front of the tiny home. Then, between a break in the curtains inside a window, Sandy made out what looked like a face. No, there were two, man or woman he couldn't tell.

As he pressed past the house, Sandy felt his front wheel roll off the pavement toward the dew-slicked grass at the edge of a slope. He touched his brakes, his rear wheel locked and the bike slid down the hill, flipped as it hit a shallow gulch and sent Sandy over the handlebars.

# Chapter 2

Sandy sat up in the base of the gully. Old Blue was yelping across the way. A family had been stirred from slumber to dread, a cross still glowing in their yard. Sandy was stuck in a ditch with eighty-seven wet papers to gather and deliver somehow before anyone could figure out he struck the match.

He rolled over on all fours, began collecting the papers scattered around him, then froze at the sound of something headed his way. It began as a tinkling, like a tiny bell. There was steady creaking and the grate of old metal scraping coming toward him, all together and at once. It slowed and stopped.

"Shhh, tha's it ol' boy, shhhhhhhh."

Sandy heard the raspy voice of a man saying something he couldn't make out. Then he heard Old Blue panting. Sandy crawled to the top of the gully, and peered low over the road. The flames had died. In the faint and wavering light cast by the bulb from the old oak tree, he could see a veil of smoke rising from the smoldering cross. People had come out on the porch.

In the road Sandy made out the shadowy outline of an old man on a bicycle with a dim yellow light shining down from the handlebars. The man reached into a sack slung over the back of the bike. Old Blue took something from the man's hand, and quietly wandered back behind the oak tree.

"A'in no damn sense in it," he heard a man holler from the porch.

"Naw, sah, a'in no damn sense a'tall," someone else said. "Third damned time this year, and this time right in the yard. They gon' keep messin' roun' 'til somebody burn the damn house down."

"Mm'hmm," came the steady reply from the man on the bike.

"Ain' yo' damn house, I don't reckon."

"Well, now, tha's a fact," the old man replied in a clear yet somber voice.

"I don't care if they's jus' boys."

"Naw, suh," Sandy heard the man on the bike say, casting a gaze his way.

"Bunch of damned fools. Bunch a damned hooligans, what they are. Somebody ought'd take a strap to ever' last one of 'em. I don't give a good hot-damn. I know they jus' a bunch of damned kids, but this the third time this year, now, and ain' no damned sense in it."

"Ah-right now," the old man on the bike said. Sandy watched him slowly walk the bike backwards then turn it toward the road. "Seein' you got everything pretty much under control, I guess I be muddlin' 'long," he called out to no reply. "I 'spec I be seein' you on Sunday, if not before."

The old man pushed off and began to pedal up the slight grade of Misty Hollow.

Sandy tried to muzzle a gasp, as the pale light from the bike strayed from the road and caught the rim of his basket at the edge of the road.

"Mmhmm," he heard the man faintly.

Sandy lay on the wet grass as the shadowy outline moved ponderously toward him, reprising the tinkling, scraping and grinding he'd heard earlier. He pictured someone sinewy and severe, a retired railroad brakeman perhaps, headed his way.

The light flashed across his face, and Sandy quickly stood and made a pretense of picking up his papers. He waited for a greeting or a scolding, for some sign of recognition or rebuke. But the man just pulled up to the side of the road, cast his light across the scattered papers and slowly shook his head.

"Ain' nothin' more tellin' on a new paperboy than a shiny new basket on a rusted ol' bike," the old man said. "Unless," he chuckled softly, "it's a pile'a wet papers in the ditch."

Sandy wanted to say something, but couldn't imagine what.

"Yes, sir."

He stared curiously at the dented flashlight, strapped with strips from an old inner tube to the bottom of a bent and rusted basket that hung like Monday morning above the front wheel.

In the dim light from across the street, Sandy could make out the muted blue frame. The front tire was trimmed with a half-inch whitewall marked with chalk in the unsteady hand of a child. Strips of aluminum foil wandered like crumpled snakeskin through the spokes of the rear wheel.

A hank of clothesline held a small brass cowbell to the handlebars. Two flashlight batteries and a row of coins were taped across the top bar. A gunnysack with the words "Southern States" written across it hung from fraying shoestrings.

One pedal looked broken. Foam padding spilled from the torn edge of the seat. Atop the rear fender was a small lettuce crate, an empty Coke bottle inside.

"Nice bike," Sandy said.

He looked into the old man's face. He wore thick glasses and his eyes were set back beneath a deeply furrowed brow that hung over his weathered face, like a sunken rooftop on a forgotten porch.

"Well, we still gettin' 'round," came the soft-spoken reply. "And, ah, we keepin' it more or less in the road, if you know what I mean."

Sandy dug both hands into his pockets and looked up in the faint light at the old man. His skin was a deep chestnut color. He had a thin salt-and-pepper beard, and a full head of silvery-white hair, and wore broken-down wingtips with paper-thin soles and no socks to cover his bony ankles. His neck swam through his shirt collar like a penny dropped down a sinkhole. The sleeves finally stopped halfway down his hands, exposing calloused palms and gnarled fingers with nails like clouded amber.

"Now, this ain' really none'a my business, unda'stan," the old man started. "But, 'bout how long you reckon on lettin' those papers lie there in that ditch? Cause I ain' never yet seen 'em git up and stuff they'selves back in the basket."

Sandy heaved a sigh, bent over and picked up his bike. He held it with one hand, grabbed a couple papers and plopped them into the basket. He leaned the bike against a signpost but it slid down on its side, spilling the papers back onto the grass.

"This could take some time," the old man said, leaning back from his handlebars to straighten his back. "But then, it's early."

Sandy walked tentatively toward him.

"Ah, sir?" But that was all he could muster.

The old man ran an open hand down his face.

"Tha' be your way'a askin' fo' help?"

"Yes, sir," said Sandy. "Please. And, if you can't, I'll figure something out."

The old man opened his hands in front of him. "Oh, you'll figure it out, no question," he mused. "Nah sir, ain' no question 'bout that."

He paused, then rolled over to hold Sandy's bike. The boy edged back down the slope, returning with an armful of papers.

"Someone burned a cross in Jimmy Jeter's yard, just across the street, not more'n ten minutes ago," the old man. "I don't guess you saw anything?"

Sandy went cold and hollow inside.

"Me? Uhmm, no sir," he said, as the two of them arranged the papers in the basket. "Don't know anything about that."

The old man looked into Sandy's face. The boy turned away and stared at the ground.

"Mmhmmm," the old man said.

Sandy could still smell the smoke in the air. He absent-mindedly ran his thumb along the damp spines of the papers in his basket.

"Eighty-eight?" the old man asked.

Sandy looked up, puzzled and hesitant.

"Mmhmm," the old man said to himself. He threw a bony leg over his bike and looked away from Sandy. "Jus' like keys on a piano."

The old man peered off down the road.

"You know," he said, "some folks get a kick out of makin' trouble for somebody else." He positioned a foot on a pedal. "Some folks make trouble just 'cause they can. But that don' make it right."

"No, sir," said Sandy. "Don't 'spect it does."

"Mmhmm," the old man said.

He pushed off against the gravel, edged onto the roadway and began making his way into the turn. Sandy watched him disappear into the darkness as the tinkling, scraping and grinding sounds faded into the silence.

# Chapter 3

H ollis T. Smith parted the curtain inside his living room window and peered out toward the street.

"Where's my damn paper," he muttered to himself. "My day, you'd get it here by five-thirty or, by God, there'd be hell to pay."

My day. He wandered off on the thought, saw the warm, green light of summer, a sort of flaring in his mind, felt bare feet shuffling along rough boards, hand-scrubbed cotton against wiry legs. A screen door towered behind him. Clear drops of water shimmered like jewels on the glistening sides of a crystal pitcher atop a table of weathered pine on the porch of an old farm-house. It sat high in the cusp of a hickory grove, where it caught the first of the morning light and the last of the evening breeze.

"My day," he whispered to himself, saw something moving then headed out the front door.

"'Bout damned time," he called out.

"Good, God," replied a startled Sandy. "Sorry, sir," he said. "Good mornin'."

"Mornin' hell, son, it's practically lunch time."

Sandy slipped a paper from his basket and handed it to the man.

"Hang on, where's my paperboy?"

"Well sir," said Sandy, "that's me, I guess. I just started this week."

The old man squinted.

"Don't you live round here?"

"Yes sir, right around the corner."

"You the Rivers boy?"

"Yes, sir. You sold my parents our house, I b'lieve."

"Built it and sold it," the old man said, "if they live here in Hill and Hamlet."

Sandy knew the story, everybody did, about how Smitty built the houses, and the county built the roads, across the old Smith family dairy farm.

"Right about here where we're standing, used to be nothing but a dusty lane leading up to the old house," Smitty said, motioning toward a broad bend in the road. "Many a mornin', just like this one, I'd follow my dad down to the pasture. Minding cows and mending fences. Those were long days — and we got started early."

"Yes, sir," said Sandy.

"Damn right. Grew watermelons, tomatoes, butterbeans. Sold 'em up there along the ridge top road. Raised chickens, shot squirrels, kept hogs down there toward the bottom, hard by the honeysuckle swamp at the end of the road. Talk about work, boy."

Sandy gazed down the road and took a deep breath.

"See' f you can be on time tomorrow, young fella'."

"Yes, sir," said Sandy, rising up to pedal off. "Well, then, I'll see you tomorrow."

"Don't keep me waitin', now."

Coasting downhill, Sandy drifted right and rode his brakes to a stop before a dented mailbox at the gravely edge of 8600 Tempest Lane. The sky had gone a deep shade of blue. He could see the road stretched out before him and fading into the black edges of a broad, sweeping curve.

He stood straddling his bike, pulled a thick, damp paper from his basket, slapped it over the others to break its spine, opened the mailbox and stuffed the paper inside. He felt a snag then heard a tear, as he jammed it into the box.

He rolled forward to 8602. Riveted to the side of the mailbox was a white metal tube with the words Richmond Times-Daily painted in black script. Sandy stopped, folded another paper and tried to push it in, but it wouldn't go. He pulled it out, folded it tighter and forced it into the tube.

"That's two," he said as he pushed off. "Eighty-six to go."

He swerved sharply left to get the boxes at 8603 and 8605. The next house didn't take the paper, so Sandy wheeled past, veering right to 8606, the house at the mouth of the curve in the road.

Before him, Tempest Lane opened and straightened out, serene and undisturbed, a river of tar and crushed stone flowing through a slumbering village of brick and wood, the darkness punctured here and there by soft yellow light spilling from narrow windows onto a closely cropped lawns. He tried to picture the land before the houses were there, before the chickens and cows and hogs.

He imagined his bike as a dugout canoe on a perilous journey into the suburban wilderness, each driveway a tributary flowing past a tiny tribe, his small but sturdy vessel heavy with word of the world beyond. He dipped his paddle into the quiet waters and pulled forward with steady strokes, across the deep middle and into the muddy shallows flowing past the willowed banks of 8607.

"Danger," he whispered, as a black Buick came into view. He reached into his quiver, withdrew a sturdy shaft and in a single motion let it fly. Swift and true it sped through the shadows, the weight of one day's history landing with a thud on the brick porch at 8609.

It was an audacious proposition, when you thought about it, the world in eight straight columns of black and white, written and edited the day before, printed at night while all Virginia slept, and delivered to doorsteps by the thousands before breakfast for six cents a day. A hundred-and-forty-six thousand copies that day. It said so right on the flag across the top of the page, published since the days editorial writers would fight duels on Main Street to defend their honor from slander or slur.

As far as most of Richmond was concerned, the Times-Daily was the absolute and immutable truth, the north star of civic discourse in divisive and uncertain times. There was national television news at night, but it had a temporal, town crier feel to it, a breezy transience that seemed just one step above gossip when compared to the black inky word forever etched in newsprint.

And the word became news at the unerring hands of reporters, remote and almost Delphic figures with the alchemist's gift of rending order from chaos. They were all anyone might expect of a minor god — omniscient, self-directed and utterly remote, unreachable even. Readers never seemed to actually come in contact with them, but their stories became holy writ, daily gospel that, once printed, stood for all time.

And, over the next couple hours, every subscriber on Sandy's route would know the infinite reach of their wisdom: An American helicopter gunship attack killed twenty North Vietnamese in someplace called Khe Sanh; the Supreme Court listened for four hours as lawyers from the National Association for the Advancement of Colored People argued that Virginia schools had yet to comply with 1954 desegregation orders; investors on Wall Street traded 19.3 million shares, shattering the previous record, on news that Hanoi was prepared to talk peace; and President Lyndon Baines Johnson announced at the White House he would go to Hawaii to discuss the overture with generals and diplomats.

It might as well not have happened at all without the newspaper to say so, to explain it, to sort through the rumor and riddle and lies, to tell it straight, lay it out, give it a headline and assign it a place on the page that conferred legitimacy and denoted importance. It was more than a daily newspaper, by God, it was a daily miracle. And it was nothing without a thirteen-year-old boy to pick it up by the bundle in the darkness before dawn and loft it to the porch at 8609.

Sandy felt his tires roll over the flat lawn, then grind through the graveled driveway before he rose back onto the street.

Half an hour later, he'd worked his way to the end of Tempest Lane, delivering even addresses during the last bit of his route and saving the odd ones for his ride back. Against a sky just beginning to lighten, he could make out the tops of the tall pines in the forest at the downward sloping foot of the road. He breathed in the cool air off the small creek that ran along the base of the woods and heard crickets and songbirds from the swamp beyond. He pulled up to the last house on the road, 8727, where Brady Sullivan lived.

No light shone from inside. Sandy slipped a paper into the mailbox and heard something moving through a thicket at the far end of the narrow footpath that ran alongside old man Sullivan's home.

It was a brick split-level, with a shed out back, built of scavenged plywood that never got painted. A bald tire was buried to its shoulders alongside a cement driveway that had long since crumbled and grown over with chickweed. A faded green Ford on cinder blocks was slowly rusting to powder.

Old man Sullivan lived alone in the first house built on Tempest Lane, at the farthest end of the road. He wasn't happy when others moved into the neighborhood and complained about the searing shriek of his chain saw when he put up cordwood each fall. Some boys had seen lights in his basement at night. Ran a still, they said. Then there was the day the county police came to tell him there could be no more gunfire within earshot of the children's bus stop — not even in deer season.

Beyond the stories and rumors, old man Sullivan kept to himself. Tended his vegetable patch in summer. Fiddled around with his truck. Seldom spoke to the colored people who cut along the footpath that ran through the woods alongside his house and emptied beneath the tall sweet gum tree stretched out overtop the Skinquarter A.M.E. Church of God.

It was a short path across a great distance, a sliver of packed dirt and sand wandering a hundred yards or so through pin oaks, holly bushes and sassafras saplings that parted to form the link between the red brick and white plaster splendor of Hill & Hamlet and the unpaved community along Midsummer Night's Lane.

At the halfway point, the path was raised by a smooth root of an old poplar tree, then crossed a shallow stream. From there it left the forest, wound through a small flat of snake grass that skirted a dilapidated plank fence running alongside the honeysuckle swamp and past the small graveyard behind the church.

Sandy heard the noise again. He peered into the blackness of the path. He barely made out the near end of the fence, sagging toward the pathway and held up by a web of waxy thorn stems and woody vines.

There was a flash of movement somewhere beyond the fence. Sandy strained to see, when a brilliant light flooded the edge of the forest, the street and the lawn at old man Sullivan's place. Sandy turned and saw headlights cresting the hill, then recognized the outlines of Winston Coleman's burgundy Mustang, pulling up to a stop beside him.

# Chapter 4

There was only one imaginable reason for Winston Coleman to be there. Sandy's throat tightened as the burning cross, the frightened faces and the angry voice of Jimmy Jeter flooded back in a moment of dread. Sandy shored up his bike beneath him as Winston's window opened, a cloud of cigarette smoke poured out. Sandy heard the sound of an electric guitar slicing through a whiskey-and-honey-soaked voice on the radio.

"Hey Rivers, got your cousin here," Winston said, slapping the steering wheel. "The-ay's a ma-an who-o li-ves a life of da-anga," he sang along then turned down the radio and continued.

"Life of danger, huh Rivers? I don't know, man. Had you figured different." Winston tapped his fingers against the steering wheel.

After five years as a paperboy, Winston had risen to district manager, responsible for all the carriers in his district. Now it was his job to respond to customer complaints, make sure his carriers paid their bills on time each week and to keep his stable of boys on bikes in line on behalf of the company.

Dangling from Winston's rearview mirror was a plastic baby key Mary Kay Bedford had given him recently on his nineteenth birthday. Dashboard lights cast a green and amber glow across the smooth, taught skin of his face as he gazed toward the forest, rolled a hand over a chrome gearshift knob and shoved it into neutral.

"Lightin' crosses in people's yards. Settin' fires. That's bad business," Winston said with a measured shake of his head. "Wrong kind of people get called. Then I get one, I got'ta stop what I'm doin', come out here and take care of it. Yes sir, that's bad business, boy."

Winston reached between his knees for a cardboard carton, raised a pint of orange juice to his lips and drew a long, cold swig.

Sandy had a sudden urge to be back in the swamp, back with the opossums safe from Sullivan's uncertain aim, far from the reach of Winston's headlights, burning through the forest. His face flushed with heat. "Hell's the matter with me," he wondered.

He thought of the night, a few weeks before, when Winston dropped by his house to let him know F-45 was his. It was a high point of Sandy's life, a quietly hoped-for miracle. Half the boys in the county were on the waiting list for a paper route. Largely on the strength of Mary Kay's counsel, it seemed, Winston had chosen Sandy.

"He'll be alright," Winston told Sandy's dad. "I wouldn't worry 'bout him."

Sandy wanted to live up to the billing, especially in Winston's eyes. Now he felt as though the bones had been ground from his soul.

"We're out here to do two things," Winston said, taking a last swig of juice. "Get the papers delivered and get the hell home. Anything else's wasted time. Might as well stay in bed."

He took a final swig of orange juice and tossed the empty carton over his shoulder into a nest of faded papers and crumpled coffee cups scattered across the back seat.

"I don't wan 'a hear 'bout any more damned nonsense like what happened this mornin'," Winston added, jamming the Mustang into reverse.

Sandy's fingers were blackened by newsprint. Another ten minutes, he'd be headed home. He imagined Winston's taillights heading back over the ridge and out of sight, the sound of the radio and finally the engine fading into the calm.

"Yes, sir."

"Alright then. You'll be seein' a new carrier takin' over Wade Eckert's papers. Well, not a new carrier, exactly, just new to this route."

"Yes, sir," Sandy repeated, taken aback. "When's he start?"

"Right around five o'clock," Winston said, "tomorrow mornin'."

 Chapter 5

It was just past seven and the last light of day was fading from the face of the jonquils. Sandy stepped past them and up the brick steps to knock on Smitty's door. He carried the collection book he'd inherited with his route. About the size of a paperback novel with a faded canvas cover, it held weekly newspaper receipts, a separate page for each customer, Sandy's hip-pocket accounting office.

Paper route economics were simple and unyielding. The publisher didn't pay anybody to deliver its newspapers. Carriers bought the papers from the company and sold them for the profit they retained after paying their bills each Saturday morning, when the two-dozen or so paperboys in Sandy's district would meet in the Seven-Eleven parking lot, gather around Winston's Mustang and settle the accounts. Sandy could make as much as eight dollars a week, if he collected what his customers owed.

"Times-Daily, ninety cents," Sandy had said as Smitty swung open the door to the brick ranch house at the top of Tempest Lane.

"Ninety cents!" Smitty exclaimed. "I just want the paper, not the whole damned paper comp'ny."

"I try to collect half my route each time," Sandy explained. "That way I don't have to bother you every week."

"You mean you don't have to knock on every door on your route every week," Smitty replied. "Well, come on in, then. Le'me see'f I can find my wallet."

Smitty disappeared down the hallway. Beneath a portrait of William Shakespeare, Sandy noticed a brown-edged topographical map on a small wooden table by the window.

"That would be the old Smith family dairy farm, before we built up all this," Smitty said as we walked back in the room. "That right there," he said, pointing to a curve in a broken line of dots, "is where we're standing right now."

Sandy smiled in wonder. "Right here? But there's . . . nothing there."

Smitty chuckled.

"Oh there was plenty here alright," he said. "It just don't show up on the map." He pointed to the mantle above his fireplace to a faded photograph of a little boy and a sturdy young man.

"My dad and his father," Smitty said, "not long after they bought this place. Wasn't exactly what you'd call a coveted parcel in those days. Only two links to the outer world — old Patter's plank road running east and west, half a day's walk into Richmond. And the old Indian trail that ran down from the ridge three miles or so south to the river. Had a sawmill down there. Dad and his brother cut white oak and hickory, hauled it by wagon down that old path to the mill. That's how they got by while they cleared the land."

"Indian trail?"

"Yep," said Smitty. "Monacans. By the time I come along, 'course, the old path had become the ridge top road, run right back behind the farm house, which is been gone now a good long time. But the little store Mom and Dad built, that's still up there. Used to be a sewing shop."

"I remember that place."

"Yeah? Well, it's empty now. Know anybody wants to buy it, le'me know."

Sandy could see a pair of winding black lines on the old map, showing the paved roadways of Ridgetop and Misty Hollow roads, and the little square that marked the one-room store where the two roads merged.

"Yep, spent many a day in that little store," Smitty said. "Smelled like kerosene, chewing tobacco and peppermint. My seventh birthday, Dad le'me pick out a pocketknife from behind the counter. Had a grip made of deer antler, got my initials engraved on it. I never went anywhere without that knife."

He told Sandy of days spent roaming broad fields and forested passageways by day, sleeping out on special nights beneath a canvas tarp and listening to his father's tales by campfire light. "There was tales of gruesome battles. Fights to the death between the Monacan and the Powhatan. Fearsome ambushes and grisly fights."

"Over what," Sandy asked.

"Oh, Lord, son, everything you can imagine: boundary lines, hunting grounds, lost children, stolen wives. This whole area was disputed land. Look'a here …" Smitty reached up to the mantle and handed Sandy what looked like an arrowhead of flinty stone.

"Dad found this one day just piddlin' 'round. Powhatan maybe, who the hell knows? I sure thought about it plenty, though, when I's a boy, 'specially hustlin' home through the woods on nights like this."

Sandy turned the family treasure over in his palm.

"Was a great place for a boy," Smitty said. "I'd pull up young sassafras roots, shave 'em to strips with my knife, and boil 'em at night with brown sugar for tea. Wintertime, I'd jump on my sled right out the house and sail across the snow clear down to the frozen creek at the far end of the farm."

Sandy tried to picture Hill & Hamlet as a dairy farm.

"It's hard work, though, takin' care of a farm . . . 'bout lost the place, just before the war. Couldn't pay the help."

"What help?"

"Handful of colored families, rented from us at the far end of the property, 'side the swamp. Hog pen was down that way, worst mosquitoes you ever saw, and a kind of wooden platform where the butcherin' got done. They called the place Skinquarter. A settlement, you might say, with shacks of tarpaper and pine, little patches of squash and greens, that kind of thing."

"And, you didn't pay them?"

"Good times we did. Hard times we tried. Eventually had to give 'em land. Dad deeded over several parcels to them to tide us over. War hadn't 'a come when it did, we'd gone belly up. Time it was over, Dad was gone. I'd had 'bout enough of the farm."

"And you went into building houses instead?"

"Well, in a way," Smitty nodded. "Le'me show you somethin'."

He opened a drawer beneath the table, unrolled a sheet of thin paper and laid it atop the topographical map.

"Hill & Hamlet," Sandy read out loud, leaning over top of the table. Heavy lines drawn by hand in dark pencil marked the individual lots and streets of the neighborhood. It was framed to the east by Misty Hollow Road, the honeysuckle swamp to the west, Patters Plank Road along the north and an unpaved road through the woods to the south.

A broken line traced the footpath at the end of Tempest Lane through the woods to the unpaved road. Behind the home lots Sandy saw an area marked by faint cross-hatching.

"The bamboo forest?" Sandy said.

"Well," Smitty started, "things got a little tricky just after the war, when I sat down to lay out this place."

The old man tucked his shirttail into a pair of khaki pants.

"By that time, you see, there were maybe a dozen families living down in

Skinquarter."

Sandy looked into the map and tried to follow the thread.

"Right along here, they'd buried a good number of people," Smitty said slowly, pointing to a thinly wooded rise near a hedge of honeysuckle running alongside the swamp. "Graves were marked with river stones, and they'd built a small chapel beneath the sweet gum tree, here. That had been a kind of gathering place for . . ."

Smitty paused as if he'd lost his train of thought, then stepped back away from the map.

"I remember one night," he started again, "headin' home and passin' by that graveyard. I started runnin' so hard I tripped over the root of a big 'ol poplar tree and fell face first into that little stream down there. Wadn't till I got all the way home and out'ta my pants I realized my pocketknife was gone. Must've slipped out when I fell. Looked and looked the next day. Never did find it."

Sandy handed the arrowhead back to the man.

"So that's the story of Hill & Hamlet?"

Smitty nodded.

"That's it."

The boy walked out, Smitty closed the door and settled into an armchair by the table. He picked up the map and ran a wrinkled finger along the cross hatching he'd sketched long ago. He could almost hear the distant echoes of hymns and spirituals rolling through the bottomlands of his boyhood, could almost smell the smoke rising from a pit dug out of the sandy soil by the hands of Skinquarter people.

"I wanted to buy them out," Smitty said to no one. "But there were too many of 'em. And the graves, good heavens. I couldn't uproot all that if I'd tried. And who was going to buy a house down there?"

It was in a copy of Southern Planter that he'd read about a fast-growing kind of bamboo some GIs were bringing home from Japan. He planted some along a thicket where the natural forest thinned. The county told him they would widen, but not pave, the road that ran on the other side from Skinquarter up to Misty Hollow. He called it Midsummer Night's Lane.

Smitty put the little map on the table, sat back in his chair and let out a deep breath. "Yeah," he could hear the wind rise in the trees, "that's the story of Hill & Hamlet."

 Chapter 6

Sandy's mind raced as he walked out of Smitty's living room, across the street to Ruth and Rich Thomas' home, where the smells of a fried fish dinner poured through an open window.

"Well, for pity sake," Ruth exclaimed as she opened the door. "Rich, come look here and see our new paperboy."

A white-haired man looked up from the dining room table, where he was picking over a thin line of catfish bones. He rose and ambled toward the door, a wadded napkin in one hand.

"Son of a gun. It ain't been no time 'tall I used to see you down the end of the street, in muddy shorts bent over the creek catchin' tadpoles. Look like you found your shoes, 'eh boy?"

"Yes, sir."

Ruth opened her purse while Rich held the screen door.

"How much did you say it was?"

"It's ninety cents, ma'am, for last week and this."

"Alrighty, then."

She handed Sandy a dollar. He stuffed it in his pocket and gave her a dime's change, along with two white paper stubs he tore out of his collection book.

"Thank you, ma'am."

"Wait a minute," the old man said. "Le'me show you something right quick."

He led Sandy through the living room to a small paneled den. A black and white television sat on a coffee table and the sound was down low. Sandy could see a graying newsman in a coat and tie on the screen, and vaguely heard him say something about North Vietnamese officials lodging protests against U.S. bombing near Hanoi.

"Now, look here. What do you think that is," Rich asked, gesturing toward a dollar bill in a wooden frame hanging on the wall.

"Well, sir, it looks like a dollar bill. Is it old or something?"

The old man laughed and looked at his wife.

"It's the first dollar I ever earned after I got out the service," he said. "Started out puttin' in kitchen cabinets. First metal cabinets anybody ever seen around here. Ever damned one of 'em painted white. Started right after the war, spring of '46."

Sandy looked at the dollar bill and smiled.

"Is that right?"

"Ah hell, couldn't keep up, so damned many new homes bein' built in Richmond back then. Started out I's makin' forty-six dollars a week. Hell, you could make a house payment for two week's pay. That dollar right there come out of my first paycheck. I ain't spent it yet. Guess it's my lucky dollar."

"Yes, sir," Sandy nodded. "Guess so."

Something on the TV screen caught Ruth's eye. She leaned down and tweaked the volume. Sandy looked over and heard the shaken newsman say something about somebody taken to a hospital.

Ruth cupped a hand to her open mouth.

"My God. They've shot Martin Luther King."

"What?" Rich responded as if she'd spoken a foreign language.

Ruth sank to the edge of the sofa, tugged the hem of her dress below her knees and stared at the screen.

"That civil rights guy? Where?"

"Somewhere down in Atlanta or Alabama, man said."

"Damned fools."

Shot King, Sandy thought, suddenly wanting to give them their privacy. He watched Rich turn up the TV, thanked them and walked himself out the door.

He took the crinkled dollar from his pocket and paused to look at it in the front porch light. The sky had gone dark. The air was cool. He pulled out a leather and madras wallet. A small tear in the lining opened into his secret pocket. He slipped the dollar bill inside and headed toward the next house.

 Chapter 7

By the time Sandy had covered almost half his route, he'd collected twenty-six dollars, seven short of what he needed to pay his bill.

"Even houses this week," he'd told himself. "Hit the odd ones next week."

It was funny, he thought, how many people weren't home on a Thursday night, and how many of those who were couldn't scrape together ninety cents.

"What the hell," Sandy said out loud as he walked across an unlit lawn, the quiet shattered by the throaty growl of an engine closing fast. He looked up, saw a pair of dim headlights approaching, then the outline of a beaten pickup truck roaring down Tempest Lane at an ear-splitting pitch, leaving the smell of burning oil in its wake.

Sandy walked into the yellow light spreading from the steps of a brick Cape Cod. From atop the stoop at 8714, he looked out over a row of neatly shaped boxwoods toward an empty driveway of amber pebbles. He opened the screen door and used the bright brass knocker.

"Yes?"

Sandy heard a woman's voice from just inside the door, then what sounded like a baby's cry.

"Paperboy," he replied. "Times-Daily, ninety cents."

"Ah, just a minute."

Sandy saw a curtain part, then drop back into place, behind a large picture window beside the door. He heard the metallic scrape of a latch. The door swung open and there stood a young woman in a pink bathrobe and cradling a baby in one arm.

"I was just putting him down," she said, struggling to keep her balance as she bent to pull a terry-cloth slipper onto a bare foot. "If you'll give me one minute . . . come on in if you'd like."

Sandy stepped through the door and onto the living room carpet, scattered with small plastic balls. There was a large stuffed bunny in a blue playpen. A red toy fire truck was propped against a sofa.

"Let me get him settled and I'll be right back."

Sandy nodded as she turned on the television and gestured for him to take a seat on the couch. He noticed a large white wedding Bible on the coffee table, "David and Pam," embossed in gold on the white leather binding, "Nineteen Hundred and Sixty Five until Forever." Beside it was an ashtray, with no sign of use, the University of Virginia Cavaliers insignia enameled onto a white porcelain surface in blue and orange.

As the TV warmed up, Sandy heard what sounded like a chorus of men singing before a picture appeared.

"Bu-d-weiser," the voices chanted in close harmony, "Best reason on earth — to drink beer."

The sound faded, a new picture took shape, and there was a young housewife holding a baby in each arm. "As good as fresh brewed," said a man handing the woman a jar of Maxwell House instant coffee then giving her an odd sort of pinch on the nose. "Now, be a good little Maxwell Housewife."

Pam stepped back into the living room, her baby's cries echoing from the far end of the hall. "Sorry to keep you waiting. My husband's out of town."

Sandy turned away from the TV and saw her standing in her robe. She threw her hair back from her face and clutched a muted cordovan handbag. "Now. How much was it again?"

She looked to Sandy to be somewhere in her mid-twenties. The glow from a lamp at the end of the sofa fell across her full and lineless face, he thought, like the first light of dawn on unstirred waters.

"Good evening." It was the television, the same coat-and-tie newsman Sandy had heard earlier, only now he could see it was Cronkite, interrupting the regular programming with a special report: "Doctor Martin Luther King Jr., the apostle of non-violence in the civil rights movement, has been shot to death in Memphis, Tennessee."

"Good God," Pam gasped, pressing an open palm against her mouth.

"He died of a bullet wound in the neck," the newsman continued. "Police said they found a high-powered hunting rifle about a block from the hotel, but it was not immediately identified as the murder weapon."

Pam sank to the couch, her face never turning away from the screen. She set her purse on the carpet and reached toward Sandy, laying her hand atop his.

No woman had held his hand since he was a child, he thought, unless you counted prayer time at the Kanawha Creek Presbyterian Church. Maybe a prayer was coming, he thought, instinctively bowing his head, his eyes catching on the white wedding Bible in front of him, as she gripped his hand in hers. Sandy felt a warmth sweep through his body as they sat motionless while the news washed over them in a calamitous wave of darkness and dread.

Memphis. It sounded to Sandy so far away, dangerous and faintly foreign.

There was file footage from the day before, a speech King gave to city sanitation workers, what Sandy's friends called garbage men, on strike for safer working conditions. Nobody much cared yesterday. It got barely a mention deep inside the pages of that morning's Times-Daily. Now King's words flooded into living rooms of almost every household in the land:

"We've got some difficult days ahead, but it doesn't matter with me now," King said on the day before he died. "Because I've been to the mountaintop."

Sandy leaned forward on the couch.

"And I've looked over, and I've seen the Promised Land," King testified in a booming baritone, his face a grainy and glowing image on the insentient screen. "I may not get there with you. But I want you to know tonight, that we, as a people, will get to the Promised Land."

Sandy glanced fleetingly toward the woman. She turned her face, their eyes locked for an instant, then both looked back to the screen.

There was another scene of King speaking, five years before in Washington, a great throng of people gathered before him near the steps of the Lincoln Memorial.

"I have a dream," the youthful preacher proclaimed. "My four little children will one day live in a nation where they will not be judged by the color of their skin, but by the content of their character. I have a dream today!"

The screen went momentarily blank, uncharacteristically silent, and Sandy turned to see tears trailing down the young mother's cheek. She looked at him and tried to speak.

"Why . . ."

It was all that came out. She squeezed his hand. He felt the distance between them melt away into the space they suddenly shared, a place where, for that moment at least, the fragile beginnings of loss felt safe.

Cronkite sounded a closing, empathetic note of authority. There was a pause, then another beer commercial was playing, its simple-minded jingle a jarring backdrop to Pam's unsteady breathing.

Sandy felt confused and paralyzed, holding the hand of a young mother in his, clutching his collection book in the other. Was there a way, he wondered, to sustain the moment, to make the television go away and take the pain it brought with it?

Pam let go of his hand, sat back and wiped her eyes. She shook her head slowly, took a deep breath, then stood and turned off the TV.

Sandy wanted to stand but felt unable to move, or even to speak. Pam lowered her head, closed her eyes, wrapped both hands around her face.

"Why would anybody . . ."

She let the sentence fade, dropped her hands to her waist and stared off toward the wall. Sandy felt invisible and wished he were gone. Pam had stopped crying, so had her baby, and Sandy could think of nothing to say.

"What's his name?"

"Davey. He's almost seven weeks now. Our first."

She paused, breathed deeply and let out a sigh. "I can't help but wonder what kind of a sad, sick, sorry world we've brought him into. I don't know, I'm just so . . . I'm sorry. I'm just . . . exhausted."

Sandy rose and stepped toward the door, not wanting to leave or to stay, and certainly not to raise the matter of the ninety cents. He'd just come back next week. Maybe her husband would be there, he thought. Maybe their baby boy would be asleep. Maybe no one would be shot to death on national TV and we could all just collect our money, pay our bills and go home.

"Well, bye."

"Goodnight," Pam replied. She ran an open hand through a long shock of hair, and looked at Sandy with a pained half smile. He watched her turn, press her robe against her chest and bend over to toss a ball in the playpen. Sandy stepped out front and made his way down the steps. She moved to the doorway, stood there and watched him without closing the door until he walked out of the light.

 Chapter 8

A half hour later Sandy came to the dead end of Tempest Lane. The night had grown cool, there was no moon at all and a gentle breeze blew out of the south, rustling the trees at the edge of the woods. Sandy smelled smoke, guessed it was drifting from somewhere on Midsummer Night's Lane, and gazed into the darkness of the footpath running alongside old man Sullivan's house.

At the far end of the path, a dim light flickered from a small window at the Skinquarter A.M.E. Church. Sandy heard muffled voices and people milling outside. Car doors opened and closed, an engine cranked and slowly rumbled to life. There was the sound of tires rolling onto the graveled roadway as the engine hacked and moaned out of earshot, leaving only the sound of rustling leaves.

Counting his money by the light from a window, Sandy was a couple dollars short of making his bill. He opened his collection book to the odd pages looking for a way to make up for the no-pays that night. He stopped on the page for 8719, which hadn't paid since the middle of March. If they were home, he could collect a dollar-eighty from them. That would just about cover it. They were two houses down, and Sandy headed that way.

"They're home alright," Sandy said out loud as he approached the red brick rancher. A large metal "For Rent" sign was planted by the mailbox, an aging Pontiac Bonneville was in the driveway and it looked like every light in the place was on. The pick-up truck that had blasted past Sandy earlier was parked on packed dirt beneath a lone pine tree like a warhorse awaiting a mercy shooting. A thin crack crossed the windshield and the crumpled hood was held shut by a rusty chain.

Sandy headed up the cement steps, reached through a tear in the screen and knocked on the door. He heard the flat trebled sound of a television and panicked barking from inside. The door swung open and there stood a good-sized woman in white nurse's uniform and crepe-soled shoes.

"Evenin' ma'am. Times-Daily, dollar-eighty."

He braced for refusal and possible belligerence, but she took a long drag off the losing end of a cigarette, turned back inside and hollered above the television.

"Wa-yne, you got two dollars for the paper boy?"

The response was swift and certain.

"Yeah, I got two dollars for the paperboy, 'bout like I got two-hundred dollars for your sweet ass," a man's raspy voice shot back. "You the one wants the damned paper, you can damn well pay for it."

The woman rolled her dark eyes, drew the last bit from her cigarette and flicked it outside past Sandy's leg. She moved to one side to invite him in.

"Hang on a second, I'll get your money."

Sandy stepped inside, and a large black dog of mixed heritage bounded across the bare living room floor, jumped a low-lying center table, knocking over a pair of empty cans, and lunged toward Sandy. A barefoot man in blue jeans jumped up from a threadbare couch and cuffed the snarling cur just behind the neck by a large black leather collar.

"Aht, Firestone! Git back boy," he ordered. "He ain' go'n hurt you. Just his way a' sayin' hello."

The dog jerked against the collar, barked in rapid fire and bared an ominous set of teeth.

"Shut up Firestone," the man scolded as he gave the dog a sharp smack. "Sit, boy. Sit."

The dog rose up on his hind legs, barking fiercely, and the man struggled to maintain his balance.

"Wa-yne, would you please put that damned dog out back."

The woman came out of the kitchen, a pair of dollar bills in one hand and a freshly lit cigarette in the other.

"Sorry," she said, handing Sandy the money. "Wa-yne, would you please . . ."

"Ahright, I got 'im," he shot back, hauling the dog barking and snarling through the kitchen and out the back door.

Sandy dug into his change pocket, handed her a dime and two nickels, then tore out the receipts for the past four weeks. "Thank you ma'am."

"Look here," she asked. "Who'd I call to stop my paper? Look like we might be movin' come June or maybe even May."

"Well, you could call the office. There's a number in the newspaper every day. Or you could just call me, I'll take care of it for you."

"Whatever's easier."

"Ok. You got something I can write my number on?"

Wayne shuffled back in the room and headed for the couch, changing the channel on the television as he walked past. It was a live shot from the White House. President Johnson stood before at least a dozen large microphones.

"America is shocked and saddened by the brutal slaying tonight of Doctor Martin Luther King Jr.," Johnson said.

"Shocked and saddened my ass," interjected Wayne. "Sick and damned tired, more like it."

"I ask every citizen to reject the blind violence," Johnson continued, but that sentence, too, was abruptly cut off.

"Yeah, I can see they listenin' to that. Riots and lootin's all over the damned country already," Wayne said. He plopped down on the beaten couch and popped the top off a fresh can of Pabst, quickly pressing it to his mouth to catch the foaming head. "Couldn't wait for that, naw. Couldn't miss out on a chance to break into some damn place and steal a fuckin' television set, now, could we?"

"I pray that his family can find comfort," Johnson continued.

"Comfort? Nobody give a damn 'bout that guy King or his crazy dream. 'Been to the mountaintop.' Wonder what he saw? Bottle of cold Thunderbird?"

Sandy feigned a feeble smile and looked down at the floor.

"He don't think you're funny," the woman shot back. Then she turned toward Sandy. "You ain' got'ta laugh at his sick . . ."

Wayne waved his beer can toward the woman.

"What the hell you know?" he hollered. "You some big civil rights deal all a sudden? You ain't never give a damn 'bout him before. Now he gets killed he's some kind of saint?"

Between snippets of Wayne's running commentary, Sandy caught a phrase here and there from the President — a line about every American of good will, then a bit about prayers for peace and coming together. Something about equality.

"I can't stomach this," Wayne exploded, rising to shut off the TV.

"We got along just fine without Martin Luther King runnin' 'round, gettin' ever'body all fired up and burnin' down the damn country," he said, holding his Pabst like a pistol aimed at the woman. "And we'll get along even better once that minstrel-dancin' Johnson's gone."

"That's enough, God-damn it! Stop railing out like that in front of the boy," the woman yelled. "He don't wan'na hear it — and neither do I."

For a near-perfect split second, Wayne looked like he'd been sucker punched, like he'd caught a hard right across the jaw from the blind side of the bar. But he quickly regained his footing.

"Well now, if y'all don't wan'na hear it, nobody's makin' you stay," he said slowly, gesturing toward the still open front door with an effeminate wave of his hand.

"And, just in case anybody's wondrin', I'll rail out any damned way I want to in my own damned house — and ain't no woman gon' stop me. That guy King's the worst kind of troublemaker, Johnson's not a damned sight better and I'll say any got-damned thing I want about any got-damned person I want any got-damned time I want in my own got-damned house. And anybody don't like it can get the fuck out — and stay the fuck out!"

Sandy was already backing away toward the door. The woman grabbed her keys and was two steps behind him, slamming the door so hard it rattled the windows.

"Redneck son-of-a-Billy-Bob-bitch, talk to me like that."

Sandy headed across the floodlit yard, past the aging pickup and onto the street. He heard the big lungs of the Bonneville open up as it lurched backward. The tires ripped across the pavement as it turned onto the roadway, the headlights casting Sandy in shadow all the way up Tempest Lane.

She drew up beside him, slowed and reached across the seat to roll down the window.

"Don't worry 'bout that ign'rent dumb ass," she said. "He's all blow and no go."

Sandy stopped and looked inside, bent down and looked into her face.

"I'm alright," she said, turning away to look down the road.

"My shift don't start for another hour 'n a half. I'll just get there a little early. Gi'me time to grab a bite."

Her breathing was heavy. Her brow was creased.

"Broke a damned nail," she said, picking at a finger against the steering wheel. "Hop in, I'll give you a ride."

Sandy was done for the night. He opened the door and slid in.

"Thanks. I'll get out at the end of the street."

She nodded and looked straight ahead as the car lurched forward.

"More like May," she said. "I got your number. I'll let you know. But probably more like May."

Sandy glanced in the mirror on the passenger door. He could see clear back to her house, where someone was turning out every light in the place.

 Chapter 9

Sandy awakened in darkness, still haunted by a dream.

He was walking through a charred and smoldering landscape of rattle-trap houses and blackened lawns, each with a small cross of glowing embers in front, led by a ghostly woman in a long flowing robe toting an enormous white Bible. Sandy wanted to grip her hand but was afraid to let her know how weak he felt without her, how he might crumble and collapse if she left him there alone. And so he walked close beside her, tethered to her spirit, it seemed, by a fragile strand of faith.

He lay beneath the covers, listening to a gentle rain against his window. He remembered skating across one of the Indian lakes, hearing the ice shatter and crack beneath him and believing that if he kept gliding forward he might reach the other side without falling through. And now, in this dream, he felt he might stay just ahead of calamity long enough to be guided out of this flame-scorched place all but consumed by hatred and fear.

He looked at his clock, its soft light glowing through a cracked plastic face. It was nearly 4:45, a chance to rise a bit early, pick up his papers and be gone before anyone else showed up.

And so there he was, a few minutes before five, coasting onto the muddy paper stop in a drizzle, echoes of night tremors rumbling through his soul. He slung a bundle of papers into his basket, pulled out his wire cutters and snipped, heard the muffled popping of unbound papers deeply breathing in, and caught the headline in the glow of the dim light overhead.

"King Is Shot, Killed at Memphis Motel."

It was big and bold faced, a full inch tall, and stripped all the way across the top of the page, just below the Times-Daily flag, April 5, 1968.

No, Sandy thought, it wasn't a dream, but far worse, a kind of ceaseless nightmare in black and white. Eighty-eight times that morning he saw it. Eighty-eight papers folded and rolled, a national obituary in seventy-two-point type, stuffed into boxes or tucked behind doors, the story of a man of peace in violent times, right there among the ads for Goodyear whitewalls, two for sixty dollars, mounted and balanced.

It was cold, his feet were wet, and Sandy didn't linger along his route. But he found himself taking just a bit more care to make sure the papers didn't rip or smear, to find a way to leave them out of the rain, so they'd be in good reading order an hour or two on, when the residents of Tempest Lane — those who hadn't watched their televisions the night before, and those who had — awakened to the news that the Rev. Dr. Martin Luther King Jr. had slipped the single strand of faith that tethered his spirit to this troubled world and was suddenly, epically and irretrievably gone.

# Chapter 10

S aturday's papers were done. Dawn was breaking in pink and gold. Brilliant, widening shafts of light seared a thin, grey edge of cloud, a majestic watercolor masterpiece unrolling across the April sky. A single copy of the Times-Daily slapped against Sandy's basket as he pedaled down the gravel drive toward the back of the Seven-Eleven.

"Johnson Sends 4,000 U.S. Troops Into Capital: Violence Subsides," read the headline above a picture of Washington in flames. "Four Dead, 350 Injured; 800 Arrested," the caption read, "in capital city violence following the assassination of King." Lest anyone miss the point, there was yet a third reference to mayhem, a list of other cities where people had died — seven in Chicago, one in Detroit — and a story about a national search for King's killer.

Another photo showed the flag of Virginia, flying at half-staff. President Johnson appealed for calm, a story noted. He scratched a planned trip to Hawaii, where he was to confer with diplomats and generals over a strategy for peace talks with Hanoi. Now, instead, he was preparing to address a rare joint session of Congress to press for civil rights legislation on the eve of King's funeral.

Sandy regarded it all much as he did the sky, an elemental force in constant change he could neither predict nor control. Washington, just a hundred miles away on the map, was as remote as the moon or the stars. Of more immediate concern was paying his weekly bill, as he rose from the gravely alleyway, leaned his bike by the others against a green dumpster and took his place in the line of paperboys gathered alongside Winston Coleman's Mustang.

A car was a requirement for the district manager's job. The Mustang, though, was something more, a gleaming, rolling American sculpture, a sort of metal-flake monument to the virtues of hard work, sacrifice and thrift. The paperboys all knew it cost nearly $2,400, and that Winston had bought it on his own, putting down cash he'd saved up as a paperboy, then making monthly payments from his salary as their district manager. Just sitting there in the parking lot surrounded by boys, it was a symbol of what they might aspire to as well — a virile, throaty, almost religious totem of what any of them might acquire by committing themselves to their routes and faithfully tithing a portion of their weekly earnings to the Times-Daily paperboy bank.

"Ronnie," Sandy heard Winston say from inside the car, as he counted out bills and change. "F-29. You got $44.75 here, but where's your bank this week?"

Ronald Morgan stood at Winston's open window, sheepishly taking a chiding for showing up with just enough to pay his bill, and not a dime for savings.

"Three complaints, two from the same damn guy who bagged me last week for not puttin' his paper inside his screen porch door. Nothin' left over to bank."

Winston wore a cotton sweater, gone raggedy about the neck, over an equally threadbare oxford shirt.

"Ronnie, do me a favor," he said, digging in the pocket of his baggy shorts and passing a dollar bill to the boy.

"First, hands off the car, buddy. Hands got two things on 'em — fingerprints and newsprint, and I don't want either one on my paint, 'speshly since I just waxed her yesterday. Now, go in there and get me a pack of Marlboros, a pint of orange juice, a pack of Juicy Fruit, and bring back the change."

Morgan turned and headed into the store, while Winston logged the payment for F-29, prepared a receipt and filed the cash in a small lockbox on the passenger seat.

"F-24, Raines," Winston said, moving on to the next boy, each known to the young district manager by name, route number and, usually, nickname.

"The Slider," Winston announced, taking a crisp white envelope from Catesby Raines, the boy who'd taken over Wade Eckert's old route after Winston sacked him. Inside the envelope was Catesby's bill and his payment, $53.84, laid out in tens, fives and ones, ordered by descending value, and coins — exact change — along with a white banking slip, already filled out, and $2.50 more for his bank account.

Sandy shuddered in the morning chill. He stamped his feet and blew on his hands, looking up to see Ronnie Morgan hustling back to hand over the Marlboros, the juice, the gum and forty cents change. Winston took the money, scratched out something on a white slip of paper on his clipboard and handed Morgan's receipt back to him, containing a record of his payment and notification of his bank balance as of the day before.

"Now that's better," Winston told the boy. "Let's see here, forty cents to the bank, that gives you almost $13 in your account. You can pay me back when you bring down those complaints."

Sandy moved up and took his place at the car window.

"F-45, John-ee Rivers," Winston announced.

Sandy smiled, felt his face blush and handed over his money. Nobody had told him about the paperboy bank, and Sandy had nothing to deposit. Still, the nickname made him feel like part of the club.

"Ok, John-ee, here's the deal," Winston said. "First time, you make your bill. Congratulations. Here on out, you bank somethin' every week. Fifty cents, f'all I care. But you bank somethin' each week. You draw four and a half percent interest from the comp'ny. Your money just sits there and grows. That way you build a little somethin' for yourself. Get your bike some new tires. Salt away a little Christmas money. Save up 'case you go to college. Just a little somethin' every week. Get in the habit, you won't even miss it. Then, 'fore you know it, you got somethin' one day."

Sandy looked at the Mustang, gleaming like a ruby in the morning sun. He peered through the window into the back seat and did a double take. Not a scrap of paper, not a single cup, milk bottle or empty cigarette pack. It was all gone, and in its place was a powder blue tuxedo laid out across the seat in a clear plastic wrap. In the rear floor were the shiniest black shoes Sandy had ever seen.

Winston added Sandy's cash to the lock box and handed his receipt out the window.

"Yoo-uu, are so be-au-ti-ful, you're such a sight to see, you're the girl for me . . . Ok guys, no complaints tomorrow, right? It's prom night, and I'm not going to be in any mood to be . . ."

"Awwh yeah," someone hollered out.

"Hey Romeo," called another.

"I could have danced all night," Raines sang.

"Yeah, that's alright Slider, keep on talkin'," Winston shot back. "You still goin' steady with your right hand?"

The Slider piped down amid a hail of jeers.

"So, I'm just tellin' ya'll right now," Winston continued, "I ain't gon' be traipsin' 'round after you young Turks in the mornin' and pickin' up after your sorry ass selves. So do me a favor — do yourselves a favor. Get it right.

Don't be sendin' trouble my way, and I won't charge you double for any unwanted phone calls."

Sandy walked away from Winston's car and into the store, coming out a few minutes later to join a handful of other boys seated outside. He took a long drink from a cold Dr. Pepper.

"Breakfast of champions," Raines offered, downing the last of a glazed doughnut and licking a white crust of sugar off an ink-blackened finger.

"Trade ya," Sandy said, offering up a drink in exchange for a bite of Raines' last doughnut.

He was a year or so older than Sandy with thick, curly hair. He wore the kind of canvas work pants favored by mechanics and rode a bike the color of smoke.

"Sure."

Sandy heard a low buzzing sound, like a hive of electric bees, looked up and saw a thin cloud of dust rising from the forested edge of the dirt and gravel alleyway, trailing what looked like a bicycle, only slightly thicker of frame. The sound of the engine grew louder as the strange machine rolled up to the store.

"Lucky Pete," Winston called out, "on his groovy Mo-ped."

"Winston," the boy nodded, shutting the engine down, slipping a dingy Times-Daily canvas delivery bag off his shoulder and draping it over his handlebars.

He glanced at Sandy and Raines, looked away as if no one were there, turned his face into the sunshine and spread his arms out wide.

"What day is it Winston?"

"It's pay day, Lucky Pete."

A smile stretched across Pete's face.

"And what do I get paid today?"

"Whatever it takes to keep you one more week."

Pete clapped his hands together against the morning chill and walked inside, appearing minutes later holding a foam cup of steaming hot chocolate. He stood and sipped on it until the last paperboy was done, only then deigning to saunter over to the waiting Mustang.

"F-15. Lu-ck-ee Pete," Winston announced, as the boy pulled a paper-clipped roll of bills from his shirt pocket and handed them through the window. "How's she runn'in?"

"Better," Pete replied, "since I drained the tank and got some dry gas in there."

Part bicycle, part motorbike, the Moped was from somewhere in Italy. It could be pedaled or powered up with the engine, one way about as fast as the other.

In four years of delivering papers, Pete Stokes had acquired the trappings of paperboy legend, delivering nearly 140 papers a day, the largest route, by some margin, in the district.

"Can we deliver on motorcycles," Sandy asked.

"What do you think," Raines replied.

"Well, I ain't got a license, so I don't guess it really matters."

"Stokes' got no license neither. He don't turn 16 'till next month."

"Well, I ain't got a Mo-Ped."

"Well, technically we ain't s'pose to do it. For one thing, the engine wakes people up, then they complain. Stokes ain't really s'posed to be ridin' on the roads. His bike's got no license tag. Ain't even street legal."

Sandy stared at Pete. Somehow the words "street legal" didn't much seem to fit.

"I've only seen him do it on Saturdays," Raines concluded. "Besides, who's gon'na fotch up a nice Moped with a damn paper basket?"

There was a dull, high-pitched drone from overhead. Winston leaned out of his window and squinted toward the sky, where a tiny red and white plane was winding through a broad, sweeping arc.

"Cessna 150, tail dragger," Winston announced. "Look how she slips through the turn. Damn, she's a handsome craft."

"Mighty fine," Pete echoed, looking up toward the sky.

"One day, old friend," Winston said. "One day, for sure."

"Mmhmm. Speaking of handsome craft . . ."

"See you tonight?" Winston interrupted.

"If she's lucky."

"Alright then, pick you up at your folks' house. Eight o'clock sharp."

Pete laughed, nodded and gave Winston a sturdy shake of the hand. "Cool as a moose."

Pete strode back toward his Moped and Winston cranked up the Mustang, its boiling rumble stirring the boys. He backed out of his parking spot and wheeled across the lot, opening up the engine just enough to leave a patch of black rubber at the edge of Patter's Plank Road.

# Chapter 11

Mornings passed, the days grew longer, until at last, like dogwood flaring by the honeysuckle swamp, April opened into May, ushering in the final weeks of school and the last dance of the season at Dolly Frances Randolph's cotillion.

Along with the Westham Country Club and a select handful of parochial schools, Mrs. Randolph's was one of the few remaining vestiges of a social order fast washing away on the restless tide of expatriates pouring in from places like Louisville, Milwaukee and Westport and bringing their money and peculiar manners with them.

Country clubs and Episcopalian classrooms were beyond the means of the Rivers' modest household: at forty-five dollars for the nine-dance season, the cotillion remained just within reach. And so, having slipped through Mrs. Randolph's elaborate social screening process — and the simple arithmetic that required her to bring in a boy for every girl admitted — Sandy found himself headed downtown on the first Saturday night in May, his father's aging station wagon hurtling over the rolling pitch and Belgian block pavement of Monument Avenue.

"Dad," he asked, "why do I have to go to cotillion?"

"I want you to be comfortable around people, and I want you to know how to make people feel comfortable around you."

Hardly seemed worth giving up a perfectly good Saturday night, Sandy reasoned. He looked out his open window and onto a broad, six-lane boulevard divided by grassy medians and towering poplars. Churches of stone and Georgian homes rushed past, cradling Sandy in a cushion of Protestant grace, white-columned porches and slate roof grandeur.

The car wound through a gentle circle that wrapped around a broad stone edifice within a wrought-iron fence. Sandy looked up to catch the imposing visage of Thomas "Stonewall" Jackson, the Confederate general who Rebel pickets mistook for a Yankee officer and shot an hour's drive north at Chancellorsville.

"When were these monuments put up," Sandy asked. "Right after the war?"

"No, son. Nobody had any money for that. The war destroyed Virginia. These monuments were put up several decades later. Most of the soldiers were dead by then, those who, unlike Jackson, survived the war."

Nearby place names synonymous with bloodshed rattled around Sandy's brain: Fredericksburg. Cold Harbor. Malvern Hill. Petersburg.

"Lost a lot of good men, north and south," his father added. "Between John Brown's raid and Appomattox, more than six hundred thousand in all."

Sandy struggled to grasp the scale of the loss.

"The Times-Daily prints nearly a hundred and fifty thousand papers a day on weekdays."

"Okay, then," his father noted, "take four days of that, and you're almost there."

The car skirted a tall monument to Jefferson Davis, the sickly president of the Confederacy who boarded the last train out of Richmond as Rebel troops torched the warehouse district, freed criminals from prison and fled the city after years of siege.

"If the soldiers were already dead," Sandy asked, "why'd they build the monuments?"

"Different reasons. Pride, partly. Trying to restore a little pride after losing the war."

"Never knew a Virginian to come up short on pride."

His father smiled.

"The war left Virginia in ruins, remember. Cities blown to pieces. Livestock gone, farms destroyed. Railroads ripped apart. Richmond was gutted. Virginia people were on their own."

He veered the car around a rough patch of roadway.

"Didn't all the Presidents come from Virginia," Sandy asked.

"Well, Washington, of course. Four of the first five, in fact."

"And didn't a Virginian write the Declaration of Independence?"

"Thomas Jefferson, yeah. And then Madison wrote the Constitution. And the Bill of Rights — that was George Mason, mostly."

Sandy felt it should be making more sense, but somehow it made even less.

"Seems like Virginians would've fought to save the country, not slavery."

"Some tried. It split the state," his father explained. "The whole country was split. We were two different countries, in some ways. Big cities, factories and banks up north. Farms and rivers and fields down south."

"And slaves," Sandy added.

"Lot of Virginians knew that was wrong. Nobody figured out how to stop it. Politicians couldn't find a way to get it done, from either side. War's what happens when politics fails and the people don't demand better - in Virginia or anywhere else."

He slowed the car and steered it through a broad circle. Sandy arched his neck to look up at a bronze figure atop a massive block of stone. It towered above the pavement like a church without a steeple, stretching toward the open sky, a general and his horse, mounting the very crest of heaven and facing south. Below it was one word flanked by a pair of black marble columns: LEE.

It was a word that embodied a civilization, no less, it seemed to Sandy, than Churchill or Tut.

"When'd that one go up?"

"Late eighteen hundreds. 'Bout twenty years after he died, I b'lieve."

"Lee wasn't even alive?"

"Never would've allowed it. Wouldn't even let 'em fly the Confederate battle flag at his fun'ral. Lee hated the idea of secession. He hated the whole war. Was never part of the old 'Forget Hell' crowd. When it was over, he told his men to go back to their homes and their families. Time to move forward, not look back."

"Why'd the statue ever get built, then?"

"It wasn't about building a statue. More like a resurrection. Raising Lee up from the tomb decades after the fire, the evacuation and the surrender. Told a story a lot of people wanted to hear. Gallantry. Resilience. Defiance."

His father cast a quick glance in the rear view mirror.

"You can always make a political statement with a speech," he said. "You recast history in bronze and stone. That's what these monuments are all about."

Sandy thought about Jimmy Jeter, the flaming cross in his yard. He thought about the old man on the bicycle, wondered how he felt when he passed by these statutes, whether they reminded him of good governance, banking and valor.

"Dad," he asked, "do you think these monuments make people feel comfortable?"

His father drummed his fingers on the steering wheel.

"Nobody wants to be remembered for the worst that's in us," he said.

"Nobody wants to be defined by defeat."

The car drifted around a large statute of J.E.B. Stuart, the Confederate cavalry commander who was killed defending the northern gates of Richmond. The broad boulevard narrowed into a one-way street tightly bordered by town houses and a great domed synagogue.

"But no, son, they don't feel good to everyone. For some, they just reopen the ugliness again and again. Having to pass by all this, pay some kind of tribute, makes some people feel like they don't belong. To them, it's divisive. It's hurtful."

Sandy had passed the monuments a thousand times without once wondering what they were doing there. He'd never questioned their almost religious power to reshape the collective memory of the South, reinvent the very meaning of the Confederacy and cloak a brutal injustice behind a veil of heroism. He'd never imagined the pain they stirred or the fury they sowed in the hearts of people whose own families helped build Virginia with their bare hands.

"Think they'll ever put up a monument to the slaves?"

His father smiled and cocked his head to one side. "That's a good question, Sandy."

He glanced at the boy, then turned back to the road.

"Never knew Dixie was so complicated," Sandy said.

His father nodded and looked straight ahead.

"Dixie's about community, son. It's about believing in our people. It's about believing in all our people."

The car slowed to a stop by the curb. Sandy stepped out onto the brick walkway, breezed past the freshly trimmed boxwoods, through the double doorway of the Old Dominion Ladies Society townhouse and into the dazzling hardwood splendor of Mrs. Randolph's cotillion.

 # Chapter 12

Sandy dug his hands in his pockets and heard the steel taps on his loafers clicking against the gleaming floor.

"Evenin' young man, let's straighten that tie, shall we?"

Seized by a sudden constriction about the neck, Sandy froze in place as his tie was yanked into line and snugged around his collar by the sure and firm fingers of Phyllis van Cleft. The gaunt and bespectacled matron stood in the foyer greeting each entrant while clutching a slender, black orchestral baton, her once-ample bosom pressed to prominent display by the yoke of her strapless gown.

Correcting the sartorial deficiencies of apprehensive young boys was a specialty of Mrs. van Cleft, one in which she took evident pride and excessive pleasure. Sandy raised his chin and felt her fingernails scrape the underside of his neck. He winced momentarily, his eyes darted to her face and she stretched a wiry smile across a set of tightly clenched teeth that reminded the boy of a sprocket cut from case-hardened steel.

"Thank you ma'am," he said, as he bowed his head slightly and stepped past Mrs. van Cleft, her shoulders bare, her floor-length gown a blood red rustle of crinoline and lace as she turned to face the next entrant.

"Evenin' young lady," she implored a tall, pale and freckled girl in a cream satin dress with matching shoes and an untimely propensity toward a slouch. "Let's hold our shoulders up tonight," she said, driving home the point with a faint tap of her baton against the girl's bare arm.

Mrs. van Cleft took a unique view of hospitality, Sandy felt, warning her guests as much as welcoming them, a sort of lingering blast of winter on a warm spring night. Through her countenance alone, she put her young charges on notice that this was not the place to assert distinguishing personality traits or adolescent notions of independence. This was a stark and unforgiving social proving ground where ordinary rules of comity and common sense were suspended or abandoned so that young teenage girls and boys might be magically transformed into something else entirely, adhering to an almost liturgical code of conduct enshrined in customs adopted generations before along scrupulously gender-specific lines.

Girls were not to ask a boy to dance, nor to decline the offer of one. Boys, for that matter, could only dance with the girl they happened upon in the curious spin of a social roulette wheel known as the Grand March. Boys lined up along one wall, girls on the other, so the two sides could promenade to the music and be brought together like a giant shuffling of human cards, partners selected at random and expected to feign delight and even gratitude at the outcome, no matter how discouraging. Beyond that, exchanges of partners would be infrequent and only under the precise direction of Mrs. Randolph, who would instruct each beau to bow slightly, and each belle to return a brief curtsy, before staggering and stumbling through the ensuing foxtrot, minuet or waltz.

Efforts to break with protocol in the interest of, say, pairing up along lines of mutual attraction, were, to put it delicately, dissuaded under the watchful eye and ready baton of the ever vigilant Mrs. van Cleft. She roamed the floor enforcing the strictures of custom with a certain ecclesiastical zeal, as if the youth of Richmond had precipitated some imminent crisis of the human condition and it was her mission to rescind the laws of natural selection long enough to stave off the descent of the entire generation into some ruinous purgatory of ash and flame.

If her burden were great, her mission was noble, and she understood it with rare and unambiguous clarity. Boys, to her, were raw and splintered timber, their predilections so threatening to adolescent girls that the two had no business being in the same community together, let alone the same room. The girls were little better, Mrs. van Cleft reasoned, but their tender sensibilities were no match for primal instincts untamed.

"The problem with men comes when we mistake them for our equals," Sandy once overheard her say to a kindred matron, "because then we expect too much of them."

Still, Mrs. van Cleft held fast to her belief that perhaps three or four boys might be broken each season, that one or two of those might someday mature into men suited to wed and take their place in the upper echelon of the city's social elite. That was her mission. That was her prayer. That was the best she could hope for on this night in May, the final dance of the '68 Season, when she would meet her glory in little more than an hour, overseeing the evening finale, the Grand Waltz.

It was a moment in the making since cotillion began in February. Since then, Sandy, like everyone else in the room, had attended two required afternoon sessions at Mrs. Randolph's immaculate West End home, where they were tutored not only in the music and steps of the ancient exchange but also in the graces and politics of cotillion courtship.

A girl was not to ask for a Coke but instead to allow her partner the honor of bringing her one. He was to present it to her with a white cocktail napkin carefully wrapped around the bottle, lest she soil her dress with condensate, and the straw was to be carefully inserted so she needn't fuss with it through glove-cloaked fingers. Names and pleasantries were to be exchanged with a natural fluency and without the strain of indecision or lapse.

Conversation should flow, Mrs. Randolph instructed, "like snow melt rolling down a mountain stream," and woe to those who might freeze in its path.

Beyond the fine points of conversation, there was the fundamental imperative to show your partner good manners, an indication of one's capacity for allegiance. Girls were to remain at their partner's side, deferring to them on matters of brief discussion and dismissing all other flirtations as distractions to be rebuffed. Boys were to offer affirmation to their partner by introducing her without pause should another couple engage. And, apart from the fleeting moment it might take to fetch a Coke from a tray extended by a passing server, under no circumstances, but none, was a boy to leave his partner on the ballroom floor alone. That, in this room, was the cardinal and singularly unforgiveable sin.

Mrs. Randolph's ballroom was meant to be a sanctuary from all that was common and crass, a dreamlike place where romance might be summoned almost on demand, like music or portraiture or fine cuisine. That sort of social alchemy, however, required a certain order, without which all could quickly descend into chaos — unpredictable and horrifying. Nothing was more so than for a girl to find herself alone and available on the vast dance floor, as out of place at Mrs. Randolph's cotillion as a mule in a swimming pool — and just about as welcome.

There were no chairs in the ballroom, no alcoves or hallways where an unescorted girl might be concealed and the only way for her to be rescued from conspicuous isolation would be if someone else's partner were to desert, passing the condition from one unfortunate girl to the next, like the chicken pox. Not the sort of thing Mrs. Randolph's was all about.

Sandy stepped into the ballroom, a glistening chamber the size of a basketball court, its pale green walls matching the richly embroidered drapes across tall windows with deep casements framed in ornate molding. An enormous crystal chandelier hung from the center of the ceiling, a good eighteen feet overhead. A five-piece band tuned up on a small stage at the opposite end of the floor. Perhaps sixty adolescents milled around in clusters of two or three: boys on the right side, girls to the left.

Sandy recognized an athletic-looking boy with blonde wavy hair and surrounded by others vying for his attention: Stoney Wickett, Sandy thought to himself, the pride of Colgate Academy.

Wickett stood with a hand stuffed in one pocket as if propping himself up from a perpetual slump, a long blue and orange striped tie dangling loosely around his narrow neck, one foot askew as he dragged the toe of a scuffed and faded loafer against the ballroom floor. Sandy spotted a patch of bare ankle beneath a cuff of his khaki pants. Wickett had shown up without socks and managed to slip under the radar as he passed by Mrs. van Cleft on his way inside.

"Biggest prick in the room," Sandy muttered to himself, "and that's sayin' something."

Across the floor, amid a gaggle of girls, be spotted Hattie Newcastle. Her pale purple gown fell the full length of her slender body and ended just above the floor, all but concealing a pair of white satin shoes, the toes darkened and rubbed to nap by a season of missteps from the imprecise dance partners she'd grudgingly endured. Sandy had danced with her before, and devoutly prayed to never do so again. She'd livened the evening, he recalled, with incessant chatter and a laugh like hot peppers on a tender tongue. He could see her now, angling for her chance to be paired with Stoney Wickett, who she watched like a darkly feathered raptor wearing heavy eye liner and circling her prey.

"The perfect pair," Sandy thought, his malicious musings suddenly interrupted by the sight of a tall sax player in a black tuxedo standing in front of a drum set emblazoned in black script: The Commonwealth Classics.

The drummer ran a four count and the band opened up on cue. Sandy joined the other boys lining up along the wall for the Grand March. As if from thin air, Mrs. Randolph appeared, a beaming whirl of sky blue taffeta and ivory lace, gliding across the stage like the last gasp of spring.

"Let the dance begin," she declared, falling back into a deep formal curtsy that, by custom, opened the Grand March.

In more than a decade as a widow, Mrs. Randolph had devoted herself entirely to the keeping of the social keys of Richmond, a position that required no husband and, for that matter, seemed best served by the absence of one. Widowhood, she'd discovered, was an opportunity not to be squandered, especially when secured by the inheritance from her late-husband's tobacco brokerage concern.

A musty old trading house rooted in antebellum Virginia, the Pamunkey and Chickahominy Corn Company had begun as a humble granary and evolved. Shortly before he died, Harrison Drewry Randolph sold off to a cadre of Philadelphia speculators most of the riverside warehouses and property his family had accumulated along the northern bank of the deep-channeled river, leaving him, briefly, a rich man and constituting, more enduringly, the basis of the widow Randolph's endowment.

A member in good standing of the Old Dominion Ladies' Society, Mrs. Randolph quickly established herself as one of its more reliable benefactors. And so, when she decided, in the spring of 1954, that the city's privileged youth were in dire need of a proper cotillion, the stucco Italianate mansion that had long served as the Ladies' Society headquarters emerged as its natural home.

It was built in the early 19th century by a Welsh engineer who'd developed a prosperous iron foundry on the nearby banks of the river. He relied on coal from the Manchester pits on the river's south side, iron ore barged down the Kanawha Canal from the mountains to the west, the cheap labor of surplus slaves rented by the day from neighboring planters and the power of the river to turn its giant rolling mills. When new, the home anchored the fashionable West End of the city, several blocks from the Capitol that Thomas Jefferson himself designed as a white-columned temple to American democracy and the rights of man. Well, some of them anyway. Over time, the city enveloped the grand old villa, which found itself sitting catty-corner from the block-long building owned by the Richmond Times-Daily Company.

The commercial centerpiece of downtown Richmond, the Times-Daily building was a living, breathing, industrial wonder. Its six-story walls housed all the people, materials and machinery needed to produce a newspaper with the content of an average-sized novel every morning, seven days a week.

There were offices for the salespeople who filled the paper with retail and classified ads each day, the executives who oversaw finances and investments and the publisher who made sure the paper reflected his view of the community the paper was expected to mirror. There was the circulation department, in charge of selling the paper and getting it delivered each day. There was the newsroom, where reporters, editors and photographers told the stories of the times, and the production room, where layout designers put it all together in pictures, headlines and words. At the heart of it all were the giant presses, an incomprehensible collection of massive rollers and minute cogs pieced together into a single monstrous machine, three stories tall and a city block long.

It was an unruly yet terrifyingly efficient assemblage of motors and sprayers, floppy webbed belts and shimmering steel that somehow wedded power and precision to transform images and ideas into paper and ink. As much magic as mechanics, it was a technological treasure, heir to a noble ancestral line reaching back to Guttenberg. The Times-Daily Company treated it that way, showcasing the press behind enormous windows and lighting it with almost theatrical form, like a post-industrial Faberge egg encased in polished glass, so that Richmonders passing by on foot or by car might pause to marvel and wonder at its grandeur and grace. More than a mere tribute to industrial might, the press was a reminder of the power the newspaper wielded to shape public perceptions, its institutional authority to influence thought every bit as unchallenged as that of the First Virginia Bank to direct the economic fortunes of the state or, for that matter, as that of the Legislature to pass its laws.

At no time of the week was the press busier than on Saturday night, when great rolls of newsprint the size of Volkswagens whirred like a child's pinwheel on giant spools that sent the thin, smooth parchment racing through the veins of the miraculous machinery that turned it into the Sunday newspaper.

It all caught Sandy's attention through an open pair of French doors as he rounded the crest of the grand promenade, just behind the witless and bare-ankled Stoney Wickett. Sandy heard the sharp thwack of Mrs. van Cleft's baton employed to thwart an attempt at a last-minute reshuffling by a girl in the opposite line, as he turned to confront the reluctantly extended elbow and decidedly disappointed expression of the purple-plumed Hattie Newcastle.

She was a good three inches taller than Sandy, even without the heels on her toe-scuffed shoes. Taking her by the arm to lead her down the middle of the freshly polished floor, he felt a sudden tightening of her hand, as she slipped momentarily, and then caught herself.

"That won't happen again," she whispered, more to herself than to Sandy, though he well grasped the spontaneous sentiment.

Hardly anyone's idea of the belle of the ball, Hattie possessed, nonetheless, unbounded self-regard. Across her thin and graceless face could be read the conviction that she was suffering some grievous injustice. She knew nothing about Sandy, and that was bad enough. This, to Hattie, was a perfect waste, a missed opportunity to be with Stoney Wickett, or at least one of his friends who might be counted on to speak lustily of her in his presence. The sooner this part of the evening was over, she felt, the better.

"Face your partner," Mrs. Randolph directed as the two lines completed their fateful merger, leaving a double line down the center of the ballroom floor.

Sandy turned toward Hattie, who gazed off somewhere beyond.

"Sandy Rivers," he said with a measured bow. "I'm honored."

"Hattie Newcastle," she replied with the faintest of curtsies, suggesting she well understood just what an honor it was.

With that, Sandy stepped toward her, took her right hand in his left as his other found a spot midway down the back of her dress. He drew her, not exactly near, but close enough to prompt her to grimace and sigh.

She wasn't all that unattractive, Sandy thought, and she did have a certain force of personality. She had the decency to wear gloves, so at least no skin was touching.

"What the hell," he figured.

Over the next twenty minutes or so the accidental couple muddled through pained motions as the ensemble played numbers Sandy faintly recognized from his grandmother's record player. Hattie did her best to steer them toward Stoney Wickett and his privileged mate, so that, when time came to change partners, Hattie was positioned to engineer the outcome she sought. Her unearned suffering was at last redeemed, when the blonde and sockless boy offered up his dance partner to Sandy in exchange for Hattie, as readily as a goat might be swapped for a sow.

"Please allow me to introduce Miss Hope Stafford," Wickett said with a slight bow to Sandy, who replied in kind, receiving as his new partner the slump-shouldered, pale-skinned girl he'd seen chastened in the doorway by Mrs. van Cleft.

Up close, Sandy could see tiny cornflowers in soft blue and yellow hues stitched into her cream cotton dress. It had a loose fit to it, as though it were bought for her to grow into, and it hung from her shoulders with an easy drape.

"I forgot my gloves," she said apologetically, as Sandy took her moist palms in his own.

"Let's liven things up a bit," Mrs. Randolph proclaimed over the glistening microphone, and Sandy saw the cello player switch to a sunburst-yellow, hollow-body guitar while the pianist sat down before an electric keyboard.

"Alright Chubby,'" she joked with the reed-thin sax player, "let's twist!"

And with that the band broke into a brassy if slightly down-tempo rendition of the rock classic that threw out a generation of young spines half a decade before. It was a relief for Sandy to release Hope's clammy hands, even if his steps were no more fluid than before. He felt her looking at him through much of the dance, and at last he glanced her way long enough to exchange a quick smile, before they both looked off again.

From the corner of one eye, Sandy caught a glimpse of Stoney Wickett, both arms draped over the bare shoulders of an ebullient Hattie Newcastle. There was someone who could make a guy appreciate a girl like Hope Stafford, Sandy thought, as though suddenly discovering hidden value where little other appeared. He looked back at her and smiled.

The band labored through a medley of early pop standards that passed for contemporary hits at Mrs. Randolph's, progressing to the drummer's showcase number, Buddy Holly's "Not Fade Away," clearly a high note for Mrs. Randoph, who smiled broadly and even briefly closed her eyes while swaying to its driving rhythms.

She led the cotillion in polite applause then stepped to the microphone, her face glowing with joy.

"There will be a brief interlude for us all to catch our breath," she said, fanning her face with one hand, "and then, in just a few minutes, we'll all take our places for the Grand Waltz."

A team of men in white linen jackets appeared, each holding a tray of opened bottles of Coca-Cola, cocktail napkins and straws.

"May I get you a Coke," Sandy asked Hope, noticing the French doors along the far wall.

"Yes, thank you."

He dismissed himself with a brief nod and the upward flare of an index finger to suggest an immediate return.

Heading across the room and toward the open French doors, he saw a flickering light and heard the growl of a truck pulling away from the Times-Daily building. He felt a blast of cool air across his face, as he stepped toward the doors. There was a small balcony outside, with a bowed wrought iron railing waist-high. Perhaps five feet below was a small garden, a walkway of old brick and high boxwood hedge. He looked out beyond the shrubbery, across the street and through the glass windows of the Times-Daily building. He heard the thundering whir of the presses.

"Gentlemen," Mrs. Randolph beckoned, as the room seemed to fall away from Sandy. "Let's take a couple more minutes and then prepare to lead your partners to the center of the floor for the Grand Waltz!"

The railing was cool and solid to Sandy's grip. In one swift movement he hauled his legs over, threw his body behind and leaped to the ground, his loafers smacking against the brick walkway below.

Chapter 13

Sandy crouched for a moment, half expecting someone, Mrs. van Cleft or perhaps one of the servers, to appear at the railing above and order him back inside. Instead, all he heard were the Classics, opening up with the solemn strains of a waltz. He stood, brushed off his knees, breathed in the night air against the boxwood hedge, and looked up toward the light shining down from the ballroom where he'd stood just moments before.

He imagined the scene unfolding inside. Boys and their partners scrambling to take their places on a crowded floor, a glistening game board of polished hardwood, Mrs. Randolph and her sidekick proudly surveying the cream of the new social dominion and savoring the pinnacle of the cotillion season. And there, he suddenly realized, abandoned and mystified on the ballroom floor, would be Hope Stafford, her bare palms going increasingly damp as she wondered why she'd been left alone. It was an awkward and briefly harrowing thought, interrupted by the sound of an enormous steel door sliding open on a concrete loading dock across the street.

Sandy looked through a break in the hedges and saw a large man in dark work clothes walking past a mountain of freshly bundled newspapers by a long, white truck idling on a concrete parking pad.

"The Sunday papers," Sandy said out loud.

He pushed through the hedges, crossed the street and gazed up at a river of paper and ink rolling over giant presses behind glass windows. He walked around the corner toward the loading dock and saw the truck rumble off.

"Hey, young man," a dockworker hollered down from the loading area. "Watch out you don't get hit comin' 'round here like that."

"Sorry," said Sandy, startled. "I'm a paperboy. I've never seen the Sunday papers before on Saturday night."

The man looked at Sandy, drew the last breath of smoke from a spent cigarette and tossed it onto the concrete. "Well," he said, reaching out a hand. "Climb on up."

There was a high shrill and Sandy saw a grease-caked forklift heading from the building, cradling a palette bearing newspaper bundles, envelopes with route numbers attached to each one.

"There they are," the dockworker called out. "How many you need?"

Sandy imagined them on their way, bound for some far corner of the city or remote reach of the state. Some were headed for drugstores, where customers would read them the next morning with bacon and eggs. Others were destined for metal boxes in places like Roanoke, Lynchburg and Norfolk. Most, though, wound up on a corner lot near a crossroads, on some barren patch of clay and sand, lying in the darkness until a paperboy on a rusting bicycle picked them up then rode off into the thin remains of the night to deliver them one by one.

Even now, Sandy thought as he looked at the papers, thousands of them, each might as well have a name on it, the person who would read it, head nodding or shaking, with a smile, a scowl or a raised eyebrow. Someone would put it down to call out for a husband or wife to come look at what was in the Times-Daily that morning. Someone else would clip a coupon to save 15 cents off their next carton of Tide, rip out the box score of last night's Braves' game, underline the phone number of the crew chief who might give them their next job, or carefully cut out a loved one's obituary and place it in a frame where it would be read again and again, year after year.

Sandy peeled back the brown paper from a bundle and saw the words Richmond Times-Daily printed across the top. "Largest Sunday circulation in Virginia" beneath a boldface number: "200,670."

The paper was fat, enormous, and Sandy felt a pall of dread at the thought of having to haul the weighty tomes down Tempest Lane in just a few hours. He read the date: Sunday, May 5, 1968, and smiled.

"It's still Saturday night," he thought to himself, as if taking in a great secret the rest of the world wouldn't discover until the next day.

Then he saw the headline on the main story: "Saigon, 12 Other Cities Shelled by Viet Kong." It was large and in boldface above four columns of type.

Sandy glanced at the story. Snipers shot a South Vietnamese general in an alley near the American Embassy in Saigon. Authorities suspected a Viet Cong guerrilla attack.

Where is Saigon? Sandy wondered. And what's a "Kong"?

"U.S., Hanoi Envoys Discuss Arrangements with French," said the headline on a related story. Sandy cocked his head to one side, peeled the brown paper further back and followed his eyes as they skipped across the page.

The telephone company averted a strike by agreeing to pay union workers an additional eight dollars a week. The South Carolina governor called out the National Guard after blacks and whites faced off in a place called Gaffney. Some guy named Richard Nixon won a mock presidential nomination at Washington & Lee University in Lexington.

And there was a one-line summary note directing readers to an article in the Commentary section of the paper: "Robert Kennedy is helped and hindered by the memory of his brother in his efforts to win the presidency."

Then came a screeching roar. Sandy looked up and saw a steel door swing open. A man in work clothes blackened by ink strode out and let the door shut behind him, a silvery lunch box in one hand.

"'Night, boys," he hollered over his shoulder, striking out toward the street and carrying a Sunday paper, like a miner headed home with a bucket of coal.

"That way is the presses, son," the dockworker pointed and said. "Noisiest damn place you ever heard."

Sandy edged over to the open door, put his hands to his ears and headed up a cement stairway. There was a door covered with inked fingerprints. Sandy opened it and stepped into a large and dimly lit room that broadly fit his imaginings of hell. It smelled of solvents. Flames flared from a furnace on the far side of the floor jammed with a dozen or so peculiar machines. They stood about six feet high and looked like a giant typewriter welded to some sort of Dickensian loom. Before each one sat a man, typing with forceful, deliberate strokes.

Sandy pressed his hands against his ears. There was a shattering cacophony of metallic crashes and claps, overlaid atop a sort of hammering drone that seemed to come from the floor. Sandy took a tentative step into the darkened room and toward the furnace.

A heavy hand gripped his shoulder. He looked up and saw a large, ruddy-faced man in an ink-stained apron motioning toward the flame.

"It'll singe the hair off your head," he hollered. "C'mon."

Sandy followed, pausing as a man pushed past a cart loaded with what looked like broken newspapers made of lead. He began tossing the chunks of metal into a large bin beside the furnace, where a glass-enclosed fire extinguisher hung from the wall.

The large man let go of Sandy, reached his hand into the bin, hauled out a hunk of metal the size of a ruler and offered it to the boy. Sandy took it and saw it cover his hand in black ink. The big man shrugged his shoulders and smiled. It felt surprisingly heavy, as Sandy held it up against the light of the fire, a line of letters in raised relief. He tried to read it, but the letters were backward.

"Lead," the man hollered to him. "Lead type."

Sandy cocked his head to hear against the roaring din and found himself facing the fire extinguisher. Reflected in the glass he read the face of the type.

"Shelled by Viet Kong."

The big man pointed a chubby, ink-stained finger at the K, shook his head and scowled. Sandy nodded and looked up to the man.

"When the type breaks, or we catch a mistake, we got to stop the presses, strip out the bad type, and make a fix. We melt the bad type back to molten lead, then feed it back into the Linotype machines."

He motioned toward the machines that looked like giant typewriters where the men sat. The fellow with the cart handed Sandy two more chunks of lead.

One had a fat number printed on it, above the word, in smaller type, "Lettuce."

The other was covered with tiny dots, hundreds of them it looked like. Sandy held it against the flame, tilted it to one side and could make out the photographic image of a soldier wearing a helmet and carrying a gun.

"Photo-engraving," the man hollered. "That's how we print a picture."

He pointed to a deep scratch running the length of the image.

"We'll put a clean one in for the next press run," he bellowed out. "You can have it. Nothin' but scrap to us."

Sandy smiled and tucked the broken treasures into his blazer pockets.

"Wan'na see the presses right quick?"

Sandy nodded and smiled, as they moved near one of the large machines.

"Linotype," Sandy's new guide hollered. A man seated at an oversized keyboard leaned back and raised his hand, summoning a boy not much older than Sandy, who attached a printed page to a clip beside the typist.

From the armless, spring-loaded chair where he sat, the man looked up and smiled. Narrow eyes peered out from behind thick bifocals in heavy black frames. On the floor beside him was a sandwich wrapped in wax paper and a slender cap with the letters VFW stitched on it.

"Jack here is one of the fastest men on the floor," the big man screamed out over the deafening din. Jack nodded, adjusted his glasses then crossed his arms.

Sandy read the paper on the clip.

"AMMAN, Jordan (AP) — Jordanian and Israeli forces clashed twice along the Jordan River Saturday, a Jordanian Army spokesman announced."

The typist pointed to the paper, then to the keyboard.

"Right," Sandy acknowledged.

"He types a stroke, the machine drops a mold of that letter down this slot," the big man hollered. "When he's done typing, he yanks down on this rod, hot lead pours into the mold and we get full lines of type. We take that down to the makeup room. They lay it out on a big heavy table we call the stone. Lock it down in a chase, kind'a like a steel picture frame. Then we use that to make lead plates, one for each page."

The old man looked up and said nothing.

"Fast is good," the big man hollered. "But it's got to be right. Once you pull that rod, the type's set. Don't matter what the editors and reporters do; Jack here makes a mistake, it gets made two hundred thousand times, 'less somebody catch it 'n make a fix. That costs money, and it takes time. 'N those'r two things we ain' got a lot of here at the newspaper."

The seated man just nodded and smiled.

"Nice seein' ya son," he said, turning slightly in his chair.

Sandy looked down, expecting to see the old man's shoes, and instead saw baggy pants legs hanging empty and limp.

.   "Yes sir," the boy hollered with a faint drop of his chin. "Thank you, sir."

Sandy took a step back, and followed the man in the ink-stained apron, away from the hammering clap-trap of the Linotype machines, beyond the roar of the flames and toward a long glass window at the far end of the room. Sandy looked down through the glass and onto the presses below.

"You'll need these," the big man hollered, handing him a pair of ear covers. Sandy slipped them on and followed the man onto a cement apron running the length of the pressroom.

The presses were still, and Sandy could see what looked like an endless sheet of paper strung through massive rollers like a river of parchment winding over rapids of rubber and steel. From the far end of the press, a lean man with chiseled biceps headed his way, carrying what looked like a single sheet of bright metal the size of a newspaper page.

"New plate," the big man hollered to Sandy. 'Member that bad headline? Twenty minutes, we can make a fix." He put his hands on his hips and gave a quick nod. "From spottin' the mistake to rollin' 'em back out."

The pressman sidled up to a giant roller and locked in the new plate. It glistened like a freshly minted dime, the absolute last word in front-page news, little more than a few minutes old, as enduring as the printed word, a modern-day metallic petroglyph, cast in a moment of fury and fire and captured for all time.

Sandy stepped back and felt the pad beneath him start to quake, as the massive presses began to roll. The paper sped past in an incomprehensible blur, newsprint, pale and lifeless, running the finely tuned gauntlet of rollers and plates that transformed it into the Sunday paper, the weekly centerpiece of commerce and thought that pulled together the Times-Daily readers, reporters and advertisers and bound them in a single community that spanned the state in a conversation that encompassed the world.

Sandy followed the big man into another large room, where men scrambled to snatch bundles off a conveyor belt.

"I'll need these back," he hollered, slipping off Sandy's ear covers. "Come back anytime — long as it's late at night."

Sandy looked up at the big man, noticed a smudge of ink on his fleshy cheek and smiled. A bit of the Times-Daily that didn't make it into print.

"Thanks," Sandy said. "I will."

He shuffled out past the loading dock and hopped down to the sidewalk. Turning the corner toward Franklin Street, Sandy froze in his tracks. Youths were streaming out of the double doors at Mrs. Randolph's cotillion, climbing into waiting cars or milling around to look for their rides out front.

"Goodnight, and congratulations on another wonderful season of dance." It was the grating voice of a beaming Mrs. van Cleft, joyfully bidding her youthful charges farewell.

As Sandy crossed the street, Mrs. van Cleft caught sight of him in the headlights of a nearing car. Her demeanor shifted like a summer sky before a storm, and a bejeweled and spindly forefinger lunged forth like snake lightning.

"Sanford Jackson Rivers," she summoned, stumbling down the steps in her heels and seizing him by both lapels. His peers and their parents stopped cold to leer at her captured quarry. "Just where have you been young man?"

Sandy opened his mouth but was cut off before he could speak.

"Never in all my years at Mrs. Randolph's have I known anyone to do what you did tonight, to simply up and leave. Deserting your partner? Leaving her there on the ballroom floor? How do you think you made that young lady feel? Do you know the consternation you've caused us here tonight? Do you have any idea the trouble you made for Mrs. Randolph and me? Good God, young man, do you know what you did to the cotillion?"

Sandy gazed down at the brick sidewalk and the crimson hem of Mrs. van Cleft's dress, her words sinking in like rain water in old shoes.

"Look at me when I speak to you," she demanded. "I'm ashamed of you."

"Nice one, Rivers."

There was the smirking face of Stoney Wickett, wandering out of the cotillion with Hattie Newcastle on one arm, a thin smile peeling off her mouth as she shook her head and turned away.

Sandy felt the lead in his pockets tug at his blazer, heard a truck lumbering out from across the street and felt a sudden longing for the deafening pressroom.

"I'm going to address this with your father, young man," Mrs. van Cleft vowed. "First thing Monday morning. And I suggest you have it cleared up with him by then, if you've got it in you, which, looking at you now, frankly, I doubt."

Her castigation complete, she turned on one heel, dismissing Sandy in a parting gesture of contempt. "Misjudged that one," he heard her mutter as she walked away. "Pathetic."

Sandy felt a welling up in his eyes, from shame or anger, he couldn't tell, pulled inky hands from his pockets and wiped them full across his face. From the far end of the sidewalk, he caught the gaze of the last person on Earth he wanted to see.

She stood in the soft light of a gas lamp at the edge of the street, staring at Sandy as though he were some curious object of public disdain, her pale and freckled face gone a flat and formless expression of . . . what was it, exactly? Sandy searched her face for clues, then locked his eyes on hers.

"I'm sorry," he moved his mouth to say, the words not quite coming out, as a faded red Falcon pulled to the curb, its passenger window rolled down.

"Let's go Hope," came a man's voice from behind the wheel, as the young girl leaned down to open the door, clutched at her dress as she stepped inside, glanced back one last time at Sandy, and smiled.

# Chapter 14

Dawn wandered in as though it might not stay, spreading the first tenuous light of day across the eastern sky, a soft and silent sea of blue, its seamless surface cut by a fiery blade of rose-colored light beneath a line of clouds.

"Early bird," Sandy hollered out, as he rolled up to the mountain of Sunday papers listing against the red clay surface of the vacant lot.

Catesby Raines glanced up and gave a faint-hearted smile. "Hell'd you expect?" he mumbled, as Sandy leaned his bike against the telephone pole and peered into the pile of papers in search for bundles tagged F-45.

An overbearing beast of newsprint, each Sunday paper weighed a good pound and a half, a dozen news and feature sections stuffed to overflowing with inserts — ads from Food Fair, Sears and Richmond's rival department stores, Thalhimers and Miller & Rhodes.

Sandy dragged his bundles together, five in all, hauled one up into his basket and dropped another into a large canvas bag.

"Not too bad today," Catesby offered, giving a kick to his own bag to make room for several papers he then forced into the engorged pouch.

"Why does Winston call you that?"

"You mean my nickname," Catesby responded.

"Yeah."

"Couple weeks after he became district manager, that's when I started my route. It's mostly the length of Ridgetop Road. I got about a hundred papers," Catesby began.

"My third day on the route, my bike slid out from under me on a wet curve in the road. I look up and here comes a milk truck. Brakes locked, skidding sideways across the road. Scared the hell out'ta me."

"Damn, Catesby."

"The truck went grill down in the mud in the ditch. I got off with a few bruises and scrapes, but my basket was all bent up. I'd barely gotten up myself when the milkman comes running up."

"What the hell?"

"I'm telling you, he was more shaken up than I was. 'You alright son? Anything hurt? You okay?' He was panting like he'd run the mile. He leaned in close to my face and I could smell a vile mix of coffee and stale cigarette smoke on his breath. Like to gagged."

"Damn."

"He reached out his hand and kept asking me, 'You alright, son? You alright?'"

"How old was the guy?"

"Hell, it was Whit Whelan," Catesby said. "The milkman. You seen him around here. I don't know, fifty or so, I guess."

"Were you okay?"

"I was fine. Embarrassed mostly. The bike was pretty heavy with all my papers and all, and it just kept pullin' and pullin' me right down that hill. I tried puttin' on my brakes, felt the rear wheel break loose, 'n me and the bike and the papers was down, just slidin' 'cross the road, like it was glazed with ice."

"Damnation."

"Anyway, Whit Whelan took me up to a house beside the road. It was pitch dark and all. He knocked on the door, guy opened it, let Whit Whelan use his phone. He called the circulation department. Was all upset."

"What'd you do?"

"I tried to make a joke about it. 'No use cryin' over spilled milk,' I said. Then he kind'a seemed to snap. 'I ain't worried about the damned milk,' he said. It was weird. He called the paper company before he called his own office. Fact, he never called them at all until after Winston showed up, come to think of it. Once he found out I was okay, Winston left me sitting in the kitchen and went out front to the milkman for — what looked through the window like — some kind of heart-to-heart."

It was slowly getting lighter. Sandy could see a stripe of mud running across the toe of a sneaker.

"I felt bad for the old guy," Catesby continued. "Figured Winston was going out there to give him hell. Then I saw him put an arm on Whit Whelan's shoulder, even patted him once or twice on the back. I couldn't see all that good, but it looked like Whit Whelan was cryin' or something."

Sandy pulled up his canvas bag, and let it rest atop the papers in his basket.

"Anyway, Winston and I gathered up the papers, got into his car and delivered my route together that morning. He told me I'd scared the hell out of the milkman and I needed to learn how to ride a damned bike. 'Steer more, slide less.' That was his advice. Smart ass. Ever since, he's called me the Slider."

Sandy smiled and looked down.

"Funny thing, though, when he dropped me back off to pick up my bike, there was a huge tow truck pulling the milk truck out of the ditch. Whit Whelan was standing beside my bike. He'd worked the basket back into shape and wiped off the mud and grit."

Catesby hammered his fist into the last of his papers, stuffing them into his basket.

Few months later, I quit my route. That was a mistake. So, I let Winston know, anything shakes loose, gi'me a call, 'n here I am. New route. Same nickname."

The rose-colored cloud had turned a brilliant orange. A half-moon hung low at the far edge of sky, its soft light spreading like a veil of gold across the tops of the trees to the west.

"That's that," he said. "See ya."

Sandy hauled the heavy bag across his shoulder. His basket could hold no more papers. He'd have to come back for the rest.

"Largest Sunday Circulation in Virginia," the description line of the Times-Daily read. "Saigon, 12 Other Cities Shelled by Viet Cong."

A faint breeze blew cool on his face. He heard what sounded like soft bells chiming from somewhere near Jimmy Jeter's place across the road. There was a low and muffled purr, like someone breathing, or humming. He strained his eyes but saw nothing, only what looked like some kind of shadow moving with the wind through the gently rising bend in Misty Hollow Road.

Chapter 15

The school year was winding to a welcomed close, and with it summer beckoned, its promise of warm and endless days drifting like a siren call into Sandy's open window. It was Friday night and getting late. Sandy lay listening to the transistor radio playing soft and low from the nightstand beside his bed.

"This is Brother Shiloh, coming to you from the city of the monuments."

The voice was rich and self-assured, the night-time deejay for WLEE radio, spinning out the love songs, pop tunes and protest ballads at the heart of the Top-40 play list.

"America's music," Shiloh called it, a cultural barometer of sorts, helping to shape and capture the youthful nation's mood.

That week, Sandy could have tuned into any Top-40 station in the country and heard "Cry Like a Baby" performed by the Box Tops or Bobby Goldsboro's "Honey" and "Tighten Up" by Archie Bell and the Drells. Pretty much anyone between the ages of nine and thirty-five could sing along with each hit, whether they made fifty dollars a week in Selma or five hundred in San Francisco.

"It keeps us all singing from the same hymn book," Sandy once heard Brother Shiloh say. "It keeps us on the same page."

If television were the electronic hearth the country gathered around each evening, Top-40 radio was the family snapshot above the mantle, ever changing, like the family itself, to mirror the nation's passions, possibilities, heartaches and dreams. More agile, more fluid, more reflective of the whole than the black and white television tube, the Top-40 hit list was a musical mosaic in constant motion, a kaleidoscopic window into the rich and fertile bounty of gospel, country, rhythm and blues, rock, soul, classical, bubble gum, torch songs, jazz, spirituals and Broadway show tunes that songwriters drew from to craft numbers that careened from the profound to the inane: An Ecclesiastes-inspired "Turn, turn, turn" one moment, and "Yummy, yummy, yummy, I got love in my tummy" the next.

"It's who we are," Shiloh liked to say of those two-minute operettas that formed the staples of Top-40 radio. "The only medium that can move at the speed of American life."

Into that expansive yet rigid format, Shiloh managed by sheer force of personality and will to raise his own presence in the precious seconds he had between hits, news and commercial jingles for new cars, soft drinks and hair care products. Nobody Sandy knew had ever seen Shiloh. His voice sounded tall and lean.

He had come a year or so before from someplace up north — Buffalo, Sandy thought he'd once said. Before that it was Memphis, or Tucson, an itinerant disc jockey making the grinding climb up a market ladder measured in rungs of twenty thousand listeners or so, on a journey that had finally brought him here. In this bastion of conservative thought and commercial appeal, he'd made the airwaves his own in the prime evening slot when all of Richmond, it seemed, was listening from their kitchens, cars and bedrooms. He called Top-40 radio, and those who listened to it, into places neither one might otherwise go.

And so, this late into a Friday night, Sandy wasn't surprised to hear the soft strings and low pitched flute, then the gently pulsing bass line of the British rock band that Shiloh liked to play to close out his show. Sandy didn't need to look at his clock to know it was eight minutes to eleven, and the thought crossed his mind, six sweet hours to sleep.

"'Faith, hope, charity and love,' a great man once said, but the greatest of these, my friends, is love." What other deejay would sign off like that, Sandy wondered, and smiled. "Shelter each other through this long night of trial. Work for good, pray for peace and, always, keep the faith."

It was a special talent, Sandy figured, maybe even a gift, to be able to say the right words at just the right time, so there was never a moment of empty air.

"Nights in white satin," the singer's reedy but clear voice began slowly as the strings rose and swayed between his words, "never reaching the end . . . "

Sandy turned slightly in his bed, felt the music sweep through him and closed his eyes.

Moonlight wandered like a silken stream across the glistening face of wet stones, and Sandy followed the narrow, meandering lane up a hill past long rows of cottages with sagging steps before the road melted away into a great forest of towering oaks and deep shade. He was riding, then running, then skipping along, the road turning to sand, smooth and cool beneath his bare feet. He was struggling now, up a steep slope, climbing over the fallen trunks of ancient trees, their bark long gone, their core rotting away and returning to soil alongside soft green clumps of thick moist moss. Why couldn't he find his way back . . .

"What was that, and what did it mean," the boy wondered the next morning as he set off in the dark, adrift on the ebb and flow of words from a dream.

Tomorrow was Mother's Day, he reminded himself. He could make a card and gather her jonquils from the edge of the honeysuckle swamp. He also thought of Pam, her pink robe, white Bible and tears.

Sandy wheeled into the empty gas station and climbed off his bike. "Regular Leaded," he read off the gas pump, "23 cents a gallon."

He unwound a faded pink air hose and kneeled to fill his tires, squeezing each one to feel it harden and swell. He stood and looked across the street toward Jimmy Jeter's house, then got back on his bike, hoping he hadn't disturbed Old Blue.

Headlights swung around the curve at Misty Hollow Road and flooded the darkened landscape as Winston pulled his Mustang into the paper stop. "'Bout time you got here," Winston hollered, as he stepped out of the car. "It's almost five fifteen."

Sandy smiled and squinted against the glare of Winston's lights.

"How you hangin'?" Sandy asked.

"Feelin' lucky just to be alive," Winston replied, searching for the district manager's bundle. He pulled a Times-Daily and held it up against the light. "Morning like this," he said, breathing in the cool air, "good just to be alive."

A large photo caught his eye. A close-cropped soldier held a framed collection of colorful ribbons bedecked with silver and bronze. "Medals Galore for a 21-Year-Old," the caption read. He was a warrant officer from Michigan, just three years older than Winston, at the Valley Forge Army Hospital in Pennsylvania recovering from wounds he'd suffered flying a helicopter in Vietnam.

"Silver Star, Bronze Star, Distinguished Flying Cross and Air Medal," Winston read aloud from the cutline. "A hundred and twenty combat missions."

He stared at the picture while Sandy leaned in.

"Now there's a guy's doin' somethin' with his life," Winston said, looking out over the pile of papers in the dirt, past the creaking carcass of the summer vegetable stand and into the darkness beyond. "A hundred twenty combat missions. That's somethin'."

Winston looked at his Mustang. It had been idling a bit rough and was getting worse.

"Graduation's three week's off," Sandy chipped in. "You'll be a free man."

"That's what they tell me."

Winston shrugged his shoulders and let the paper drop to his side.

"The old man wants me to go to college, though, so I don' know 'bout all that."

"Which one you goin' to?"

"You don't just pick one, dumb ass. You got to apply."

"Well, where'd you apply to?"

"I was supposed to've done it two or three months back."

Sandy heard a distant whistle wail and thought of the tracks by the river.

"I don't know, I just wan'na do somethin' with my life. Not hang around some college classroom four more years then get stuck in a nine-to-five job."

Sandy straddled his bike.

"You got a good job. District manager and all. Could just keep that 'till somethin' better comes along."

"Yeah, well. I go full time come June. Assistant circulation manager. Got my own desk and everything waitin' downtown. Ah, hell, let's don't worry with it now."

Winston stepped out of the light and leaned against the car door.

"Get those papers delivered and I'll see you when you come up to pay your bill. How much you got for your bank this time?"

"I ain' bankin' this week, Winston. I come up short. Had to tap my change jar to make my bill."

"What the hell's goin' on?"

"I don't know. I had 8719, you know that house with the old pick-up truck, move out on me first of the month. They owed me for three weeks."

"Should'na let 'em skip out on you. Dirty bastards."

"The woman was nice, I didn't think . . . "

"Cheatin' a paperboy's lower'n dirt," Winston cut him off. "She knew what she was doin' alright."

Sandy spun a pedal with his foot. "Then I had two complaints this week from that day it rained."

"Tuesday. I remember the damned complaints. Then you had 'nother on Thursday, 'member, when we had the high winds 'n you left a paper on the porch and it blew all to pieces. Hell, I spent five minutes pickin' it up."

"That damn guy makes me put it on the porch."

"Not when the weather's kickin' up, dumb ass. Get off your bike and tuck it up inside the screen door. That way it won't blow to kingdom come and I won't be pullin' Sears Roebuck ads for garden tillers out of a damned holly bush before breakfast. Still got the damned scratches to prove it."

Sandy looked off toward the south. The red light of a radio tower blinked slowly through the distance. "I didn't know, about the holly 'n all."

Winston just looked at the younger boy.

"Then I got this one woman. Ah, never mind."

"What?"

"I don't know. Just skip it."

"Look here, John-ee Rivers, you 'sposed to be makin' money on this route. Thas' the idea. Now what the hell's goin' on?"

"I don' know, man. I go to this woman's house Thursday night. It's dark in there, like nobody's home. I ring the doorbell anyway, 'n here she comes in her damned bathrobe. Hair's all gone crazy. Place smells like a still."

"Ok. So she's been drinkin'. Who cares?"

"Well I care, because she ain' got no money. Or she's got it but can't find it. Or she's got a headache. Or she's on the phone, it's somethin' ever' damned week like she just can't seem to do anything at all if it means reachin' into her wallet and payin' up."

"Ok, Rivers. What's her name?"

"Beales. I think that's it."

"How long she owe you for?"

"Six weeks."

"Six weeks? That's two seventy. That's, les' see, hell boy, that's almost half a damn week's pay for you. No wonder you're goin' to the cleaners. You keep this up you'll be in the poor house — and takin' the paper comp'ny with you."

"Well what the heck'm I s'posed to do? March in there and take it from her? She lives alone. Drives an old Buick that 'bout chokes the life out of you ever'time it bellows up the road belch'in out smoke."

"Cut her off."

"What?"

"You heard me. Tell this Madame Beales this week she either pays up or you're stoppin' her paper. That'll sober her up right damned good 'n quick."

"Stop her paper? Dang, Winston, I can't do that."

"You sure's shootin' can."

"C'mon, Winston. She'll complain and the paper company'll . . ."

"I'm the damned paper comp'ny, far as you're concerned, and you're in charge of your route. Eighty-Seven Nineteen walked out on you, right? You lost two dollars and seventy cents. Thas' 'bout like workin' three days for nothin'. You seen anybody from the paper comp'ny comin' 'round offerin' to make it up to you?"

Sandy looked off to the side.

"No, sir, 'n you ain' gon'na neither. You lose money out here, you're on your own. Let her call circulation. You know what'll happen? They'll send her to me, and I'll tell her straight up just how it is. Hell man, how many people like that you got not payin' you?"

"I don' know."

"I bet it's . . . damn. Look here Rivers, when you pay your bill this morning, bring your collection book with you. You 'n I's goin' through it page by page, and I'll damn-well find out where all your money's gone and get you pointed north so you can go out and get it back. Now bring that damned book."

"Alright, Winston. I'll get it after my route."

"And don't come up there without it. Hear me?"

"Alright."

"Damned right."

Winston took hold of the wire basket and rocked it back and forth.

"Alright then. Get goin'."

Sandy shoved off into the darkness, heard Winston's car door open and close, the gurgling roar of the Mustang as it ground its way out of the vacant lot behind him, onto the pavement and down the long road.

Chapter 16

An hour or so later, the eastern sky had opened into a rich, milky hue. Sandy heard fluttering from the eaves of rooftops and tittering from the telephone line overhead. Soon, he figured, the lawnmowers would come out, and no one could hear the birds. Small clouds filled the sky like hot dumplings swelling in a great pan of blue.

"Rain's coming," thought Sandy, as he pedaled over a dirt and gravel lane, his canvas-covered collection book bouncing in the basket before him. He slowed as he neared the large metal dumpster, winced at the stench it cast, then pulled around the back of the Seven-Eleven.

The store hadn't yet opened. Only two other paperboys were there, the Slider and, surprisingly, Pete Stokes, sitting beside Winston in the Mustang.

"Let's have it," Winston said through the driver's side window.

Sandy handed over the collection book like he was giving his report card to his father. Winston stretched back against his seat, laid the book across the steering wheel and flipped it open.

"Eighty-six hundred," he read out loud. "Owes you one week's pay."

"I collected odds this week," Sandy explained, pointing to the paper divider he'd placed in the middle of the book to separate addresses, even and odd.

"Eighty-six-zero-two, owes you for three weeks."

"They were out of town a couple days and I . . . "

"They back yet?"

"Yes sir, they got back 'bout a week ago."

"Yeah," Winston said, without looking up.

"Eighty-six-zero-four, one week due, eighty-six-zero-eight, eighty-six-twelve. What's the deal with eighty-six-ten?"

"For rent. Nobody there."

"Eighty-six-twelve, Sunday only. Owes you for three weeks. I don't like that."

"No, sir."

"Folks get the paper got'ta pay for it. If they get it on Sunday, they Ought 'a get it all week."

"I think the guy travels during the week. Never see a car in the driveway, 'cept on weekends."

"Guy got a wife?"

"Yeah, couple little kids too. But she's home with 'em all week, I don't think goes nowhere."

"Eighty-six-fourteen, one week due, eighty-six-sixteen, one week. Eighty-six- twenty, what about eighty-six-eighteen?"

"Not sure. Never took the paper, far as I know."

"Eighty-six-twenty-two, three weeks back."

"Got a kid away at college, both of 'em work, said they'd pay me in full the middle of the month."

"Eighty-six-twenty-four, current, more or less; eighty-six-twenty-six. There's no eighty-six-twenty-eight."

"An old woman, widow I think, doesn't take the paper."

"A widow?"

"Well, I don't think she's got a job or anything. Ain' nobody lookin' after her. Carport's all full of boxes and crap and the screen's 'bout torn off her porch."

Winston lowered the book to his lap, stared out through his windshield and cocked his head. He turned toward Pete, who smiled, shook his head and looked away.

"Alright Rivers, look 'a here," Winston said. "Forty-five cents a week. I want you to remember that. That's what you need from every house on Tempest Lane. 'Bout the price of a dozen eggs, 'bout like buyin' a gallon a milk."

He said it slowly this time.

"For-ty-five cents a week. Every week. Now, you're gettin' up five o'clock ever' damn mornin' come rain or shine. You're ridin' your bike right past these houses. You got no business ridin' past 'em without gettin' paid for it."

Sandy stared deeply into Winston's face. He couldn't remember ever feeling quite so inept.

"I don't like seein' people not paid up. I don't like seein' blank spaces in your collection book. An I don't like empty mailboxes where mornin' papers should be. Thas' money jus' sittin' there. You could easily be makin' another fifty, seventy-five cents a week here with no extra work at all. Adds up. We ain' out lookin' for charity here. Ever' damned one of these people needs the Times-Daily. How the hell else they gon' know what's goin' on?"

Sandy looked at Winston and nodded. He thought about the big man in the ink-stained apron, the Linotype operator who'd lost his legs in the war. He thought about the lead in the furnace, the presses, the ink and the fire.

"You talk about that mother back there not gettin' the paper? Where she gon' get her grocery coupons? How she gon' know when Food Circus has got hamburger meat on sale? She needs to know that. It's your job to make sure she does. Where she gon' get paper to cover the table when the kids make a mess with their paints and glue? Who she gon'na vote for come November? What's she doin' not gettin' the Times-Daily and why aren't you takin' better care of her?"

"I don't guess I'd thought of it exactly like that."

Winston reached behind him to pick up a paper and held it up as if it were some kind of reward. Sandy could see the picture of a young helicopter pilot.

"And that widow woman? Nobody needs the paper more 'n her. How's she ever gon' get rid of that junk 'less she looks in the classifieds and hires a guy with a truck to haul it off? How's she gon' find somebody to fix her screen porch? How's she know when her friends die off? We're not just deliverin' paper out here, Rivers, we're making sure our people are part of the world. We're making sure they don't drop off the face of the Earth. We're bringing them a dose of redemption each morning for forty-five cents a week. Hell, boy, even the Bible calls on us to take care of the widow."

Winston reached into his glove compartment and pulled out a stack of dark blue papers, subscription forms for signing up new subscribers.

"Here you go," he said, handing a fistful to Sandy.

"Hey, Winston, gim'me some of those," Slider said.

"Get out of here, 'n wait your damn turn," Winston said, as the larger boy stepped back.

"Now listen, Rivers, I want you, this week, to go to every house on Tempest Lane that's not taking the paper seven days a week, knock on every single door and ask every last one of them why the hell not. Even better, what day you wan'na do this?"

"Well, I collect on Thursdays."

"Okay then, build yourself some extra time in Thursday night. I'll put you down for a dozen promotional copies that morning. You're entitled to promo papers, thas' exactly what this is, 'n they won' cost you a penny.

"Now, you take 'em and carry 'em 'round with you in your Times-Daily bag. Anybody don't take the paper every day, you give 'em a copy for free. But when you give it to 'em, you stand there and go through it with 'em. Try 'n get 'em to invite you inside so you can sit down in the living room and give 'em the feel of it, not just standin' out there on one foot tryin' to wrap up and move on."

"What if they say 'Thas' all great, but I ain't got the money?"

"It ain' never the money, Rivers, and it ain't the paper either. They all want the paper, and they all got forty-five damn cents a week. It's makin' a decision that's hard. It's pullin' the trigger, man. It's goin' on and just damned doin' it. That's the problem for most ever' damned one of 'em, 'n thas' your job, just to help 'em get there. Hell man, thas' all sales is. You don't talk anybody into doin' somethin' they don't want to do. You just make it easy for them to do what they already want to do any damned way."

Sandy looked down at the subscription forms. Each had a line drawing of a slender man in a suit and tie sipping coffee at a kitchen table. A young woman in an apron smiled as she handed him a morning paper.

"Get the Richmond Times-Daily brought to your door each day before breakfast," it read. "Because, in today's fast-moving world, what you don't know can hurt you."

Winston flipped back through Sandy's collection book, working his way through the odd-numbered addresses, scowling now and then when he came to the pages for customers owing two or three weeks back. Then he came to 8617.

"Here's a ticket in here, Rivers, for the week ending March 30," Winston said. "Today's May 11."

"That's that Beales woman I told you 'bout."

Winston counted the small square tickets, each representing a week's worth of papers.

"Hell, Rivers, this lady owes you for seven damn weeks. Three dollars and fifteen cents. It's like you out here workin' half a week for nothin'. Lucky Pete, we got a paperboy here loves his job so much he's willin' to work for free."

"Oh it's good work alright," Pete chimed in with a broad smile. "Maybe we ought'a start chargin' 'ole Rivers here for lettin' him be out here at all."

Catesby laughed and turned away.

"What you laughin' at, Slider?" Winston slurred. "Nobody pulled your chain."

Winston ran a hand across his face and looked up at Sandy.

"Alright, alright," he said, holding up the collection book, opened to 8617 Tempest. "This Thursday, you go to this woman's house, this eighty-six-seventeen, and you show her this page. And you point to every ticket on the page and tell her she owes you for seven, hell, by then it'll be eight, weeks. Two months. Three dollars and sixty cents."

Sandy envisioned her reaction.

"Then you tell her, 'Ma'am, I have to pay for your papers every week. Every Saturday I have to pay the paper comp'ny for your papers, whether you pay me or not. And I've been payin' for your papers now for two full months. Deliverin' them, and payin' for them.'"

"You could ask her," Lucky Pete chimed in, "if she'd like you to come read 'em to her while you're at it."

"Naw, don't be a smart ass. Just tell her, 'Ma'am, I simply cannot keep on doin' like this. You owe me three dollars and sixty cents, 'n I need the whole bill, paid in full, before I gon'na bring you one more paper.'"

A long truck rumbled down Patters Plank Road hauling thick logs strapped down with heavy ropes and rusted chains.

"Look here now," Winston said. "She ain' gon' like it. She may even throw a fit. You just stand there, be polite and all, look her in the eye, and tell her, 'Ma'am, I've been patient. I've worked with you on this, 'n I'm not bringin' you any more papers until this bill's been settled.'"

Sandy just stared straight ahead.

"Look, I've done it before," Winston said. "Pete's done it too; hell, we've all had to do it, man."

Sandy looked at Pete.

"People like that pay me in advance," Pete allowed. "I got it now so 'bout, I'd say, a third of my route pays like that."

Sandy looked back to Winston, saw him raise his eyes skyward momentarily, then look away, pretending not to hear.

"I just tell 'em, it's comp'ny policy. You fall three weeks behind, you have to pay two weeks' advance for the next six months," Pete said. "Comp'ny policy."

Winston shuffled through the papers piled in his back seat, pretending to be distracted so as not to be brought any further into it. "Company policy my ass," he thought. Not only was there no such company policy, the very idea of paying a paperboy in advance was unheard of. Hell, people didn't pay in advance for anything, not their electricity, their water, their telephone, not even their mortgage. Somehow or another, though, Lucky Pete had convinced upwards of thirty-five households that if they didn't fork out two weeks' worth of payments in advance, they'd wake up next morning without a paper.

"And then there's premium service," Pete went on. "You want it delivered on the porch, that's premium service. And premium customers pay two weeks in advance. Hold your papers while you're on vacation? Premium service. Anything at all they want, I say 'Yes Sir, Yes Ma'am, you're a premium customer now. Two weeks advance. Comp'ny policy." He smiled and winked at Sandy to finish the thought. "Lucky Pete Enterprises policy."

Winston had long waited for the day when one of Pete's customers might call him on a matter of policy. What the hell would he tell them? But the call had never come. They'd gotten used to it, he guessed. Anyway, it was Pete's deal, he figured, and, as long as it stayed that way, Winston let it go.

"Good luck," Winston said, giving the collection book back, as Sandy handed over that week's payment.

"And one more thing," Winston finished. "This is the last time you pay your bill without puttin' somethin' in the bank. Last damn time for that."

Sandy nodded, took his receipt and turned away. A man was opening the heavy glass doors at the Seven-Eleven, and Pete and the Slider were walking in.

"Buy you a doughnut? They've got chocolate."

"No thanks, Catesby," Sandy replied.

He tossed his collection book into his basket as though he'd failed an exam, climbed on his bike and headed home.

# Chapter 17

Sandy raced along the tar and pebble pavement, breathing heavily and pedaling hard, as if he might somehow catch the long, slender image stretched out before him. Sunlight, soft and golden, lit the sweetly scented lawns alongside Tempest Lane, casting sharp shadows across the grass.

It was eight-thirty, a cool wind blew into Sandy's face, and he looked up to see a solid line of dark grey clouds pressing in from the west. Just minutes before, he lay in his bed, enjoying a post-delivery nap. He'd heard the phone ring, his mother's summons and then Winston's voice on the line: "Brady Sullivan's phoned in a complaint."

Sandy thought for a moment as he held the phone.

"He's out'a his tree," Sandy said. "I put it in his box, for sure."

"Look Rivers, I ain' callin' for a conversation. You know Sullivan. Claims it got stolen or sump'in."

Sandy didn't say anything.

"He ain' blamin' you, 'n neither am I. I'm jus sayin', the man ain' got his paper. You want me to take him one, I can. I got to be out that way shortly anyhow for somethin' else. Or, you can take care of it yourself'n save yourself the thirty-five cents for the complaint. 'S'up to you."

Sandy glanced toward the high-backed chair in the dining room, saw the paper he'd brought home for his parents.

"Aw-right Winston, I got it."

"Tha's good. I got'ta get going. See ya."

"Okay," said Sandy. "Happy Memorial Day."

The first raindrops surprised Sandy, who hadn't noticed how fast the dark clouds were moving. He crested the rise toward the end of Tempest Lane, saw the wooded edge of the road before him and bore left, over the narrow ditch at the edge of Sullivan's front yard.

The old man appeared unshaven at the screen door of his red-brick split-level. He wore a sleeveless undershirt with a yellow stain down the front, and a belt he hadn't yet buckled.

Sandy grabbed the paper, laid his bike against the grass, hopped up the few steps leading to Sullivan's small stoop and turned his face from the overpowering smell of burnt sausage.

"'Em damn boys back dere 'gain, I guess," Sullivan said, motioning with a bare arm toward the narrow path running alongside his yard and glancing over his shoulder toward Skinquarter. He sounded like he was talking with marbles in his mouth. Sandy looked at the man through the screen. His lips were too big for his gums. Sandy quickly looked away, wondering exactly what had to happen each morning before the old guy put in his teeth and buckled his belt.

"'F'i don' git it by sis- or sis-thirdy, 'dey come 'long ever damned time 'n steal it righ'd ou'd my box. I ain' caught 'em yet, but day I do, dey be sum dam sorry soul den, I guran-dam-tee-ya."

"Yes sir," Sandy said, as the old man opened the screen door and stepped barefoot out onto the small cement stoop. "Well, Mister Sullivan, here's your paper. I'm awfully sorry 'bout any inconvenience."

"Aw, hell, it ain' yer damned fault."

The wind picked up and blew in the front skirt of the storm, a soft and rolling shower sweeping across Sullivan's freshly cut lawn. The old man looked skyward and squinted against the rain. He saw tall pillars of darkening clouds, just as lightning flared out of the west beyond the trees at the end of the road.

"Son-av-a-bish," Sullivan sputtered. "Can't remember lass time we had mornin' thunder. We gon' have a reg'lar damned day-luge. Come on in, boy, git ou'd de rain."

Sandy thought about the gums and the skillet with the grease all burned black.

"I be aw'right," the boy hollered back, bounding down the low brick steps toward his bike as thunder rumbled dull and distant through the trees. "Thanks anyway."

Sandy picked up his bike, threw a leg over the bar and rode off, his head bowed low against the rain. Standing to pedal hard, he cut his front wheel to the right and felt his bike slide out from beneath him.

"God almighty," he sang out as he went sprawling across the lawn. The rain pelted the pavement in strong, straight lines, turning Tempest Lane into a long, black mirror of glistening tar.

Sandy scrambled to his feet and picked up his bike. He looked toward the trail leading between Sullivan's yard and the densely wooded edge of the honeysuckle swamp and quickly made for a spot beneath the broad and sheltering boughs of an ancient poplar tree midway down the path.

He leaned his bike against the tree, rubbed at the wet grass on his legs, and gazed back through the darkened tunnel of ferns, wild sumac and sassafras that shielded the path from the storm. Vines snaked over the trunks of aging oaks and elms, weaving themselves into a fragrant arch that shrouded the pathway like a cathedral. A taupe-feathered bird fluttered and fed on a mulberry bush nearby.

Lightning flared and a crash of thunder crackled just overhead. Sandy leaned into the sturdy poplar like a lost soul at the base of a steeple.

The rain fell in the forest like applause, the extended ovation of a thousand pale leaves receiving the cool, moist kiss of spring. Sandy looked past a thin stand of scrub pine at the edge of the swamp. The rain pummeled the shallow black water around the broad, smooth pedestal of a once-regal cypress split in two by some long ago storm. Sandy began to imagine the tops of the giant trees hurtling down in splintered shafts of shattered timber.

He turned and looked down the path toward Skinquarter, saw the rain streaming down the smooth, green stalks of bamboo that formed a dense thicket behind Sullivan's yard. The tall, thin reeds looked strangely out of place, almost foreign in this world of hardwoods and pines. From out of the thicket, as though it sprang from the bamboo, a narrow stream boiled over its shallow banks and raced across the sandy trail into a wandering patch of thorns.

"Fingernails," Sandy thought to himself, drifting back to that day, some years before, when he rode his first bike to that very spot and squatted down by the sunlit stream.

"Hey boy," a deep voice called out, taking little Sandy aback. "Wha'chu doin' ova' he'a?"

A big man towered over him from the other side of the stream in faded denim overalls, no shirt underneath, his tank chest glistening with sweat.

"You loss' yo young mind?"

"No sir," little Sandy replied, feeling his stomach tighten and remembering his mother's edict that he never set foot on the path to Skinquarter.

But this wasn't actually the path to Skinquarter, he had reasoned. This was the path off Tempest Lane; the path to Skinquarter began on the other side of the stream, a good three or four feet away.

"I'm just lookin' for crayfish."

"Mmhmm," the man allowed, looking down the path past Sandy. "They's crayfish in there aw'right."

The boy looked down at the creek, then back up at the man.

"Well, son, I wooden' be messin' 'roun these parts if I's you."

He pulled a raggedy ball cap off a head of hair gone mostly grey, and swatted away a mosquito near his face. "'These woods is seen a mighty hauntin'."

He stepped over the stream, past the boy, and shuffled with a limp toward a fallen log in the shade of the poplar tree. He lowered himself and settled in like a king on his moldering throne, crowned himself with the raggedy cap, heaved a deep breath against the afternoon heat and looked off toward the swamp.

"'That's some ol' black wa'da back they'a," he said in a deep and hardened voice, each phrase carved out of the steamy air like words cut into a cypress trunk. "Old and black. Blackened by time."

Sandy rose and drew nearer. Not a whisper of air sifted through the dense woods.

"Swamp wa'da, see boy, don' nev'a move. It jes sits there, year aft'a year, collectin' up all the evil and magic that pass through these parts. And they's a lot done passed by he'a."

The boy sat in the cool sand in the path in front of the man, near his creased and faded shoes. His hands were calloused and crusted, he had a wandering left eye, and he spoke with a smell like hog's breath that could burn the forest down.

"You see that ol' tree?"

The man pointed to a tall, thick cypress. It had a scarred-over wound, as if a large limb had sheared off ages ago and disappeared into the rich loam below.

"That's where they hung young Martin, you know. Y'assah, right there from that tree."

"Who's Martin?"

"He's the slave boy tried to lead them Yankees 'cross the riva' that night."

The old man furrowed his brow.

"Ain' you nev'a herd' 'bout young Martin?"

The boy shook his head.

"Lawd knows," the old man declared.

"He tried to lead them Yankees to Richmond. Y'assah, happen' right down by the riv'a, not far from this very place. Wuz a cold night, and rainy, they say. Lil' Martin got down on his knees and pray'd to God. He say, 'Great Father in Heaven come down this night. Part the wa'das and lead us to freedom. Part the wa'das, and lead us to the crossin' place.' And he got down in the riv'a, and the Yankees followed him down on horseback."

Sandy could see it all in his young mind, the soldiers in the darkness and the horses they rode, the icy water swirling around the slave boy in the dark.

"But the wa'das, they rose, and the horses went down, and the Yankees, they drown, mostly, jes like Pharoh's men when the sea broke loose on 'em out of Egypt. Jes like Pharoh's men, they drown. And the big Yankee cap'n, he grab poor Martin, not much older'n you, and he hang'd him from the thickest limb on that very tree right there. The limb's gone now, God destroyed it in a storm. But the evil trickled down into the wa'da below, and blackened it over time."

Sandy could almost see the slave boy's body, swinging in the darkness from the cypress tree. Sure enough, the limb was gone.

"He's still here; he ain' gone nowhere," the old man said. "I seen him myself, once or twice. He still roams these parts late at night, when the air in the swamp is silent and still. He's searchin' for the crossin' place, they say. Still searchin' for the crossin' place."

Sandy stared at the old man's wandering eye. Beads of sweat hung like pearls on a thread in a deep crease along his forehead. He wiped his brow and Sandy noticed his fingernails, thick and yellow and sharp at the tips, like thorns.

"Yes, sir, these woods has seen a mighty hauntin'," the old man said, heavy hands on swollen knees.

"This is an ol' Indian trace right here," he continued. "At one time, this trail ran from the riv'a clear ov'a to where Patter's Plank Road is t'day. That ol' road's a trade route. Run all way to the mountains, at one time. But this trail here, it won' no trad'in trail. Na'sah. This w'uz a secr'it trail. This was the kwee-ah-ka-sin trail. You know what a kwee-ah-ka-sin is?"

The young boy shook his head.

"Kwee-ah-ka-sin wuz a secr'it burial place for the old Indian chiefs. When they'd die, a dozen braves'd carry the body 'long this trail to the riv'aside.

Won' nobody else 'llowed on this trail but them braves. 'N they'd stay right there wi'd him fo fo-teen days 'n fo-teen nights. Don' nobody know exactly why, but thas' how long it was, fo' certain."

"Wha'd they do all that time?"

"Oh, they had it all organized and ceremonial-like," the old man said.

"First day, they gon' bay'd the body in the riv'a, to prepare it for the next life. And they'd chant all day, and all night long. And they'd take dried tabacc'a leaf, and rub it in their hands, 'n scatt'a it all ov'a the riv'a."

"And then he'd go up to heaven?"

"Ah hell naw, boy. They din' know 'bout no heav'n 'n hell. To them, that riva' was sacr'it. And the big king, he gon' to the next world. And, if they don' take care of him good befo' he go, he gon' come back and fix a mighty hauntin' on 'em."

A bevy of starlings chattered in the shadows.

"Ain't nobody ever found none of them secr'it bur'al sites. Folks tried to find 'em, so they could dig 'em up, steal the bones and trade 'em to the old chief's enemies. You grind up those bones, mix 'em in the warm blood of a fresh-killed copperhead, then drink it in the las' light of a quarter moon, you gon' git all his strength, his courage, and all his women too. So they be wantin' to hide all them bones."

That all sounded right to Sandy.

"Now, way I got it figured, they bring 'em back here near the swamp fo' proteshun'. Lot'ta things back he'ah don' nobody wanna fool with. Cotton-mouth, fo' one; mosquitos, fo' 'nother. And quicksand."

"Quicksand?"

"Deadlies' thing in the swamp. Suck a man down in half a minute — keep him down there for all time."

The boy stared through the forest toward the broad swamp waters, fertile and still and dark, their thick, acrid sweetness just beneath the soft scent of honeysuckle. A slender shaft of sunlight fell across a patch of barren ground.

"Anybody ever get sucked down 'round here?"

The old man lifted his cap, ran a hand through his sweat-soaked hair and leaned back on the log.

"I ain' gon' talk 'bout that."

"Anybody?"

The old man stroked the grey stubble on his chin, leaned over toward a thicket of thorns, then glanced back over his shoulder toward the swamp, as if someone might be there. He looked up into the trees and squinted against the sunlight.

"Some things," he said, running a finger along the edge of a long thorn, "are ev'n worse than we can imagine."

The old man's voice dropped low. His breath was edgy and raw. He leaned forward and looked at Sandy.

"You know what happens when the quicksand gets you?"

The boy shook his head, thought of leaving, scooted his hands beneath his bottom and started to get up.

"Sit down boy, we ain' goin' nowhere," the old man scowled, laying a hand with the weight of what felt like a railroad tie on top of Sandy's thin shoulder.

"First thing that happen, the lungs fill up wi'd wet sand. Once the chokin' stops, the breathin' follows. Then the heart sieze up, like a stone."

He balled up a hardened fist in front of the frightened boy's face.

"It take a few minutes," the old man went on, "but then the blood starts to cool, from the feet all the way to the brain. Then the muscles go all numb. Time melts away into the daw'kness b'low, and then disappears in the wada'ry void."

Sandy thought of his mother. He blinked hard, felt something warm dribbling down his cheeks and over the dust on his face. A mosquito worked the papery rim of his ear.

"But they's a funny thing 'bout quicksand," he started in again. "Funny thing is, it don't kill you outright. It kind'a hangs the body halfway between heav'n 'n hell. Kind'a like young Martin left to hang on the tree. And th'only way you can tell a life ain' crossed over yet, is by the finga'nails."

He lifted his hand from Sandy's shoulder and held it alongside his head. Sandy felt a sharpened nail graze his cheek.

"Yeah, that's right," the old man whispered, drawing his face so near the boy could feel the heat off his skin. "The finga'nails don' stop growin'. They just keep gettin' long', and long'a 'til they come up out'd the ground, long 'n waxy, 'n reach up taw'ad the sky. They reachin' up and tryin' to grab somethin' to pull they'sev's up out'd the daw'kness b'low. Jus' sump'in to stop they'sev's from hangin' there between heav'n 'n hell. And all they need is ta catch a young boy like you, catch him by the pants leg, or the socks, or the shoes, and pull him down into the daw'kness where the time slip away."

He reached into the bib pocket of his overalls, and pulled out a pocketknife, rusted along the edges of a chipped and worn deer antler grip.

"I ain' gon' hu'cha boy," the man whispered, pulling open the knife. "I'm gon' show ya sum'pin. I'm gon' le'cha feel the wax on the fing'a-nails."

The big man leaned back on the old ivy-covered log and reached down with the knife to cut a fresh sprig of thorns.

"Got-damit," the man hollered out, jerking his hand from the thorns and shoving a finger to his mouth. A bulb of blood pooled at the edge of his lip.

"Aha, ha, ha, haaa," he bellowed. "Yeah, I tol' you, boy. They down there, aw'right, and they tryin' to pull us down there wid 'em. C'mon on now boy, les you 'n me go down there wid 'em — just you 'n me! C'mon now, got-damit! Jus you 'n me!"

He lunged for Sandy, as the boy rolled hard across the sand then scampered toward the poplar and tore off running with his bike. He jumped on and started pumping, too frightened to slow down where the sand vanished beneath the gravely edge of the road, too frightened to look back to see an old man laughing with a chest-belching roar and waving a waxy sprig of thorn toward the summer sky above the short and narrow passage to Skinquarter.

Chapter 18

A distant rumble of thunder from the departing storm shook Sandy from his remembering. He noticed goose bumps on the grass-covered skin of his arms. Rain had washed pollen onto the path, where it meandered in pale streams of yellow and green like watercolors adrift on a canvas of sand.

The forest fell silent in the wake of the storm, a brief pause in the rush of spring. There was an angry chattering, a flash of red, and a cardinal vanished into the mulberries. Sandy heard water rushing down the small stream, a gray squirrel scratching his way across a broad poplar limb and what sounded at first like country music playing softly through Sullivan's kitchen window.

Sandy shook the rainwater off his bike and wiped the seat with his hand. As he began to turn the bike around, he heard voices from the church at Skinquarter rising with the driving bass chords of a piano: "Walk together children, don't ya git weary, there's a great camp meetin' in the promised land."

Sandy edged his bike toward the stream as the singing grow louder, then he crossed over the water to a place where he saw a cluster of mud-caked cars beside a white clapboard building slung low beneath a sweet gum tree.

"Gon'na walk and never tire," the voices rang out as the boy drew nearer to the church. "Gon'na sing and never tire; gon'na shout and never tire."

The path rose from the stream and the forest gave way to low scrub pines and brush. Sandy walked his bike up the path and, through the lingering drizzle, the little church came into view.

It sat at the end of Midsummer Night's Lane — a single-story frame building of broad pine timbers and knotty slabs. It had a tin roof dented by hailstorms and time. A small wooden cupola served as a steeple, shimmering in the rain. Over the front doorway hung a white board with hand-painted black lettering: "The Skinquarter A.M.E. Church of God."

Behind the church, alongside a stand of oak and maple trees, was a small, well-tended cemetery. A large green tarp hung from ropes and poles above a freshly dug grave. At the church entrance, wooden steps led to a gently sagging porch. By an open set of double wooden doors, a large woman in a dark brown dress stood by a grey-haired man in a suit and tie, clutches of church bulletins in their hands. To the right of the open doorway was a hand painted sign: "Welcome to Our House of Worship and Prayer."

Sandy had passed by the church before, but never during services. He turned to leave and then, from across the narrow field, he noticed an old bike he'd seen before. It had a lettuce crate tied atop the rear fender, and it was leaning below an open window beneath a broad wooden eave.

"The bicycle man," Sandy whispered to himself.

From inside the church he heard the deep voice of a man say, "We are gathered, dearly beloved, on this Memorial Day, to pay tribute to an American patriot, to remember a son of Skinquarter, and to celebrate the life of a child of God."

The singing had stopped and, standing now beneath the window, Sandy heard the message:

"Stapleton Moses Marable was not yet twenty-one years old when a sniper's bullet took his life last month in the faraway place of Vietnam. In a very real sense, this young man's life had just begun, though he had already journeyed a great distance."

Stapleton Moses Marable, Sandy turned the name over in his mind. Mose?

Looking up through the window from below, Sandy saw only the ceiling, sharply pitched pine slats painted the pale blue of the sky, with soft white whirls and feathery flourishes that reminded him of clouds. From along the high center of the ceiling, three pan-shaped light fixtures hung from the slats, suspended above the congregation like brown hubcaps, each with a large ceiling fan.

"Like so many of you here, I can remember Mose as a baby in his mother's arms, the very first Sunday she brought him here to this place, wrapped in a blue blanket to keep him warm against the biting chill of a December day," the man said softly from inside. "I can remember him as a young boy, playing with pebbles and marbles in a large glass jar beneath the shade of the sweet gum tree. And I remember the last time he stood in this church, on the Sunday evening before he shipped out, when we gathered as a congregation to bless him, to offer such strength as he might take from the communal force of our collective prayers, and send him off on behalf of our nation, with a Christian commission and a charge to serve."

Sandy leaned his bike against the side of the church and climbed up. His feet on the crossbar, he steadied himself with both hands on the ledge of the window, his eyes just over the sill. From there he could see the front of the sanctuary, where a large photograph of a young black man in an olive green uniform was propped up in an easel beside a light wooden casket with polished brass rails.

Twin boys, eight or nine perhaps, stood at opposite ends of the casket, facing the congregation like bookends in matching shirts and ties. Each held a small American flag. To the right of the casket was a large, freestanding spray of red roses, white carnations and blue chrysanthemums. There was an aging upright piano, chipped in places and worn to bare wood. On a small, black stool before it sat a middle-aged woman in a violet dress, a golden brooch pinned high on her chest. A man and two women, draped in long robes, sat behind her on folding chairs. Seven rows of crowded pews spread out from a narrow center aisle.

From the rear, Sandy saw mostly the backs of heads. He could make out several women seated along the front row beside two men in military uniforms. Half a dozen people stood pressed against each other in a corner in the back.

The preacher — a short, balding man in a tight-fitting black suit — stood at a simple pine altar with a darkly stained cross. On the wall behind him hung a large portrait of Jesus, preaching from a hillside overlooking the sea.

"Many of you were here on that day we bade him farewell," the reverend recalled, slipping a piece of paper from the inside pocket of this jacket and carefully unfolding it in his hands.

"And, in the letters he wrote, until his final hours, Mose told his mother what your prayers meant to him. Listen for the voice of Moses Marable as I read from his last letter home."

He cleared his throat, looked reverently at the paper, then softly and slowly began.

"'In less than two months, I'll be headed out of here,' he wrote. You see, his unit was nearing the end of its tour."

"'Goodbye to K-rations — and lemon grass soup!'"

People nodded, a few sighs rippled through the congregation, the fleeting comfort of memory shared, and the pastor went on with the letter.

"First thing I'm going to do is take Clifford and Jenks down to the river.'" The pastor paused and looked down toward the boys astride the casket. A bittersweet smile stretched across his thick face, then he returned to the letter.

"Sometimes out here it seems like a dream, like home is so far away. But then I close my eyes, and it's like you're all right here with me.'"

Sandy looked toward a grey haired woman on the front row, heavy shoulders rolled forward, staring deeply into some imagined distance beyond the casket before her.

"'That's how I know when I get out of here, when God brings me back home, everything will be just like before. And when I get to feeling scared or lonesome, I think about the night everybody said prayers for me, and I feel right strong, on the power of that faith.'"

The reverend paused, took a deep breath, gently folded the paper and laid it in a dog-eared, black Bible lying open atop the altar.

"Listen, brothers and sisters, to a child of God: 'I feel right strong on the power of that faith,'" he repeated, looking out into the sanctuary.

"You see, dearly beloved, Private Stapleton Moses Marable was a man of faith. Private Stapleton Moses Marable was a man of God. Today our hearts grieve, but, you know, way deep down in my soul, I feel right strong today, brothers and sisters. I feel right strong."

Heads nodded from the pews, someone whispered a soft "Amen," and someone else echoed gently, "Mmhmm."

Sandy glanced around the room. There were other pictures of Jesus, praying in the garden at Gethsemane, and speaking with children beneath a tree.

"Private Marable was named for a great prophet who led his people out of the bondage of Egypt and into the freedom of the Promised Land. And, I say to you today, brothers and sisters, Private Moses Marable lived up to that legacy. For he, too, led his people to safety. He, too, led his people from harm."

"You see, it was his job on that morning to walk point for his unit, to be the first man out front, with two dozen behind, as he led that patrol across perilous ground. It was his job to lead them to safety, and to sound the alarm when danger showed its face, as surely he knew it would."

The preacher picked up his Bible and held it to one side of his head.

"'Man hath no greater love than this, that he would lay down his life for his friend.'"

He placed the Bible back on the small altar.

"Private Marable was down by the time the others heard the shot. A bullet the size of a lipstick tube passed clean through his chest and out the base of his spine. And, as he lay at the edge of that faraway road, in the dust and the dirt by the road, this young man's life slipped away."

The tiny sanctuary drew silent, but for the rhythmic swish of the ceiling fans.

"No one will ever know exactly what Moses was thinking as his soul drifted from this troubled world to the next, as his spirit crossed over the Jordan and into the Promised Land. But I like to think that was his way of coming back home.

"I like to think, brothers and sisters, he was remembering the shade just outside this door, beneath the old sweet gum tree where he used to play as a child. I like to think he was remembering how cool that shade felt in summer, when the soft breeze of evening blew through."

Sandy saw tears streaming down the reverend's full cheeks, as the holy man struggled to smile through quivering lips.

"And I like to think he was remembering the banks of the river, where he used to take his young cousins fishing at night. I like to think he was remembering the riverside."

The pastor pulled out a white handkerchief, wiped his eyes and stuffed it back in his suit pocket.

"We are gathered today, dearly beloved, to pay tribute to an American patriot, to remember a son of Skinquarter and to celebrate the life of a child of God. But we dare not, in this remembering, brothers and sisters, lose his last thoughts in the midst of our tears; we dare not let our sorrow lay silent his voice. Could it be God sent Moses to lead us today?"

A soft chorus of "Amens" rippled through the pews.

"Today, brothers and sisters, I want to go down with Moses. I want to go down by the riverside. It's a great distance, my friends, but I want to go there with him because somethin' inside of me's feelin' right strong today."

Someone said "yes" and heads gently nodded.

"This war is costing us our sons and daughters, as all wars surely do. And it's a high and mighty price to pay.

"For it comes attached to the endless sorrow of unrequited dreams. It comes shackled to the bottomless heartache of losing those we love. And it comes bound to the heavy and sullen burden of grieving widows, mournful mothers and children with fathers forever gone.

"The cost is high and mighty, as in all wars before," he said, closing his eyes and facing skyward, "but, oh God, it hasn't ended there."

The preacher began to regain his voice, rising on the strength of his words.

"This war is roiling our nation. It's imperiled our very soul. Win or lose, we cannot triumph now, for this war has already taken far more from us than it could ever repay. It has changed us forever. It has changed who we are. It has divided us, as a people, right here at home. Our purpose, our meaning, our very measure as a nation, all are in danger of being lost forever in this ill-conceived and misguided quest to dominate and to destroy."

His voice grew steady and somber.

"It is not for us to rule far-off lands. Brothers and sisters behold, the hand of God is mighty, and the hand of God is just. Could it be that God sent Moses to lead us down by the riverside this day?"

A soft wave of consensus rolled through the room.

"Mmhmm," a woman nodded. "Tha's right," another said.

"If this is to be a great nation, Doctor King once told us, then this must become true," the pastor pressed on, "that we, the people of this mighty land, shall one day find it within ourselves to lay down the burden of war."

He looked out across the tiny sanctuary as if taking stock of all the pain and loss in the room, as if gathering his flock beneath the broad eaves of the church to shelter them from the storm.

He opened his mouth to speak, and started soft and low.

"Gon'na lay down my sword and shield."

A woman called out from the rear of the sanctuary, "Down by the riverside!"

The reverend held out his hands before him, his palms opening to cradle the woman's response.

"Gon'na lay down my sword and shield," he repeated, voice rising.

"Down by the riverside," several others in the church called back to him.

"Let us all follow Moses Marable today," the pastor sang out as the people called back, "Down by the riverside!"

"I feel right strong, brothers and sisters," he testified, "I feel right strong today."

"Down by the riverside!"

"Ain't gon'na study war no more," he shouted.

"Down by the riverside!"

"In the name of Moses Marable, and in the mighty name of God."

"Down by the riverside!"

The reverend stretched his arms open wide, held his palms toward the heavens, closed his eyes and began to sing.

"I'm gon'na lay down my sword and shield."

The woman at the piano sustained a single chord and nodded to the three robed singers, who rose from their folded chairs, followed by the congregation.

"Down by the riverside," they sang back in layered harmony, as the reverend gestured for all to join in.

Sandy let it pour over him, the piano, the choir, the preacher leading his flock from the silent reverence of its grief and loss into the boisterous release of its sorrow and pain.

"I ain't gon'nna study war no more, ain't 'a gon'na study war no more, ain't 'a gon'na study war no mo-o-ore . . ."

Sandy's eyes swept the room. People were standing and singing, from the front row to the rear. In the far back corner he fixed on a sight that froze his gaze. It was the old man he'd once seen on the strange bicycle, wearing a tattered tweed jacket and crimson tie. Standing beside him, silent and still, was the only white man in the room. Sandy couldn't quite make out his face in the crowd, so he stretched to get a better view. It was Winston Coleman, looking him straight in the face.

# Chapter 19

Dawn broke warm and moist and grey. Soft clouds swirled low across the scalloped face of the sky. Sandy coasted toward a mailbox slouched over a rusting pole at the end of Tempest Lane. It was the fifth day of June. He paused to look into the forest at the end of the road and take in the sweet breath of the honeysuckle blossoms peering yellow and white from the edge of the swamp.

More than a week had passed, but every time he drew near to the end of Tempest Lane, Sandy remembered what happened at the little church through the woods and thought about his recent conversation with Winston.

"I saw you lookin' in," Winston told him the day after the funeral. He was waiting at the paper stop when Sandy rode up on his bike, and leaning against the burgundy Mustang, engine running, as if he wanted to talk.

"An' I saw you high-tailin' it back down the path when we started comin' out the church and headin' back toward the graveyard."

Sandy didn't much know what to say. Winston pulled out a cigarette, lit up, took a drag, then watched the smoke drift off in the damp air.

"Mose was a couple years older'n me," Winston began. "When I got my first route, the route you're deliverin' now, Mose had the next street over."

"Midsummer Night's Lane?"

Winston nodded and took another draw from his cigarette.

"That was the only route they'd let him have. No white guys would take it anyway."

There was a long pause. Sandy heard the distant rumble of a lone truck headed toward the city down Patter's Plank Road.

"I 'member the first time I saw him — I'd seen him around, just walkin' around, you know — but I mean the first time I saw him up here, gettin' his papers 'n all. I'll never forget that. It was January, colder 'n hell. It'd rained the night before, 'n the streets had a kind of glaze to them, solid ice in spots. I came rollin' up here, 'bout like you did just now, hit the edge of an ice patch 'n went down flat on my ass."

Winston laughed for a second, Sandy looked the other way, then turned back toward the district manager, trying to imagine him falling off his bike.

"Hell, I's what, ten, maybe 'leven at the time? And there I look up 'n see Mose, standing over me laughin' his head off."

"'You wan' me to strap sum skates on that bike for ya,' Mose hollers out. I can hear him now," Winston said. "I'll never forget that."

Sandy smiled, shook his head and listened.

"Then, I got up, 'n Mose picked up my bike, leaned it against that pole right there. It was right dark, but I saw him lean down, take the cap off my front tire. Next thing I hear's the air startin' to bleed out.

"Wadn't like I could do much about it. He's 'bout twice as big as me at the time, 'n I just figured he gon' let ever' dam bit of the air out've my tires. Then I heard Mose say, 'If you sof'en 'em up a little, they won't slide so much.' That was all he said. Then he put the cap back on, let a little air out the back tire, and headed on his way. Sure enough, he was right. I didn't slide anymore."

Winston stared at the creosoted telephone pole.

"He kind'a looked out for me that way. I's just a little kid, what the hell'd I know? We'd bump into each other up here, couple times a week. He bought me a carton of chocolate milk one time off Whit's truck. Mostly, though, he just kind'a looked out for me, you know. I don't really know why. I's just a dumb kid."

Sandy studied the older boy. It was hard to imagine him being looked after by anyone.

"Then one mornin' he said he's goin' in the Army."

"Drafted?"

"Naw, signed up. Enlisted. Said he wanted to go, and, if it worked out right, the Army'd pay to send him on to college afterwards. That was almost two years ago, I guess. Said he wanted to help out his country and see the world. That's exactly what he said. Few weeks later he was gone, and I ain't seen him since, 'til the other day, when we buried him out back behind the church."

Sandy couldn't think of anything to say other than, "Who took over his route, I mean, when he left to go into the Army?"

"I did, for a few weeks. Then another guy took over from Midsummer Night's Lane."

"What happened to him?"

Sandy saw the tip of Winston's cigarette go a bright orange as he pulled a final drag from it, dropped it to one side then rubbed the embers in the dirt with the toe of his shoe.

"Let's you and me get going now," Winston said. He slung open the door and climbed into the Mustang, threw it into reverse and hollered out through the open window.

"How'd it go with that old drunk woman?"

"Great," Sandy lied, flashing back on the hateful scowl with which she met the news that he was cutting off her paper for non-payment that night, just before she called him an impudent punk, assured him she'd report him to the newspaper company, then slammed the door in his face, vowing in a voice he heard only too clearly through the open living room window that she'd be dead and in her grave before he saw one penny of the three dollars and sixty cents she owed him.

"Told ya," Winston shot back. "Just got'ta be firm sometimes."

"Yes sir," Sandy acknowledged. "Just got'ta be firm."

"See ya Saturday," Winston called out as his tires chirped against the pavement and the Mustang roared off into the darkness.

Sandy watched the taillights disappear down Misty Hollow Road, loaded up his papers and pedaled off. He turned the conversation over in his mind as he worked his route all the way to the far end of Tempest Lane, where he stood straddling his bike, reached into his basket, pulled out a paper and, just before he folded it to stuff it into the aged and dented mailbox, glanced at the two-deck headline stripped across the top of the page: "Kennedy, Two Other Persons Shot After California Victory Statement."

It was the sixty-ninth time he'd seen the headline that morning, and it still hit him like a jolt to the body. "What the hell's wrong with people in California," Sandy wondered out loud. "What the hell?"

He glanced back toward the crest of the road behind him, remembered the morning Winston had come over it to talk to him about the cross he'd burned in the Jeters' yard, and found himself wishing the burgundy Mustang would come charging back up over the small ridge again.

He thought of his fourth grade teacher, bursting into the room nearly five years before and telling her students with tears in her eyes that President Kennedy had been shot in Dallas. Now it was his brother, Bobby, the paper said, shot in the kitchen of a Los Angeles hotel.

There was enough light for Sandy to read the story softly to himself: "Robert F. Kennedy, brother of the assassinated President John F. Kennedy, was shot early today. His condition could not be immediately learned, but a reporter saw blood gush from the senator's face."

It had happened while Sandy was sleeping, after Bobby Kennedy gave a victory speech, "a moment of political triumph," the story said. Kennedy had been the projected winner of the Democratic primary race in California, adding momentum to his bid to overcome Vice President Hubert Humphrey as his party's candidate for the presidential elections just five months off.

There was a small, one-column picture of the young U.S. senator from Massachusetts and his movie-star smile gazing out from the page with eyes that seemed to be racing ahead of his time, fixed on some grand and distant vision he thought everyone could see.

Sandy lifted his own eyes, turned away from the paper and watched a finch disappear into the shadows along the path to Midsummer Night's Lane.

"Two brothers," Sandy said to himself, looking away from the paper and back toward the fragrant woods. He thought about the people all along his route and suddenly could see them, every one, as if in a single moment, unfolding their paper, from their box, from their porch, or walking into their kitchen and seeing it lying there for them, its grim message stark and cold on the page. Just like Doctor King, he thought, only two months before.

He held the paper in his hand as though it were a thing of great evil, a Godless force with an awful power to bring darkness into the world. For an instant he thought about putting it back in the basket, thought about turning his bike around and taking the papers out of every box, quietly unfolding each one in the soft, grey light and just taking it back. And when finished, he would ride right here to the edge of the honeysuckle swamp, take them into the graveyard behind the Skinquarter church and bury them in the soft, dark soil. Then he'd go back and do the same for the papers of April, and for the papers from that November nearly five years before. Just bury them all by the honeysuckle swamp — Dallas and Memphis and the Ambassador Hotel — and just like that, the loss and horror would be gone. If he could somehow bury this bearer of evil, and keep it out of the kitchens along Tempest Lane, maybe then none of it would ever have happened, at least not for them. And it would never, ever happen again.

"Hey boy, you lost?"

Sandy turned and saw Brady Sullivan standing behind the screen door on the front porch of his house wearing boxer shorts and a faded undershirt.

"No sir." Sandy pretended to laugh. "Poor dumb bastard doesn't even know yet," he thought, stuffing the paper into the box.

He took one last glance down the path that led past the swamp and the graveyard before he heard the screen door slam and saw the old man head down the sidewalk to pick up his copy of the Richmond Times-Daily.

Chapter 20

There was no way to explain it really, just why these kinds of tragedies happen. Part of the chance you take when you put yourself out there, day after day, around the huge crowds, talking to people, asking for support. Still, it seemed especially cruel for it to happen twice to one family. No way to know. No way to really understand. Just keep them in our thoughts and prayers.

It wasn't a fully satisfactory explanation, but it may have been the best any eighth-grade history teacher could do on the last day of school, a day when the shock and sadness of the morning news was eclipsed and quickly overtaken by the thrill of summer and its magical promise of ease.

And, while Sandy didn't expect WLEE to make perfect sense of it either, he found himself looking forward to lying in bed that night and listening to the radio.

"We've lost three now we can never replace — Bobby, Martin and John," the deep-voiced dee-jay intoned at the close of his show. "And remember that, in times like these, it's more important than ever for us to work for good, pray for peace and, always, keep the faith."

Sandy replayed it all in his mind the next morning as he ground his way up the long hill toward Misty Hollow Road, arced left and glided down the gentle grade to the paper stop.

The sky had lightened. A half-moon hung low in the west, a crystalline caravel setting sail across a boundless sea of blue. Sandy hauled a full bundle into his basket. He cut open another and began fitting in papers around the sides, more details on the grisly killing and an eyewitness description of the gunman, a young man from Jordan with two last names.

Sandy looked across a patch of milkweed running wild across the paper stop and out into the darkness beyond. There was a tinkling sound, like distant chimes, and he turned toward Jimmy Jeter's house across the road, squinted against the light bulb hanging down from the old oak and swinging gently in the breeze. He heard a sort of scraping sound, and for a moment he thought to hide.

The sound grew nearer, something emerged from the shadows, the old man on his bicycle, turning off the smooth pavement to the vacant lot.

"Bad news draws a crowd, I reckon," the bicycle man said.

"I guess so," Sandy replied.

He handed the paper to the old man, who edged into the dim light pooling at the base of the telephone pole. Straddling his peddler's pack of a bike, he ran a weathered hand across a face sketched with stubble, then pinched his chin between his fingers as he read down the page. His eyes fixed on a small picture, the sharp-featured face of a man with deep-set eyes.

"Sirhan, Sirhan. Kind of damn name's that?"

"Hell'f I know," Sandy replied. "Maybe thas' what they call guys over there in Jordan. Says sump'in in there 'bout Palestine."

"Mmmhmm."

The old man set the paper down across a leg and heaved a deep breath that seemed to empty his body of everything but the bones.

"Well, it don' much matter. Won' him, 't'ad been somebody or another."

He handed the paper back to Sandy.

"What's that s'posed to mean?"

"Somebody'd a done it, one way or 'nother. Hell, you know that, boy. In this country? Hell, he was on his way to the White House. You know what that'd mean? This country ain' gon' stand by let that happen. Naw sah, not again."

Sandy tried hard to follow.

"Bobby Kennedy wanted to change things. He wanted to shake it up. This country wadn't 'bout to let that happen."

Sandy stared blankly at the old man's face.

"Aw, now, folks wan'na change, some folks anyway. Passed the Civil Rights Act. Voting rights. Housing rights. That's all good. That's change. But lot of folks fightin' it anyway they can. Lot of folks just can't get on board. Makin' trouble for the rest of us," the old man went on. "But change is comin', like the man say, just not quite yet, you see. Bobby got his'self crosswise wid' all that."

The old man dismounted his creaking bike and walked it toward the vegetable stand. The bins were mostly empty, but the old man followed a sweet fermenting smell toward a far corner of the table. He groped around until he found three tomatoes that had gone soft and damp, smashed in the bottom of a bin. He picked them up, dropped them into the burlap sack hanging from his bike, then wiped his hands on the outside of the bag.

"Seed," the old man said to Sandy. "I take 'em home, dig me a lil' place in the garden, 'n drop the whole damn tomato right in. Long 'bout late September, I have me all the fresh tomatoes I can eat."

White light flooded the vegetable stand, washing over new canvas the color of wheat. A car turned into the paper stop and Winston hollered out the open window.

"Got any fresh watermelon?"

"Naw, not today," the old man shot back, "but I got me some tomatoes, good 'n ripe."

"Oh, I can smell that," Winston said, climbing out of the car. "Who you got helpin' out this mornin'?"

"Oh, him? Tha's my understudy. He's in trainin'. Got a long way to go, but he's gon' work out alright I 'spect."

"I hear he's right strong on the grilled items."

"Oh yeah," the old man came back. "He got a way wid' a flame, now."

So that's the way it was, Sandy thought to himself. That's how Winston found out about the cross.

"Only, he's 'bout moved away from that line altogether, 'n shifted over into fresh produce. You know, melons 'n greens 'n such," the old man chuckled.

"Is that right," Winston chimed in, walking toward Sandy, feigning a rabbit punch to the boy's ribs and clamping a headlock on him.

"Yes sir," Sandy let out, as Winston gave his scalp a knuckle rub.

"Tha's what I like to hear," Winston said, letting go of the boy like a man who's finished up petting a pup. Winston turned his back to the vegetable stand and hauled himself onto the wooden edge of an empty cantaloupe bin, the old man stooped at his side.

"Well now, when you gon' be movin' into that downtown office mister graduate?"

Winston dangled his legs above the packed clay.

"Well, that ain' exactly a done deal."

"I thought you're movin' in to become the next circulation manager or something."

Winston turned his face toward the fading moonlight.

"Been a little change in plans."

"That right?"

"I got'ta break away from this place, try somethin' different, try somethin', I don't know," Winston said, "just somethin', even if it don't work out."

Nobody said anything.

"I mean, what if a guy felt like he had a chance to do somethin' that mattered, somethin' he'd always wanted to do?"

The old man looked skyward, ran a hand across his face, then spoke in a quiet voice.

"You mean like Mose?"

Winston straightened up and heaved a deep sigh.

"Well, at least he didn't waste his life sittin' around here, goin' nowhere and get'in' old."

He was sorry the instant he said it, but there was no pulling it back inside.

"Oh, no sir," the old man said, "that he did not."

Winston reached out, grabbed hold of a bony shoulder and gave it a quick shudder. The old man just stood there, his pants slung over his narrow waist like the burlap bag draped over the frame of his bike.

Winston leaned back against the empty bins. He saw a bat fluttering in the milky sky, its wings a desperate torrent, beating the air to keep this unlikely aviator with failing eyesight darting and diving for prey.

"There's so much we miss every day of our lives," Winston said out loud. "So much we don't see, or hear, right in front of us."

He watched the bat jerking in and out of the darkness, a near sightless rodent that had no business in the air and yet somehow managed to thrive.

"I've always wanted to fly," Winston said at last. "I know I can do it, and now I've got the chance."

The old man lowered himself onto a bundle. Sandy dragged another over and sat beside him.

"I went down to the Army recruiter's place a few months back," Winston said. "He told me they need helicopter pilots, and he set me up to take a test, see if I could get into Army flight school. I didn't wan'a say anything about it, 'cause I wasn't sure I'd pass. Hell, it was harder'n any exam I ever taken. Took most of the day. But I made the cut. Did right good on it, matter of fact."

Sandy was listening carefully, and wondering what kind of questions might be on a flight school test.

"So he got me signed up. Said, after I do my basic trainin', I'll be headed to flight school. This time next year, little longer at most, I'll be a helicopter pilot."

"Tha'd be so cool Winston," said Sandy. "No bird."

Winston nodded, smiled and looked down at the ground.

The old man shook his head, broke off a strip of wood from a melon crate and scraped it across the dirt.

"Did you happen to ask him why it is they need helicopter pilots so bad?"

"Said they need 'em for all kind of things. Movin' supplies around, gettin' guys in position, reconnaissance, special ops, secret missions, all kind of things."

The old man pounced back.

"All kind a things, huh? They tell ya 'bout what they really need 'em for? They tell ya 'bout flyin' into a hot combat zone to pick up the dead and the wounded? Tell ya 'bout flyin' a big ol' bus in over the treetops so the gotdamn Viet Cong can shoot you down in the jungle? They tell ya how well those damn things fly when the VC knock that big prop off the top? Tell ya what one of those damn things look like when it bursts into flames?"

"Ah come on man."

"Ah come on, nothin'. Didn't tell ya 'bout all that, now, did they?"

"You startin' to sound like my old man."

"Well, hell, Winston, ever stop to think your old man might have a damned point?"

"He's got a point, alright. Point bein' I can go to college like all the other losers around here and waste another four years of my life."

"Wastin' your life? Hell you talkin' 'bout boy?"

"Talkin' 'bout sittin' on my ass in a classroom, listenin' to some professor ramblin' on 'bout . . ."

"Talkin' 'bout gettin' a damn education, so you can make somethin' of yo'self."

"Hell, you get a better education in the Army. They pay for you to go back to school if you want, and I might just do that, I don't know. Meantime, seein' the world ain't gettin' an education? Learnin' to fly, somethin' useful, that ain't gettin' an education?"

"Then go talk to Mose 'bout a damn education! Trouble is, you'll have to talk mighty loud. He kinda hard of hearin' down there in the . . ."

The old man's voice trailed off. He waved both hands to signal he was through.

Winston dropped his face in his hands. He hauled himself down off the stand, slid a bundle next to the old man, sat down and leaned over toward him.

"I did talk to Mose," he said, calm and quiet. "Well, listened mostly. Went to see him last night. I stood there a long, long time. Just listenin' mostly."

The old man reached a thin and wrinkled hand over toward Winston, who took it in his own.

"I'm so sorry," Winston said. "I'm just so sorry."

The old man's body began to shake.

"So many gone," the old man whispered, gripping Winston's hand. "So, God help us, many gone."

He covered his eyes with his free hand and with the other shook Winston's arm.

"You know," Winston started in softly, "time I finish flight school, Vietnam'll be over with anyway. We got Hanoi by the throat, everybody knows that. The peace talks'll get all worked out. It can't go on much longer now."

The old man raised a hand to signal he understood, or perhaps had heard enough.

"I just want somethin' a little bigger, you know. That's always been my dream."

The first orange and rose fingers of dawn reached into the feathery edges of a slender cloud. The old man stood and leaned forward, put his hands on the vegetable stand.

"Dreams," he whispered, almost to himself. "Lot of dreams buried out there behind the church th' other day. Lot a dreams buried. Lot a dreams gone." He climbed on his bike, tugged at the burlap sack, felt the weight of the tomatoes inside, then rode off into the soft light of dawn.

 # Chapter 21

Two days later, Winston went public with his plans.

"I'm go'nna miss you guys," he told the paperboys gathered around his car to pay their bills. "But I'm leavin' you in good hands."

Pete Stokes stood by, his winning smile at its early morning best, a bright red and black "For Sale" sign taped to the side of his Moped. He was buying the Mustang. He'd need it for his new job as district manager.

"Lucky Pete'll take over startin' tomorrow," Winston said. "He knows the territory 'bout as well as anyone around, 'cept me, that is. I'm headin' down to the beach for a couple days. . ."

"Y'ain' goin' alone I hope," Catesby called out.

"Not as 'lone as you'll be tonight Slider," Winston replied to light laughter. "I'll tie up a few loose ends back here next week, 'n then I'm on the Greyhound to Fort Polk, Louisiana."

"Hey," someone hollered out. "They don't call it Lose-e-anna for nothin.'" There were a few groans, Winston raised his eyebrows and cocked his head slightly.

"Guess not. Hey dingo, promise me you won't lose that great comedic sense of yours. I can tell you're goin' a long way on it."

"Whachu gon' be flyin' Winston?"

"It's called a Huey, my man."

"Hell's that?"

"Well, it's a little chopper carries 'bout nine infantry. Goes around a hun'erd 'n fifty miles an hour, got about 'leven hundred horsepower, little stronger than this baby right here."

He gave a slap to the hood of his Mustang.

"Sheeit-fire," someone said.

"You goin' to Vietnam?"

"Probably so, if it's still goin' on time I get my wings."

"We'll look out for Mary Kay for you," someone hollered out.

"Oh yeah," another chimed in. "I'll keep an eye on her."

"Well men, as they say in the Army, line up beside the Mustang and let's pay our bills and get the hell out'a here."

It was Pete, stepping in for the first assignment of his new job, and smoothly putting an end to the catcalls before someone went too far. He walked around the side of the car and climbed into the passenger seat, while Winston slipped behind the wheel to do the weekly accounting one last time.

Several boys scuffled for a place near the front of the line. Sandy shuffled back to the rear. He'd counted his money that morning on his way out the door — thirty-three dollars and forty-three cents — and stuffed it in his pocket, alongside the crumpled white envelope he'd found in his parents' mailbox the night before.

"Master Rivers" was all it said on the front, and when he opened it, Sandy was surprised. Inside were three one-dollar bills, two quarters and a dime. There was a note, in a barely legible hand-written scrawl.

"Dear Master Rivers," it began. "I'm sorry for falling so far behind with my bill and for treating you rudely the other night. I promise to do better from here on out." It was signed, "Kitty Beales, 8617 Tempest Lane."

Winston, Sandy'd thought when he read it.

Sandy had stopped her paper that week but didn't bother to phone in the cut to the circulation department. Instead, he delivered the spare paper to the older woman at 8628, the one success he'd scored in his sales mission the week before. Now that 8617 was back, he'd need to up his daily count.

"And heerrrrrre's John-ee," Winston announced, as Sandy approached his window. "There's a man who lives a life of danger," Winston sang out, tapping a long yellow pencil against his steering wheel and slapping an open hand against a baggy pair of cut off khakis. "Wha'cha got for me today, John-ee Rivers?"

Sandy pulled the money to pay his bill from his pocket and handed it through the window to Winston.

"I'll be needin' to add a paper."

"That's what I like to hear," Winston said. "Lucky Pete, give John-ee Rivers here a start slip," he said, as Stokes pulled a form from the clipboard on his lap.

"You got a bank slip I can fill out," the boy asked.

"Got one right here," Pete sang out.

Winston passed Sandy the forms and the pencil. He watched as the boy filled out the papers then handed him more cash.

"And for the bank," Winston said to Pete, who looked down to mark the figures on a form in the clipboard, "three dollars and sixty cents."

Winston looked up at Sandy.

"How much does that give John-ee Rivers in his bank account?"

"Three dollars and sixty cents, sir," Pete shot back.

"Good luck, Rivers," Winston said, reaching his right hand through the window, his smile reflected in the face of the speedometer. "And keep Lucky Pete here straight for me, will ya?"

"Sure thing," Sandy said, offering his small hand, grey with newsprint, to the older boy, who gave it a tight, firm squeeze. "Sure thing."

Chapter 22

June crept into July, and that month into the next, as sun-bleached days of barefoot ease drifted past in a sultry haze. By midday the August heat closed in so tight that Sandy felt he might choke on his next breath of air. The grass had gone dry, like pins of straw beneath his feet. Tar bubbled along Tempest Lane and pop against his tires like black taffy on the boil as he rode home from the pool each afternoon. There was even a sound to the heat late in the day in a hum that seemed to emanate from somewhere between the wilting leaves and the hardened earth and hang beneath a heavy sky.

Nights were little cooler than the days, and Sandy spent most of them atop a thin cotton sheet, lying flat on his back as still as the curtains that hung lifeless against the open window by his bed. Not even a whisper of breeze slipped through from outside, only the sounds of a summer night - the mournful howl of a distant hound, the wail of a freight train rolling east or the high-pitched trill of cicadas. Night after restless night he would lie there like this, in the pine-mottled light of the moon, his hair moist and matted against a warm pillow he would turn over continuously for the fleeting relief of its cool underside.

For what seemed like endless nights he tossed and sweated in the dead weight of persistent hours, until something, the dull ping, perhaps, of a June bug flying into his window screen, stirred him enough to notice the moon had shifted along its broad arc across the sky.

The moon was a source of endless wonder for Sandy. He sometimes propped a pillow atop his windowsill to dream in its eternal glow, suspended in darkness, it could seem to him, by some ancient celestial thread.

There were times its light shone soft and undefined, a feather-edged pool of mercy wandering the warm and gauzy heavens, a shimmering jewel whose beauty waxed and waned in the unfathomable rhythm of tides. Other times it sailed, silver and bold, across a satiny sea of clouds. Still other times its light grew thin, a sliver of gold, a careless stroke against the ink-washed patina of night.

Sandy pulled back from the window sill, saw the trees outside in a lightning flash, rolled onto his side and let the cool wind lead the edge of the storm into his room. A crack of thunder shattered the night, and Sandy closed his window just enough to deflect the deluge. He strained his eyes, peered into the darkness, and saw a burst of lightning mirrored against the watery surface of King Lear's Court. He fell back in his bed and lay there, listening to the lilting lyric of rain; slapping like pollywogs in shallow puddles against the waxy leaves of boxwoods outside his window and gurgling down the gutter spout.

He pulled the top sheet over his shoulders for the first time in weeks and imagined rainwater slaking the parched throat of the dry stream bed that crossed the path to Skinquarter. When Sandy awoke early the next day, the storm had passed, leaving in its wake a cool wet morning and a clear orange sky. He was soon on his bike and headed up Merry Wives Way.

"I know to you, it might sound strange," he sang out loud, "but I wish it would rain!"

Sandy rolled into the paper stop and ignored for a moment the mountain of Sunday papers awaiting him. Finches chattered in the tall grass at the edge of the vacant lot, and a pair of starlings pecked at the edge of a small puddle in a fold of canvas atop the vegetable stand. He thought of the blistering afternoon before, dusty husks of corn baking in a field near the railroad tracks.

"To the world outside my tears, I re-FUSE to ex-plain," Sandy sang, pointing a finger to a bulging bundle, "I just wish it would rain."

The celebration carried him through his route and back home, where Sandy napped briefly. He rose, showered and got ready for church, where a grateful congregation gave thanks in prayer for the overnight respite from the August heat.

"And, oh Lord, as we praise you for bringing us the sweet blessings and cool waters of your heavens, the rains that will nurture and nourish our vegetable gardens, lawns and fields, we ask also your blessings upon our leaders this day, and upon the citizens of this great nation, as we together, and as one people, prepare to weigh the worth of men and choose one to guide us forward through troubled times."

It was as close as the Rev. Ennis Stout would ever get to bringing politics into the pulpit. But in the Sunday after the Republican national convention in Miami put Richard Milhous Nixon and Spiro Agnew on the GOP ticket, there was little doubt as to his message.

"Be in our hearts, oh Lord, we pray, through this time of testing and trial, and guide us, that we might use this season of decision to render the civic judgments necessary to the functioning of our democracy, lest we stumble on our journey to your kingdom."

Sandy's head was bowed, but he opened his eyes briefly and noticed a trace of black ink still on the fingers he held folded across the lap of his wrinkled khakis.

"And let the people of God say," the pastor concluded, as Sandy breathed out with the rest of the congregation, "Amen."

The Kanawha Creek Presbyterian Church was an unpretentious house of worship atop a rolling glade of pine and grass at the foot of Ridgetop Road. One of his earliest memories was of crouching in the shade and taking his turn churning ice cream from a cedar tub, just outside the sanctuary where he sat in a long dark pew, listening to Pastor Stout.

The man was tall and lean with a thick head of white hair that swept back from a bony forehead as square and taught as a jon boat stern. His career as an Air Force chaplain before coming to Kanawha Creek shaded his sermons from time to time with talk of spiritual grace readily linked to national might. He spoke in steadily cadenced and measured tones, his sermons rolling over the sanctuary and lapping against the ear like warm mineral springs in autumn.

"Please rise, as you are able," he said, as the rich chords of the church organ took flight, "while together we give thanks and praise through song."

Sandy pulled the worn blue hymnal from the rack in front of him as he stood, thumbed his way to page 252 and sang along.

"When morning lights the eastern skies, oh Lord, thy mercy show, on thee alone my hope relies, let me thy kindness know."

Sandy imagined the sun rising above the pines along Tempest Lane. It was a thought of comfort and assurance, very much at home with the familiar Biblical themes echoing through old hymns, quiet reminders of place and time. He glanced up at the arched ceiling and the long white walls, saw morning light stream in through tall side windows and fall in slanted lines across broad shouldered men in dark suits and white shirts and silver-haired women in pastel shades of linen and silk.

Seated beside Sandy was a young mother in a floral patterned dress, there with her two small boys, each with shiny brown shoes and neatly combed hair. She wore little makeup, only bright red lipstick against a deeply tanned face. Sandy imagined her putting it on that morning, pictured her in front of a small mirror seated at a white vanity. He briefly envisioned her in a satin slip, the white edge where her tan ended running the breadth of her chest. He took a deep breath and looked straight ahead.

From the front of the sanctuary, a pulpit and matching lectern hovered above the congregation, twin pillars from which the pastor and his associate might look out and render both the guidance and grace to be had from scripture well studied and sermons well told. Choir pews flanked each side of the altar, women in dark robes facing identically clad men along the opposite wall.

All of it — the pews, the ceiling, the choir loft and even the light — directed the congregation to the sanctuary center piece, a brilliant stained-glass window towering behind the altar, a jewel-like portrait of Jesus as a shepherd, returning a single lost sheep to his flock.

Through countless Sunday mornings for as long as Sandy could recall, that shimmering backlit image of Christ had been the visual backdrop for every word of holy sacrament and song, the set piece for every sermon he'd ever listened to or ignored and every daydream he'd entertained in between. It was there year after year, a finely crafted mosaic of color and light, watching over him when he knelt and plucked a cup of grape juice from the communion tray and awaited his gaze when he lifted his head from every whispered prayer.

There was no photograph or painting Sandy had looked upon more than this window, a deeply embedded totem in his spiritual landscape, a compass point marking the true north of faith, a vision forever constant, its meaning reaffirmed and renewed one season to the next.

Jesus walked alone along a rugged path of dirt and stone. He wore brown leather sandals and bore a straight and sturdy staff. At his feet two sheep beckoned. And, in the crook of one elbow, he cradled a small lamb, lost and frightened, perhaps hurt, but found, ultimately saved, and returned to the fold.

"O gracious Lord, revive my soul and bless," Sandy sang as the congregation wound up the hymn. "And in Thy faithfulness and love, redeem me from distress."

He closed his hymnal and settled into the pew as Pastor Stout stepped away from his pulpit to address his own flock.

"Greetings in the name of our Lord," he said with a broad smile. "Jesus taught us to welcome the stranger in our midst. And so, if you are visiting with us here today, I invite you to stand so that we can recognize you."

Several pews in front of Sandy, a woman with bluish hair like spun glass nudged a young girl beside her. She leaned forward, hesitated, then rose at the matron's urging. She was tall with light brown hair that rolled past her round and freckled shoulders and onto the scooped back of a cotton dress.

"Welcome," Pastor Stout said, as the young girl clenched her church bulletin in one hand. "We're glad you're with us."

"That must be some kind of living hell," thought Sandy, watching the girl standing there as all the congregation gaped. "Better her than me."

She sat down, the woman leaned over and whispered something and Sandy saw the girl nod slightly.

"The roses here today," the pastor said, gesturing toward a brilliant pink bouquet, "are to celebrate the birth this week of Mary Louise Starkey, the first daughter of Chris and Becky Starkey, who report that baby and mother are a little tired but otherwise doing fine."

The pastor's smile faded with the soft din of light laughter.

"And please keep in your thoughts this week Missy Forrest, who goes into the hospital on — is it Tuesday?" he asked, looking toward a white-haired woman in a dark blue dress, who nodded from the front of the sanctuary. "Alright," he confirmed, "goes into the hospital on Tuesday for cataract surgery. We will certainly keep Missy in our hearts and prayers as her eyes mend over the coming weeks."

The pastor turned back toward his pulpit, as a man in a dark suit rose and stepped to the lectern. "Please follow along with me in Mathew, Chapter 15, verse 10, for our New Testament reading," the reader said.

Few actually opened their Bibles. Sandy looked down toward his lap and folded his church bulletin, as he heard something about the Pharisees taking offense at Jesus and his teachings.

"Let them alone," the reading concluded. "They be blind leaders of the blind. And if the blind lead the blind, both shall fall into the ditch."

Pastor Stout rose, bowed his head in brief prayer, looked out over the congregation and began. "One desperately hot and humid morning, just a few weeks back, Missy Forrest came into my office, as she often does, with a tightly sealed Tupperware bowl in her hands."

Knowing smiles flickered and light laughter trickled through the sanctuary.

"I stood up to greet her, naturally, extended the hand of fellowship and reached with the other for what I dearly hoped would be a dozen of Missy's freshly baked chocolate chip cookies. But Missy stopped me, set the Tupperware down on my desk, and said, 'Pastor Stout, there's something I need to talk to you about.'

"I could tell by the tone in her voice that this was serious. And then, in her typically selfless, uncomplaining, yet matter-of-fact, way, Missy shared with me the problem she'd begun to experience with her eyes. It had been going on for well over a year, she explained, and it had gotten progressively worse. And, as I listened carefully to this faithful servant of the Lord, struggling with one of the inevitable burdens of age, I began to realize that it wasn't the failing of her eyes that troubled Missy so much as the feeling that she might be somehow less useful, perhaps somehow even less of a person, without them.

"'I'm afraid,' Missy confided, 'I'll no longer be able to lead our Senior Sundays worship class.'"

The pastor looked down and smiled at the woman, who stared forward as if he were speaking of someone else, then he slowly walked back to the pulpit.

"Be still," the young mother beside Sandy said, giving the boy beside her a quick pop on the leg. She wore a pair of wicker and cork slip-ons with lime-green canvas tops that set off a pair of lean and shapely legs. Probably a wicked tennis player, Sandy thought to himself.

"Ya'll quit," she whispered. Reaching into a canvas purse that matched her shoes, she pulled out two small Tootsie-Rolls, which she quietly unwrapped and handed to her boys.

"Missy's cataracts, fortunately, are correctable. And, through the surgeon's skill, and the grace of God, her eyesight will return, or very nearly so. And, when it does, she'll take her place once again reading the scripture lessons, making announcements, setting calendars and otherwise leading our Senior Sundays worship class, as she's done so very splendidly now for lo these many years."

He pressed his open palms together in front of his chest.

"But, in our conversation — which ended, you'll be relieved to know, with two cold glasses of milk and those marvelous chocolate chip cookies — she reminded me of something that's so often lost in our political conversation these days. You see, as her sight began to dim these recent weeks and months, Missy came to understand a basic truth: We cannot direct others, without the vision to lead."

The pastor leaned back, drew a sip of water from a glass behind the pulpit, looked up toward the balcony and continued.

"The history of the world can be largely told as a continual crisis of leadership. On that point, the Bible is clear."

He held up a large black volume for emphasis then reverentially laid it back down on the pulpit. He spoke of the Egyptians enslaving the Israelites, of Moses leading them from bondage, of the rise and fall of families, tribes and nations ever since, and the link each story shared to leadership.

"Jesus himself was crucified," he said, "nailed to a cross and left to hang and to die, not for any wrong he'd done, but because the governors of the Roman empire lived in stark fear of the day when a true leader might arise from the masses and use the force of moral authority to topple their tyrannical reign of terror and turn their whole world upside down — a crisis of leadership in the making, my friends, a crisis of leadership, writ large."

He paused, folded his hands before him, dipped his chin against his fingertips, and pressed on.

"As this election year gathers steam, we must ask ourselves, as citizens, do we face a crisis of leadership in our nation today? Are we enslaved, as a people, by the pursuit of material possessions, by jealousy, by lust, by greed, just as much as the Israelites were enslaved by the Pharaohs of Egypt? Does the American family, the American tribe, have a leader to look to who will guide us with the staff of confidence and truth? Or do our own elected officials today, for all the power and might they possess, live in fear that somewhere, somehow, a true leader might emerge who will... turn... their... world... up... side... down?"

He let the question hang for an uneasy moment, then drove it home.

"Might they be blind leaders of the blind?" the pastor asked slowly, stretching his long neck out over the pulpit. "For, if the blind lead the blind, both shall fall, Jesus warns us, into the ditch."

He stood back up straight.

"What does our Christian faith teach us about leadership? What does the Bible say? Well, leadership, the Bible tells us, requires three things.

"First, is vision, the ability not just to see, but to be able to look far out over the horizon and to know which way to lead because you know where it is that you want to go," he said. "A leader without a vision is no real leader at all, but is instead merely someone who holds a finger to the wind and sets the ship of state on a course that will veer and tack with no more purpose or direction than the next fickle breeze. A ship so guided will never bear a storm, and it will never arrive at any meaningful destination, because there is no grand purpose for the voyage, no higher calling other than simply to follow the wind."

Sandy looked down at his Weejuns, faded against the freshly waxed tile floor. He glanced at the bright wicker shoes the woman beside him was wearing, watched her slip out one bare foot, rub it against an ankle then slide it back into her shoe. The younger boy beside her had his head in her lap, and she ran her fingers through his blonde curls.

"You cannot lead, my friends, without vision. And, when we look at our leaders today, we must ask ourselves, as Christian voters, what vision, what purpose, what noble calling guides them forth? Is it vision to sit in the halls of power perusing the latest polls, and then from those polls try to divine some semblance of a national course, like trying to predict the future by reading entrails or scattering bones on the floor? Is that the kind of vision the Bible tells us we need, or is that leadership that is flying blind?"

Sandy glanced at his church bulletin. There was a family picnic scheduled for the Sunday before Labor Day. He felt the last days of summer slipping by.

"Second thing's what I call character. Some call it courage, some call it integrity, still others call it strength of heart. I believe the Bible teaches us it's all of those things – and one thing more."

This was it, Sandy thought. Pastor Stout would never utter the name Lyndon Baines Johnson from behind the pulpit, but here it comes, sure as rain on the tail of a cool wind in spring.

"When you lead, my friends, you're out there alone," he said. "That's why leadership requires one thing more. It requires faith, the great power to be summoned by our belief in the people we profess to lead, and the even greater force to be found through our faith in God."

He repeated the end of the last sentence, paused, and smiled.

"When you look at our leaders today, do you see men of vision? Do you see men of character? Do you see men of faith? For if the blind lead the blind, both shall fall into the ditch."

Sandy thought about President Johnson, lying awake in the White House night after night, listening to the pounding of the war protesters' drum from the park on the other side of Pennsylvania Avenue. He recalled Johnson on the television that April night Doctor King was killed, and the time, days before that, Johnson told the nation he'd been beaten down by the steady toll of national division and the unceasing weight of the war.

"And yet, we know that great leaders can rise from difficult times. We know this, too, from our history.

"The greatest leader of all, led from the heart. He commanded no army. He presided over no Congress. He raised no taxes and spent not one penny in campaign funds."

Sandy gazed into the stained glass window, the rocky path, the frightened lamb, the strong but gentle man with the sturdy staff and ruby colored robe.

"Jesus," the pastor continued, "led with vision. He led with character. He led with faith. And, two thousand years later, He is leading still, by the enduring force of the words He preached, and by the powerful example of the life He led. Two thousand years on, we believe in Him still, this carpenter's son who was born in a stable and lived to be called the King of Kings. Two thousand years from now, who might be remembered that leads us today?"

He paused, looked out on the congregation and let the thought sink in.

"Ah, you might say, but Jesus was the son of God — He had a special constituency."

There was light laughter and relief at a line that seemed to give the congregation permission to shift in the pews, a sort of seventh-inning stretch for the spirit.

"But the world was unkind to Jesus," the pastor continued. "Indeed, by contemporary measures, he failed. He suffered defeat. And yet, today, long years later, when we look at Calgary, we see, not loss, but victory. We see, not death, but eternal life. And we know what has endured is not simply the memory of this great leader, but the people he led: Christians, forever bearing eternal witness to Christ."

He leaned forward, an almost smoldering pillar of virtue steadying himself against the pulpit.

"We know that, while His body has turned to dust, his vision has endured," he said. "That vision remains as clear today as ever it was, his character has become imbedded in our own and his faith is an undimmed beacon that guides us through the long night still. And that, my friends, is what it means to lead. That's what God calls our leaders to be. And that's the kind of leadership our nation needs — today, tomorrow and always. Thanks be to God. Amen."

The man who'd given the New Testament reading suddenly appeared near the front of the sanctuary and led half a dozen church elders in passing shiny brass collection plates up and down the aisles.

The young mother beside Sandy fished out a pair of nickels from her purse and handed one to each of her boys. Sandy reached into his pocket, pulled out a quarter and dropped it into the passing plate with a quick prayer.

The organist played a lofty chord progression that seemed to build on itself like a thundercloud rising clear to heaven with a soul-stirring force.

As he watched the plate make its way through the pews in front of him, the young visitor turned to receive it and Sandy caught a quick glimpse of her face. There was something familiar he couldn't quite place. He looked at her hair, falling like sunlight across her shoulders, then caught a flicker of her face once again, as she turned to pass the plate down the pew. Somewhere, Sandy was certain, but where, he wondered as he stood to sing.

"Glory be to the Father, and to the son and to the Holy Ghost," Sandy sang along,

". . . world without end, A-men, Amen."

"As we all remain standing," Pastor Stout implored, his arms stretched open and wide, "I'd ask that you exchange a sign of peace with those around you."

Sandy reached over the pew in front of him and extended his hand to a middle-aged man, who gave it a bone-crunching squeeze.

"Peace of," Sandy said, then went suddenly blank. His gaze caught on the young girl several rows to the front, now turned and looking him square in the face.

Sandy felt a rush of recognition. A flood of warmth tinged with terror swept through him. The entire sanctuary seemed to fall away, every pew and all the people in them, until all that was left were her eyes fixed on his against the bejeweled backdrop of the stained-glass window of Jesus and the lost little lamb. In a single moment he wanted to disappear, to hide like the boy beside him behind the hem of his mother's dress.

The girl up front tilted her head almost imperceptibly, brushed a lock of hair back from her face, looked deeply into his eyes and smiled. Three months had passed since that night at Mrs. Randolph's cotillion, and something about Hope Stafford had changed.

"Please be seated," he heard the pastor say.

Hope bit her lip slightly then turned to sit down.

Sandy turned to the woman beside him and saw she was smiling. He felt like a child, dropped his head and tugged at a button on his blazer. "My goodness," she whispered. "It feels like about a thousand years since a boy looked at me like that."

"No, no," he said quickly, "it's just that . . . "

"Mmhmm," she cut him off, laying a hand across his elbow. "I know exactly what it is."

The organ opened up, Sandy rose to sing the closing hymn, with an unfamiliar longing for the service to continue just a little longer. Wasn't there something more the pastor might say about Jesus or leadership or even Missy's cookies?

"Praise ye the Lord, the almighty the King of creation," he heard the congregation intone before realizing he'd stood without his hymnal, his vacant gaze directed instead toward the back of Hope's cotton dress. She glanced over her shoulder and caught him, smiled and turned back around.

The woman beside Sandy extended her open hymnal for him to share. He took it from her and held it open as everyone sang.

"Let the Amen, sound from His people again, gladly for aye we adore Him!"

# Chapter 23

Word that Hope Stafford would spend the last two weeks of summer with her grandmother fell on Sandy's ears like unexpected rain on a summer day. And the words "Would you like to join us for supper," fell as naturally from the lips of Varina Teale as the pastor's benediction.

And so, soon after swapping his Sunday khakis for a pair of white Levi's and his favorite madras shirt, there he was, sailing on his bike along the gracious lanes of Westover Farms, gliding past the wide and meticulously groomed lawns opening up from the expansive colonial homes of aged brick and stone that anchored this rolling redoubt of suburban exclusivity in Richmond's west end.

Pumping hard toward the crest of Canterbury Lane, he came to a large, black mailbox imbedded in an ivy-covered casement of weathered brick that matched the walls of the stately home behind it. In front of the mailbox, attached to the brick, were wrought iron letters fashioned in Old English type and spelling out the word "Teale."

A walkway bordered by boxwoods opened at the edge of the street and led past an oak tree it would take three men to reach around. Its boughs stretched out over most of the lawn, shading a sea of summer-green before the two-story slate-roof home.

Sandy turned his bike down the wide driveway, slowed, got off and began to push. A screen door opened and Hope scrambled out from a side porch.

"Hey there," she called out, a glistening glass in her hand. "Thought you might be thirsty."

Hope wore a white cotton shirt, sleeves rolled up to the elbow, and sky blue Keds with no socks. She flicked her head to one side and threw her hair back over her shoulders as Sandy approached her.

"Thanks," he said, taking the glass from her hand. "Mmm, lemonade."

"Fresh made," she said, gently wiping a bit of pulp from his lips with her thumb.

Hope smiled and took hold of his handlebars, her long shirttail riding up the back of her faded pink shorts.

"Let's take it around back," she said.

Sandy followed her down the driveway to a small slate patio between the garage and side porch, where she nudged down the kickstand with her toe.

"You got a paper route?" Hope asked, looking at the large basket.

"Yep," Sandy said, taking a long swallow of lemonade. "How'd you know?"

"My brother used to be a paperboy," she said, running a finger along the wiry edge of the basket. "Plus," she said, looking up at Sandy and tilting her head to one side, "I kind'a remember you havin' a special interest in newspapers."

Sandy felt his face grow warm. He turned to look down the long driveway toward the road.

"Hope, aren't you goin' invite your comp'ny inside?"

Sandy looked toward the porch and there was Varina Teale, wearing a brilliant floral blouse and pistachio-colored slacks.

"I've got fresh deviled eggs here'f anybody's hungry."

Hope looked at Sandy and smiled.

"Yes ma'am," she replied, turning toward the door and motioning toward Sandy to follow. "Sounds good Gra'ma."

Sandy looked down at a large cobweb a banana spider had laced in the shadows between low wooden steps and broad-leafed shrubs. He stepped inside the porch as the woman set a tray down on a glass-topped coffee table. Deviled eggs formed a neat circle along the fluted edge of a large, white plate, alongside small triangles of toast.

"They look delicious, Mrs. Teale," Sandy said, as the woman stood up and motioned for him to take a seat. He slipped into an end chair and picked up the scattered remnants of that morning's Times-Daily. Hope took a spot on a faded couch, folding her legs beneath her knees.

"Oh lem'me take that," Mrs. Teale said to Sandy, reaching for the mass of Sunday papers. "I'll go get the table ready."

Sandy helped himself to a deviled egg. Hope nibbled at a piece of toast.

There was light and not altogether easy banter between them. Earlier this summer, Hope explained, her mother had gone back to work, selling menswear in the big department store downtown. "I've spent most of the summer at my grandparents' place in the country," an old soybean and corn farm that fronted the York River outside Gloucester. "I love it down there.

I love the water. I love the peace and quiet. I love the light on the fields in the late afternoon."

Sandy stared at her frayed white collar, its worn cotton fibers against the soft, smooth nape of her neck. Her skin was more freckled than tanned, far darker than he remembered her pale shoulders and face in the ballroom at Mrs. Randolph's cotillion. She seemed sturdier, too, not quite the waif he'd danced with that night in May. Just looking at her made Sandy feel a bit sturdier himself. Perhaps he'd grown stronger, he thought, in the months of delivering his papers. He took another deviled egg from the plate and slipped it whole into his mouth.

"Sandy, Hope, ya'll wash up now," Mrs. Teale's voice trumpeted from the kitchen. "Supper's ready."

Sandy followed Hope through the doorway. "There's a bathroom just down the hall," she gestured to Sandy, who followed her directions, passing by a pale blue wall of photographs.

In a thin wooden frame, there was a black and white shot of a lean man with a thick shock of hair wearing a dark suit and standing in front of a large and gleaming locomotive with the letters N&W painted on its side. There was another photograph of the same man, clustered around several others in mountainous territory, standing on a gleaming steel bridge. There was a broad ribbon in front of it and the men were holding a huge pair of mock scissors. In a wide, black, wooden frame, there was a color picture of the same man, grown a bit portly, standing beside the construction site of a large structure Sandy recognized as the Southern States Building downtown, one of the most prominent features of the Richmond skyline. And another, also color, of the man, heavier still, his hair gone grey and thin, standing beside a Piedmont Airlines pilot in front of a glistening new terminal at Byrd Field.

Master Teale, no doubt, Sandy thought to himself, as he rinsed the soap off his hands in the small hallway bathroom, his eyes fixed on yet another color photograph of the lead character in the family exhibit, this time standing erect in front of a split rail fence, a double-barrel shotgun slung open across his chest, with half a dozen ducks laid out at his feet.

"Guy gets around," Sandy mumbled to himself.

"We're in here," Hope called out.

She and her grandmother sat at a long, wooden table in a dining room with pink wallpaper and an ivory colored ceiling. There was a third setting, for Sandy, at the head of the table.

The dining room looked out over a spacious, sunken den with a stone hearth and a large picture window. Looking out from the table, Sandy saw the broad arms of an enormous live oak with limbs as thick as his waist. In the shade of the tree he saw the deep-green lawn slope downward from the house and fall away to a dense row of rhododendron and wisteria. Along the horizon above the hedge row, and framed by the distant tree line formed by pin oaks, white birches and sugar maples, Sandy eyed a shimmering ribbon of silver. He squinted slightly then cocked his head.

"It's nice to have a man join us for supper, isn't it Hope," Mrs. Teale said, as Sandy edged into his seat. "I hope you like Smithfield ham."

"Is that the river?" Sandy asked, gazing deep into the vista before him.

"Well le'me see now," the woman replied. "The Indian lake is out to the west, so it couldn't be that. The Ches'peake Bay is east, and we're lookin' south ..."

"Gra'ma," Hope cut her off with a smile. "Yes, Sandy, it's the river. Pretty, huh?"

Sandy stared off into the distance, his eyes following the sculpted flow of lawn through the thicket and into the water below.

" I've never been in a house before where you could look right out the back window and see the river." He paused, realizing he'd said something not only stupid but borderline rude, referencing, as it so directly did, the family's financial station and highlighting its disparity with his own.

"I've been to the Confederate cemetery downtown," he said, hoping to recover. "That place has got a great view of the river. Well, most of the grave sites anyway."

There was a briefly awkward silence before Varina Teale dealt with the comment in the most graceful way she knew how: "Help yourself to some ham, Hope, then pass the plate to our guest. Here son," the old woman said to Sandy, reaching toward him with a small wicker basket lined with white linen that covered half a dozen steaming biscuits. "Help yourself."

Sandy took two from the basket. "Thank you, ma'am," he said, and passed it to Hope, in exchange for a large white platter neatly spread with matchbook-sized slices of reddish brown ham.

"Gra'ma says if you can't read the Bible through it, it's sliced too thick," Hope offered.

"Ever tested that one out on Pastor Stout," Sandy queried with a smile, casting a glance at his hostess, who cocked her head slightly and brought the corner of a white linen napkin to the edge of her mouth.

"Hope," she said, "have some of those fresh Hanover tomatoes and pass the bowl to Sandy."

A bowl of warm butter beans followed, then another of cinnamon-colored apple sauce from the kitchen of some aunt or cousin near Winchester.

"Oh," Mrs. Teale exclaimed, lifting herself from her chair as though she smelled smoke, "I forgot the coleslaw."

Sandy watched her scurry around the table and into the kitchen.

"I don't know where my mind went," she said, hustling back to the table and carrying a large yellow and white bowl of freshly made slaw. She paused by Hope's side, spooned out a small serving, then handed the bowl to Sandy.

"Hope," he said, "are there any more biscuits?"

They both watched him pick up a tomato slice from his plate, lay it inside a fresh biscuit, then spread a fork full of coleslaw atop the tomato. He picked it up with both hands and took a bite, the warm cake-like biscuit melting away into the milky sweetness of the slaw. He put the biscuit down, wiped his mouth with his napkin then turned to Mrs. Teale.

"That's the very best coleslaw and tomato biscuit I've ever had," he said, as a broad smile worked its way across her face. "In fact, it's pretty much the very best thing I've tasted all summer."

# Chapter 24

Hope's laughter filled the forest like chipped ice in a tin bucket, as Sandy followed her along the winding footpath through the hedge at the end of the Teale's backyard and down the wooded slope toward the river.

"I must say, Sandy Rivers, that was some kind of table manners miracle," Hope said, pausing at a narrow point in the path to lift a long, thin limb and make way for him. "Did you practice those lines just to get on Gra'ma's good side, or are you just lucky?"

Sandy leaned to one side of the limb and took a step forward.

"Well, Miss Stafford, just maybe a little bit of both. You know, luck only takes a guy so far," he said, looking at Hope. "And, now and then the occasional miracle presents itself."

"And what exactly would you know about miracles, Sandy Rivers?"

He looked at the way the sunlight fell through the trees and across the freckled skin of her face. "I know a thing or two about miracles," he said.

Hope smiled and let the limb snap back, whisking the side of Sandy's arm with a knot of hairy, spiked-green devils the size of ping-pong balls.

"Hell's that?" Sandy burst out.

"Chinquapins," she shrugged, picking her way through the woods.

"There's a little nut inside it," she continued. "Ripens in the fall. Pretty tasty. My Grandad taught me how to eat 'em. Time you get past the thorns and the crusty shell, though, there's hardly enough to make it worth your while. That's part of their protection, I guess. More trouble 'n they're worth."

She glanced back over her shoulder and smiled. "Kind'a like some paperboys I know."

Fair enough, Sandy thought to himself, considered a mild retort but nothing approaching parity came to mind.

The leaves along the pathway were still damp from the overnight rain. At the base of the hill, a dense row of young juniper trees ran alongside a dilapidated plank fence. Hope ducked beneath a thick clutch of limbs, put her hands on a sunken top plank, then threw both legs over the top, landing at the edge of the field. Sandy followed her over and onto a narrow footpath leading through shoulder-high grasses, wildflowers and cane. Over the straw-colored top of the field, Sandy could see a slight rise, railroad tracks glistening in the afternoon sun, and beyond that a long thin line of trees.

"So, where's your grandfather Teale?" Sandy asked, leaning down to pull a bull thistle off the hem of his jeans. "I figured he couldn't have gone far at dessert time, when your gra'mother offered me the choice between her coconut cake and his last Moonpie."

"Yeah," Hope laughed. "You passed that test at least."

"Turnin' down a Moonpie's not a nat'ral thing."

"Oh, that much was clear."

Hope paused to get her bearings at an overgrown patch of the path, shaded her eyes with one hand then spread open a curtain of grass before her.

"Okay, then," she said out loud, pressing on.

"Well, Daddy Teale spends most weekends at the river."

"You mean, the river he can't see from his dining room window?"

Hope furrowed her brow but didn't turn around.

"The Gloucester place," she said. "Gra'ma spent her summers there when she was little. Daddy Teale goes down there to hunt and fish, mostly. Piddle around in the fields. She doesn't go much anymore."

The footpath widened and the field gave way to a rise at the rock-strewn base of the railroad tracks. Hope scrambled to the top, looked down both sides of the empty tracks, then turned and reached back to Sandy.

Hope's hand felt strong in his as she helped him up the rocky slope. From atop the tracks, Sandy could see the full reach of the hot field behind them. He turned and, through a shaded clearing in the trees beyond the tracks, he saw the water's broad sunlit surface, framed on one side by an enormous poplar. A soft breeze swept toward him, carrying the pungent scent of the river.

"Got a penny?" she asked.

"For your thoughts?"

"No, you crazy boy," she said. "For the train."

Sandy listened for a moment, heard only the soaring trill of cicadas in the warm grass and trees.

"It'll come along in a while," Hope said, stepping over the tracks and onto the heavy timber ties in between. She knelt to press an ear to the silvery rail.

"Hot," she said, as Sandy reached into his pocket.

"Got two of 'em," he said, stooping over to lay one on each of the tracks.

"For good luck," said Hope.

She stood and scrambled down the graveled rise toward the thick-stalked pokeweed leading toward the trees on the riverbank.

Sandy followed, stumbled at the base of the track bed and tumbled into a knee-high patch of hairy-stemmed green plants with small, tooth-rimmed leaves shaped like arrowheads. He bounded up, more embarrassed than hurt, wishing Hope's back had been turned to him when he fell, and followed her into the shade of the trees. Suddenly he felt as though his left arm were being torn into by hornets and set on fire at the same time.

"Owww," Sandy screamed. "Damn!"

Sandy slapped at his arm, but nothing was there. He scratched at it, but that made the pain and burning worse.

"Hold still," Hope said, glancing at the small red welts appearing on his arm then back toward the spot where he fell in the weeds.

"I can't," Sandy shouted, swatting at the air. "It itches like crazy!"

Hope grabbed Sandy's right hand.

"C'mon," she said, leading him in a gallop toward the tall poplar at the crest of the bank.

"My arm's on fire!"

"Let's go," she hollered, kicking off her Keds and scampering barefoot down the bank toward the river. She waded into the shallows, past the moss-mottled trunk of a fallen tree, working her way downstream to a hollowed out spot in the bank where the water was still. At the water's edge, there was a dense stand of grassy plants with round and pulpy leaves. Hope reached in, grabbed a long thick stem and yanked. She waded back upstream to where Sandy was squatting at the river's edge, frantically splashing water on his arm.

"It's not helping," he screamed. "It's getting worse."

"Get up," Hope said, dropping part of her harvest onto a muddy rock on the bank and shredding the rest in her hands.

"Gimme your arm."

"What the hell's that?"

"Duckweed," she shot back. "Now gimme your arm!"

Sandy held it out as if he never expected to get it back. "What the . . ."

Hope started to wipe the wet leaves and stems across his arm, as Sandy jerked it away.

Hope stood knee deep in the water, heaved a great sigh and brushed her hair from her face with a muddy hand.

"Sandy Rivers, give me that arm or I swear I'll throw you right straight in this river, white pants 'n all."

He surrendered his left hand, and she rubbed the mash of moist foliage into his skin. Sandy looked down into the shaded shallows, where the water curled gently around Hope's bare legs.

The August heat had drawn the water down, exposing brown and yellow stones, smooth and round, and the wandering roots of ancient trees in the mud and clay edge of the riverbank. Further out where the channel deepened, the broad surface of the river ran smooth, like wet lacquer glistening in the afternoon sun, with swirl marks here and there, as if someone had run a finger across it before it could dry. There was a ragged white line of riffles toward the far side, where the water rushed past the grassy bottoms of grey rocks. Beyond that he saw the shaded darkness beneath a dense wall of trees on the southern shore. He'd hardly noticed while he was watching the river, but the burning, itching and stinging had eased, as if it were flowing out of his arm, until somehow it just disappeared.

"Now hold it there just like that," Hope ordered.

She dropped her handful of duckweed into the water, where Sandy watched it float and bob downstream, then she bent over to pick up more from the rock. She broke the stems, tore the leaves and squeezed it all together in her hands. A thin milky sap oozed out, and she worked it into his skin.

"Feel'in better?"

Sandy just looked at her, felt her soft strong fingers kneading his arm.

"Nettle grass is evil stuff," she said, stooping over to rinse off her hands.

"Duckweed?"

"Well, that's all I've ever heard it called," she said, carefully picking her way over the rocky river bottom and onto the edge of the muddy bank.

"It's a miracle plant."

"I thought we'd pretty well established here that you're not the resident expert on miracles," Hope said, kicking the water off one leg and then the other.

She eyed him at a sort of angle then tapped the side of his head, the way a woman might thump a cantaloupe she wasn't convinced was quite ripe.

"You can't hardly talk about miracles unless you actually believe in them."

"Well I damned sure believe 'n this," he sputtered. "Two minutes ago I'd about cut my arm off to stop the pain. Now all a sudden it's like it never even happened."

"Oh it happened alright," she said, wringing out her shirttail and leaning into the bank as she walked up toward the broad boughs of the poplar where she'd left her shoes.

Yeah, it happened, he thought to himself, following her up the hill, just like leaving her stranded and alone in the ballroom that night. Running around acting like a damned fool.

Sandy watched her stoop over the thin grass and moist clay at the base of the tree. "Can't get much muddier, I don't guess," she said, reaching for a shoe and crouching down to sit. "These shorts are prob'ly ruined already."

"Hang on," he said, reaching for her shoulder.

She stood and faced him, a thin muddy streak running beneath one eye. She cocked her head suspiciously to one side, as he motioned her toward the large tree.

"You just stay right there," he said, turning back to get her Keds.

Hope smiled softly to herself and leaned back against the gnarled trunk of the tree.

"What are you doin'?" she laughed, as he knelt on the thick hump of a root by her feet. She watched his spindly fingers working to untie one shoe. A faint breeze blew through his hair, gone light brown with the sun, and she could see the bone line of his shoulders pressing through his madras shirt.

"Lift please," he said, taking hold of her right ankle with his hand.

"Careful now," she admonished. "I'm ticklish."

He cupped her heel in one hand and swept the sole of her foot, rubbing off the sandy mud and gently working his fingers over her toes.

Hope started to snicker and let loose a light kick.

"Quit," she giggled.

"I got'ta get 'em clean first, don't I?"

Sandy looked up and caught an unexpected glimpse of her stomach, smooth and taught beneath her shirttail, then saw her smiling down at him.

"Now hold it up a second," he said, letting go of her foot as it dangled before him, sunlight sparkling off the veil of river silt clinging to the downy hair along the length of her leg. "Let's see if the slipper fits." He opened the shoe beneath her, carefully plucked a burr from the tongue and tossed it aside as she pointed her toe and slipped it into the shoe.

"Finally," Sandy sighed. "I've searched my kingdom high and low . . ."

"You're a goof," she laughed, reaching down and grabbing a hank of his hair. "Am I s'posed to hop home on one foot?"

"Patience, fair maiden," Sandy replied, taking her left foot in his hand. "If I might have the other one now?"

Hope settled back against the tree, pulled her arms up behind her and rested her head against her open palms. She could hear the simpering of the river flowing past and the ringing of cicadas high in the trees. She closed her eyes, breathed in the sweet scent of the shade and felt his hands warm and firm on her feet. From a great distance she heard the high moan of a whistle break the summer calm.

"Our pennies," she murmured, reaching down without looking to run a hand through his hair. "The train's comin' for our pennies."

Sandy felt her fingers, still cool from the water, against the back of his neck, smelled the fertile, fragrant river on her leg as it brushed against his cheek while he tucked and tugged the laces into a bow.

"Tight enough?"

"Perfect," she said in a low pitched near whisper, as Sandy got up off his knees.

"You know, Hope," he began.

"Shhhhh," she said slowly, her eyes still closed as if fixed on a dream. She reached her arm around his waist and drew him to her side. "It's comin' for our pennies."

Sandy felt a warmth sweep through him as he edged against the tree. She let her head fall against his shoulder. The breeze blew through her hair. It reminded Sandy of green acorns on a freshly cut lawn, like honeycomb on waxed paper, baby oil on sunburned skin and the spray of the foam where the sea meets the shore. It smelled, he thought, like a part of summer that might never end.

From across the field came a low, fluted moan, like a child blowing across the rounded mouth of a milk bottle, a single note of longing, then a sound that rose and fell like a drop of rain, a plaintive, pleading voice, like the bending of the soul, followed by three soft and measured tones.

"Mourning dove," Hope said, gently rolling her head back and forth against the sturdy trunk. "Coo, coo, coo."

The two of them waited in silence and listened, heard the five-note sonata once more.

"Are there two of them?"

"Of course," replied Hope. "They're always in pairs. They mate for life, you know."

Sandy said nothing, just listened — to Hope's voice and the cooing of the doves.

"Daddy Teale told me that he won't hunt for dove. Says you kill one it's like killing two. Says a good sport won't do that."

The whistle blew again, much closer this time, and Sandy felt the dampness from her shirttail bleeding through his pants leg. The thought raced through his mind to look into her eyes, to wipe the thin smudge of the river from her cheek. But her head was against him; her face turned away.

"Hope," he whispered, or rather, imagined he might, as a prelude to all he wanted to tell her just then. Instead he said nothing, just drew in the scent of her hair and silently prayed that the train might somehow forever draw nearer yet never quite arrive.

There was a low, whining whir as two brownish grey birds with long thin tails flew over the tracks and toward the trees. A thick flock of blackbirds exploded from the field and arced northward toward the forested hill across the hot grass and cane. A thunderous roar broke from the west and Sandy felt Hope tighten her arm around his waist.

It was a huge, black locomotive, like the one in the picture with Daddy Teale. It hurtled past them and down the tracks in a furious, ground-shaking blur, the hot rails sagging ever so slightly beneath the weight of the rampaging beast, like twin steel backbones groaning with the strain of a spine-wrenching load.

What it was hauling, Sandy couldn't yet tell. Certainly not coal, not on a train that fast. Flat cars sped past, a few bark-stripped timbers chained to steel beds, then box cars, a dingy yellow or dust-caked blue, some with open doors showing nothing inside.

Sandy stood up straight to try to count the cars, but they were speeding by too fast, until finally, as quickly as the train had arrived, a rust-colored caboose fled past, the fleeting coda to the long train bound east.

"C'mon," Hope said, stepping out toward the narrow pathway leading back to the tracks. She scrambled up the slight hill and over the rocky track bed to where two long and shiny ovals of copper sat glimmering in the sun. Against the glassy surface of the silvery rails, the flattened pennies looked oddly new.

"Here you are," Hope said, handing Sandy the thin rolled remains of a penny as he joined her on the tracks.

"Another rough day for Lincoln," Sandy mused, staring at the Great Emancipator's barely discernible visage stretched across the elongated face of the coin.

"We'll drive a nail through 'em when we get back to the house and string 'em on twine necklaces," Hope said. "They'll bring us good luck the rest of the summer."

Sandy rubbed the warm coin between his fingers. He looked back toward the river, the poplar tree and the matted spot where he'd tumbled into the nettle grass, then turned toward Hope.

"I'm, you know, just really sorry," Sandy said, watching the play of the light on her hair. "I guess I kind'a panicked."

"That's what we do when we're hurt and scared," she smiled. She looked past Sandy and toward the river. "Fortunately," she smiled, "God gives us a cure for all that."

"You think that's how it is," Sandy asked, following her down the track bed and back into the field, "for every bad thing in the world?"

"Yes I do," she replied, making her way to the field. "That's what I believe."

"Is that somethin' else you learned from your granddad?"

"Don't you worry 'bout how I know what I know, Sandy Rivers," she said, stopping in the field to turn back once more. "You'd do well, for that matter, to never doubt me again."

Chapter 25

The next two weeks blew past Sandy amid a swirl of back-to-school preparations, subscribers returning from vacations and repeated visits to the Teale's place on Canterbury Lane, where he and Hope passed their days together with afternoon walks to the river, lemonade on the porch and conversations stretching long after dark. All too soon, they both realized, they'd return to school on different sides of town, and separate worlds apart.

It wasn't until the last week of August that Sandy finally met Daddy Teale, as he and his wife sat with Sandy and Hope around a small black and white television on the side porch one night watching the national Democratic convention in Chicago.

"Damned protesters," Daddy Teale opined. "Ought to stay the hell home."

Daddy Teale, though, wasn't surprised when Vice President Hubert Humphrey was named the party's presidential candidate, promising to pick up where Johnson's peace diplomacy left off and bring an honorable end to the war in Vietnam.

Mrs. Teale rose to answer the telephone, then called out from the kitchen to her husband, just as he crammed a handful of parched peanuts into his mouth and washed them down with a swig of Budweiser. Mr. Teale hauled himself out of his seat with both hands and a wheeze, swept the papery brown peanut skins off the front of his shirt and ambled inside to take the call.

"One of the members, I expect," Grandma Teale offered, returning to her place on the small sofa beside Hope.

Daddy Teale, Sandy had sussed out over time, was a former public relations executive who'd become the president and face of the Old Dominon Banking and Loan Association, referred to in the Teale household as "The Association" but better known to the general populace, and uncharitable editorial writers, by its ill-considered acronym, ODBAL. Its members were banking executives, one of whom was already hammering away at Teale to develop a strategy for seeing to it that ODBAL coordinated with its sister associations around the country to work quietly behind the scenes to help defeat Humphrey in November.

Through the porch doorway Sandy could see the old man hunched over the kitchen table with the nub of a pencil in one hand scribbling on a napkin, nodding as he listened and gesturing into the air with his pencil as he spoke.

Sandy mulled over the scene as he rode his bike home that night. Why would a grown man take something like a political race so seriously? Why not just show up on Election Day, cast your vote and go home? Besides, that wouldn't be until November, which was an eternity away.

The next Saturday night, Mrs. Teale dropped off Hope at Atlantis pool, where Sandy paid fifty cents for her to be his guest for the summer's-end teen dance. A band called Silver Spurs played under the rain shelter of corrugated steel. "Here's one by the Spencer Davis Group," the lead guitar player, Rick Montayne, announced, before belting out a hard-driving rendition of "I'm a Man."

The band took a break while Sandy stood in line at the snack bar, where he ran into Catesby Raines. When Sandy returned with two bottles of Nehi grape drink, Rick was leaning on a folding table and talking with Hope.

"This is my friend Sandy," she said looking down, her face slightly flushed. "I'm kind'a here with him."

"Lucky man," Rick nodded, hardly acknowledging Sandy, who handed Hope her drink. The guitarist was two years ahead of Sandy in school and a good head and a half taller. He had deep set eyes and go-to-hell smirk.

"You want somethin' to drink," Hope asked him. "You've been singin' and all."

He snatched a dark red guitar pick from between his teeth and reached out his hand. "Yeah, I could use a sip." Rick turned up the bottle and took a long swig, pulled it from his lips with a crude slurping sound and handed it back to her.

"Here you go, Hope," Sandy said, offering her his bottle instead. "That one's all yours," he said to Rick.

"You hang onto it, little man. I got somethin' better backstage."

"It's okay," said Hope, taking the bottle back from Rick and tipping it to her lips for a long, cool draw.

The older boy pulled a pack of Marlboros out of his shirt pocket, flipped opened the box and a cigarette popped out like it was on a string.

"Oh, sorry," he said, extending the pack toward Hope with a vaguely inquisitive look on his face.

Sandy shook his head and smiled. "That's alright man, she doesn't . . ."

"Thanks," Hope said, plucking a cigarette from the pack.

Sandy stared at Hope, but she turned from his gaze and looked instead at Rick.

"Light?"

"Ah, no thanks," Hope replied, tucking the cigarette into her shirt pocket. "I'll save it for later."

Rick smiled and lit up.

"Okay. Better get back."

"Good luck," she replied, as Rick glanced back over his shoulder and smiled.

"What the hell was that?" Sandy wondered to himself.

"Nice guy," he said to Hope instead.

She took a swig from her drink.

"You were kind'a rude to him you know," she said.

"Me?"

"That whole business about the drink."

"I just thought he might, you know, want his own."

"Oh sure," Hope said. "That's close."

"Well you were the one who was sooo concerned," Sandy said. "You know, 'All that singin' 'n all.'"

"What's it to you?" Hope replied. "So I gave the guy a sip of my drink?"

"Nothing," Sandy snapped back. "That's fine."

"Fine."

"Good."

"Great."

"Perfect!"

Sandy took a gulp from his Nehi bottle and sat down in a webbed chair.

"Well, are you just gon' sit here?" she asked.

Sandy spread his hands apart above his lap. He didn't look up at Hope.

"'Cause I don't feel like just sittin' around."

"Do what you want," Sandy fired back. "Nobody's keepin' you here."

"Aww-riiiiight," a voice blasted from the big, boxy amplifier toward the front of the rain shelter. "How's everybody doin' out there?" It was a pudgy guy behind a set of drums, a kid Sandy had seen Rick Montayne hanging around with by the bleachers one day when neither bothered to dress out for gym class.

There was a blare of feedback from someone's guitar and Sandy saw Rick Montayne walk over and adjust some knobs on an amp.

"We're gon' kick off this set with a li'l somethin' from the Turtles," the drummer shouted out, before clicking off a four count with his sticks.

Sandy recognized the bass line that started off the song.

"Imagine me 'n you, I do, I think about you day 'n night, it's only ri-i-ight, to think about the girl you love, 'n hold her tight, so happy toge-the-er."

Sandy found himself tapping his foot.

"I like this one," he said to Hope, stood to face her and saw she wasn't there. He scanned the tables by the makeshift dance floor, and saw Hope standing near the low wooden bandstand. She and Rick Montayne were looking directly at each other, while he crooned out the lead vocals and played an electric guitar.

"I can't see me lovin' nobody but you, for all my li-i-ife," he sang.

Sandy felt a burning inside his chest. He saw Catesby standing by the pool in a dripping swimsuit, and walked over toward him.

"Where's your girlfriend?" Catesby asked.

"She's not my damned girlfriend," Sandy spat back. "I just brought her here 'cause she wanted to come."

"Oh yeah," Catesby shrugged. "Sure thing."

"Papers'll be huge tomorrow," Sandy said. "Labor Day sales 'n all."

Catesby cast a blank look.

"Who gives a rip?"

Catesbuy turned, lunged into the pool and toward a gaggle of other boys.

Sandy looked beyond them to where his red bike stood leaning against the outside of a tall chain-link fence. He put his hands in his pockets and walked back toward the rain shelter, where several older teenagers gathered near the band.

Sandy heard a voice boom out over the PA system.

"This one goes out to a special lady named Hope."

Startled, Sandy looked toward the stage and saw Montayne backing away from the microphone, looking toward the chubby drummer and ripping into the opening riff of "Louie-Louie."

Sure enough, there was Hope, this time with a lighted cigarette in her hand, bobbing to the music just in front of the small stage.

"A Lou-ah Lou-a-yeh, oh baby! I said a me gotta go," Montayne sang out. "Yah, yah, yah, yah!"

Sandy felt his body turn as if by remote control. By the time he realized he was walking, he was halfway out the gate.

"Hey pussy, where you goin'?"

It was Catesby calling out through the fence as Sandy climbed onto his bike.

"Nowhere special," Sandy yelled back. "See you bright 'n early tomorrow."

Catesby hollered something back, but Sandy was already pedaling toward the parking lot.

"Ok, let's give it to 'em — right now," Rick Montayne shouted out as he leaned into the bridge, his electric guitar wailing out from the little bandstand.

Sandy reached into his shirt, grabbed a thin and misshapen copper coin, gave a yank, felt the thin cotton twine around his neck give way, and tossed it into the wild grass by a curve in the hill rising away from Atlantis pool. He rose in his pedals and pumped as hard as he could, the hot night against his face, an even hotter dampness in his eyes, and a part of summer he'd once thought might never end fading farther and farther behind.

# Chapter 26

Indian summer lingered mercifully into fall, bringing warm clear days of brilliant sunshine that lit the maples, poplars and oaks of Hill & Hamlet, turning its autumn foliage into a rustic palette of reds, yellows and browns cast upon rain-replenished lawns of every perceptible shade of green.

Not until the first day of November did Sandy need his hooded sweatshirt. He felt the soft fleece against his neck as he stepped out the back door and breathed in the cool morning air, rich with scents of moist grass and fallen leaves. He'd put his bike behind the back of the house the night before, a safeguard against Halloween hooliganism.

He looked up into the darkness and saw a lone cloud that vaguely resembled a large horse silhouetted against a golden moon, nearly full and hanging low in the western sky. He bent down, squeezed his tires, mounted up and headed out.

"I need someone to deliver F-29 tomorrow," Lucky Pete had told him the day before. "It's 120 papers, for just one day. I'm in kind of a jam, and there's a quick three bucks in it for you if you'll take it on."

All it required, really, was that Sandy get up an hour earlier than usual, deliver the route as Pete laid it out for him on a set of white index cards, then ride back and take care of his own papers. And so, as youthful trick-or-treaters combed Hill & Hamlet the night before, Sandy had carefully taped the index cards to the back of his basket, so they could guide him through F-29.

To get to the paper stop for that route, though, Sandy had to cut through the narrow pathway in the woods behind Skinquarter. He'd ridden it plenty in daylight, even a time or two at night, riding home from the Teales' place last summer. This, though, still felt like Halloween night.

No sooner did Sandy reach Tempest Lane than he ran over the slick and pungent remains of a pumpkin someone had smashed and left to rot in the road. He noticed a pale yellow porch light shining down on a row of painted plywood tombstones planted on the lawn at 8703 Tempest.

"Here lies Jon, he tied one on," Sandy read off one in the amber glow, "crashed his car, and now he's gone."

Better keep an eye on those kids, he thought.

Further down the road, he passed a neat brick Cape Cod house, where a large maple was festooned with a paper skeleton against an angel hair cobweb. Pam's house, Sandy thought to himself as he rode past, marking her baby's first Halloween. He imagined her suckling her son, slipping a soft round breast from her nightgown as she cradled the infant in bed.

The vision momentarily took the chill off the air, until a flickering red light next door broke his train of thought, illuminating a large, squat jack-o-lantern with a gaping grin, beside a straw hag in a pitch-black hat.

Just hours before, he thought to himself, all of Hill & Hamlet had been alive with little goblins and ghouls dressed up like ghosts and haints. There were princesses and pirates, mummies and cowboys, baseball players, movie stars, magicians and thieves, a teeming panoply of suburban fantasies and fears set loose upon the placid porches and chicory pocked lawns of those who now lay fast asleep, at ease in the solace and sanctity they purchased from the youthful and teeming horde for the price of a caramel apple, box of raisins or miniature Milky Way.

Sandy felt decidedly less comfortable in the empty night alone, as he crested the hill near the end of Tempest Lane to see long white belts of toilet paper streaming eerily from the tall pines and roof of the old Sullivan place.

"Sum-bitch," he muttered beneath his breath, as he pressed his brakes and approached the darkened path.

"Everything's good," he consoled himself, bringing his bike to a stop where the pavement broke up at the edge of the woods. "It's only a damned game, really, just something for the kids. A rite of autumn, like burning leaves."

He sniffed the air, as if for smoke, but all that was there was another season of broken limbs and downed trees left to molder away in the honeysuckle swamp beyond the crumbling plank fence.

"Le'me just get my eyes adjusted here," he said to no one, buying time. He looked back down Tempest Lane, imagined children laughing nearby just hours before, but heard only the baby-like cry of some animal off in the darkness. "Probably a cat," he shrugged as he straddled his bike and pulled the hood on his sweatshirt over the back of his head.

He peered deep into the blackness before him and saw in the distance a soft green something glowing by the edge of the path. Phosphorous, he figured, or a glowworm, perhaps.

From somewhere far beyond the woods, something let out a high whining howl. A breeze rushed through the trees overhead, and Sandy heard the moaning of a young pine limb rubbing against an old oak.

"Okay, let's go," he said to himself, rolling slowly forward into the woods. There was just enough moonlight trickling through the forest gloom for Sandy to follow the narrow path. Dull shadows fell across the footway as he passed by the old poplar tree, recalling the grim tales he'd heard there as a child.

He had a sudden image of young Martin's lifeless body as it hung by the swamp, then imagined the slave boy traveling this way by the light of a pale and silvery moon, searching still for the crossing place. His bike wobbled momentarily toward the edge of the path, as the moon slipped behind a cloud. Something prickly, like thorns, tugged against the hem of his pants, and he could almost hear the raspy voice of an old man.

"The finga'nails don' stop growin'," the voice echoed inside his head, as he pedaled deeper into the tunnel of blackness before him. "They reachin' up 'n tryin' ta grab somethin' to pull they'sev's up out'd de quicksand b'low . . . Ha, haa, haa, haaaaaa!"

He felt his front wheel plunge into the edge of the creek, heard the splash of shallow water beneath him, thought of the river and suddenly pictured a party of Monacans, with painted faces and long glimmering knives, ferrying the bloody body of a fallen chief to sacred burial grounds. His arm rubbed against something smooth and hard, as he passed alongside the dense stand of bamboo.

An impenetrable darkness encased him, as the moon slipped behind a veil of cloud. Navigating by memory, his palms cold and damp, he felt the landscape seem to shift beneath him, like hay lifted on the prongs of a pitchfork and tossed. A dry branch slapped against his face and snapped. Something yelped out again from afar. Rite of autumn or not, he thought, if spirits ever rose to roam abroad, surely this would be the night.

"I ain' ever doin' this again," he vowed out loud to the emptiness.

He struggled to fill his mind with wholesome and comforting themes, to conjure up some reassuring vision of protective saints. He thought of Brother Shiloh, Jesus and Lee, Pam's warm breasts, milky and full.

"Halfway through," Sandy urged himself on, rising from his seat to pull his bike up the slope leading out of the woods and into the tall grass alongside the churchyard. A single light bulb swung bare in the breeze beneath the chapel eave, casting moving shadows out to the side and toward the edge of the graveyard.

He whispered a prayer for Moses Marable, saw the casket and empty grave in his mind.

"Just a closer walk with thee," he sang out as he pumped his bike through the narrow field and past the small wooden church at the edge of Midsummer Night's Lane, its thinly whitewashed steeple standing sentry against the inky sky. "Daily walking close to thee . . . "

There was a sound up ahead, a mad beast, he imagined, hideous and huge, crashing through the brush by the bend in the road just opposite the church.

"Let it be, dear Lord, let it be," Sandy croaked out, his voice gone faint with fear. The thin cloud swept from in front of the moon, and in the pale curtain of light that opened before him Sandy saw a flowing specter in white, suspended in the air like a corpse from a tree, like a shriveled zombie risen from the quicksand below, like a face-painted warrior on a mission from . . .

"Yeee-aaaaahhhhhhhhhh," the ghoul shrieked out as Sandy rode past.

"Go-o-od daaamn," Sandy let out, his eyes clenched shut, his heart a heaving mass of molten stone about to burst through his bone-dry throat. "Yaaaaaaaaaaaaaaa . . . ."

He was on top of both pedals with all his weight and leaning out over his basket, his legs pumping like pistons. He felt his bike surge forward beneath him, as though it had somehow taken flight, as though the chain were no longer attached to his wheel. He pictured a young Yankee officer in a blue, bullet-riddled coat, astride a massive black steed, galloping close behind. He glanced down to make sure he was still bound to the road, then heard the clatter of another set of pedals from behind.

"Hy-aaaaahhhhhhhhhh," there was another shriek, much like the one just before, then laughter, wild and unchastened, as Sandy rounded the bend and tore down the moonlit road.

"What the hell," he hollered out loud, not daring to look back, then saw a white flowing figure pull up on a large bike by his side. Sandy stared into the face of the beast, squinting hard at its pointy nose, beady eyes, and the pale ivory bed sheet flowing around it all.

"Good God almighty, Winston," Sandy hollered out, sitting back on his seat and letting his bike coast. "You scared me into the next lifetime."

Both bikes coasted to a halt, as Winston struggled to catch his breath against high-pitched laughter that made his whole body heave. "Go-o-od daaaaamn," he mimicked Sandy with an exaggerated reprise of his cry, triggering another round of gut-wrenching mirth that finally drew to a breathless collapse. Like the last wheezing gasps of a run-down pick-up, Sandy thought to himself, that's hauled its last load of manure.

"Ohh, Lordy," Winston said, his words flowing over residual giggles of delight like rivulets across the lawn as a storm subsides. "I'll never forget that as long as I live. What was that sound you made again, Yaaaaaa . . . oh mercy, my sweet mercy me!"

"Very fuckin' funny."

"Hey, John-ee Rivers, seriously," Winston said, feigning a respectful tone. "Trick or treat!" Then it started again, another bucket-load of incontinent laughter.

"I am not be-lievin' you did that," Sandy said, getting off his bike and letting it drop in the middle of the dark and empty road. "You scared the liv'in hell out'a me!"

Winston unwrapped himself from the bed sheet, closed his eyes and turned his head upward, ran a hand across his face and sighed. "Oh, Lordy me, that was good."

"How the hell long you been there like that?"

"'About ten minutes," Winston replied. "I didn't wan'na miss you — flyin' past me like that!" Another belly roll of laughter followed. "I'm sorry, man, but if you could've heard that scream . . ."

"How the hell," Sandy started, then remembered Winston's best friend. "Oh yeah, Lucky Pete."

Winston smiled, stuffed the sheet in the dented basket of his aging black bike, veteran of countless early morning encounters past. "I ran into him last night at the Bridle 'n Post," Winston said. "He told me you were takin' F-29 today. I figured you might just swing by this way."

Sandy said nothing but looked far down the lane to where it intersected with a blacktop road. In the dim light of a tired streetlamp, he could make out a three-legged dog hobbling past a small stack of paper bundles, just where Pete told him they'd be.

"When'd you get home?"

"Coupl'a days ago."

"How long you around?"

"Few more hours."

Winston pulled a Marlboro out of his shirt pocket and lit up, drawing the two of them inside the pale pocket of flame.

"I finished up basic at Fort Polk," he said, pulling a long drag from his cigarette. "Got a few days leave. Felt good to get the hell out'a there. They don' call it Lose-y-anna for nothin', remember?"

He let the smoke drift out of his mouth.

"Next stop's Fort Wolters. Somewhere in Texas. Primary flight school. Gettin' down to the good stuff."

"You mean you haven't learned how to fly yet?"

"Not 'less you count gettin' knocked on my ass flyin'," Winston shrugged. "But I'm done with foxholes 'n rifle butts. From now on it's stick 'n rudder, avionics, navigation, radio communications, all that stuff."

Sandy nodded his head as if he understood.

Winston nodded back.

"Well, old man, few months at Wolters, then I'm on to Fort Rucker, Alabama, then 'nother eight months from there, things go right, I'll be a helicopter pilot," he said, pulling another drag from his cigarette. "If I don't wash out."

Sandy weighed the thought.

"Sounds right tough."

"No tougher'n ridin' through Skinquarter alone in the dead of night," Winston replied, giving Sandy a stiff shot to the shoulder.

"Damn," Sandy said. "Your fist feels like a hammer. What all they got you doin' down there?"

"This 'n that," Winston said. "Hey, do me a favor while I'm gone."

"Oh, yeah," Sandy shot back facetiously. "I guess after all this I owe you one."

"This one's easy, but it's important."

Sandy looked up and saw Winston's face in the fading moonlight.

"Look after Mary Kay, for me, will ya? She ain' takin' this whole Army thing all that well."

Sandy nodded, leaned over and picked up his bike.

"Well," he said, climbing onto his seat, "you got one thing right. Keepin' an eye on Mary Kay won't work no hardship on me."

"Just remember," Winston cautioned, firing another right at Sandy's shoulder.

"Oww! Damn, man." Sandy rubbed his shoulder. "You gon' see her 'fore you leave?"

"She's makin' me pancakes, then droppin' me off at the bus station."

Sandy paused, expecting something more. Winston looked up, stretched his neck and sank the back of his head into his shoulders.

"Hey Winston, you know a guy named Montayne?"

"Fast Rickie?"

"Yeah, I guess."

"Used to play on my little league team. Not much of a first baseman, but a helluva guitar player. Ran into him last night, in fact. Said he's got some kind'a band."

"Silver Spurs, I heard 'em last summer."

"Yeah, that's it. He's hell on the guitar."

"You saw him last night, at the Bridle 'n Post?"

"Yeah. Didn't talk to him, exactly, but he was there."

"Was he, you know, with anybody?"

"Yeah," Winston said. "He was with that smart ass, what's his name? Guy plays drums, I think, in his band. How come?"

"Nothin' really."

Winston looked back down the road toward the little wooden chapel. The moon rode low in the west, the last of its orange light fading off the face of the hand-painted sign welcoming the faithful to The Skinquarter A.M.E. Church of God.

Sandy stared at the darkened doors, remembered the morning he saw Winston inside for the eulogy that spring.

"Sky-y pi-lot," Winston sang softly to himself.

"That what they gon' call you?"

Winston looked down and kicked his shoe against the street.

"Naw. That's what they call the military chaplains over in 'Nam."

Sandy thought it over a moment, looked back at the chapel and listened.

"Each unit has its own chaplain. Sort of like havin' your own preacher along."

"Is it just for pilots?"

"For everybody, really. Pilots, grunts, everybody."

The light bulb beneath the eave flickered, then died, then flared back to life.

"I guess he's s'posed to watch over you," Winston reasoned, "or help guide you to heaven, to the sky, if, for some reason . . ." He looked toward the little church. "Let's hope it worked for Mose."

Winston took a final draw from his cigarette, then gave the glowing butt a toss.

"Well, sir, you don't want those bird cage liners turnin' yellow on you."

"Reckon not," Sandy replied.

The two boys rode together the few blocks to the paper stop, where Sandy leaned his bike against a telephone pole and searched in the pale light of the streetlamp for the bundle marked F-29.

"How's Lucky Pete doin' as district manager?" Winston asked, as Sandy hauled up the weighty bundle with both hands.

"Oh, he's alright," Sandy said, catching his breath. "I kind'a liked that other guy."

"Shheee," Winston said. "How much you bankin' this week?"

Sandy thought for a second. Things were going well on his route, and he was picking up extra dough subbing on F-29. Plus, he was trying to save up a little money for Christmas presents.

"Three dollars," he replied, throwing a leg over the crossbar, straddling his bike and pulling out his wire clippers.

"Tha's what I like to hear," Winston said, as Sandy popped open the bundle. "Le'see what we got here."

Winston pulled out a paper and tilted the front page toward the light.

"Johnson Orders Bombing Halt," Winston read out loud the first of at a two-deck headline stripped overtop the width of the page. "Saigon, Viet Cong to Join Paris Talks."

He leaned toward the paper and squinted into the dim light.

"That mean the war's over," Sandy asked.

"Not hardly," Winston replied. "What it means mostly is that we're three days from a presidential election and Johnson and Ho Chi Minh have finally found somethin' they can agree on."

"Wha'da'ya mean?"

"Neither wants Nixon to win," Winston said. "Le'see here, Johnson's sayin' the talks will pick up again the day after the November fifth vote. Now ain't that a pretty coincidence?"

"Hell's the election got to do with bombin' Vietnam?"

"Johnson wants ever'body to think he's endin' the war. Wants 'em to think 'ol Hubert'll finish the job. Wants 'em to figure this ain' no time to be changin' horses in midstream, you know, don't throw out the Democrats and put the Republicans in."

"Ah, c'mon, Winston," Sandy said, biting a smile and shaking his head. "Who the hell'd mess around with the war like that — stoppin' the bombin', startin' the bombin', talkin' peace, not talkin' peace — nobody'd do all that just to win a damned election."

Winston looked at the boy, opened his mouth to speak, then let it go.

"All I know is the Army brass thinks this war'll prob'ly last another year," Winston said. "The Viet Cong'll get the message once Nixon gets in."

Winston tossed the paper back on top of the others in Sandy's basket.

"You think he'll win?"

"Hell'f I know," Winston shot back. "Humphrey damned sure won't win in Virginia, 'less that damned fool Wallace strips votes 'way from Nixon."

"Wallace? Who the hell'd vote for that ign'rnt sum'bich," Sandy proffered. "Hell, I heard him talkin' on TV th'other night. He sounds 'bout like a third-grade drop-out with his mouth full of marbles."

"Well, buddy, obviously you ain' never been to Ala-fuggin'-bama," Winston countered. "But, anyway, we'll know soon enough, won't we? 'Meantime, I got'ta get on home to pack."

He pulled something from his pocket, another cigarette Sandy figured, and rose up on his pedals as the bike rolled forward.

"Good luck with flight trainin'," Sandy said, gripping his handlebars and steadying his bike. "And, don't forget to pack your sheet."

There was a soft plop, and in the dim light cast by the streetlamp Sandy could see a Milky Way bar the size of a matchbox bounce across his basket of papers.

"There you go, John-ee Rivers," Winston said, turning to ride off in the darkness, "Happy Halloween."

# Chapter 27

Sandy worked his hands, one over the next, up the ladder on the back of a huge, yellow moving van. "Just don't look down," he told himself, as he reached toward the hulking figure above him against the glare of the city lights.

"I got you, c'mon up," Catesby Raines hollered over the din of the crowd, hauling Sandy up to the flat top of the truck.

"I ain't standin' up," Sandy vowed out loud, breath steaming in the cold night air. He rubbed his hands together quickly then crawled on all fours past a handful of others seated on a canvas tarp.

"I got us a good spot over here," Catesby said, striding across the roof like a cat on a rail as Sandy picked and pawed his way behind, nodding at strangers and gritting his teeth.

"How's this?" Catesby asked.

Sandy drew up beside him and peered out over the edge of his perch at the noisy throng alongside the six-lane boulevard stretched out below. About thirty yards away, atop a flatbed truck festooned with flowing bolts of brown and yellow fabric, was the longest pair of women's legs Sandy had ever seen sprouting from what looked like a thicket of vines and rising to the papery base of a honey-colored costume resembling a giant peanut shell capped with a black stovepipe hat.

"The Virginia Peanut Growers Association Welcomes You," he read on a white streamer spanning the length of the float, "to the 1968 Tobacco Festival Parade!"

Following from astride a white stallion rode a small man in a grey flannel uniform, Klondike hat and knee-high riding boots glistening like wet ebony beneath brilliant street lights. Behind him a dozen other mounted police rode in a pair of single-file lines. "Virginia State Troopers," read the gold embroidered letters on a banner the two lead riders bore. "Keeping the Old Dominion Secure."

Close behind came the Maggie Walker High School band in sparkling red and white uniforms blasting out a brassy rendition of "The Horse."

"Man," Sandy shouted over the blare of trumpets and horns to Catesby. "This is swift."

Catesby nodded and smiled.

"I never seen the parade like this before," Sandy hollered, recalling the times he'd come to the annual event since childhood, straining at curb level to catch partial glimpses of passing floats and performers from behind a curtain of overcoats, baby strollers and wide-girthed enthusiasts.

"It's a different world up here," said Catesby, who only that morning at the paper stop had invited Sandy to join family and friends to watch the parade from atop one of the trucks in the fleet of his father's moving company.

"Look a' that," Sandy blurted out, pointing to a float built to look like a giant milk bottle. "River Bend Dairy" was painted across its side, and men in white suits stood at its mouth and tossed small cartons of chocolate milk to the crowd.

"Wonder if ol' Whit Whelan's in there," Sandy hollered.

"Could be. Here, try some of this," said Catesby, handing him a steaming cup of apple cider.

"Damn," Sandy said. "Hits the spot."

"Scooch up," Catesby said, motioning Sandy forward. "It's alright, you ain' go'n fall."

Sandy inched toward the edge of the roof, where he slid first one leg and then the other gingerly over the side.

"Even if you fall," Catesby quipped, "you'd just land in the crowd."

Sandy looked down and saw a man carrying a small boy on his shoulders, a knot of cotton candy clutched in a sticky little hand.

"Hell-ooo Richmond," a deep voice boomed out, as a miniature radio tower moved past atop a float decorated to look like a broadcast studio. A stocky man with a long, grey ponytail stood there. "This is Big Lee Radio's Brother Shiloh, comin' at you live from the City of the Monuments."

Sandy stared at the passing icon, as Shiloh looked up toward the top of the truck and waved. "Raines' Moving and Storage," the dee-jay announced in a voice exploding from a set of large black speakers. "Keep the faith."

Across the lamp-lit skyline Sandy saw a cloud of billowy, white sails on a mast of what resembled a 17th century English caravel. "Susan Constant," read the name on the bow of the vessel, perched atop the bed of an eighteen-wheeler. On deck, at the foot of a brilliant, yellow Elizabethan flag emblazoned with a black cross stood a flinty-looking man with a dark-red beard and wearing tin helmet. He had a short, thick sword at this side.

"Captain Smith," someone hollered out, drawing a scowl from the old salt. He raised a brass telescope to one eye and peered suspiciously into the crowd as his tall ship sailed past.

Next was a float depicting a field of stalks with broad golden leaves. Standing atop the porch of a small cottage and looking out over the field was a portly man in a cavalier's hat, baggy black pants and a wide black belt with a large silver buckle. At his side and waving to the crowd stood a tall girl wearing a loose buckskin halter and matching skirt. Her skin was painted a tawny brown. Two brightly colored feathers were woven into a band encircling a head of long hair that streamed down her bare back as she stared up toward the moving van then turned away. At their feet were bundles of large yellow-brown leaves tied at their narrow stems.

"Tobacco — America's First Cash Crop," read a sign made to resemble parchment in Old English lettering, and then, in smaller letters below, "Courtesy of the Old Dominion Bankers Association."

Sandy's eyes flashed back toward the oddest of couples, the middle-aged Englishman and the young Indian girl, but the float had moved on from his view.

"Did you see who that was," Sandy called out to Catesby.

"You mean John Rolfe and Pocahontas?" Catesby said then took a long draw of steaming cider.

Sandy stared at the float. Couldn't be, he thought to himself. He turned back toward the parade and strained to take it all it in, the rolling midway of attractions passing before him in a kaleidoscopic caravan of spectacle and noise.

A gleaming white pickup truck towed a float sponsored by the Eastern Shore Watermen's Fleet: a wooden row boat outfitted with lines and oars. A pair of men in bright yellow hip waders worked their way alongside, over blue and brown crepe paper meant to resemble shallow water and a mud-bottomed channel alive with plastic oysters and crabs.

There was a man in blue denim bib overalls leading a lumbering bull with a shiny brass bell clanging beneath its neck. A small boy, similarly dressed, was perched atop its broad back, bearing a banner that read, "The Virginia Cattlemen's Association."

A green and yellow tractor pulled a float made to look like an orchard. Young women in red gingham dresses with matching bows in their hair tossed out apples to the crowd. "An apple a day from Winchester V-A!" read the white paper streamer running the length of the float.

Sandy waved and held up his hands, hoping an apple might be hurled his way. A woman smiled and waved back, then tossed an apple toward a group of children reaching out toward the float.

"Yeeeee-hiigh," a man screamed out far to Sandy's right, as a chorus of others quickly mimicked his high pitched, blood curdling cry. Sandy looked toward the ruckus and saw a white-bearded man in a grey flannel uniform marching forward, eyes fixed ahead, back straight as a rail. He wore a matching grey cap with a glistening black brim and black boots that reached his knees. He carried in front of him with both hands, on the end of a long silvery staff, an enormous Confederate battle flag, its stars and bars fluttering in the November breeze.

As far as Sandy could see, great masses of people rose as one from their curbside seats or folding chairs. Men took off their hats, women held babies high, and all who could applauded and cheered, as a long row of men in uniform marched four abreast, followed by men playing brass bugles, trumpets and horns. A whistle blew, the band members held to march in place, and a sound like rolling thunder pealed out from the dozens of drummers bringing up the rear.

Sandy instinctively leaned back on his haunches and hands, pulled himself up to his feet in a single motion and stood erect at the high edge of the truck, the fresh chill of the night sweeping over his face.

The drums pitched up a rhythm as familiar to Sandy as his own heartbeat, a deliberately punctuated, pulsating roll, like the broken punches of a battered fist pounding the sky and cueing up the opening strains of some national hymn. Finally it began, on a single, collective note that gathered the brass, the woodwinds, the cymbals and drums, and the voices that blended with Sandy's own, mysteriously, inexplicably, combining the untempered tenor of rebellion with the practiced precision of a hand bell choir.

"Oh I wish I was in the land of cotton, ol' times there are not forgotten, look away! Look away! Look away, Dixie land!"

Brass cymbals crashed at the end of each verse, fanning the crowd to a fever pitch as all in attendance clapped in time.

"In Dixie land I'll take my stand, to live and die in Dixie! Away! Away! Away down south in Dixie!"

The music stopped, the drums played on, the crowd cheered, a whistle blew and the columns of grey-flanneled men sallied forth, healthy and whole and close to home, the myth and memory they evoked as clear and crisp as the hammer and anvil clash of the metallic taps on their heels as they marched.

"Yaaa-wh-oo," Catesby sang out, cupping his hands to his mouth.

"Yaaaa-wh-oo-ooo," someone answered from below.

Hard on the boot heels of the Confederate tribute band, a large flat-bed truck hauled a miniature model of Richmond. Green fields and brown woodlands gave way to the long boulevard dotted with monuments to Jackson and Lee. The railroad wound along the river, the old Jefferson Hotel was perched high on a hill, and higher still was the grand Capitol that Thomas Jefferson himself had designed.

Looming over it all atop a throne of orange and yellow chrysanthemums, like some royal vision draped in purple taffeta and bearing a silver and jewel-bedecked crown, sat the Tobacco Festival Queen, the lustrous and beaming embodiment of the fertile and feminine promise of the Old Dominion herself. In one white-gloved hand she held a large bouquet of red roses. The other hand was stitched through the arm of a grey-haired man Sandy vaguely recognized as the governor, the Virginia state flag flying at his side, a warrior woman with one bared breast and a single foot on the chest of a slain foe. "Sic Semper Tyrannis!"

"Isn't she magnificent," intoned the satiny voice of the grand marshal, an athletic-looking actor in a black tuxedo, riding in a white Cadillac convertible decorated to look like a Lucky Strike cigarette.

Beside him sat the Marlboro Man, easily identified by his range-riding garb. To the other side was a young boy dressed up in the maroon and black uniform of a hotel bellhop. "Call for Philip Moor-issss," the boy yelled into the microphone, as the grand marshal held it in front of his face. "Call for Philip Moor-isss!"

The crowd cheered, a few final floats drifted past on their way into the baseball stadium just down the boulevard, and the crowd disintegrated into an unstructured mob scrambling to beat the rush back home.

"Where we s'pose to meet your brother?" Sandy hollered out to Catesby, as others filed past and began climbing down the back of the Raines' moving van.

"Ball park," Catesby replied. "He's helpin' tear down floats."

Sandy made his way down the ladder at the rear of the truck, and followed Catesby down the street to the ball diamond.

"My brother told me to meet him by home plate," Catesby said. "He won't be long."

The parking lot was packed with pickup trucks, school buses and cars. Sandy saw several horses, like those the state troopers rode, being coaxed into a large metal trailer. He brushed past a group of players in the Maggie Walker band, bundled up in jackets and blankets.

The diamond was lit to full daylight, as if for a game, and had a backstage feel to it, fully encircled by floats in various stages of disassembly.

"Another year, ol' fella," a man in a yellow slicker and hip boots called out.

"Yah, sir," the driver towing the watermen's float replied. "'Be back nex' year, Lord willin'."

Sandy saw the Winchester apple girls and what looked like half the Confederacy crowded around a steaming cart where two women were busy handing out hot dogs.

Men in olive green jump suits were beginning to take apart the float bearing the large model of Richmond, parked far out in center field, and Sandy saw the Tobacco Festival Queen being ushered into a waiting car by a man in a dark suit, while a woman in a long white coat trailed behind with the roses.

A small gaggle of youths had gathered around second base, where Brother Shiloh was signing autographs.

"I'll be right back," Sandy shouted.

"Don't be long," Catesby shot back. "You know what a prick my brother can be."

Sandy was already moving across the infield when someone hollered something out, and the reply caught Sandy's ear.

"Better not," he heard a girl shout back, "or I'll tell ol' Powhatan!"

He looked toward the voice just as she turned his way, a broad and saucy smile fading from across the painted skin of her face.

"Poca . . . Hope?"

She stood there, looking at him for a moment, startled and not quite sure what to do.

"'Scuse me, ma'am," a man in a dark brown animal skin said as he passed between them, carrying a large bear head in one hand.

Sandy closed in the space between them. "Hope," he said her name again, thought to reach out and wrap her in his arms, held them partway open, then let them drop at his side.

"C'mon Sandy," she said, breaking the moment and stretching out her arms. "Even bears hug."

He felt the heavy paint on her face as she pressed against his cheek, felt the soft, fraying edge of the brown buckskin along her back and her cold bare skin against his hand, closed his eyes and breathed in the rich smell of her hair.

"I missed you," Sandy said. He felt her pull him close, as she did that afternoon long ago by the river, and for a moment the whole carnival around them fell away into the night and disappeared.

"Yeah," she gently nodded. "I miss you too. Kind of."

She let go of Sandy, he leaned back to look at her and saw instead over the top of her shoulder two young boys tearing tobacco leaves off Hope's float, as a man dressed in black Elizabethan garb stood by smiling and taking it all in.

"John Rolfe: Daddy Teale?"

Hope smiled and nodded, tapped a finger on the point of Sandy's nose.

"That's funny," she said. "You know, Daddy Teale remembers you too, from that night he came to pick me up at the pool."

Sandy sighed and looked up into the lights.

"Said it reminded him of somethin' my own Dad might do. He didn't mean it as a compliment."

No, Sandy thought to himself, he wouldn't have.

Hope cocked her head and looked at him, confident he'd have no suitable retort, but giving him the chance to try.

Sandy looked down, saw Hope's feet in deer skin moccasins on the dew-covered grass, her bony ankles and long legs rising up to the fringed edge of the skirt above her knees. Her face glistened like fresh cut cypress, the light falling like rain across her painted skin, and she stood like a silent and shivering fawn against the color and chaos and noise. She opened her mouth to speak, and Sandy saw the gauzy mist of her breath vanish against the autumn air.

"There goes the queen," Hope said, as the car bearing the tobacco monarch edged its way out of the park.

"No," Sandy said, shaking his head and fixing his gaze on the beaded front of her halter top. "Pocahontas is the only real queen Virginia's ever had."

Hope smiled and shook her head.

"You always had a gift for sayin' how you feel — and a funny way of showin' it," she said, crossing her arms and staring at him. "Funny way of runnin' off and leavin' people whenever it seems to suit you, and then somehow thinkin' they owe you somethin' in return."

Sandy wanted to react. There were things he could toss in, like sawdust on a fire, but something — instinct, self-preservation, maybe just good sense for once — held him in silence.

"My toes are numb," Hope said, bouncing on the balls of her feet. "It's freezin' out here."

Sandy pulled off his jacket, wrapped it around Hope's shoulders and zipped it up front with her arms still crossed inside.

"Now you'll get cold," she said.

"I'm fine, I got my sweater."

Hope tilted her head one way, then the other.

"My hair," she laughed.

"Lemme get it," he said, using the empty sleeves hanging limp at her sides to turn her around. Sandy slipped a hand against her neck, gently lifted her hair from inside the jacket collar and let it fall across her shoulders and tumble down her back. Hope laughed and shook it back from her face. Sandy clutched the sleeves and pulled her back against his chest as she turned her head to one side.

"I'm sorry," Sandy said, his chin on her shoulder, his cheek against hers. "Are you gon'na tell Powhatan?"

"I might."

He felt the warmth of her breath on his face.

"I just got a little tense that night at the pool, I really don't know why."

He slipped his hands in his jacket pockets, just at the curve of her hips.

"Sandy," she said, as he drew her against him. "Were you jealous?"

"I don't know," he replied, desperately groping for another word for it. "Just kind'a confused, I guess."

They stood looking off into the distance. A man in leather chaps and a cowboy hat was hurrying a woman in tight woolen slacks.

"Do you think we can bury the tomahawk?" Sandy asked.

Hope smiled.

"I will if you will."

Neither one said anything. They just looked out onto the scene as if watching it all from afar.

"Hope? Hope!" someone called out.

"Daddy Teale," she sputtered to Sandy, breaking from his embrace and looking up to see her grandfather from across the field.

"Should I . . ." Sandy said.

"No!"

Hope stood off from the boy and hollered out to the old man. "Comin'!"

She turned quickly to Sandy.

"My Dad's going out of town for Thanksgiving. Me and my mom are spending the holiday with my grandparents."

"Could I . . ."

"Yes!"

Hope turned back toward her grandfather and ran toward him, the fringes on her buckskin skirt dancing against the backs of her legs.

"Next Wednesday," Sandy hollered. "I'll come over Wednesday night."

"Yeah," Hope hollered back, glancing over her shoulder. "You've got to come — if you want your jacket back!"

# Chapter 28

S andy blinked his eyes against the pearl white glare of a brilliant moon, full and round as a river stone, before a radiant curtain of blue. Bottle-green leaves, pointed and small, clung stubbornly to the shrubs in front of 8728 Tempest Lane. Moonlight poured over a cluster of mums at the edge of the lawn, the last gasp of autumnal glory in muted shades of orange and red.

Pedaling past the hedge and across the lawn, Sandy tossed a paper onto the brick porch. He saw the crisp edges of his shadow against a sparkling screen of frost-covered grass, a boy on a bike, its bulbous tires tracing a narrow line through the jewel-like finish of the silvery lawn.

The Tuesday paper felt tinsel thin. Sandy rolled it with one hand as he rode, side-armed it onto the stoop as he swept past and watched the paper unfurl, bringing to the edge of a rubber welcome mat the news of Richard Nixon's choice for national security advisor.

"I don't know why he can't just pick an American for that job," Mrs. Teale had offered at lunch the Friday before, when her husband mentioned over sandwiches of leftover turkey and cranberry sauce that the brilliant Harvard professor might be tapped. "And, of all people," she added, "a German."

"He was born in Germany," Daddy Teale said, "but he's lived here for thirty damned years. Been a naturalized American citizen ever since World War II."

"I don't care, it's not the same," she countered. "It's like being a Virginian — either you are or you aren't. You can't just hold up your right hand and make it so."

Less than a month had passed since Nixon squeaked out a narrow win. Now, six weeks before he would take office, even supporters were at odds over the key aides he might name.

Mrs. Teale set a slice of cold pumpkin pie in front of Sandy, as Hope gave her grandmother an incredulous look.

"Comp'ny first," Mrs. Teale replied, turning back to bring more for her husband and grandaughter.

"Thank you, Mrs. Teale," Sandy said.

"Thank you, maa'm," Daddy Teale added.

"Coffee?"

"Yes, please."

"Go ahead," Mrs. Teale said to the others, as she poured her husband a cup.

"What exactly is a national security advisor anyway," Hope asked.

"Harry Truman set it up after the war," Daddy Teale explained. "He wanted someone who could cut through bouts between the generals and the diplomats, the politicians and the spies, give him a short list of options so he could made a decision 'bout what's best for the country."

"So that's what this German guy's gon'na do?"

"He's a U.S. citizen, Hope," Daddy Teale jumped in. "Same as you 'n me."

"But isn't . . ."

"Was a time when folks in this country understood that bringin' good minds in from overseas was a good thing," Daddy Teale said, reaching for the sugar bowl. "Immigrants built this country, after all, though some families don't like to remember it that way."

"And some haven't been here long enough to forget," Mrs. Teale chimed in.

Daddy Teale brought his coffee cup to his lips, then paused and set it down.

"Well," he said, pushing his chair back from the table. "I hope you all will excuse me, while I go pack my carpetbag. My surname seems to have been dropped from the king's peerage."

Hope rose to follow her grandfather out of the room.

"Oh let him go," Mrs. Teale said, as Hope paused and turned to look at Sandy.

"He's been lookin' for a good excuse to leave all day," Mrs. Teale said. "Wouldn't spend a full holiday weekend at home, would he?"

Sandy stood, following Hope's lead onto the porch. Sunshine poured in through louvered glass panes. A small gas-fired heater simmered in the corner. He sat on the sofa and picked up a newspaper lying open there.

"Giving Thanks," read the boldface headline over the lead editorial, just beneath the date, Nov. 28, 1968. "They sailed in tiny ships of wood — the adventurer, the soldier, the refugee — driven by the wind and guided by the stars across dark and uncharted seas," Sandy read softly to himself.

"I want to hear," Hope said, leaning back into the cushion on the end of the sofa, pulling her feet beneath her and settling in.

Sandy glanced at her and smiled.

"There was no guarantee they would get here, no telling what they might find," he read aloud. "But they understood that, then as now, life is a contest between fear and faith. Their choice became their destiny, and it forever changed the world."

It was the story of Jamestown, retold to underscore Virginia's legacy as the site of the first permanent English settlement in America, some fourteen years before the Pilgrims set foot on Plymouth Rock.

And, indeed, a year before the Mayflower arrived, the editorial continued, settlers led by Captain John Woodlief fell to their knees in prayer on the banks of the river, "declaring a perpetual day of thanksgiving to Almighty God for delivering them to this land of hardship and hope. Three and a half centuries later, that first Thanksgiving Day still sets the tone for our nation, as we pause to take stock and give thanks as one," Sandy read aloud.

"Americans, President Johnson tells us, may be less inclined this year to offer God thanks than to ask for His mercy and guidance. Some of us, though, are indeed thankful this feckless and accidental president will soon be leaving the White House."

Sandy paused to clear his throat, heard what sounded like an enormous acorn thump against the porch roof and tumble down the gutter spout.

He read off a national litany of woe: half a million soldiers fighting half a world away; the Rev. Dr. Martin Luther King Jr. shot down in a savage rebuke of the bold example of non-violence he set; Bobby Kennedy murdered by a deranged assassin in a hotel kitchen.

"Still, as our lame duck president rightly recalls, there is much for which we owe our thanks," Sandy read.

A liberal democracy had been tested and passed the test. The nation was moving toward a kind of miracle of American democracy, the peaceful transfer of presidential power. Far from ending the Civil Rights movement, Dr. King's death renewed it. The country was moving toward putting a man on the moon. "And the peace talks in Paris, led by a competent new president, surely means peace is at hand in Vietnam."

Sandy looked up from the page and glanced at Hope, to see whether she was still listening.

"Is that it?" she asked.

"No, there's more," Sandy said, turning back to the page to finish.

"And so, on this Thanksgiving Day, we pause to give thanks for the resilience that defines who we are as a people, the proud heirs to those hardy explorers who arrived on the banks of the great river so long ago, the native Americans they met there and the Africans who unwillingly joined them in chains," he read.

"Nearly four centuries on, we have become the new Americans. We are the new pioneers. No less than those bold adventurers who first set foot on that swampy patch of sand at the river's edge, we have arrived at a place and a time that has never before existed in the history of the world. It is a time of turmoil. It is a time of wonder. It is a time of hope. And, if we are to prevail in this 'New World,' we must gather the strength to be found from all of our waters, from all of our varied tributaries and streams. That is the promise of American democracy. That is the power of choosing as one. Our choice will become our destiny. We, too, can change the world. And that, above all else, is what we pause to give thanks for, on this Thanksgiving Day."

Sandy lowered the paper, let his hands fall into his lap, and stared out past the lawn and the forest to where a sliver of autumn sunlight glistened off the river.

"An'body want another slice 'a pie 'fore I put it away," Hope's grandmother called out from the kitchen. Neither of them answered, and a moment later they heard the refrigerator door close.

"G'bye Hope, I'll see you Sunday night."

It was Daddy Teale, standing in the porch doorway, a faded wool jacket draped over the weather-beaten duffle he clutched in his hand.

"I'll prob'ly be gone," she said, rising to throw her arms around her grandfather's neck. "Mom's gon'na meet us at church then I'm goin' home with her."

"Alright, darlin'," Daddy Teale said, patting her back. "We'll see you for Christmas then."

"Yes sir. Can't wait."

Sandy stood and shook Daddy Teale's hand on his way out the door. He heard plates and silverware clattering in the kitchen, then the sound of water running in the sink.

Daddy Teale climbed into a hulking green Buick with mud-caked tires, settled in behind the wheel and glanced up through the windshield toward the small kitchen window over a cracked and peeling trestle of rose bushes gone bare. The Buick coughed up a black seam of smoke as Daddy Teale backed it out of the driveway. Hope scrambled down the porch steps, stood barefoot on the cold pebbles and waved.

"I love you," she hollered out as the car lurched onto the road with a gurgling roar. "See you for Christmas."

Sandy could still remember the sound of her voice, as he guided his bike across the yard, the last of his papers bouncing in the wire basket beneath the full moon. He turned the phrase over once more in his mind, as his bike rumbled off the frost-shrouded lawn and his tires kissed the broken lip of the pavement at the edge of Tempest Lane.

 Chapter 29

The ragged hounds of winter tugged at the rumpled blanket of fall, stripping the stems of jonquils bare in the frozen mulch at the base of the steps. Sandy moved into the light from the small brick home, pressed a frigid finger to the doorbell and eyed the spruce wreath on the stained pine door.

"Merry Christmas," Ruth Thomas sang out as the door swung open. "Come on in, it's freezin' out there." Scents of cinnamon and nutmeg mingled with the smell of fresh cut fir as he stepped into the living room.

"Yes ma'am," he said. "It's gotten right cold."

"Who's that, Ruth?"

Sandy recognized the faintly hoarse voice of Rich Thomas, slipping from the kitchen in his socks, holding a pot of steaming milk in one hand and running the other through an unruly lock of silver hair.

"Times-Daily," she said, as she brushed against him in the narrow hallway, reaching for her purse.

"How 'bout some hot cocoa, son," the man asked. "I'z just makin' a cup."

"Better not, thank you. But it sure smells good."

"C'mon, have some. Only take a sec."

"He's got no time for that triflin'," Ruth admonished, hustling back into the room with a dollar in one hand and a white envelope in the other, as her husband shrugged and turned back to the kitchen.

"Ninety cents?"

"Yes ma'am."

Sandy took the crumpled bill, stuffed it in his pocket, and handed her a dime. His eyes fixed on a cardboard box overflowed with electrical cords sprouting out of long plastic stems.

"Got to get my candles in the windows," Ruth said. "Only what, now, six days 'til Christmas?"

Sandy nodded as he tore off the receipts for two weeks of papers, gave them to Ruth and let the thought sweep through his mind. Six more days. Six more papers. Hope they're not too big on Christmas morning.

"Hold on a minute son," Rich Thomas exhorted, walking back into the room and looking toward the mantle. Winding sprigs of holly with shiny red berries and waxy leaves were woven beneath a large mirror. "Now wha'd we do with that card, honey?"

"I got it right here," she said, handing Sandy a small white envelope.

"Paperboy," it said, in scratchy red ink.

"Thank you," Sandy said.

"Go ahead, open it," the man insisted.

Inside was a white card with a bright drawing of Santa Claus, wearing red pajamas and reading a paper called "The North Pole Holler."

Sandy looked at the card and smiled, opened it and saw a crisp dollar bill inside — straight from the bank, he figured — folded over beneath the words in black ink, "Read All About It: Santa Claus is Comin' to Town!"

"Merry Christmas," the couple had written, "Ruth and Rich Thomas."

Sandy looked up at the two of them.

"Thanks," he said, smiling. "Merry Christmas."

He walked down the steps and back into the night, working his way through the even-numbered houses along Tempest Lane, past shrubs strung with colored lights, a brick split-level with a rooftop-Santa's sleigh and a picture window with canned snow stenciled on in the shapes of flakes, stars and Christmas trees.

"Have some — they're hot out'd the oven," the woman at 8612 insisted, as Sandy picked a warm pair of bell-shaped sugar cookies off a red paper plate she held through the door, while two small children in faded pajamas scampered behind her around an artificial tree.

He picked up two more dollars in Christmas tips by the time he got to a brick Cape Cod where a pair of floodlights threw a soft white veil over the front lawn and a manger scene. It was about the size of a doghouse, made of rough-hewn struts and boards. Assembled around it, as if frozen in place atop a sheath of scattered straw, were replicas of a donkey, a camel, the three wise men, Mary and Joseph. All gathered near a tiny manger, with a doll serving as baby Jesus.

"For Unto Us, a Child is Given," read a sign atop the manger, beneath a star of silver tinsel. "Unto Us, a Child is Born."

Through the broad picture window, Sandy saw a tall man, reaching to lace a line of tiny white lights through the limbs of a shapely Fraser fir. Pam, his wife, held her baby in one arm and, with the other, directed the trimming.

Sandy glanced back toward the manger and read the sign above it once more. He felt a blast of cold that cut clear to his bones as a sharp wind scraped the landscape like a rake through splintered ice.

"Well, hey there," Pam said as she opened the door. Warm air flooded over Sandy like the breath of summer. "C'mon in here out of the cold."

Sandy smiled and thanked her as he stepped inside, saw the baby's face wince from the wintry air that shot in, as the little fellow rolled back his head and sneezed.

"Oh, my goodness," Pam said, bundling the boy close to her chest. "We're fighting our first cold. Hank, this is Sandy, our paperboy."

Her husband set the last of the lights in place, leaned back to momentarily assess his work, stepped down from a low footstool at the side of the tree and reached over to shake Sandy's hand. "How're you doing," Hank said with a semi-professional air that seemed a good fit with his orange woolen vest.

"Fine, thank you, sir. And you?"

"What do you think, honey?" he asked his wife, turning away from Sandy.

"Still a little thin around the bottom," she replied, as her husband took their son from her arms.

"And what do you think, big fella?" he asked, holding the boy high over his head. The baby just stared in wide-eyed wonder and kicked his chubby legs. There were six or seven packages, wrapped in ribbons and bright paper, spread across a red skirt beneath the tree. Wha' do we owe you?" Hank asked, setting the baby down on the carpet and reaching for his wallet.

"Ninety cents, for two weeks."

"Oh," said Pam, dropping to her knees at the edge of the tree, "we've got a little something for you." She pushed aside a box of ornaments and pulled out a small box wrapped in red paper. "Here we go," she said, pushing herself up. "Merry Christmas!"

Sandy took the package, absent mindedly gave it a shake, then looked at Pam and grinned.

"What is it?"

"You'll have to open it and see," she laughed, as Sandy fumbled with the taut gold ribbon.

"Chestnuts roasting on an open fire..." Nat King Cole's slate-and-granite baritone peeled out from the dining room.

"Why don't you take it with you and open it when you get home," her husband suggested.

"Oh no," Pam insisted. "I got it for him. I wan'na see him open it."

Sandy held his collection book between his knees and pulled the ribbon into a knot.

"Nice try," Pam laughed, reaching out her hands to take the package from him.

"Hawaiian Surf," Sandy read aloud, as Pam peeled back the wrapping paper from the box. "Soap on a Rope."

There was a drawing of a dark brown tiki doll on the front of the cardboard box, and the clove-laden fragrance of a man's cologne.

"Hank loves it," Pam said, handing the box back to Sandy with a wink. "And so do I."

Sandy glanced toward Pam's husband, who rolled a large blue ball toward his son.

"Thanks," Sandy said, turning back toward Pam.

He suddenly wished he had something to give her in return, and silently vowed to make sure they got a good dry paper every day from now on.

"Well," said Sandy, backing toward the door. "Thanks again."

"Merry Christmas," said Pam, following him to the door.

"Yeah," her husband called out as Sandy headed into the yard, "Merry Christmas."

Sandy picked his way down the steps and over the frozen grass behind the manger scene, pausing to force the box of soap into a back pocket. "Getting colder," he thought to himself, raising his hands to blow warm breath on them and smelling the sweet and pungent spices of Hawaiian Surf.

It was an exotic scent, Sandy thought to himself. He pictured Pam barefoot beside him, palm trees waving on a moonlit beach, her thin white dress billowing in the balmy breeze, a smooth and rounded bar of soap dangling delicately between her breasts.

A blast of arctic air cut against his face, rasping away the tropical dream.

"Tiny tots, with their eyes all aglow, will find it hard to sleep to-night," he sang to himself in the darkness.

He imagined Christmas Eve and suddenly wondered whether he'd be with Hope. "Still haven't bought her a present," he said to himself as he worked his way down Tempest Lane, finishing the last house on the even side at the forested end of the road.

He tried to tuck his collection book in his rear pocket, but the Hawaiian Surf box blocked its way. He looked around in the darkness, pulled out the soap and tossed the box in the woods.

"Hey boy," a man hollered in a gruff voice as a porch light flared on from across the street. Sandy froze, looked up, and saw Brady Sullivan, holding his front door open with one hand and cupping the other to his mouth.

"C'mon over, I got your money here."

Sandy hadn't reckoned on collecting from any odd numbered houses that night, but he could use an extra dollar with Christmas coming, and here was a bird in the hand.

"Yes sir," he called back. He bounded up the steps and toward the door, where the old man beckoned him inside a living room heavy with the smells of fried eggs, sausage and burnt toast against the scent of cedar.

"Just finishin' up my dinner," Sullivan said, grabbing a dirty plate from a coffee table and turning toward the kitchen. "Be right back."

Sandy didn't hear him, but stared instead toward a darkened corner of the living room, where a scraggly tree seemed to have grown straight through the hardwood floor.

It was vaguely conical and leaned awkwardly to one side. It reached nearly to the ceiling and had scaly green needles peppered with small blue berries frosted with a natural, waxy glaze. And, fixed upon its uneven limbs, were life-sized models of what looked to Sandy to be every kind of woodland bird.

There was a robin, its rust-colored breast full and round beneath dark grey wings, beside a nest with three small eggs the color of a cloudless sky. Below it was some kind of finch, with a downy, brown-spotted white breast. To one side was a swallow, a dark silky blue hood forming a shimmering helmet slung low over a noble and assertive brow. And, above all the rest, peering proudly from atop the high loft of the tree, a red cardinal was perched and poised to fly, crowned with a magisterial tuft of ruby-colored feathers protruding like a spike from the edge of a hatchet-shaped yet oddly regal face.

"Ohhh," Sullivan noted as he ambled back into the room, "you like my angel?"

Sandy smiled, taking the gesture as an invitation to step closer toward the tree.

"Cardinalis," the old man said. "It's Latin for important."

"What else," Sandy smiled in reply, "for the Virginia state bird?"

There must have been a dozen birds on the tree, he thought, gazing at an oriole with a soft yellow belly and white-streaked black wings. Behind it was a blue jay, menacing and erect, a long beak stretching out from a narrow ridge of bone between small black eyes.

Beneath the tree, upright on a small patch of straw, was a bobwhite quail, its odd bottle-shaped body and small head colored in the ornate earthy patterns of brown, black and gray. A few chicks nearly disappeared into the leaf-carpeted floor meant to resemble a forest or field.

"You like that little fella there?"

"They're amazing," Sandy nodded. "Where did you get them?"

The old man chuckled.

"Well, if you got a minute, I'll show you," he said, turning toward the hallway. "Come on."

Sandy followed him down a narrow wooden stairway, through a basement den paneled with knotty pine, and into a darkened room. "Wait a second," the man called out, reaching behind an aging washing machine to flick on a dim light above a heavy wooden workbench.

Wood chisels of varying sizes and shapes hung from a perforated board along the wall. There were fine-toothed saws, a large hand drill and various other tools for shaping and fashioning wood. Thin paintbrushes sprouted from an empty shellac tin atop a pale green clock radio, and a large plastic bottle of white glue leaned against a block of rubber wrapped in sandpaper.

Locked in a wood vice was a small telescope-shaped figure made of cork and wood, black and white feathers glued to the sides.

Suspended from the floor joists were half a dozen lengths of what looked to Sandy like fishing line, each with a small hook at the end. From one dangled the unmistakable red head of a hand-crafted woodpecker, a hairy bug of some sort clutched in its long and sharp beak like a soybean caught in chopsticks. Sandy glanced back toward the vice, its jaws stuck fast around a bird in the works. He beamed like a child who'd just uncovered a great secret and turned back toward the old man.

"You make these?"

Old man Sullivan nodded and smiled, picked up a charred wooden pipe from the edge of the bench, tapped it against the side and let a blackened pinch of ashes fall out on the cement floor.

"This is my flock, you might say," he chuckled, pulling a foil pouch of Sir

Walter Raleigh tobacco from his pocket and tamping some into his pipe.

"It's kind'a fun breathin' life into feathers 'n wood," he added. "Keeps me busy through the winter time — and brings in a little pocket change."

"How'd you learn to do this?"

"Oh, just payin' attention mostly," Sullivan replied. "I watch 'em in the woods 'n fields. Sometimes I come across one that's died, 'n I bring it home to study, then bury it out back."

Sandy saw several rows of small cardboard boxes stacked beneath the workbench.

"You sell 'em?"

"A few. Little shops here 'n there," the man replied, gesturing with his unlit pipe. "Spe'shly this time'a year. Some folks like to give 'em as gifts."

He reached under the bench, pulled out a brown box, opened it and handed it to Sandy. Lying on its side in a bed of fresh wood shavings was a light, smoke-colored bird with short hair that made it look like a bald chick, a greyish-brown body with black spotted wings and a long, thin dark tail.

"It's beautiful," Sandy said, drawing the bird in the box near for a closer look. "How do you do the eyes?"

"Tricks of the trade," the man replied, opening a workbench drawer of small clear plastic bins— like those from a tackle box — holding glass beads of different colors and shapes.

Sandy looked back at the bird, shook his head and wondered how long it must have taken him. A white tag hung from a thin string around the bird's neck: "$7.50."

"That's what they sell for in the stores," Sullivan said. "I get about half."

Sandy traced his finger across the finely fashioned edge of the bird's smooth and seamless neck.

"Coo, coo, coo," old man Sullivan said slowly. "Mourning dove." He struck a wooden kitchen match, filling the air with a sulfurous smell and drawing the flame to the edge of his pipe.

Sandy looked past the haze of smoke and into the creased and wrinkled face of the old man. He clutched the box in his hand as if he suddenly couldn't think of putting it down, couldn't imagine leaving without it, couldn't picture being with Hope at Christmas without carefully wrapping it first and placing it under her tree.

"Is this one for sale?"

"I reckon so," the old man replied. "I give her to you wholesale, if you want her. Three seventy five 'n she's yours."

Three seventy five and she's yours, Sandy repeated in his mind.

"But I can't give her just one," he muttered to himself.

"What's that?"

"I'll need two of them, a matched pair."

The man stroked a fleshy chin dusted with grey stubble, shook his head and pulled two other boxes from beneath the workbench. He set them on the work surface and opened one. There was a brilliant yellow goldfinch inside it, and, in the other, a tiny green and white bird with a bright orange flourish in a circle about its neck.

"That there's the last dove I got," he said. "How 'bout this hummingbird?"

Sandy leaned forward to feign interest.

"It's really nice. But just one dove by herself won't do."

The old man stood up straight, drew deeply from his pipe and let the sweet smoke roll from the side of his mouth. "Okay," he said. "I got'cha."

Just over the old man's shoulder, on a wooden shelf against the wall, Sandy noticed a photograph of a woman who looked to be in her late 50s with an open-neck sweater and long, dark hair, standing beside a wooded lake.

"Well, sir, tell you what. You want two, I can make you 'nother. Gim'me, le's see here, three days. I'll get it done over the weekend. You come back Monday, it'll be ready for you. I'll sell you the pair for seven dollars even."

"That'd be great!"

"It's a deal then," the old man said, stretching out a chapped and craggy hand to shake on the bargain. "Leave this one with me, and I'll make her a mate."

Sandy paused at the top of the stairs. He looked at the young juniper that old man Sullivan had cut from the forest at the end of Tempest Lane, dragged in through the cold to his living room, then trimmed with the wood-and-feathered bevy of birds he'd brought to life on long wintry nights in his basement shop. Sandy was still thinking of the tree as he went home by starlight, and of the woman in the picture downstairs. Christmas was coming, the holy birth of a child.

Chapter 30

Two days later, just before dawn, a powdery snow fell. It started as just a light dusting, silvery glimmers floating past a porch light near the top of Tempest Lane, and had only begun to stick as Sandy delivered the last of his Sunday papers and headed home to bed. When he awoke, a good two inches had gathered in the boxwoods outside his window, a perfectly good reason to miss church, even if it was only three days before Christmas.

Missing church, though, was the last thing on Sandy's mind. Seated later that morning in a dark wooden pew, a green sweater vest beneath his blazer for warmth, his faith was rewarded. For there, just two rows behind him and across the aisle, sat Hope Stafford, in a black turtleneck sweater and brown and red paisley skirt that flowed nearly to her ankles. Beside her sat Varina Teale, ensconced in a cloud of advent purple gathered snugly about her hips.

"Hark! The herald angels sing, glory to the new born king!"

Sandy was still singing to himself several hours later, as he stepped off the icy pavement at the end of Tempest Lane and into the path through the forest, remembering the final hymn from earlier that day, the charge the Rev. Ennis Stout had made from the pulpit for all to share the joy of Christmas and the peace of Christ with someone around them, and the broad latitude the boy had accorded the pastor's words in crossing the aisle and walking two rows back to extend the hand of fellowship to Mrs. Teale and her paisley-draped granddaughter.

Hours later, just as he had hoped and impertinently prayed, Sandy was on his way to the big, brick house on Canterbury Lane, this time on foot, cutting through the narrow path to Skinquarter on what had turned into a brilliant and cloudless afternoon, the snow-covered forest glistening in the sun like the polished face of a priceless jewel.

Sandy wore a plaid coat, woolen gloves and a yellow stocking cap. He clutched a brown A&P grocery bag. In it were two small cardboard boxes. One contained a matched pair of handcrafted mourning doves, nestled together in a bed of straw. The other held a small green and white hummingbird with a bright orange neck. Brady Sullivan had hollered out to Sandy on his route early that morning that he would have the second dove ready by mid-afternoon. When Sandy stopped by on his way to the Teale's, he struck a deal with the old man, who nodded and let him take all three birds for ten dollars.

"Peace on Earth, and mercy mild," Sandy sang out to himself, "God and sinners reconciled!"

There was an odd absence in the forest. Sandy stopped singing to listen for the faint echo he normally heard in the woods, but there was only the snow-muffled silence of a wintry world gone uncommonly mute. He paused to look down at the pathway. No footprints disturbed the silken cape of snow, dimpled here and there by dried twigs torn off in the morning wind. A cluster of chokeberries lay broken open on the crust of snow, like garnets spilled and bleeding upon a carpet of pearl, and there, just ahead and arching over the trail, were tall stalks like poles the color of grass in May, bowing beneath the aching weight of snow on bamboo.

Sandy smiled to himself and walked forward. He cocked his head at a clutch of finger-shaped leaves, lilting like ballerinas in satiny slippers of ice. He peered deep into the bamboo forest, curtained in summer by an impenetrable wall of shadow and brush, and saw instead an airy and soundless sanctuary where traces of sunlight glanced off the surface of snow-caped leaves in a hall of mirrors suspended like spoons in some magical grove.

A raucous chatter broke the stillness, and Sandy turned to see a black and white woodpecker with a brilliant red head bombing through barren limbs by the honeysuckle swamp, its once forbidding gloom glazed over and buried beneath a cold and glassy calm. Sandy kicked away several inches of snow, leaned down to coax an amber cobble from the frozen grip of the ground and sent it sailing toward the swamp. It ricocheted off the ice with a curdling sound before vanishing into a bank of snow at the edge of the bog.

Even the graveyard by the old church had been transformed into a picture-card vision of splendor and peace as Sandy trudged slowly past. Small, snow-capped headstones of brown and grey rose from the freshly quilted surface of the cemetery. The wooden chapel with chipped paint glistened like a temple on high beneath the diamond-bright mantle of winter.

Hope was still wearing the long paisley skirt when she opened the front door to invite Sandy into the fir and nutmeg scented home of Varina and Daddy Teale. "Merry Christmas," Sandy said, the side of his face lit by the orange remnants of a fading sun, all that remained of the afternoon.

"My prince," she smiled with a low curtsy, as a blast of warm and smoky air tumbled from the living room on a rolling wave of Tchaikovsky. "Come at last to save me from the wicked mouse king!"

Hope twirled back from the open door, the hem of her long skirt flaring around her knees, rising tiptoe in her black stocking feet, one arm tilted upward before her and the other sweeping low behind her waist.

"Sorry," Sandy said, turning as if to walk away. "I was looking for someone who used to live here. A girl named Hope? Guess I knocked on the wrong..."

"No," she commanded, lunging back toward the door with outstretched arms. "The Sugar Plum Fairy will soon return, and if you're not here..."

Sandy stepped inside, pulled the heavy door behind him, reached down to unbuckle his boots and saw a small program on a table beside the door.

"The Richmond Ballet presents the 1968 Nutcracker Suite."

"Quickly," she said, leading him by the hand toward the living room. "The others don't believe you're real."

Sandy heard a delicate tinkling that sounded like icicles melting, then the playful pulsing of strings against the hollow drone of an oboe that brought to his mind the image of an elfin-like figure padding weightless across the wafer-thin surface of the frozen swamp.

"I've just journeyed through a magical forest dusted with sugar," he told her, "with long green licorice glazed with butter cream frosting and cinnamon candies strewn across the ground."

"Then it's not just a dream."

"Oh, it's more than a dream," he said, shedding his coat, tossing it over a wing chair with his grocery bag and recalling the cemetery smothered in snow. "I barely made it through the land of the dead."

"I'll lead you to safety."

Sandy followed her into the den, where a fire crackled in the stone hearth and a large fir tree stood in a corner, a single strand of white popcorn and red cranberries strewn about its girth.

Through the picture window winter bore down upon a frozen canvas of white, falling away to the railroad tracks and the distant river beyond, its bare and frigid surface faintly shimmering in the steely blue shades of twilight.

"No one will find us here," Hope whispered.

"Promise?"

"I promise."

Sandy saw the firelight flare soft and yellow against her face, wanted to throw his arms around her and warm himself against her, but instead he stood there, rubbing his half-numb hands together in front of his chest.

"You must be frozen. Go warm yourself by the fire. I'll make us some hot chocolate."

Sandy took a seat on a braided rug while Hope warmed a dented kettle of milk on the stove and poured cocoa and sugar in a measuring bowl.

"Where's Mama Teale?"

"She and Mom've gone out to dinner," Hope hollered down from the kitchen. "I'd a gone too, but . . ."

She came down the steps to the den bearing a matched set of mugs.

"Daddy Teale?"

"Gloucester," she replied, bending down to hand Sandy his cocoa. "Careful, it's hot."

Sandy cradled the mug, felt the warmth against his hands, and stared at a pair of marshmallows melting along the rim. "That leaves just you and me," she said, "to take care of the tree."

Hope sat down beside Sandy, tucked her feet beneath her and tilted her head toward a large cardboard box marked "Christmas stuff" in a handwritten scrawl. Beside it was a large salad bowl brimming with popcorn and a smaller one filled with firm cranberries. In a wicker basket atop a wooden stool were a spool of dark thread and a pincushion stuck with several large needles.

"Ow!" Sandy winced, lowering the mug from his lips.

"Told you it was hot," Hope said, leaning forward to run the corner of a paper napkin along the sticky line of marshmallow tracing his upper lip. "You got'ta let it cool a minute."

She sat back, raised her own mug, pursed her lips and gently blew the steam away. Sandy felt her breath against his face, the smell of chocolate laced with the scent of Hope, a wave of warmth sweeping through him like wind off a fire.

"Oh, I see," he said. "You mean like this?"

He closed his eyes and imagined for a moment he was exhaling the smoke of a cigarette, as effortlessly as Rick Montayne might slip a guitar pick from between his teeth, and blew across the top of his mug.

"No, no," Hope said. "Too hard. You don't want to blow all the taste away."

Sandy tilted his head slightly and smiled. She leaned the tiniest bit closer.

"Watch me," she said.

Hope wrapped both hands around her mug and held it nearly touching his, her long hair falling alongside her face.

"It's not a stormy furnace blast across the desert. It's more like a sigh, set loose across a meadow in spring, like the first breath from the first baby born on the first Sunday morning in May, like this . . ."

Sandy closed his eyes and felt it once more, the steam of chocolate and the essence of Hope, wafting against his wind-burned cheeks.

"Now," she said. "Let's see if you can do it."

Sandy felt her fingers pressed against his, as they brought their mugs together. He thought of the softest thing he knew, then imagined himself breathing against the snow-dusted edge of the bamboo leaves, gently enough that they wouldn't shudder.

"Uh, uh, uh," Hope whispered slowly. "You can't do it with your eyes closed."

Sandy looked up and saw only her face, freckles cast like cinnamon across a pool of cream poured over the bones of her cheeks, the sweet milky dew on the downy brim of her lip, like the summer river dried on her legs. Sandy felt his head moving as if by some command, until only the warm mugs, held side by side, were between his face and hers.

He looked deep into her watery eyes, like emerald lagoons in the flickering fire. Softer this time, he thought to himself, as soft as the wisp of a horsetail cloud, as soft as snow falling in the soundless woods, as soft as the wings of a mourning dove chick just emerging from its shell. A veil of steam glided over her face and hung like a halo before her brow.

There was a popping, scratchy sound, like nails on an electronic chalkboard, and Hope straightened up. "The record," she said, springing to her feet and bounding across the room to the large wooden cabinet that held the stereo. "Let's just listen to the radio."

She turned a small brown knob until she heard a rich and familiar voice pining away about a blue Christmas.

"Well," she said, "might as well get started."

Sandy hadn't exactly understood what Hope meant when she spoke about stringing popcorn earlier that day in church, but one look at the single garland draped around the tree and all was suddenly clear.

"You've got to double the thread, or the popcorn'll fall off," Hope explained, tying off the thread and handing it to Sandy.

"Now," she continued, "the way I do it, you do three pieces of popcorn, then one cranberry. Then three pieces of popcorn, and just on like that."

Sandy watched and nodded.

"Well," he demonstrated, "way I do it, I do three pieces on the needle, kind'a like that, then two pieces . . ." he popped in his mouth.

"No, no," said Hope, grabbing a fistful of popcorn, "it's more like this." She stuffed the whole handful against Sandy's mouth as he struggled against laughter to take it in.

"Oh, the weather outside is frightful, but the fire is so delightful," a steady voice crooned from the radio, as they worked their needles through the white puffs of corn and the red berries. "And, since we've no place to go, let it snow, let it snow, let it snow."

Hope stood, stretched, and put a log on the fire.

"So, how come you're spending Christmas in Gloucester?"

"Gra'mama thought it might be nice, her and Mom and me and Daddy Teale."

"What about your dad?"

"He's traveling, on business."

"At Christmas?"

"He travels a lot," Hope shrugged. "They're some ham sandwiches in the kitchen. Want one?"

An hour or so later, they had dressed the tree, its branches entwined with a winding necklace of popcorn and cranberries that seemed to have grown through its limbs like ivy. They began taking small wooden ornaments from the Christmas box — a black one in the shape of a steam locomotive, a large, white milk bottle with the words "River Bend Dairy" painted across the front in banded script, various cookies and pies, a brightly painted pony of yellow and red.

"Have yourself a merry little Christmas," Sandy heard over the radio. "Keep the yuletide bright . . . "

He pulled out at last a gold painted angel carved in wood.

"That one was Mom's when she was little," Hope said, looking at the angel's faded wings of silk and straw.

Sandy stood on the stool, placed the angel atop the tree, then got down to admire their work.

"Not bad," said Hope.

"Yeah. Not bad."

A high wind whistled through the trees outside.

"Let's turn out all the lights," she said, "and see how it looks by the fire."

Sandy walked toward the hall, flicked off a small table lamp, and picked up his bag from the chair. He walked through the darkened living room and toward the amber light of the fire.

Hope stood by the tree, her back to Sandy, and he could see her face reflected in the window glass. She turned, and he saw she was holding a long, slender box.

"Let's go over by the fire."

They sat down on the rug before the stone hearth, and Hope handed him the present.

"Merry Christmas, Sandy," she said. "I hope you like it."

Sandy looked at the package, and the bright red bow. He shook it, then looked back up at Hope as if searching for some clue beyond her gleaming smile.

"I don't know if I can wait until Christmas morning."

"Oh no," Hope replied, bringing herself upright on her knees. "You have to open it now. We're leaving for Gloucester in the morning."

Right, Sandy thought to himself. This would be the last he'd see of Hope until who knew when.

"How come you've got to spend Christmas there?"

Hope's smile faded, she patted her legs and Sandy picked up, a moment too late, on the pretty-sure-we've-already-covered-this look on her face.

"How come you're wearing cologne?"

"Who said I was?"

"Weeelll," Hope replied. "Have I been sitting right here beside you?"

He shrugged.

"Well, I'm not."

"Then that's some fancy soap you're using."

She paused for a moment and looked at him.

"Well, what is it?"

"What's what?"

"English Leather," she concluded with an emphatic air of victory and a slap to one thigh. "My brother wears it. I know that smell. English Leather."

"Well, if it means that much to you," Sandy started in, putting his present on the floor, "it just so happens to be not English Leather."

"Is too, don't even try to lie to me."

"It's Hawaiian Surf, if you must know."

"Woo-ee, Ha-waii-an Surf is it?" Hope waved her hands in a mock island dance and rolled her eyes. "If I must know."

Sandy looked off toward the picture window, saw the reflection of the room as if he were suddenly looking in on somebody else's Christmas.

"Where'd you get it?"

"I don' know."

"Well, where d'ja buy it," Hope asked. "Are you afraid to tell me or somethin'?"

"I didn't buy it."

"Ok, then, who gave it to you? Did she wear a grass skirt?"

Sandy narrowed his brow and shot her a glare.

"C'mon, Sandy. Let's see, now, was it Catesby?"

"No, it wasn't Catesby. What difference does it make?"

"Mighty sensitive all 'a sudden," she said. "I'm not going to be jealous or anything. We're just friends."

Sandy felt a cold and sudden space between them, a confusing place that didn't exist just moments before, as if part of Hope was some kind of stranger.

"What the hell's that s'posed to mean," he said, halfway hoping for an apology he somehow knew better than to expect. "I know we're just friends."

"Good," Hope shot back. "Because that's all we're ever gon'na be."

"Right."

"Yeah, that is right," she piled on. "It's not like I'm looking for a boyfriend or anything, and if I were . . ."

"Go on 'n say it. You think I care?"

"I know you don't care, Sandy Rivers, I never want you to care, I never want anything from you except a simple answer to a simple question."

Sandy said nothing, asked himself what he'd possibly done wrong, looked back at the window and wondered whether maybe he had accidentally stumbled into the wrong house after all.

"So, God-damn it, what's her name?"

"Pam," Sandy blurted out. "Her name's Pam. She's a customer on my paper route. She has a baby boy, a husband about a hundred years older than me and I guess she had some wild idea that I might want to use this next time I wanted to be with somebody special."

Hope let out a huff, looked at him sideways, then turned and stared off into the fire.

Neither said anything for what seemed to Sandy like a long while. He looked up at the tree. A strand of popcorn and cranberries had slumped gracelessly between two sprigs, and he stood to tuck it back across a limb.

"Go ahead and leave," she said, without turning from the fire. "I know you want to."

"Okay," Sandy said, staring at her long, straight back. "G-bye."

He crossed the room, hopped the low stairs by the fading light of the fire and made his way into the front hallway.

"Now, damn it," he thought to himself, "where the hell'd I'd leave my boots?"

He got down on all fours, feeling his way along the darkened floor.

"Great," he said out loud.

He stood, ran a hand against the wall and groped for the light switch. He felt her fingers against his arm, warm and moist, just like that night at cotillion. He felt her arms around his waist, her head against his shoulder.

"Can't leave without your present," she said, running the package against his ribs.

Sandy stood there, paralyzed, his arms at his side.

"I didn't really mean to say those things," she said. "I don't know why . . ."

"It's alright," he whispered. "It's alright."

Hope eased her grip and stood next to him in the dark. He could taste the chocolate sweetness of her breath, as she took his hand in hers.

"Come back and open it by the fire, then you can go if you still want to."

The fire had faded to embers. In the orange glow, they sat, and he unwrapped a small box, the words "Jacob & Oliver" emblazoned in gold on its glossy lid. He rose to his knees, opened the box and out tumbled the black-fringed edge of a green and blue patterned length of silk with gray wool stitched to the back. Sandy fingered the fabric, ran his hand along the silk, and gazed spellbound at the design, like something from an Italian painting he'd seen in a library book.

"Here, let me see it on you."

She pulled the scarf from the box, wrapped it around his neck, leaned forward to loop one end beneath his chin, sat back and smiled.

"A good-looking guy in a handsome scarf," she said. "Not much better 'n that."

"It's so warm," Sandy said. "And soft."

"Nothing wrong with that either, now you mention it," she said, leaning her face against the tail of the scarf where it draped across his chest.

"Whew," Hope said, leaning back up and waving a hand before her face. "That Caribbean Sunset's something else."

"Hawaiian . . . come on," Sandy said, flicking an end of the scarf against her hair.

"I want to hear more about this Pam," Hope said with a smile and raised eyebrow. "Sounds like she's keeping a pretty close eye on you."

"It's no big deal," Sandy shrugged. "She's, gosh, a mom. We're kind of friends."

"Ooou," Hope said, taking the ends of the scarf in both hands and rubbing it against the back of his neck like she was shining a pair of shoes. "I am going to have to hear more about that."

"I wouldn't get too sassy if I were you," Sandy said. "Santa's still watchin', you know."

"Mmm," she replied, leaning back and holding herself up by the ends of the scarf.

"Better watch out."

"Have I been a bad girl?"

Sandy opened his mouth but went dumb as a stone. He looked at her, shook his head and tried to suppress a sheepish smile. Outgunned, outflanked and utterly outdone, the boy reached for reinforcements in the grocery bag. Out came a cardboard box with Sir Walter Raleigh's picture against a background of red.

"For me? Oh, Sandy, how did you know?" Hope chuckled and let go of the scarf. "You really shouldn't have."

"Not much of a wrapping job," Sandy acknowledged, as Hope ran a fingernail beneath a small strip of tape that sealed the lid of the box.

"Well, I just can't wait to find out if I stick it in my favorite pipe, or just put a pinch between my cheek and gum."

Hope slipped off the lid, shot Sandy a quick and curious gaze, then slowly drew back the wrinkled curtain of white tissue covering the pair of mourning doves, lying side by side in a nest of fresh pine needles.

There was a short gasp, Hope pressed an open hand to her mouth and her eyes grew suddenly moist. She stared at the matched set of birds, the fine taupe-colored feathers, glassy eyes and downy crown, felt her lips start to quiver and her breath come and go. She looked up at Sandy as if to make sure he was really there, saw his face go blurred through the dampness in her eyes, pressed the box to her heart and slumped against his chest.

Sandy wasn't quite sure what to do. He wrapped his arms around her and held her there, felt the bones of her back through her sweater as her whole being seemed to heave and shake.

"Shhhh, Hope," he said, rubbing his hand across her shoulder. "Everything's alright, darlin'. Everything's alright."

She pressed her face into his shoulder and went limp in his arms. He would sit and hold her right there, forever, he thought, until the embers died, the mourning doves came to life and took flight and the stone hearth crumbled to sand. He felt her face against his neck, smelled her hair, her skin, her breath, until at last she pulled away to look down at her birds.

"I can't believe," she started to say, but couldn't finish. She sat up, gave her head a quick shake, set the box down between them and ran both hands through her hair.

"Gimme a minute," she said, standing to slip through the darkness into the kitchen. Sandy heard her blow her nose, then he turned on a small table lamp, took the birds from the box and placed them in the light.

"They're beautiful," she said as she walked back in the room. She picked one up, and carefully turned it over, while Sandy told her about old man Sullivan and the basement shop of wonders in his home.

Hope nodded, stood, and looked at the tree.

"Let's put them on."

"Yeah," he said. "You pick out the spot."

She stood on her tiptoes to reach a limb overhead, opened the spring-loaded clip disguised as an ear, and slipped it onto a sturdy sprig.

"There," she said, stepping back. "Where you want yours to go?"

"That's easy," said Sandy. He took her place by the tree, then pinned his bird on a separate limb next to hers, and slightly below it, then stepped back and stood by Hope to admire the tree.

It was a thing of glory, Sandy thought to himself, a perfectly shaped fir tree dressed in popcorn and cranberries, a family collection of wooden ornaments and a pair of doves that seemed to have just flown in from the wintry fields outside.

"They look like they belong together."

"Yeah. Somebody once told me they mate for life."

Hope smiled and nodded. "I've heard that too."

Sandy replayed the moment over in his head as he walked the long journey home that night, all the way past the tiny wooden chapel at Skinquarter and the makeshift nativity scene in front of Pam's, braced against the cold by the memory of the fire and the soft woolen scarf she'd wrapped around his neck when she saw him off at the door.

"Merry Christmas, Sandy," she'd whispered in his ear.

"Merry Christmas, Hope."

 # Chapter 31

Rain like silent teardrops hung from gnarled and barren boughs, cast like frail and crooked hands against the light at the crest of the hill. The streetlamp seemed to float unmoored in the pre-dawn mist and fog as Sandy stood on his pedals and pumped up the long grade. He leaned his bike onto Misty Hollow Road and glanced up at leafless limbs reaching out from the edge of the forest like the hollow bones of the gods.

January had fallen with the weight of dread. Holiday light and warmth were gone, replaced by a blanket of darkness and gloom. For weeks Sandy struggled to keep the joy of the season alive, to warm his soul on the embers of memory, until the fondly recalled carols and lingering hints of nutmeg and clove only kindled dispiriting reminders of how very distant Christmas had already grown and how long it would be until spring.

"Winter," Winston once told him, "is when paperboys earn their keep."

It was also when many quit, and who could blame them, Sandy wondered, tugging at the hood of the poncho he wore like a pup tent over his sweatshirt.

In the closing hours of a moonless night, stars were lost behind clouds. Weeks after it had burned out, the sole source of light for the paper stop had yet to be replaced atop the telephone pole on the deserted lot. Navigating largely by instinct and rote, Sandy heard his tires swishing through shallow puddles as he pulled onto the darkened paper stop, where mud, cold and gritty, splashed against his ankles.

"Perfect," he said out loud, as the wetness and chill pressed through his woolen socks and soaked into his sneakers.

Sandy climbed down from his bike, propped it against the telephone pole, pulled the canvas bag out of his basket, slung it over the seat of his bike and slogged over to the mountain of Sunday papers piled atop the soggy ground. This kind of fog, even rain, could almost be counted a blessing in the middle of January. Better, at least, than ice or snow.

He slipped off a pair of rubberized work gloves and stuffed them in his poncho, then tucked his bangs under the wool stocking cap beneath his hood. Fishing a cardboard matchbook from his jeans, Sandy leaned over the pile of papers, struck a match and searched by its tiny yellow flame for his papers.

"Damn it," he cursed, as the match sputtered against his fingertips.

"Have a light," a raspy voice beckoned, as the faint glow from an aging flashlight pierced the darkness from the edge of the stop.

"Good God," Sandy stammered and jumped back. "Who's there?"

He recognized the low and breathy laughter of the old man with the crazy bicycle, though weeks had passed since Sandy had seen him.

"Good God," the old man mocked, laughter spewing from his chest like hot root beer from a broken bottle. "You sca'yd boy? You sca'yd a' the dawk?"

Sandy felt like a fool. What the hell?

"Naw," he said, "I ain' scared 'da dawk.' You scared 'da dawk?'"

"Oh yeah," the old man feigned. "I'm scared half'ta death of it." Uncorked laughter welled up once again, and the old man wheeled his creaking bike forward and aimed the flashlight taped to his handlebars toward the paper stack.

"Now, I ain' sca'yd when somebody offer me a light. But then, me'be I don' scay all that easy aft'a all."

Crazy, Sandy thought to himself. Complete lunatic.

In the wavering light, Sandy found the envelope to F-45 and read the tag noting there would be six more bundles along with it.

"You been out here all night or somethin'?" Sandy asked to no reply as he hauled the first bundle up, slipped it into his basket and reached into his hip pocket. "Great," he said out loud. "Forgot my damned wire cutters."

"Ahh now, you off to a good start today," the old man taunted, as Sandy heard him rummage through the lettuce crate attached to the rear fender.

"Don't bother," said Sandy, already busy twisting a piece of wire back and forth until it snapped in his fingers, releasing the papers as they filled the space in his basket.

"No sense gettin' all in a huff wi'd me. I'm just tryin' to help." He pushed his bike a bit closer, and in the amber-white glow of the flashlight Sandy could see a bold, black headline through his basket.

"Peace Talks Expanded in Paris."

There was a picture beside it. Sandy couldn't read the cut line, but he could make out the corpulent profile of Nixon's national security advisor.

"Send any damned body they want," the old man chimed in, "ain' gon make a damned bit a differ'nce."

"Why not?"

"'Cause this war ain' gon' end in Paris," the old man said. "It's gon' end right where it started, in Vi-et-nam."

He handed Sandy his wire cutters.

"It's gon' end when we tell the North Vietnamese to surrender or we're going to stop holdin' back on 'em," Sandy retorted, turning to grab another bundle of papers.

"Holdin' back on 'em? Hell, boy, we done kil't damned-near half a million of 'em. You say we holdin' back on 'em?"

Sandy was momentarily taken aback, before assuring himself that couldn't possibly be right. "Damned right we're holdin' back. You think we couldn't just bomb their damned swamps and rice paddies and grass huts off the face of the Earth if we wanted?"

"What the hell you think we been doin'?"

"Winston said we been holdin' back. Mostly 'cause of the damned Red Chinese, so they wouldn't come piling on like they did in Korea," Sandy wheezed under the strain of the heavy bundle. He let it go and it fell by his feet then popped open of its own weight. The wire broke with a ping and the papers tumbled out like a broken deck of cards onto the muddy lot. "Great."

Sandy bent down and began to pick up his papers, as the old man pressed his case.

"Did the Red Chinese ask us to go there?"

"I don't know," Sandy shot back. "Winston said they want us to get out. Hell, there's a blue billion of 'em, runnin' 'round with their little red caps 'n all."

The old man chuckled. "Well, the thing 'bout havin' a billion people is, first thing, somebody got to feed 'em. They ain't nobody yet figured out how to do that. Not Pharoah, not Moses, not Mousy Tung or whoever that damned guy is." The old man covered his mouth for a cough. "So, when the day comes 'long they got that all figured out, maybe then we'll get to worryin' 'bout what comes next."

Sandy looked off in the darkness. Cold, damp air poured under his collar.

"Did the Vietnamese ask us to come?" The old man was pushing on it again.

"Hell'f I know," Sandy conceded. "Somebody must've wanted us to."

"Nobody asked us to go over there, did they? Went all the way over there on our own."

"Ah, damn'it to hell," Sandy said, wiping the mud off a front page against a pants leg.

"Okay, but thas' right, ain' it? Nobody asked us to go over there," the old man said. "We damn well went over there on our own, now ain' that right?"

Sandy grabbed the canvas bag from his seat, slipped it over the top of a bundle then dragged it back across the mud.

"Now'd we gon' over there on our own, why can't we just say, 'Alrighty then, we done what we went there to do, now it's over and we're goin' home and just leavin' the whole damned mess behind.'"

Sandy leaned over the bag, made a clean snip of the wire and felt the canvas fill and tighten against the papers inside.

"You mean just say 'Hey everybody, we won!' And come on home?"

"Yeah, sump'in pretty much like that."

"Jus' like that?"

The old man began to rise to the notion, started waving his hands in the dark.

"Yeah, boy, pretty much 'zackly like that. Fact, thas' not a bad way to put it. We won, and now we comin' home. Ain' that what ol' Nixon's fixin' to do?"

Sandy didn't quite know what to say, felt like the old man had the better of him, but couldn't exactly fathom how.

"Ah hell," he let out, "why'd I get myself dragged into a conversation about this with you, anyway? Ain't you ever heard 'bout the damned dominoes?"

"Dominoes?"

"Yeah, the damned dominoes," Sandy shot back with newfound authority. "If Vietnam falls to the communists, all those other damned countries over there will fall too, just like a line of dominoes."

"Dominoes, shit," the old man said. "Nixon dud'n know dog hair from sawgrass. Countries ain't dominoes. The world ain't no board game. And we ain't got no damned business flyin' helicopters and fighter jets all the way to damned Vietnam, messin' with those people over there. Got plenty 'nuff trouble of our own right here at home without goin' halfway 'round the world lookin' for more."

Sandy let it go, thought about Winston flying over the kind of jungle hamlet he'd seen in the paper the week before. He threw a leg over his bike and hoisted the canvas bag across his shoulder. "How long you think it'll take 'em to end the war? Might be over 'fore Winston finishes pilot school?"

The old man didn't say anything. Sandy wondered whether he'd heard his question.

"I don't know why he's going to Paris any damn way," Sandy followed. "What the hell'd the French know about Vietnam?"

"The French? Sheed, boy, they been there forever. They ran the damned place for, I don't know, couple hun'erd years or somethin'."

"Well if the French know so damned much about it, why'd they leave?"

"Vietnamese kicked 'em out. Just like we gon' get kicked out."

Sandy looked at the old man, the rough edges of his face and the glint of one eye in the faint glow of the flashlight. He wondered how anyone could be so ignorant as to think the United States of America was going down in defeat to people in straw hats and rubber sandals.

"We gon' get kicked out, huh? Just like that?"

"Nah, I didn't say nothin' 'bout 'jus' like that.' But we damn sure gon' get kicked out," the old man said, his breath pressing a soft wave of steam into the dark fog. "Tha's where it's gon' end."

Sandy leaned forward to hand the wire cutters back. He heard them land in the jumble of tools in the lettuce crate on the old man's bike. He pulled on his gloves, steadied himself for the perilous ride, then lumbered off into the dark.

"Dominoes," he heard the old man mutter. "Dominoes, my ass."

Over and over the words tumbled through Sandy's mind that morning, as he worked his way down Tempest Lane, stuffing the thick Sunday papers into rusting mail boxes and paper tubes at the muddy edges of frigid lawns, steering clear here and there of the brittle and greying carcasses of Christmas trees left by the roadside. He picked up a paragraph here and there about hopes for the Paris peace talks, reading by the glow of a street lamp or the glimmer of a porch light someone forgot to turn off before they nestled into bed the night before seeking the solace of shadow and tugging a thick flannel quilt over a cold bare shoulder to shield it from the throes of winter.

# Chapter 32

A harsh wind cut like wolf's teeth through the darkness and gnawed at Sandy's face until his cheeks felt like they'd been sandpapered and sprayed with salt. An arctic blast swept down the collar of his coat, past the sweatshirt and flannel pajama top he wore underneath, and chilled his chest to the ribs.

"Bitch'n hell, it's cold!"

He barely touched his brakes, felt the rear wheel start to give way on a glaze of ice, eased off, put both feet out and veered toward a frozen mat of grass at the edge of Tempest Lane.

"No you don't," he steadied his heavily laden bike, as it leaned sharply to one side. "Whoa baby, whoa."

There was little fear of anyone hearing. It was just before six in the morning, 9 degrees above zero and a wind from the north made it feel more like 9 below. It was the coldest part of the day, for that matter, a good hour before dawn. Only a damned fool would be out here in the middle of February, Sandy thought to himself — or a paperboy.

Through two pairs of gloves, his hands felt like they'd been packed in ice, his fingers numb to the knuckles. He reached for a paper to slip into the mailbox at his side but could barely grip it tightly enough to pull it from the basket.

His parents wouldn't be getting their Times-Daily that morning. He'd set it on fire in the wire basket at the paper stop, taking off his gloves to thaw his fingers by the flames. It was strangely hypnotic, he thought to himself, watching the paper burn, flames lapping at the edges and working their way inward on the page, turning straight columns of news and neatly ruled photos into the kind of charred and blackened relic that might be unearthed from some ancient tomb.

"Apollo 11 Mission a Go for Summer," Sandy read below a kind of drawing, an artist's conception of a lunar module descending upon the cratered surface of the moon. The page smoked, then curled, then burst into flame, the fire peeling back the thin sheet of ash like the hand of some unseen reader working its way, page by page, through the paper.

"Roastin' hot dogs for breakfast?"

It was Catesby Raines, rolling into the vacant lot, his round cheeks red and golden in the light of the roaring fire.

"Wadn't expectin' comp'ny," Sandy replied, "or I'd a put a couple more on the grill."

Catesby laid his bike on the frozen ground, pulled off his gloves, stuffed them in the pocket of a faded Army surplus coat and took up a place opposite Sandy by the fire, rubbing his palms in a kind of wintry prayer.

"Good thing it's Thursday," Catesby allowed. "We got us a good fat paper to burn."

The boys stared into the fire, a gust of wind kicked up and Catesby turned away and rubbed his eyes.

"Damned smoke," he said, shuffling over to the bundles by the light of the flames.

The fire faded to smoldering embers, darkness filled the void and the frigid air caved in around the boys.

"Here, light this one," said Catesby, offering his own fuel to the cause, another copy of the Times-Daily that would go unread that day.

"Damn, it's freezin' out here," Sandy said, as they watched the flames engulf an ad promoting snow shovels and rock salt from Hatcher's Hardware.

"This ain't nothin'," Catesby shot back, watching sparks from the fire soar into black sky. "You should'a been out here two winters ago."

Sure, Sandy thought to himself. It was always like that. Whatever the hardship, whatever the trial, Catesby was sure to have seen worse before.

"Damned papers' so cold you couldn't light 'em with a blowtorch."

Here we go, Sandy figured.

"Ha'da steal gas from the station to make us a fire. 'Cept, your fingers'r so frozen you ha'da stuff 'em down your crotch to thaw 'em out enough to pick up the hose. Then, damned metal's so cold your skin froze to the nozzle."

Sandy tugged at his pants leg, pulling at the long pajama bottoms he wore underneath.

"Ha'da wait till Winston pulled up, lit a damned cigarette, then blew smoke on my hand till he got it unstuck."

"Oh I know all about blowin' smoke."

"Okay, smart ass. Don't b'lieve me, ask Lucky Pete."

"I ain't askin' him nothin'."

The boys watched the last pages of the second paper go up in smoke, their spirits dimming with the fading light of the flames. Sandy pulled on his gloves, turned toward his bike and stumped his toe on a broken bottle frozen in the ground. Boots, he'd learned the hard way, didn't work on a bike. So Sandy had put on three pairs of socks, slipped a plastic sandwich bag around each foot to break the wind and keep them dry, then stuffed the whole package into his tennis shoes. Still, his toes were cold.

"Damnation," he let out, "that hurts like a mother."

"You're alright," Catesby assured him. "Should'a been out here two years ago."

It was all the colder, Sandy thought, as he rode off from the paper stop and pressed into the darkness after he'd stood by the fire. Now, halfway through his route, his toes were as numb as his fingers. His breathing quickened and his teeth began to chatter.

"I got'ta do somethin'," he said out loud, carefully leaning his bike against a station wagon covered in frost. He trudged across a frozen lawn to the base of a loblolly pine, dropped down on his stomach onto a thick carpet of pine needles and pushed up on the palms of his hands.

"One," he breathed out, straining to keep his back straight. "Two," he wheezed, his lungs filling with air, and on he pressed with the push-ups, past twenty, then twenty-five. The warmth began in his shoulders, spread quickly to his chest then pressed upward toward his face and head. "Thirty," he declared with finality, then dropped flat onto the pine needle bed, rolled over and lay on his back.

A wind swept high through the limbs overhead, where the big tree listed and moaned. Through an opening in its broad, full boughs, Sandy saw a dense cluster of stars. A waning moon sailed like a silver slipper upon a boundless sea of night. A jagged shard of thin cloud seemed etched into the sky as though someone scratched the inky skin of the universe with broken glass and lay bare the gauzy base beneath.

Sandy connected the dots of three stars aligned in a row. Then he saw the whole thing before him. "The Big Dipper," he said out loud, and smiled.

"Why are the stars always so clear when it's really cold outside?" he'd asked his father years before. He remembered walking up the long hill toward Misty Hollow Road on a winter's night, hustling to keep up with the big man in the long woolen overcoat. They walked to the gas station by the paper stop. His father put a nickel in a red vending machine and they shared a pack of peanuts on the walk back home.

"Cold night," his father answered, "clear skies."

Cold night, Sandy thought to himself, lying still in the pine needles. He watched his breath briefly cloud his view then quickly disappear. How long since that night his father showed him the Big Dipper? And now here it was, right where they left it. That same constellation, it occurred to him, those very same stars, pricked that ocean of darkness in the same pattern of mystery that steered ancient mariners to faraway shores. The thought shot through Sandy that even Columbus himself had looked upon this very sky for guidance, one bitter cold night long centuries before. Now others, it seemed, would follow the stars.

Staring at the silvery crescent, Sandy thought of newsprint crackling in the flames and astronauts bound for the moon. "Mission control, we're headed back to the module," he said out loud, rising to pat pine needles off his coat and pants. "Crossing the lunar landscape, stark and barren and cold."

Sandy played with the daydream as he completed his route, his cold seat a cozy cockpit, his handlebars the panel for an array of lighted instruments and his basket the fireproof cowling to shield him from the intense heat of re-entry.

Heat, Sandy thought to himself, imagining the radiant salvation of warmth.

"Mission accomplished," he said aloud, stuffing the last of his papers in the box at 8700, his flight of fancy quickly turning to visions of a steaming hot shower back home.

Chapter 33

The next few weeks ground by in a mix of snow and rain. Wintry days crawled past grim and grey like an endless stream of soggy newsprint, story after mind-numbing story of peace talks bogged down like soft tires in cold mud until one morning, toward the end of his route, Sandy unzipped his plaid coat, pulled his arms through, then stuffed the heavy woolen garment into a side basket.

"There's that damned thing gone," he said to the mid-March darkness, looking up toward a dim yellow porch light two houses away and realizing that, for the first time in months, it seemed, he was warm.

He breathed out toward the light, saw his breath roll off in a soft shroud of mist that floated through the darkness like a long goodbye. It was not the frosty tight wisps swallowed up by the air like ice pepper on a frigid morning, but the languid fog of breath that lingered low and still.

Winter was over, it would soon be spring, and Sandy imagined himself putting it all — the coat, the gloves, the long underwear and the layers of sweatshirts, all of it — into a wooden crate he would nail shut and never be cold again.

He climbed on his pedals, hauled his bike up the hill near the end of Tempest Lane, began to pick up speed, felt his front wheel hit a rock, then heard a sharp metallic ping.

"Damn it," he said, pulling off the road. In the glow from the porch light, he could see a broken spoke lying limp at the base of his rim. He reached down, pulled out the spoke and tossed it in the yard. A light fell over his basket, lit the street and widened into the trees beyond, as Sandy turned and heard over his shoulder the winding moan of an aging milk truck cresting the hill.

It came to a stop at the edge of the road. The engine idled unsteadily, like an old mule choking on each labored breath. Through the windshield he saw in the softly lit cab the gaunt face of a bony man, his shoulders slumped over, a tuft of white hair sprouting out beneath a faded blue and red Richmond Braves ball cap, as Whit Whelan opened the driver's door and stepped down out of the truck.

He held a wire basket in one hand, loaded with quart bottles of milk that clattered against each other as Whit rounded the front of the truck and struck out across the lawn toward the front porch of a brick split-level.

"Mornin' son," Whit called out to Sandy as he passed.

"Mornin'," Sandy shot back, watching the lanky figure disappear in the dark, then quickly re-emerge.

"Feels like spring out here," the old man said.

"Yes sir," came Sandy's reply. "I'm gett'in warm. Kind'a thirsty too."

"Thirsty?" Whit said, not looking up, but quickly crossing the street and cutting up the lawn of the house on the other side.

"Like chocolate milk?" Whit asked when he returned moments later. "I'll sell you half a pint for a dime."

Sandy reached a clammy hand into an empty pants pocket.

"Can I write you a check?"

The old man laughed.

"River Bend ain't much on credit," he said, stepping up into the cab of the truck. "But I'll swap you for a paper if you've got one to spare."

"It's a deal."

Sandy glanced at the dozen or so papers remaining there and picked out one with no evident dog ears, creases, smudges or tears, the one his parents wouldn't get to read that morning.

The old man reached into the back of the truck and handed a cold cardboard carton of milk to Sandy, who offered the paper up in return.

"Any word from Winston?"

"Lucky Pete's in touch," Sandy called back. "Says he'll be in Vietnam come June."

The milkman stood in the cab door, pulled his shoulders back and let out a deep breath.

"He will, will he?"

"That's what Pete says."

Whit stared off into the darkness, put a hand along the small of his back, stretched with a grimace and sat down at the wheel. "Aw'right, young man," he called out. "You be careful out here, now."

Sandy watched the truck creep back over the hill and rumble out of sight. He tore open the carton and tasted the cold sweet milk. "Damn, that's good," he said to himself, wiping his mouth against his shoulder.

"Here," he remembered Hope saying, handing him a tall glass of lemonade, clear droplets of water streaming down its sides. "Best thing in the world for a hot afternoon."

Second best, Sandy thought to himself, picturing her barefoot in an old pair of shorts, her brother's oversized shirt hanging low off her shoulders, a faint constellation of freckles twinkling across her face beneath a summery veil of sun-lightened hair.

He breathed in the wetness of March, the earthy fragrance of the slumbering swamp, felt a longing for the world to awaken, to drive off the long tail of winter with the delicate scent of honeysuckle, the bright pastels of dogwood, the sound of a dove cooing softly at dawn.

"Dear God," he prayed in a whisper, "thank you for the end of winter. Thank you, for the coming of spring. Thank you for the promise of summer. And thank you, dear Lord, for Hope."

He took a long, lingering drink of the chocolate milk, felt it rich and thick in his throat, then set off to finish his route.

# Chapter 34

It wasn't yet four-thirty and Catesby was already there, stretched out on the threadbare canvas tarp he'd laid atop the hard-packed clay at the paper stop. He couldn't see Sandy, but he heard him coming down Misty Hollow Road.

"Hey lazy bones, it's show time," Catesby called out. "You've already missed a dozen of 'em."

Sandy felt his tires roll off the smooth pavement, his front wheel wobbling slightly from the broken spoke he'd yet to fix. He braked to a stop, climbed off his bike and leaned it against the vegetable stand.

"Told you to wait 'til I got here to get started."

"Yeah, sorry 'bout that one," said Catesby. "Look a' that!"

"Where?"

"Damn, man, missed another."

Sandy followed the sound of Catesby's voice through the darkness, walked past the wire basket, made his way to the edge of the tarp and kneeled down.

"Wow, did you see that one!"

"Gi'mme some space, will ya?"

Sliding his hands across the worn canvas, Sandy lay back and looked up at the sky. A quarter moon, gone amber-orange, hung low to the west, just above a ridge of pine. Something flared at the edge of his vision, streaked across the far corner of sky and in less than a second was gone.

"Damnation," he sputtered, raising his head startled and thrilled. "Shootin' star!"

"No, a bird," Catesby laughed. "Been seein' 'em just like that for the past twenty minutes."

"Wow, that thing was movin'."

"About seventy thousand miles an hour," Catesby proffered. "Around a hundred times the speed of sound."

"How'd you know that?"

"It's called science. Ever heard of it?"

Sandy's science teacher, in fact, had told his class about the meteorite shower, stressing that it would peak shortly before daylight. "Anyone able to watch it and write a one-pager on what you see can pick up two extra points on your final grade when school lets out next week," she'd said.

Sandy and Catesby made plans to gather early to watch.

"How many you reckon we'll see?" Sandy asked.

"I've counted fourteen so far," said Catesby. "It's a clear night, we've got ourselves a right good post. Should be good viewin' 'til dawn."

Sandy scanned the star scape, saw a speeding streak of light out of the east, pointed and exclaimed just as Catesby did the same.

"How does a rock go that fast?"

"Not much to slow it down up there, 'till it slams into the atmosphere and pretty much burns up."

Sandy combed the sky for another.

"Most of 'em are no bigger'n a grain of sand. A few are 'bout the size of a softball to start, then they break up and, like I said, catch fire and disintegrate. That's why we see 'em in the dark."

Catesby paused. Sandy waited for him to continue.

"Now 'n then a big one gets through. One came blazing into Arizona or someplace out there about fifty million years ago. 'Bout the size of a steamship. Naw, bigger'n that I guess. And thick, like a big hunk of iron."

Sandy tried to imagine something that big hurtling through space and crashing into the honeysuckle swamp. He leaned back, glanced westward, saw the slender tip of the crescent of orange slipping behind the tops of the pines.

"Did'ja see that one!" Catesby sprang up and pointed across Sandy's face.

"Where?" asked Sandy.

"Right there! Right overhead!"

Sandy lay back flat on the tarp and locked his hands behind his head, just as something shot across the southern edge of the sky in a vivid bolt of blue, went white in an instant and vanished into the void.

"Eww," shouted Catesby, rising up on an elbow. "Did'ja see that one!"

"Yeah," said Sandy. "Wow, that thing was . . ."

"Shh," Catesby, said, motioning with his hand. "Listen."

From out of the darkness, they heard the low rumble of Old Blue across the street, then a man's voice.

"Mmm, mmh," he said. "I ain' never seen the like a that!"

There was the sound of a woman laughing, then the high-pitched squeal of a child.

"I didn't see anything! Where is it?"

"You got'ta look, son, just keep watchin', they're more comin'."

Sandy stared off into the darkness.

"There's people down there 'cross the street," he whispered.

"Yeah," said Catesby, "front of Jeter's house. You don't have to whisper. It ain't like they don't know we're here."

There was a low whining roar, like a locomotive howling through a narrow tunnel. Sandy turned to his right and saw what looked like a giant fireball screaming across the blackened sky. In a split second the sound went shrill, like a bullet through the air, and the flaming specter rocketed in a brilliant reddish-yellow across the horizon and out of view.

"Lawd, sakes," the woman's voice called out from the house across the road, as Sandy scrambled to his feet and hollered.

"What the hell was that!" he cried out.

"Sweet Jeezus," a man's voice came from across the street.

"Whoah," said Catesby, leaning up on his haunches. "Did'ja hear that?"

"Sounded like it almost came crashin' right through the house," someone called back to him in the darkness.

"Great Gawd a-mighty," another man's voice called out. "You boys see that?"

"Yes'sir," Sandy called out. "Where'd it go?"

"Prob'ly out in the ocean somewhere between here and Florida," Catesby said.

There was a brief silence, and then, from across the street, howls of laughter broke out.

"Be damned if tha's so."

"Yeah, look like it headed for downtown Richmond," a woman hollered back to laughter all around. "Mighty glad I ain't livin' on Church Hill!"

"Be one bad barbecue right about now."

"I heard that!"

Sandy looked toward Catesby and started to chuckle.

"Hell you laughin' at?"

But Sandy couldn't stop.

"Sheet, boy," he heard someone murmur in the darkness, "Florida my ass."

"Yeah, Catesby," Sandy mimicked, "Florida my ass."

"I been to Miami," he heard someone scoff. "Took me two days on the Silver Meteor. Hey boy, you think that ball 'a fire stopped by the Main Street station to pick up a ticket!"

"Yah, ha, ha," a chorus of laughter rang out.

"Yeah, travelin' light tonight, get it?"

"Yes, sir, travelin' light, alright!"

"Hey," Sandy called out to the party across the street. "Ya'll keep it up you gon' hurt his feelings. He's the sensitive kind."

"Ah, naw," someone shot back, "we don't wan'na do that, now!"

"Why don't you take yourself a nice hot swig of shut the fuck up?" Catesby told Sandy. "What the hell'd you know about anything?"

Sandy was laughing too hard to stop, too hard to notice another meteorite screaming through the sky, high overhead, too hard to notice the bobbing headlights of the lumbering panel truck. It veered sharply off the road, bombed into the paper stop, locked up its wheels and went into a hard slide across the clay before slamming against the telephone pole near the wire basket, as the two terrified boys jumped up.

The engine died. All went briefly silent. A thin veil of dust drifted past the headlights and the cab door slid open with an angry bang.

"What in the name of God are you two knuckleheads doin'? I could've killed the both of you," a stocky driver fumed at them through the open doorway of the truck. "What do you two think this is, a gol-danged campsite? Hell's the matter with you two?"

Sandy looked at Catesby. His mouth hung open like it was frozen in place, his eyes locked onto the paper truck.

"Sum'bitch," Catesby mumbled.

The driver jumped out, eyeballed a small dent in the heavy steel bumper on the front of the truck, ran his hand across the metal, clapped his palms together and turned toward the boys.

"I nearly ran over the both of you," he stammered, voice quivering, hands shaking, feet cemented to the darkened ground. "What the hell are you even doin' out here?"

"We came out here to . . ."

"Well don't ever do it again," the driver sputtered. "I damn near killed you both."

Sandy looked at Catesby, then down toward the ground. Neither said anything as the driver climbed back up in the truck, hauled open the big door to the rear and began tossing out bundles of the Times-Daily.

Catesby walked over to where he'd left his tarp.

"Le'mme give you a hand," said Sandy, as the two boys shook off the dirt.

They folded the canvas and Catesby laid it flat in his basket, as the driver tossed out the last of the bundles and slammed the truck door.

"We're sorry," Catesby called out, as the man, still shaken, waved him off with a chubby hand.

"Damned kids," he muttered, settling into the driver's seat and jamming the truck into reverse. "See'f you can get through the rest of the mornin' without givin' somebody a heart attack."

The boys stood there as the old truck backed out, then rumbled over the hill.

Sandy dug his hands into his pockets without saying anything. He stood there for a moment, looking straight up at the sky, hoping for some celestial sign of redemption, but saw only blackness and motionless stars.

"What's his problem?"

"Yeah," said Catesby. "Wu'den our damned fault."

"Shouldn't be drivin' so fast's what I say."

"Damn right. Outright hazard to the road."

"Let's report his ass."

"Yeah. Let's tell Pete. He'll fix his wagon."

"Stubb-fisted, bald-headed, sawed-off half man."

"Out here raisin' hell with us."

"Yeah, like we ain't got the right to be here? We're paperboys, got-damnit. We own this place."

"Without us, he's out 'a job."

"Got-damned right."

"He can bite me."

"Yeah, and the piece of crap truck he rode in on."

"Yeah. Piece 'a crap."

"Did you see his face when he's lookin' at the bumper!"

"That sum'bitch was leanin' down, rubbin' that damn thing like he gon'na raise it from the dead."

"Hot-damn Lazarus with four wheels 'n a cab!"

"Hallelujah!"

"Praise the Lord!"

Through the darkness from across the street someone joined in the dirt lot revival.

"Must be some mighty spirit at work over there, Jeter!"

"Mighty clouds 'a joy jus' come rollin' right on in," a man fired back, clapped his hands and laughed out loud.

"Yes, sir-ree, I ain't never seen two boys enjoy they're work so much!"

"Keep the faith, young bloods!"

Laughter faded. The impromptu roadside tent show died down. Sandy heard a screen door slam shut from Jimmy Jeter's house and Catesby made for the stack of paper bundles.

"F-55 where are you," he said, probing the darkness with the wavering glow from a Zippo lighter.

Sandy peeled back the paper covering his bundle. "U.S. Troops to Begin Leaving Vietnam," he said out loud, reading a headline by the light of the tiny flame. "Allies Urge Similar Act By Hanoi."

"That don't make no damned sense," he called out to Catesby. "If they bringin' home troops, why they need Winston over there?"

"They ain't bringin' home no damned troops," said Catesby. "Those guys comin' out, they'd be comin' anyway. They bring some home, then send so' more, then tell the North Vietnamese they got to cut troops, too. Then Hanoi'll do the same damned thing. It's not a drawdown, really. More like a rotation."

Catesby pulled a paper from his bundle, laid it flat atop his basket and held his lighter near the front page. There was a photograph of an Asian man in a western business suit, waving from the doorway of a passenger jet. "President Nixon and South Vietnamese President Nguyen Van Thieu announced yesterday that 25,000 American troops would begin leaving Vietnam within 30 days and be out by September," Catesby read aloud.

"Nixon went to Vietnam?"

"Naw," said Catesby. "Says here they met at a Navy base somewhere on Midway Island, couple hours; flight from Honolulu." He read on by himself, then gave Sandy the short version. "Hey, listen to this, Nixon's plane hit a damned albatross when it landed. Damn near grounded Air Force One in the middle of the Pacific Ocean."

Sandy wheeled across the clay in the darkness. Leaning over Catesby's shoulder, he started reading an account of three days of pitched fighting three miles from the Cambodian border. "What's fire support base Liberty?" he asked.

"Picture a fortress in the middle of the jungle," Catesby said. "Sandbags. Barbed wire. They cut back all the trees and stuff so the Viet Cong can't sneak up on 'em."

"What're they for?"

"Base camps for long-range artillery. They can rain down fire eight or nine miles away."

Sandy tried to picture it in his mind. He thought of the meteor, then imagined a gun that could fire all the way to downtown Richmond from the paper stop. "What are they doing out there?"

"Well, technically we ain't supposed to be fightin' across the border in Cambodia. That's what we say, anyway. But the Viet Cong hide behind the border, kind'a like a shield. They bring supplies and ammunition through there. You know, Ho Chi Minh Trail. Then they run attacks against our guys, and sneak back across the border so we supposedly can't go after them."

"That's a bunch of crap."

"No," Catesby shrugged, "that's how you fight when your side's got pea shooters and we've got fighter jets and napalm."

"Why don't we just go bomb the hell out a Cambodia? Teach 'em a damn lesson for comin' after our guys."

"Take a look at the map, dumb ass. We go into Cambodia, the Chinese come after us. There's about a trillion of 'em."

Sandy stared at the page by the flickering light of the flame.

"So," said Catesby, "we send our special forces, Green Berets, that kind of thing, to go after those Ho Chi Minh bastards."

"In Cambodia?"

"If that's where they are," said Catesby.

"So we say we ain't fightin' in Cambodia . . ."

"Then we send these guys across the border at night."

Sandy turned back to the story.

"For three days in a row, enemy soldiers have fired mortars and machine guns, then followed with a troop charge," Catesby read out loud. "Military spokesmen said the bodies of 399 North Vietnamese had been found beyond the base perimeter, the victims of artillery, helicopters and jet fighter planes called in for support. American losses were reported as one dead, eight wounded."

"How do they get those guys out of there? The Americans I mean."

"Hueys," Catesby replied. "Helicopters. Only way to get 'em out there. Only way to get 'em back."

Sandy stared at the sky, which had begun to lighten toward the east. Stars were beginning to fade. The west was a dark carpet of blackness and blue. The moon had slipped from view.

"Winston's there now, isn't he," Sandy asked.

"'Cordin' to Pete."

"When politics fails," Sandy said to himself.

"Huh?"

"Nothin."

Catesby snapped shut the Zippo, smothering the flame and slipped the paper back in with the others. Sandy walked away, climbed onto his bike and followed the older boy off the vacant lot and onto the road.

"D'ja see that one?" he heard someone blurt out, as an old man pointed toward the sky.

"Shhhh," he heard a woman say.

"You boys take it easy," someone said soft and low, as Sandy and Catesby pedaled past the small house. In the dim light, over his shoulder Sandy saw Jimmy Jeter tip-toeing up his front porch steps, a small boy sound asleep in his arms.

 # Chapter 35

Sunlight streamed past thick white columns at the edge of a broad arched portico, casting slanted shadows across the fieldstone walkway leading up to the doors of the Kanawha Creek Presbyterian church. Sandy watched her walk toward him down the long and sunlit passage, her head gently tilted, eyes slightly narrowed, mouth wandering into an open smile.

"Nice jacket," Hope said as she approached.

"Thanks," Sandy replied, one hand tugging at the lapel of a blue and white seersucker blazer. "Good morning, Mrs. Teale."

The woman walked up beside him, her well-worn Bible in hand, wearing a cotton skirt and a necklace of bright orange wooden beads.

"Hello, Sandy," she replied. "Hot enough for you?"

Sandy wasn't thinking of the morning heat. It was, after all, the middle of July. What was remarkable was the vision standing before him in a yellow sundress and cork and wicker shoes. After two weeks at the Outer Banks, Hope's skin faintly shimmered. Her hair was streaked with shades of gold. Her shoulders and face were dappled with freckles, like brown sugar sprinkled on cream. Tiny beads of perspiration gathered along her upper lip like dew on the edge of a violet.

"When dij'all get back from the beach?"

"Yesterday afternoon," Hope said. "I'm staying with Mama Teale for the rest of the month."

There was no better sound she might utter; nothing further he needed to hear.

"Sandy, we're countin' on you for a little arm power this evenin'," Mama Teale implored.

"Yes ma'am, I'll be there. I can crank with the best of 'em."

"That's the secret of good ice cream," the woman replied, moving her arm as if winding a grandfather clock. "It's all in the churnin'."

Bells pealed out from the steeple and Sandy followed Hope and her grandmother inside. It was surprisingly crowded for mid-July, and Mama Teale struggled to squeeze into a pew toward the front of the sanctuary.

"Don't worry," Hope whispered, "Sandy and I can sit in the balcony."

Just a handful of others were in the small alcove upstairs, strung out along the front pew. Hope led Sandy to the middle of the rear pew, its wooden back flush against a circular window of frosted glass. A few latecomers trickled in, the piano introit concluded and Pastor Ennis Stout stepped to the altar, spread his arms open wide and smiled. "Let us be glad to come to this house of worship," he said. "Let us lift up our hearts and sing."

The organ set free a mighty chord, and the choir and congregation arose as one.

"Guide me, oh, thou great Jehovah, pilgrim through this barren land," Sandy and Hope sang out, following along in the open hymnal they shared. "Let the fire and cloudy pillar, lead me all my journey through."

Sandy felt her arm brush against his blazer. He took in the rich scent of her hair, remembered that day long ago by the river, looked up from the hymnal to cast a quick sideways glance at Hope, who caught him from the corner of her eye and smiled.

"Strong deliverer, strong deliverer, be thou still my strength and shield," they sang. "Be thou still my strength and shield."

The congregation was seated, hymnals placed back in their racks, and Pastor Stout resumed his welcome.

"Please keep in your prayers the family of our dear sister Mandy Tollier, whose mother is nearing the final days of her long and gallant struggle with breast cancer," he implored. "And we pray this week, especially, not only for the brave men fighting for our country in Southeast Asia but also for the courageous astronauts who will lift off from Cape Kennedy just a few days from now on their journey beyond the heavens, bearing our nation's collective hopes and dreams on their historic flight to the moon."

He smiled broadly then shifted gears.

"And, a bit closer to home, don't forget to return this evening for what has become one of our most popular events here at Kanawha Creek, a Midsummer's Ice Cream, when we can all have our fill of fresh, homemade dessert," he said.

"Tickets are a quarter apiece, and it's the only time I know of we can eat ice cream for a good cause, as all proceeds go for postage to cover the paperback books we collect to send to our troops. And now, with hopeful hearts and watchful eyes, let us join together in worship."

The pastor sat down, and a small-framed woman with silvery white hair stepped up to the lectern and cleared her throat. "Today's Old Testament reading comes from the book of Deuteronomy," she read in a thin and halting voice. It was Missy Forrest, the sainted relic, Sandy recalled, who had struggled with cataracts the year before.

"Look down from heaven, your holy dwelling place," she began, her reading a prayerful and personal celebration of lost vision restored.

Sandy thought of the meteor shower, the shooting stars, the fireball racing through the summer night.

The pianist played a spare progression of chords. The choir rose and sang. "Great sun of righteousness, arise, bless the dark world with heav'nly light."

A soft postlude brought the hymn to a close. Pastor Stout took his place behind the wooden pulpit, bowed in prayer, raised his face to his flock, took a deep breath and began.

"In the beginning," he said. "God created the heavens and earth."

He smiled broadly, paused and scanned the congregation.

"Has anyone ever heard that before?"

Soft chuckles rippled through the sanctuary.

"If you have some dim recognition of those words, and are wondering where you might have come across them before, this is the first line, of the first chapter, of the very first book of the Bible."

Hope crossed her legs, her yellow sundress falling just above her knee.

"It is probably the very first line any of you ever remember hearing in Sunday school as a child. It is, literally, where our faith begins. In the beginning, God created the heavens and earth. That's what we, as Christians, believe.

"We may differ on exactly how God did that. The Bible tells us hH did it in six days. Took the seventh day off to rest — though exactly how He spent his Sundays before the advent of Braves baseball isn't exactly clear."

Sandy, who had barely been listening, turned over his bulletin to see where it was all headed, reading the title Pastor Stout had given the sermon: "Mission Control: Hearts of Faith in Wondrous Times."

Sandy looked down toward the front of the congregation and caught the back of Mama Teale's head.

"Now, through the wonders of modern science, anthropology, medicine, geology and math, we are finding that there might have been a bit more to it than that. And some of us Christians like to get in a big fuss and fight over the question of exactly what we mean when we read in Genesis that God made the heavens and the earth in seven days."

The pastor took a quick sip from a small glass of water.

"There are those who insist, banking their immortal souls upon it, that every word of the Bible is literal truth. There are others who see the Bible as a book of spiritual truth hung upon a series of parables and metaphors: the parting of the seas, the healing of the lame, the resurrection of the dead, the creation of Earth and all that's in it in just seven literal days."

Kind of like the weekly rhythm of the newspaper, Sandy thought, from the small Monday papers to the Sunday beasts over a predictable seven-day arc.

"And in the unholy scrum churned up by this debate, we Christians completely lose our way. We lose sight of the larger meaning of God's world and our place in it. We overlook completely the true wonders and miraculous work of God in our lives, as if somehow our understanding of God can't help but collide with our understanding of science, someone trying to tell us we must make up our minds and believe in one, or the other."

Through the stained glass window, sunlight illuminated Jesus, the sturdy staff in one hand, returning the lost lamb to the fold.

"And the whole question will be rekindled this Wednesday, when that splendid Saturn rocket, with its thousands of tons of propulsion, lifts off from Cape Kennedy like that fire and cloudy pillar the hymnist wrote of, to carry our three brave astronauts, these three pilgrims, to journey through the barren reaches of space, on their historic flight through God's glorious heavens."

Sandy imagined a sunset. He pictured himself that evening with Hope and her grandmother, churning ice cream out on the church parking lot; licking the paddle when it was done; the frozen goodness of fresh peaches, sweet cream and a hint of rock salt that slipped in from the ice; pushing Hope on the old swing behind the church.

"Brothers and sisters, there is no inevitable collision, no great unavoidable debate, no grand contradiction between the miracles of God and the wonders of science," Pastor Stout said. "And I hope that, for those of us here at Kanawha Creek, and for our nation, this will be a time of unity, and that these bold adventurers will go with our blessings."

Sandy thought of the meteor shower, his paper for science class.

"Because, you see, I believe that the more we learn about the wonders of our world — and, beyond that, of our universe — the greater we must see the true glory of God. As we unlock each mystery, as we advance, day-by-wondrous-day, we can't help but be humbled by the expanse of God's creation. We can't help but to marvel at the ineluctable completeness of God's design. We can't help but to sing out with new conviction those magnificent lines we just heard from our choir: 'The heavens declare Thy glory, Lord; in every star, Thy wisdom shines.'"

There was something to that, Sandy thought to himself, something about this man's gift for taking words from a hymn written before the American Revolution and transforming them into a kind of prayer for the lunar mission, a way to link, through verse, this ancient faith to the promise of Apollo 11.

"And yet," the pastor said, "science without faith is folly. Thy Gospel, oh Lord, truly makes the simple wise. Our astronauts are bound for the great unknown, the new frontier of space," he said, rising to the heart of his sermon. "They are well-equipped. They are well prepared. They go as our nation's pride. And yet, they head for the moon with no guarantee they will get there safely, no telling how this could go. On some level, these brave men will be soaring through the heavens on faith — the faith bold men have always found to leave their fears behind, so that they can follow their peoples' boldest dreams."

Sandy scanned the congregation. All eyes were fixed on the tall man in the pulpit.

"Not all who journey venture forth in faith. When the Soviet cosmonaut Yuri Gagarin became the first man in space seven years ago, he was reported by the Kremlin to have said this: 'I don't see any God up here.'"

"Yuri Gagarin. First man in space. April, nineteen sixty-one. Pierced the heavens, slipped the surly bonds of Earth, in the words of the poet aviator John Magee. But rather than touch the face of God, Yuri Gagarin journeyed into the great unknown only to declare 'I don't see any God up here.'"

The pastor brought his glass once more to his lips, took a sip of water, then looked out on the congregation. "'I don't see any God up here,'" he repeated with a dark and somber tone.

"Well, we have to ask Yuri Gargarin, just exactly where did you look? What exactly were you expecting to find? Did you think God would be standing there, some exalted haloed vision, waiting since the Creation for a Godless

Communist cosmonaut to come sailing by so he might prove to you and your comrades that this world and all He created, this boundless universe we all share, really does exist? What exactly did Yuri expect to see?"

Was it a punch line, a cue for the needed relief that laughter might bring? The stern set of Stout's jaw seemed to suggest otherwise, and the unease set off a general yet orderly shifting in the pews.

The pastor then posited a series of questions. Didn't the Russian pilot see God, he wondered, in the moon and the stars, in the sun and the speeding comets, in all the majesty of the cosmos? Did he not see God as he looked down on Earth? Hadn't Yuri Gagarin come face to face with God, then chosen to turn away?

"Now, I don't mean to be hard on this man," the old Air Force chaplain continued. "He was killed, we are told, in a plane crash this spring. May God have mercy on his soul. May he, despite his avowed disbelief, come to abide with God, as the prophet Isaiah sings praise 'to him who rides the ancient skies above, who thunders with mighty voice.' And was it really the thundering voice of Yuri Gagarin who questioned the existence of God? Or was this line that's been attributed to him really just more of Khrushchev's propaganda? We will surely never know."

Hope uncrossed her legs and straightened up in the pew, until Sandy could feel her shoulder lightly against him. She tucked a hand into a dress pocket, and Sandy could see what looked like kite string hanging across her wrist.

"What we do know is this," Pastor Stout declared. "When the first man lands on the moon this week, he will be bearing the Stars and Stripes of the United States of America, not the Hammer and Sickle of the Soviet State. He will bear the proud symbol of American democracy, not the sorry reminder of repression and fear.

"For, while the Russians may have beaten us into space, the first trip to the moon will be a very different kind of journey. A journey of peace for all mankind; not a mission of conquest by the powerful few. A journey powered by government of the people; not the forced dictatorship of a petty tyrant. This, my friends, is an American journey. This is a journey of faith."

The pastor paused to let the thought sink in.

"Americans," he said, "are a people of faith."

He held up something small and shiny.

"This is the coin of our realm," he said. "Cast in copper, secured by gold and backed by the full faith and credit of the United States. Upon it are written these words: 'In God we trust.'

"That's what we believe, as a nation. That's part of what binds us as one."

"My friends, there are no words to convey the stark and irrepressible differences between our two countries any more clearly than these: 'In God we trust'— 'I don't see any God.'"

Hope looked straight ahead, slowly worked her hand from her pocket and let it rest on the top of her leg, practically touching Sandy's own hand.

"One nation, under God," Pastor Stout intoned, a rising firmness in his voice, reaching his hands to the right of the pulpit, palms facing each other as if he were about to take a handoff from some unseen quarterback. "Another nation," he said, swinging his hands to the left, "that sees no God. That sees no God in the wonders of Earth; that sees no God in the face of the heavens. That sees no God in the purpose of its people."

Sandy glanced at his own hand, so near to Hope's.

"We are embarked, as a nation, on a noble quest — a quest of discovery and faith. We have no idea what lies beyond the heavens. We literally can't imagine what's out there that's part of God's plan. The Bible tells us, Psalms 19, 'The heavens declare the glory of God; the skies proclaim the work of his hands.'"

Sandy didn't know exactly which came first, the wave of heat sweeping through his chest or the touch of Hope's moist palm, open and warm, enfolding itself around his hand like new ivy clutching a knot of pine. Sandy wanted to close his eyes, wanted everyone in the sanctuary to disappear, melt away and leave them alone in the balcony.

"Brothers and sisters, we journey, as a nation, into the heavens this week. We reach into the skies proclaiming the work of God's hands."

He felt the tips of her fingers roam the edge of his knuckles, turning his hand sideways, then placing something in his palm, a hank of string, a small, thin, undefinable something with ridges running along its curved surface.

"What, exactly, is it we expect to see? What if faith is how God chooses to reveal the secrets of His universe, my friends? What if that's the only way?"

Sandy looked down, opened his hand, and saw a knotted length of kite string pulled through a tiny hole in a small seashell, amber and white.

"I made it for you at the beach," Hope whispered. "Try to hang on to this one — if you can."

She moved to pull her hand away, Sandy caught up her fingers in his, and they sat there, a thin ray of sunlight falling across their shoulders, clutching the shell and string necklace in the fold of their hands.

"And so, as our brave astronauts venture forth this week, as they ride the ancient skies above, pilgrims on a mission of national faith, let us hold them in our prayers," Pastor Stout concluded. "Let faith and the fire and cloudy pillar, oh God, lead them all their journey through. And let all the people say, Amen."

 Chapter 36

A paper-thin crescent of moonlight clung to the western edge of the sky, its gently curved rim shining clear and gold like the glint off a wedding ring. The eastern horizon had begun to lighten behind a veil of cloud streaked with pink.

Sandy stood in the remnants of shadow at the edge of the paper stop, thinking back on a warm field in summer and the sound of a mourning dove, the second beat of its five-note sonnet, rising, then falling, as if the bird's very soul were being opened and aired before it moaned its three-note refrain. Was it a somber plea for mercy, a eulogy for the dawn, or a kind of prayer that might break your heart, he wondered, if you listened closely enough?

Sandy heard it once more, this time from a short distance, beyond the scrub pines in the wild grass beside the lot. There was a call, then an answer, then a third dove weighed in, as Sandy turned and saw it posted high on a telephone line stretched out above Misty Hollow Road. He squinted into the dim light and saw a rumpled figure grinding his way up the road on the creaking carcass of an aging bike.

"Hey there," Sandy called out, as the old man brought his bike to a halt by the vegetable stand.

"Guess we all know the big news today."

"Yes, sir."

Sandy pulled a paper from his basket, held it toward the light of dawn, then read the front-page headline aloud. "Historic Trip to Moon Off to Flawless Start."

There was a picture of the Apollo 11 capsule, fixed atop a Saturn rocket, sailing through the sky and trailed by a plume of flame. "On the Way to the Goal," the caption read, near a photo of the cratered face of the moon.

"Three American astronauts left Earth for the moon yesterday atop a colossal rocket, perfectly launched, beginning a space travel adventure that several hundred thousand people have worked toward for nearly a decade," Sandy read from the article.

"Mm, mm, mm," the old man said with a shake of his head.

"That's somethin' ain't it?" Sandy proffered.

"Oh it's somethin' awright," the old man agreed. "It's somethin' we gon' live to regret."

Sandy was beginning to grow accustomed to the old man's contrarian ways.

"We ain' got no business sendin' a spaceship to the moon," the old man said. "We messin' 'round now with somethin' we don' understand."

"Wha'd you mean by that?"

"Good Lord want us to go to the moon, he'd a made some kind a' 'rangement fo' the thing. 'Stead, here we done gon' on, take it 'pon ourselves to go on up there on our own. I'm just sayin', ain' no good go'na come of it."

"Well hell," Sandy said, "what're we s'posed to do, sit back and let the damned Russians take over the moon?"

"Oh, mercy," the old man came back. "You ever heard a' anyone tried to make a phone call to Moscow? Sheed. I had a nephew tried to get through one time. Those damned boys couldn't even get dial tone."

Sandy looked at the old man in the pale light. "That first mornin', when you helped me pick up my papers. How'd you know so much about my route?"

The old man ran a hand across his face, then waved the hand sideways, as if he wasn't in the mood to respond.

"Was this your route or something?"

"The widow at 8609," the old man asked. "Brick house with green shutters. She still Sunday only?"

Sandy nodded; his hands hung loose at his side.

"Old man Sullivan. Still come out in his boxer shorts?"

"So that's it," said Sandy. "It was your route."

The old man's craggy face seemed to fall into itself.

"Not mine," he said. "It was my son's route. I helped him on the heavy days."

"Your son? What's his name?"

"My son's name is Gabriel."

"Where's he now?"

"Now? Where's he now? Well, ahh. Whew. Well, he's in heaven, boy. He's. Mmm. He's gone to be with the Lord."

Sandy looked away, felt his eyes widen, then turned back to face the old man.

"I'm sorry," he said. "I didn't know . . ."

"It's alright son," the old man said. "It's alright. My boy's in heaven now. I guess the Good Lord called him home."

"I'm sorry."

"Mmhmm."

"What happened?"

"What happened?"

"I mean. I'm sorry, I don't really know, I mean, your son . . ."

The old man looked skyward, touched his chest as though he were patting dust off the old jacket, then spread his hands wide.

"How many times have I asked that myself? How many times have I asked that myself? What in the name of our sweet Lord Jesus happened? After so much time, I'm still not sure I know what happened. Well, I guess I know what happened, I just ain' ever been able to figure out why."

Sandy breathed in the smell of the grass and the sweet ferment of cantaloupes going bad in the wooden vegetable bins nearby.

"I know it was a cool mornin' in late March, and the fog was layin' low and thick across the road. It was a Thursday, papers was big and all, and I used to come along now and then and help him on those big days you know — Thursdays mostly, and Sundays too. Yeah, always Sundays," he said. Then he smiled.

"We used to talk, 'bout nothin' mostly, but we'd just get to talkin' and carryin' on, 'bout . . . just nothin' really. Sometimes we'd split us a grape drink from out'da machine at the gas station. We'd just laugh and talk, just him and me out here all alone in the dark and the quiet. But we's together, you know. On the heavy days."

Sandy leaned back and gripped the wire basket with both hands.

"Anyway, it was mighty dark, and the fog, like I told you, was hangin' low and thick. He was young and strong, my boy. Had a big ol' heavy bike. But he was strong. 'At boy once ate nine eggs at a sittin'. He'd ride out in front, and I'd pedal 'long behind, shoutin' out, 'Wait up boy, I can't keep up.' Damn, 'at boy was strong."

The old man looked up and sighed.

"And," he began, paused, then started up again.

"We got our papers. He took two bundles and I took the other'n. Just laughin' and talkin', you know, right here at this place, all by ourselves. And he sprung on out ahead, headed right down that road, darker'n midnight, and the fog all around. And I hollered out, 'Now wait up a damned minute, I'm comin', I'm comin'.' And I heard him laugh."

Sandy strained to see the look on the old man's face, saw him gaze beyond the little sewing shop and toward the broad curve in Misty Hollow Road,

"And next thing I know, I seen lights burnin' through the fog, jumpin' 'round like some kind of wild fire in the darkness, and it come up over that hill and swerved right 'round that curve . . . and it hit . . .'"

The old man's voice halted, he turned his head to one side and let out a deep sigh. "The milk truck hit my son. Knocked him right through the air."

The old man paused, his breath gone quick and shallow.

"It happened so fast," he began again. "But I could see it all like it was all slowed down, like every second was somehow froze up solid in the lights and the dark and the fog 'n all, and I heard everything. The truck, it turned that big heavy bike into a crumpled knot of steel. And my boy, oh dear God in heaven, I heard him hit the street. I can't forget that sound. Still wakes me up at night."

The old man stared into the roadway as if it were a stage, the horror unfolding before eyes weary of a scene he couldn't stop watching. "I dropped my bike and I run to him, and I seen him in the lights, lyin' on his back. I tried to pick him up, but he just crumpled. That strong young body crumpled in my arms like a rag doll. I called out to him, 'Gabriel, my son,' but he didn't say nothin'. Lord save us, he was gone. Just like that," he said, his thick lips quivering, voice beginning to crack. "Just like that, my boy was gone."

The old man took a knee by the wire basket, grabbed a hold of Sandy's leg and started to sob. "When I seen him like that," the old man choked out the words, wiping his eyes with the palm of his hand, "I jus' wanted to lay right down and die right there with him. I wanted to lay down and die."

Sandy crouched down beside him, saw the old man's face wet with tears.

"'Wait up boy,' I hollered. 'I'm comin', I'm comin'.' But it won't no use. I jus' couldn't keep up, I guess."

The old man's tears ran down his unshaven face.

"I hollered out to you. If only you'd waited, if you'd just waited for me. And I kept thinking it over and over and over again," the man said, his chest wheezing, heavy and raw.

"Why Lord, oh sweet God in heaven why? Why couldn't he have just waited just that one day, just one half a minute and everything'd be alright.

Everything'd be just fine. My boy would be right here with us now, and everything'd be just fine. But Lord God almighty, he went up ahead, just rode on off by his'self into the darkness and the fog. And the driver, he never even seen my boy, he jus, jus, oh Lord God almighty, my precious little baby boy. My little baby . . ."

The old man's voice seemed to drown in a torrent of sobs. Sandy reached out a steadying arm, dropped to his knees and felt the frail body beside him quake. He reached both arms around the old man and felt his grizzled face sink into his shoulder.

"My God," Sandy said. "I'm so sorry . . ."

The old man leaned into him like a willow in a storm.

"I'm so sorry," the boy repeated, holding the old man as if he might come apart bone by bone. He flashed back to that morning, it seemed long ago, the first time he saw the old man. Already, then, he thought to himself, he'd already lost his son.

Sandy held him like that until the old man quieted and the rolling and shaking and sobbing stopped. The old man patted him on the shoulder, leaned back and pushed up from the ground.

Sandy rose beside him, pulling himself up on the wire basket.

"I'm sorry," the old man said with a heavy sigh. "Happens 'bout ever' time I tell it. That's why I mostly just keep it to myself."

"They ever catch the guy?"

"Catch him?"

The old man paused and looked Sandy in the face.

"Catch him, boy? Lord in heaven, it was Whit. Whit Whelan killed my boy."

Sandy stared stunned and speechless as the old man went on.

"I know he didn't mean to. I know he dies with it a little each day, just dying with the memory of it all. And I know, Lord I know, I got to forgive him for it. I know Jesus forgive Pilate. I know Jesus forgive Judas. And Lord knows Jesus forgive me, all so I'd know how to forgive Whit Whelan. I know it, I know I got to do it. But it jus ain' nowhere in my heart to let it go."

The old man clenched one hand into a fist, looked skyward than looked back down again. "And I searched my heart, ever' last corner of it. And it just ain' nowhere in there to let it go. I want to. I need to. But I feel like lettin' go would be like lettin' go 'a Gabriel. Like lettin' go of his mem'ry, you know. Kind 'a like jus', I don't know . . . leavin' him there alone in the road."

The old man turned to look at Sandy. The tears had returned to his eyes. "And, God save me, I can't do it. I don' reckon I'll ever be able do it, to my dyin' day. And sometimes I think I'm dyin' with it, jus' like Whit is. I'm dying a little bit with it each day, with the mem'ry of it and the not lettin' go. I 'spect it gon' take him and me too one day jus' like it took Gabriel. It gon' take us bit by bit, 'stead 'a all at once. God knows, it gon' take us bit by bit."

The old man braced himself against the wire basket. Sandy laid a hand against his quivering back, heard the cooing of a dove. Kill one, he remembered Hope telling him, and you might as well kill two.

The old man straightened himself up, pulled a dingy handkerchief from a jacket pocket, wiped his face and blew his nose. "And then I think," he said, his voice gone thin. "I got to go on. God took Gabriel from us, but he left me here. He left me on purpose, and I got to go on and find that purpose, if I can. I got to try to find it ever' day. How close we got to get to dyin' 'til we see why we're here to live?"

Sandy clasped his hands and took a deep breath.

"The man from the milk company, he come 'round couple days after that," the old man began again. "I always figured Winston told him where we lived. Winston knew the place and all. The man come 'round, give my wife a thousand dollars. A thousand dollars cash. He said it really wadn't Whit Whelan's fault, but the company felt bad jus' the same. Said he wanted us to have the money. She signed some papers. He told her he was sorry. Then he left."

A cool breeze rustled the canvas draped over the vegetable stand.

"A thousand dollars for my dead boy. I kept thinkin' 'bout those lights, jumpin' round in the dark so wild like. I swear that milk truck was gon' too fast. Just too damned fast. My cousin, he said maybe I get a lawyer, but we done already signed the papers and all. And, tell the truth, I didn't have it in me to fight about it. I didn't have nothin' left in my heart on the thing."

The old man tugged at his jacket, put his hands on his hips and stared off at the road.

"The newspaper comp'ny sent a letter. And Winston, he come around to the funeral. There was talk about some kind of memorial fund, to help boys like Gabriel go to college and all, but nothin' much ever come of it.

"Winston said he'd asked the paper comp'ny to give us some money direct, but they said paper boys don't work for the newspaper comp'ny. Said paperboys were little businessmen. Private contractors. Said, if the comp'ny give us money, might have to do the same next time some other boy gets hurt deliverin' papers."

Sandy stared out at the road as the old man spoke, watched the scene unfold across the empty blacktop.

"Winston got the paper to put our boy's picture in the obituary. We didn't have to pay nothin' for it. I heard Winston's so mad he paid the money his'self to put Gabriel's picture in the obituary. But I never knew that for sure."

The old man heaved a great breath of finality, swatted at something across the front of his neck and turned toward his bike.

"Anyway, that was that," he said, walking across the lot. He took his bike in both hands and turned back to face the boy. Sandy could read the words "Southern States" in red across the burlap bag tied to the crossbar.

"We buried my son down by the church. They found somebody else to carry the route, and that was that."

Sandy stood still, took in the smell of the morning and stared at the old man, bathed in the first golden light of the day.

"But somehow, I don' know's I understand it, but somehow I feel him most out here. It's like a, like a kind a hauntin' almost, but a good hauntin'. Somehow, I feel like he's still out here. Some part of him, anyway, still here. That's why I still come out here myself, every Thursday and Sunday mornin', helpin' out on the heavy days. Just kind'a helpin' out on the heavy days."

Chapter 37

Darkness stealthy and sudden closed in, strangling the light from the sky. A cloud the color of charcoal towered behind the woods at the end of Tempest Lane. A torrent of dust stung Sandy's eyes as he pedaled into the wind, and a sudden train of snake lightning ripped through the cloud like a ribbon of quartz through black granite.

There was a loud thunderclap, Sandy made for the end of the road, leaned left and took sanctuary inside the tunnel of foliage over the path that led to Midsummer Night's Lane.

"If I can just beat the storm," he thought to himself, feeling the dark path go cold.

He heard a sound like pebbles on a soggy tarp, then the sky exploded with rain, pelting the leaves of the old poplar tree at the edge of the path. Sandy jumped off his bike, leaned it against the huge tree and sought refuge beneath its broad boughs.

Rain poured in great sheets through the forest, rushing in rivulets along the vines and sagging wooden fence at the edge of the old graveyard. Sandy couldn't make out, through the darkness and rain, where the bamboo bounded the path. The honeysuckle swamp was boiling with the furious storm. The great cypress tree loomed like a spirit at the water's edge, and where, Sandy wondered, had all the animals gone?

There was a crash as Sandy's bike blew over and fell across the path. He clung to the trunk of a young sassafras tree and looked up toward the ceiling of cloud. Rain gushed into his eyes. Sandy dropped his head, put a hand across his brow and turned his face up again. Lightning flared like the gnashing of teeth in a great spark that lit the sky, tracing a jagged arc that seared a hole through a swirling ocean of clouds. There was a low rumble, then a deafening crack, as thunder split the heavens just overhead.

Maybe this, Sandy thought, is what the bicycle man was talking about when he warned of dark things to come. Maybe this is the kind of thing that made Moses think God had parted the waters to free the Israelites. Maybe this is what the president had in mind when he said a transcendent drama would soon unfold.

A blistering bolt of lightning struck just beyond the swamp. Sandy felt a concussive boom, heard the terrifying sound of live wood shattering, then the falling of some ancient tree. He reached under his shirt and gently fingered the shell that hung from his neck on a string.

Rain washed over his body and drenched his clothes, the canvas shoes and cotton shorts he'd put on for dinner at Hope's. He'd been sure he could beat the storm. He saw goose bumps on his forearms, from fear or cold he couldn't tell, and he crouched low against the thick trunk of the poplar. Water overflowed the small creek at the path, raced wild across the forest floor and flooded a bank of ferns. Sandy tucked himself into a ball, pressed his chin to his chest, drew his arms over his head and began to shiver.

"Can you come over for dinner tonight?"

He replayed Hope's invitation that morning, in the stifling air outside the church. There was no hint of the storm until late in the day, when he heard the boxwoods scraping against the screen outside his bedroom window.

"We can stay up and watch the men on the moon."

It was too far to walk home after midnight, he'd reasoned. He'd need to have his bike. There was no hint of any storm, not until he heard the boxwoods scraping and pulled down his window. It had been blistering hot outside the church. Even the pastor had prayed for rain.

"We can make a butterscotch sundae and share it on the porch."

There'd been no talk, no thought of a storm. Not until he felt the wind and the dust against his face. He could knock on the door at old man Sullivan's house. A five-minute bike ride and he could be back home, stretched out on his bed listening to the rain. Five minutes and he could be warm and dry. There was, though, no riding in this.

Thirty seconds worth of fuel. That's all they had left, Sandy thought to himself, when they landed; all that was left when the voice of Apollo 11 Commander Neil Armstrong came crackling over the radio back to mission control just a few hours before. Cowering beneath the roar of the storm, Sandy replayed it in his mind, just as Cronkite had brought it into his living room that afternoon.

"Oh boy," was all the grey-haired newsman could say when the tiny lunar module finally touched down on the cratered face of the moon. The most trusted man in television, wearing a gold tie to mark the historic moment.

And, when the moment came, the moment Cronkite had been preparing for since Kennedy vowed eight years before to put a man on the moon, the newscaster took off his dark-framed glasses, rubbed his eyes, shook his head in wonder and relief and told the world, once again, "Boy."

Cronkite, thought Sandy, looked shaken. After traveling a quarter of a million miles, Armstrong didn't like the landing spot the computers picked out, a crater, he said, the size of a football stadium, strewn with rocks and lunar debris. So Armstrong took over the controls, eyeballing the thing to a site some four miles away. Mission control in Houston warned that he had thirty seconds of fuel remaining. Armstrong's heart rate doubled. Then he set it down.

"Houston, Tranquility Base here," Armstrong radioed in. "The Eagle has landed."

"Roger, Tranquility," mission control relayed back into space. "You got a bunch of guys about to turn blue. We're breathing again. Thanks a lot."

Sandy looked at his bike in the mud and the sand, its missing spoke, the wobbly front wheel. "Tranquility Base," he said to himself. "Fire Support Base Liberty."

Sandy whispered a prayer for Neil Armstrong. He said another for Winston. He thought of Pastor Ennis Stout, then saw in his mind the stained glass window, the Good Shepard and the little lamb. He had left his flock to save just one, lost and afraid and alone.

Sandy retold himself the story, wondered whether it had been raining that day, or dark. Then he pictured the sturdy staff Jesus held in the sunlit window, looked down the path and saw a thin ray of light streaming in from Midsummer Night's Lane. The back of the deluge had broken. A few scattered drops still fell. Dark clouds rolled off to the east, and eventide shimmered like moonlight off the tiny wet leaves of bamboo.

Sandy rose from his crouch, stretched his legs and leaned his face into the soft wet tail of the storm. Cool air swept in, Sandy picked up his bike, and shook off the rain from the seat. He was a five-minute ride from home. He thought of the men at mission control and the little spaceship on the moon. He waded across the muddy stream, pushed his bike past the bamboo, up the hill past Mose and Gabriel to the glistening black roadway on the other side.

 # Chapter 38

It was nearly eight o'clock when Sandy arrived at the Teale's, an orange sun low in the sky. Hope bolted out from the side porch and raced toward him across the lawn, bare feet wet and covered in bits of grass, brown hair kissed by summer and flowing over her shoulders like lace. She threw both arms around him and ran a hand down his matted hair.

"I can't believe you rode over here in that storm."

She wore a faded shirt her brother had outgrown that fit her like a dress atop a pair of white shorts.

"Come on, you know how I am when it comes to Mama Teale's coleslaw."

"You're crazy," she laughed. "Let's get you out of these wet things."

A half hour later, Sandy walked down the stairs and toward the dining room. He had a hot shower behind him, luxuriously dry skin and a faded shirt and baggy khakis from Daddy Teale's closet. He heard the dull drone of a television from the side porch and the sound of his tennis shoes banging against the rotating drum of the dryer in the utility room.

"Sorry I'm late," he said, as Mama Teale appeared at the kitchen door carrying a large glass bowl. "Didn't mean to make you hold dinner."

"Well," she replied as Sandy took a seat at the table, "it's not like the chicken salad's gettin' any colder. We're just glad you're here."

Daddy Teale shuffled in from the side porch, laid a crumpled newspaper on the kitchen table and stood in the dining room doorway. "Well, well," he announced, "storm survivor."

Sandy smiled and rose to greet Daddy Teale.

"Don't get up," he dared Sandy, who, to Hope's relief, didn't take the bait.

"Good to see you, sir," Sandy said, reaching over a casserole of baked beans to extend his hand as Daddy Teale moved to the head of the table.

"Big night," he said. "Those biscuits ready yet?"

"Comin' as fast as I can bring 'em," Mama Teale hollered out from the kitchen.

"Did you see that story in the paper today?" Daddy Teale asked, looking toward Hope, "about that British guy who rowed across the ocean?"

"Can you believe that?" Hope said to Sandy.

Mama Teale swung behind Sandy carrying a basket of steaming dinner biscuits. She placed them down in front of Daddy Teale, who plucked one out and dropped it on his plate. "Know what the guy said when he got to Florida? He said, 'I'm fed up with rowing,'" Daddy Teale chuckled. "Now I can damned well b'lieve that. Sandy, would you like to ask grace?"

Sandy said a quick blessing and, before they raised their heads, Hope added a coda. "And thank you for guiding Sandy safely through the storm."

"And be with our astronauts tonight," added Mama Teale.

"And thank God for the good folks at Evinrude," Daddy Teale put in with a chuckle.

Sandy paused, cautiously peeked out over the table to see whether any further bids might be forthcoming, caught Daddy Teale buttering his biscuit, then quickly closed his eyes. "Amen."

Through two helpings of fresh tomatoes and chicken salad, Sandy listened as Daddy Teale held forth on the strengths of the Republican Party, the mysteries of the universe and the primacy of American might. "Never thought I'd see anything like this in my lifetime," he said, pointing a fork of baked beans and molasses toward Hope. "Or yours."

"I read in the paper," Hope said, "they might not ever get home."

"Well," Daddy Teale replied, "they've tested the equipment much as they can. Still, if it fails on the moon, nobody there to fix it."

"What would happen?" Mama Teale asked.

Daddy Teale looked across the length of the table to his wife.

"Let's hope," he said, "it didn't come to that."

"Why'd we send a man up there anyway?" she asked.

"Because it's there," her grandfather shot back. "Like that guy said about climbing Everest. Because it's there."

"Still," Mama Teale interjected, "the billions and billions of dollars. All the problems we got right here in Virginia. And now Vice President Agnew's talkin' 'bout goin' to Mars. Sometimes I just wonder whether . . ."

"Good God, Varina," Daddy Teale cut her off. "Even that damned liberal Muskie said goin' to the Moon's gonna drive us to do more here at home. For heaven's sake, nobody's ever set foot on anyplace that wasn't somewhere here on Earth. Nobody's ever done this before. Lot a' folks believed it couldn't be done. Don't even try, just give up now."

"I think," she countered, "what I was tryin' to say was . . ."

"Didn'ja' ever think about? Hang on. This is an investment in our future, an investment in these kids' future," Daddy Tealed continued. "You got no idea what this whole space program means to this country. It's set us head 'n shoulders above the Russians. Our satellites. Weather forecasting. Good for the farmers."

Daddy Teale took a quick sip of sweet tea, but lifted a finger from a raised hand as if to hold his place.

"Transistor technology," he jumped back in, wiping his mouth with the back of his hand. "Hell, you got a radio now the size of a pack of cigarettes you can listen to the ball game anywhere you want. This stuff's comin' right straight ou'd the damned space program. Medicine. We're learnin' 'bout zero gravity. Solar power. Good God, it's a whole new world now. It's changin' everything. This is going to mean somethin' to these kids. There are, what, twenty thousand companies with a role in this thing. Godamit, Varina — this is jobs!"

Hope's grandmother sighed and patted the edge of her mouth with the pointed corner of her napkin. She knew better than to tug on that cord again.

"Well," she said, and let the thought lie.

Her husband, point registered, caught his breath and reached toward a small bowl of sliced peaches and cottage cheese at the edge of his plate. "Speakin' 'a jobs," he turned toward Hope. "What'd your dad hear from that outfit in Raleigh?"

Hope looked down at her plate, bit her lower lip and glanced quickly at her grandmother.

"Nothin's definite, now," Mama Teale said in a tone suggesting a quick change of subject.

"Nothin's definite? Hell's that s'posed to mean?" Daddy Teale asked with a mocking chortle. "Hope here's enrolled at All Saints. She checks into her dorm little more'n a month from now. Those Episcopals ain' expectin' you to show up late, 'n besides . . ."

"Excuse me," Hope sputtered, rising from her chair and turning toward the kitchen.

"For God's sake," Mama Teale blasted her husband. She threw her napkin on her plate, pushed her chair back from the table as the back door slammed, started to get up, then looked at Sandy.

"What the hell's the matter with everybody," Daddy Teale blurted out. "Why's everyone around her so damned thin-skinned all a sudden?"

Sandy was already on his way out the back door.

"Hope," he called out, as she made for the narrow woods at the edge of the lawn. "Hope, wait!"

Picking his way through the thin trees, Sandy caught up to her at the edge of the field on the far side of the woods. "Wait up, will ya'? What'd I do?"

She kept going, slowed to a walk, and Sandy came up behind her on the narrow footpath through the tall grass.

"Hey, what's going on?"

"Why don't you go back and ask Daddy Teale? You and him seem to know more about everything than anybody else."

"I don't even know what just happened."

"Maybe it's nobody's business, okay?"

"Hope, please," he reached out to take her hand, grabbed her wrist instead and she jerked it away.

"Leave me alone."

"Hope, quit it," he said. He took hold of her elbow and pulled her around to face him. She made a fist with her free hand and punched at his chest.

"No," she said, as he tried to hold her in front of him.

"It's none of your damned . . ."

"Stop it Hope," he said, wrapping his arms around her back and pulling her in tight. "Shhh."

Sandy felt her body heaving next to his and thought of the Christmas before. He felt her eyes warm and wet against his neck. Below the broad field lay the river, swollen and muddied by rain, and the railroad tracks roaming the edge of the field like quicksilver in the twilight. He thought of her putting the pennies down the day the train came, the smile on her face in the sun.

"Shhh," he repeated. "Everything's alright."

He lowered his arms to her waist, running his hands down her wrists, enfolding his fingers in hers. "Remember that night at Mrs. Randolph's?" he said, leaning his head back to look in her eyes.

Hope said nothing, nodded, then nestled her face back into his shoulder.

"You were so . . ."

"And you left me standing there on the dance floor," she cut in. "I felt like an orphan or some kind of freak."

"Well, you're not an orphan."

"Oh, thanks a lot," she said, pushing back from him. "You can go now. That's your specialty after all." She turned and walked off slowly. Sandy followed her down through the field. She plucked a long sprig of dried grass, clutched it between her teeth, turned briefly to face him then leaned into the gravely slope to the tracks.

Soon they were sitting close on a rail and looking out on the river, flowing fast against the coming of night. Their feet were bare and muddy, and Sandy thought of the time he put her shoes on beside the tree on the bank.

Hope leaned her head on his shoulder. Sandy reached for her hand.

"Wasn't my idea, just so you know."

"Yeah, I kind'a gathered that."

"My parents," she paused. "I don't know. I guess my dad's takin' this job in North Carolina. They're sellin' the house. Mom's movin' down to the place in Gloucester for a while. See how things turn out."

Sandy took the stem of hay from her lips. He tasted her as he held it between his teeth.

"That left the 'problem' of what to do about 'Hope.' So, Daddy Teale made a phone call to a woman he knows who's the headmistress at a boarding school down that way."

Sandy swung an arm around her shoulder and pulled her against him.

"So, wha'd you decide to do?"

Hope let out a shot of breath, almost a laugh, but not quite.

"Things have a way of gettin' decided for you around here," she said. "I mean, when Daddy Teale makes a phone call, it's not exactly a suggestion."

A soft breeze blew the hair back from her face. A cotton ball cloud slipped off to the east, unveiling a pale quarter moon reflected in the water below.

"I'll come see you on weekends."

"How," she shot back, "on your bike?"

"I'll figure it out, smarty pants."

"Sandy. It's sixty-five miles away."

"Okay, I'll go Greyhound. I'll hitchhike. Or, Gimme a ticket for an air-o-plane."

"Hmph," she said, laying a hand across his knee. "That sounds nice."

A small cloud drifted just beneath the moon, making it seem to be cresting a wave.

"The moon was a ghostly galleon," he whispered, "tossed upon cloudy seas."

"What's that?"

"It's from The Highwayman. My dad used to read it to me at night."

Hope stared off toward the river.

"The road was a ribbon of moonlight, over the purple moor, when the highwayman came riding, riding, riding, the highwayman came riding, up to the old inn door."

"I like that," said Hope. "A river of moonlight. That's pretty."

"Ribbon," he said, running a finger through her hair. "Ribbon of moonlight."

"Ribbon of moonlight," she nodded. "I like that too."

"Alfred Noyes," said Sandy. "That's the guy who wrote it."

"What's it about?"

"He's a robber, this highwayman. That's what they called them. And every night he rides up to the old inn, whistles a tune, and the landlord's beautiful daughter comes to her window."

"Does he love her?"

Hope glanced sideways at Sandy. He looked straight ahead, then smiled. "He lives for her."

The moon slipped briefly behind the cloud, then peered out over the rim.

"A ghostly galleon," said Hope. "Over the purple moor."

She turned to face him. Saw the fragile shell hanging on the string from his neck, took it between her fingers, held it to her lips and kissed it.

"Mmmm," she said, closing her eyes. "I can still taste the salt from the sea."

She slipped the straw from Sandy's mouth and held the shell to his lips. "Here. Try it."

Sandy closed his eyes, kissed the edge of the shell, felt himself flooded with the scent of Hope.

"Yeah," he said, his eyes still closed. "I can taste it."

She pulled gently on the string. He felt the heat off her brow.

"Hope," he whispered soft and slow, savoring each sound in her name.

He felt her against him, the touch of her skin, felt a soft warm dampness against his cheek, felt it move like some small animal against the open edge of his mouth, felt the tilt of his head, the bones in her face against his, felt her pour herself into him, opened himself and took her inside.

He wanted it to last forever, prayed it might never end, refused to even open his eyes lest he find it had all been a dream. When they parted, he kept his eyes closed still, rested his head against hers, felt the breeze off the river and took in the earthy scent of her hair. He held her and pulled her close until the moist warmth of her back bled through her brother's old shirt. He touched the smooth steel rails beneath them, heard a soft breeze high in the trees, felt her chest rise full and warm.

"I love you, Hope."

"I love you too."

They sauntered as one through the moonlit field, their arms draped over each other's waist, saying little or nothing all the way through the thin forest that opened to the edge of the lawn. Hope stepped on Sandy's bare toes, and from her bedroom window Mama Teale heard them laughing.

Sandy felt nothing beneath him, not until his feet touched the cool linoleum kitchen floor. They saw the dining room lights turned down, and a note on the table there.

"Daddy Teale's watching the moon coverage upstairs. I'm tired and going to bed. There's ice cream in the freezer. Feel free to help yourself. Mama Teale."

Hope looked at Sandy and smiled.

Cronkite's voice, weary and drawn, tolled in a low buzz from the porch.

"Go ahead," Hope said. "I'll make us something good."

Sandy slumped onto the old porch sofa and propped his feet on the glass table top, where an open section of the paper lay. In the flickering glow of the TV, he could make out a large ad. Goodyear had nylon cord tubeless whitewalls on sale for $13.95. Trade in an old tire and mounting was free.

Next to the ad was a syndicated piece from The New York Times.

"It would be hard to describe our race relations as anything but a disgrace, and Vietnam makes the Bay of Pigs look like a regrettable incident," the article read. "It is harder to concentrate the mind on creating a just and decent society than it is to mobilize the intelligence and machinery to go to the moon."

Perhaps the moon mission, the column suggested, might inspire the nation to higher good. "The goal was to do something no man had ever done before," the article continued. "The whole idea of America was to create a society nobody had ever created before, and it could be that the moon men, with their concentration, purpose and time schedule, have shown us the way."

"Never quite thought of it like that," Sandy thought to himself. He turned the page and saw a cluster of ads.

"How to Commit Marriage," starring Bob Hope and Jackie Gleason, was playing at the Patter's Plank Drive-In. Sidney Poitier was appearing in "The Lost Man," at the Booker-T downtown.

"Unfasten your seat belts," read an ad in bold face on the opposite page. "Unwind on the Pocahontas." In agate type below was the schedule for Norfolk & Western's blue-chip passenger service from Norfolk to Cincinnati, with stops in Suffolk, Petersburg, Lynchburg and Bluefield. Sandy remembered the smooth feel of the rails, then shook his head at the thought of it: To get on a train at the mouth of the river and wake up the next day in Ohio.

"Air conditioned," the ad boasted. "Scenic domed. Dining car. Reclining seats."

Sandy looked up from the paper. Cronkite was describing the lunar module, recounting the dangers of the landing several hours before and praising the cool, steady hand of Neil Armstrong, the Navy aviator who flew seventy-eight combat missions over Korea off the deck of an aircraft carrier.

Sandy stared at the screen, caught bits and pieces from Cronkite's measured commentary. Wapakoneta, Ohio. Tranquility Base. Live television pictures from the moon.

"How's this look?"

She stood in the porch doorway, her brother's shirt hanging low off her neck, and slung her hair back from her face. In one hand she held a bowl of vanilla ice cream topped with warm butterscotch and a mountain of whipped cream; in the other a single spoon.

"Looks pretty good from here," Sandy said, dropping his feet from the table and sitting up straight.

"Any better from here?" she smiled, stepping toward the couch and sidling up against him.

"Yeah," he replied. "It's better from here."

"Close your eyes," she told him, as Sandy leaned his head back, took in the musty smell of the aging couch, and readied himself for a spoonful of ice cream.

"I got a little on me," she said, running a finger coated in warm butterscotch along the edge of his lips.

"Mmm," said Sandy. "Finishing this sundae could take some time."

"Look Sandy," she said, turning toward the television and a fuzzy grey image of what resembled the side of a tree house wrapped in tin foil and propped up on spider legs. A man in a cumbersome white space suit with what looked like a large backpack was slowly making his way down the spindly strut of the craft.

"Neil, we can see you coming down the ladder now."

It was the voice of mission control, assuring Armstrong that the camera mounted on the spaceship was transmitting images of his epic descent.

"Okay," the astronaut radioed back. "I'm at the foot of the ladder."

Sandy reached an arm around Hope.

"The surface appears to be very, very fine grained, as you get close to it," Armstrong said. "It's almost like a powder down there. It's very fine."

Sandy glanced at Hope, then turned back to the screen.

"I'm going to step off," the astronaut said.

Sandy leaned forward on the little couch. Hope set the bowl down on the glass. Armstrong let go of the ladder.

"That's one small step for man," he said, "one giant leap for mankind."

The camera stayed fixed on Armstrong, as he took his first steps on the moon. Sandy heard Cronkite in the background, sighing and chuckling, relieved and amazed.

"Neil Armstrong," the newsman finally declared, "thirty-eight-year-old American, standing on the surface of the moon."

From the perfect peace of their side porch nest, Hope and Sandy felt far from the gaze of the world. Off in the vast cold universe, a man wandered the face of the moon, a quarter of a million miles farther than any man ever walked before, tethered to Earth by radio waves bounced from satellites to earth stations and the electronic box before them.

Hope got up quickly to turn down the sound.

"Don't wanna wake up Mama Teale," she said. "Can you still hear it ok?"

Sandy nodded and sank into the worn cushions.

It was nearly midnight. The ice cream was gone. Through the open kitchen window in the house next door, the soft strains of strings wafted over the lawn, someone playing Beethoven on the stereo in the dark.

Sandy felt his body go limp in the oversized clothes. Hope leaned against him and nestled her head between his shoulder and neck.

Cronkite somehow stayed with it, finding new ways to talk of the mission, the men, their families, even their spacesuits and the exotic new materials used to make them. Teflon. Neoprene. Spandex.

Daddy Teale was right, Sandy thought to himself. This was going to change the world.

He heard her breath, steady and shallow, imagined the infinite reaches of space. He squinted at the TV. There was a blurry picture of a young girl walking with a man in a grey suit and gold tie across a crater-pocked landscape covered with powdery dust, her shirt hanging down to her knees. A man played cello behind them, and a woman played violin.

An enormous June bug popped against the porch screen. Sandy opened his eyes, looked out and saw the quarter moon low to the west, reflected off the windshield of Daddy Teale's Buick. He didn't hear the seasoned newsman sign off for the night, or notice the screen go dim, aimless electrons racing like ants across the flickering electronic void.

 # Chapter 39

"Sandy," Hope whispered, taking him by the shoulder. "Sandy, wake up!"

Sandy stretched his legs, opened his eyes and saw sunlight, soft and orange, wandering the length of the lawn, casting long shadows just beyond the Teale's porch.

"What!" he said with a startled stare, lifting himself from the couch.

"I know," Hope shot back, rising to head toward the kitchen, "we fell asleep."

"Your grandparents . . . what time? My papers," he said in a confused whirl of thought. "I got'ta go!"

He stood, saw his bike leaning against the side of the garage, looked down at his bare feet and Daddy Teale's baggy pants.

"I'm comin' with you," Hope said, appearing back on the porch to hand Sandy his dry shorts and shoes. "You can change in the bathroom."

Hope tiptoed upstairs to the guest room, turned down the sheets on her bed, jumped in, rolled around, then got back up and put on her shoes.

"C'mon," she whispered to Sandy through the bathroom door.

"Good morning Grandma," she dashed out on a napkin. "Can you believe we put a man on the moon??? Gone to help Sandy deliver his papers. Be back soon! Love, Hope."

"Let's go," she said to Sandy, pushing her brother's old bicycle from around back and through the pebbled driveway out to Canterbury Lane. Songbirds chattered from a high oak, wet lawns glistened in the morning light, and a man in a terry cloth robe toddled to the end of a long brick walkway, stooped over and picked up his Times-Daily.

"Mornin'," he called out as Hope and Sandy rode past.

"Good mornin'," they both replied.

"Damn," Sandy said out loud, looking at the waiting papers on the sidewalks along both sides of the road. It must be, what, he thought to himself, six-thirty?

"Come on Sandy," Hope called back to him, standing on her pedals at the crest of the hill.

A lone car swept past them along the old river road. Sandy smelled bacon cooking somewhere. As they rounded the broad bend in Misty Hollow Road, Old Blue stirred and growled.

"Don't worry 'bout him," Sandy hollered through labored breath. As they turned into the paper stop, Sandy felt a knot in his chest. His bundle lay alone on the muddy lot. He slung it into his basket, as the image flashed though his mind of sidling up the next morning to a bundle with 89 complaints attached, pink envelopes fluttering like tiny flags.

Hope straddled her brother's bike and quickly took it all in: The sagging vegetable stand, the puddles of mud, the wire trash basket, blackened and charred. The wild grass at the unkempt edge of the lot. The empty gas station, its idled pumps standing silent sentry over the domain of paperboys and Old Blue.

"Okay," Sandy said. "Let's ride."

Hollis T. Smith stood at his mailbox as they approached Tempest Lane.

"Is this today's paper, finally, or tomorrow's?"

"Mornin' Mister Smith," Sandy called out, handing him a paper as he slowed his bike, then rolling on past.

"Take a couple of these," Sandy said to Hope as he braked for the next mailbox. "Do the first two boxes, skip the third, then hit the fourth."

"Got it."

Hope reached out to take the papers — and froze.

"Sandy, look."

He glanced at the banner headline, tall block letters as thick as a thumb. "Man Walks on Moon."

They stared at the page.

"First time I've ever seen a color picture in the paper," Sandy said.

An artist's rendering took up half the page, depicting the lunar landing craft's descent to the moon. "How'd they do that?" asked Hope.

Sandy thought about his night in the pressroom, the hot lead and fresh type, the giant spools of paper speeding through rollers of ink. "Durn if I know. But it's pretty slick."

However historic, the papers were small. It was still Monday, after all.

"Hey son," a voice rang out, "any way I could get a copy?"

It was Rich Thomas, at 8600, in his pajamas, leaning out his front door.

"Yes'sir," Sandy shouted, rising on his pedals through the wet grass and up to the porch, where two bottles of cold milk stood aside the door. Sandy pulled out the top paper, noticed a small tear, but presented it as though it were a prize.

"Would you look at that," the man said. "That there's a keepsake."

Sandy smelled freshly brewed coffee and faintly burned toast.

"Yessiree, this 'un's goin' in my scrapbook."

"In that case," said Sandy, "take this one instead."

He handed Thomas a paper with no creases or tears, culled from the center of his basket, and took the torn paper back in exchange.

"Need some more," Hope called out from the side of the road.

It was puzzling, Sandy thought to himself, looking down Tempest Lane. Why were all the cars still there? Why was Thomas just now getting his milk?

Oh yeah, he remembered. National holiday, declared by Nixon to mark the event.

A wave of relief washed over him. Folks would be sleeping in a little late. If it wasn't a day off for Sandy, at least he'd been granted a reprieve for oversleeping.

"Okay, 8609 gets it on the porch," he said, folding a paper, tucking it up good and tight for Hope. "Just ride across the grass and toss it up there."

Sandy coasted downhill, stuffed a mailbox as Hope made her way across the lawn. There was a loud metallic crash as the paper slammed into the base of the aluminum storm door, followed by the panicked yelping of a dog from inside.

"Damn, Hope," Sandy called out. "Didn't mean for you to throw it through the door."

"Well I didn't know," she sputtered, laughter spewing out like water sprinkled on a drought-scorched lawn.

"It's not funny, Hope."

"Sorry."

Sandy pedaled up beside her, heard the door open at 8609 and suddenly felt his own laughter tumble out.

"Skip it," he chortled, gesturing to 8611 and its overgrown grass. "On vacation."

Hope watched Sandy roll a paper in one hand, guide his bike with the other near a rusting white tube at 8610, and slip the paper inside as he coasted past.

"Pretty nifty," she called out. "Now can I have some?"

He rode slowly alongside her, handed over several papers, and together they worked their way down the road.

"This must be your sister," a thin and dark-haired man said to Sandy, walking out to his mailbox to pick up his paper.

"Cousin," Hope shot back to the man. "Vist'n from Gloucester."

"Thanks a lot," Sandy said as they rode out of earshot. "Now every time he sees me it's gon'na be, 'How's your cousin from Gloucester?'"

"Didn't want me to tell him the truth did you?"

She grabbed Sandy's basket and gave it a shake.

"Hey," he said, regaining control of his bike. He slowed as he approached 8712 and a red and white mailbox with faux fins on the back and a Cadillac medallion affixed to the lid.

Sandy rolled a paper and swiped it against the front of the box. The lid dropped open, he thrust the paper in, caught the base of the medallion with his hand and flipped it to close the box just as his bike crawled past.

"Show off," said Hope.

A voice startled Sandy, who looked up to see Pam standing barefoot in the amber pebbles at the end of her driveway.

There was the sound of rubber skidding across wet tar, as Hope brought her brother's bike to a halt. She put down both feet, straddled the high crossbar, and stared at the tall blonde in the sheer knee-length pink robe.

"Good mornin' Sandy," Pam said softly, looking directly at him. "Who's your helper today?"

"Oh, hey," he stammered, braking to a stop. "This is my friend."

Pam arched an eyebrow, stepped toward the boy, then glanced sideways at Hope.

"Pretty good friend," Pam said, "to be out this early in the mornin'."

"Yes ma'am," Sandy said, forcing a smile.

"Let's see here," Pam said, resting one hand on Sandy's handlebar and reaching the other into his basket. "I think I'll take . . ." she found one she liked, ran a finger along its spine and slipped it out, "this one."

In the still morning air he could smell her perfume and could see she hadn't yet brushed her hair.

"Thanks," she said to Sandy, "and this time I've got a little news for you."

He shot a glance at Hope, who watched intently and lowered her chin.

"I'm goin' to have another baby," said Pam. "Here, feel."

She took Sandy's hand and pressed it to her robe. Through the thin fabric he felt her tummy, tight and round, felt a surge of heat well up inside him, like doing pushups in the cold.

"Right here," she said, slightly moving his palm. "Feel that?"

Something pushed at him from inside her, like the round back of a small spoon. Then he felt it again.

"Wow."

Sandy felt a broad smile sweep across his face, as he looked into the young mother's eyes. "That's . . . incredible."

She smiled and tilted her head.

"It's a little fist," she said, holding his hand to her stomach. "Or maybe a shoulder, or heel."

Sandy felt something sweep downward. He followed it with his open palm, his fingers tracing the under curve of her belly until the tips of them grazed the edge of bone.

"Better get goin', don't you think." There was a stern tone to Hope's voice. "'Less you wan'na take it from here."

Sandy took a deep breath, felt Pam's hand fall away from his, and straightened up on his seat. "Okay," he said, wrapping his warm palm around an ink-stained handlebar grip. "Take care," he looked at Pam, "of . . . everything."

"Bye Sandy," he heard her say as he pedaled off. "See you soon."

Sandy rode right past the next mailbox, looked straight ahead down the road, then veered over in front of Hope toward 8717.

"Thought I had this side," she let out from behind.

"Oh, sorry, you're right."

Hope pulled up beside him for more papers.

"Mighty friendly neighborhood."

There it was, thought Sandy.

"Yeah," he responded. "Folks mostly get along."

"Well, does she have a name? You seem to have suddenly forgotten mine."

"Ah, yeah," Sandy said. "I think it's, ah, Pam."

Hope's eyes widened like the flame of a torch.

"You think?"

"Pam," Sandy said, looking at Hope. "Yeah, her name's Pam. Let's go."

"The Pam who gave you the fancy-schmantsy soap-on-a-rope? What was it again, Hawaiian Nights?"

"Surf," Sandy said. "Hawaiian Surf. Better get goin'."

"Better get goin' nothin'. You can finish this yourself."

Hope climbed high on her pedals, began pumping with long sure strokes, and shot off down the road as Sandy clambered to catch up.

"Oh, c'mon now, Hope. Stop. Hope!"

Tempest Lane sailed past her on either side, parked cars and sunlit lawns. Through an open window she heard a radio. From behind a backyard chain link fence, a black dog jumped and barked.

Hope crested the hill, saw the end of the road, and braked to a halt. Before her stood the forest at the edge of the honeysuckle swamp, the narrow little path to her left.

"Damn it," Hope said out loud. "What am I s'pposed to do now?"

"Mornin' missy," an old man called out. "You hadn't seen my paperboy have ya?"

Hope turned toward the house at the end of the road, saw an old man in shorts and a sleeveless undershirt headed toward her down a driveway of chipped cement.

"Hope," Sandy called out, coming over the hill, "wait a minute."

Hope looked past the old man, then turned away toward the tall trees.

"Where am I gonna go?" she asked out loud.

"What?" Sandy asked, skidding to a stop beside her.

"Nothing. Never mind."

"Good mornin' Mr. Sullivan," Sandy greeted the man. "Runnin' a little behind, I guess, but here's your paper, sir."

Hope leaned over her handlebars and stared into the forest in search of clues for escape.

"Man Walks On Moon," old man Sullivan read out loud. "Now that there's sump'in I never thought I'd live to see."

Hope tapped a foot on the pavement. "Just tell me how to get home from here."

Sandy ignored her. "Did you watch it last night?" he asked the old man instead.

"Watch it? Hell, boy, I was up half the night."

"Me too."

"Whad'ya think?" the old man asked.

Hope turned toward Sandy.

"Well sir, for me, it was magical."

Hope rolled her eyes and turned away.

"Fact is," the boy continued, "I don't know I'll ever have a night quite like that one, long's I live."

"Know what'cha mean," the old man put in.

Hope thought for a moment how he'd looked when he showed up soaking wet at the Teales's, having ridden to her through the storm.

"You know," the old man let out. "I couldn't help but come out here in my yard, take a look at that ol' moon. I thought about it long 'n hard, just couldn't believe that man was really all the way up there, the moon lookin' so shiny 'n all."

"Kind'a like a ghostly galleon," Sandy said, "tossed upon cloudy seas."

The old man smiled and nodded, then looked at Hope. "Who's your understudy?"

"This is Hope," Sandy said. "Hope, this is Mister Sullivan. He's the one who made your Christmas present."

She looked at the old man, a thin tussle of grey hair atop an unshaven face. "You," she said incredulously, "made those mourning doves?"

The old man chuckled. "I guess I did."

"I love them," she said. "I've never seen anything more beautiful."

Old man Sullivan looked at the girl. "You must be mighty special," he said. "The boy had me custom-make 'em just for you. Wouldn't take just any bird. Said it had to be a matched pair."

She looked at Sandy. He was still breathing hard from the chase down Tempest Lane.

"She's special alright," Sandy nodded. "Reckon you can pretty much see that for yourself."

The old man looked down at his paper, turned and walked back inside.

"Hope," he said. "I'm sorry. But what was I supposed to do?"

Hope turned a meek smile.

"I'm sorry, too."

Sandy rolled his bike toward her. "I meant what I said last night on the tracks."

"Me too," Hope said. She reached out across his handlebar and laid a hand atop his.

"We call this the honeysuckle swamp," Sandy said, gesturing toward the

259

forest. "That path cuts through the woods, past a grove of bamboo on up to Midsummer Night's Lane. If you just keep straight by the little church, and down toward the blacktop road, it'll point you back toward Mama Teale's."

The sunlight had warmed up the morning. A brown tabby cat crossed the road.

"I can finish these on my own."

Hope looked at Sandy and squeezed his hand. She slung her hair back. Tiny beads of sweat lined her brow. "Oh Sandy," she said in a tone of mock passion. "I've got a little news to share with you. Right here, can you feel it?"

She pressed his hand to her cheek, and poked it from inside with her tongue.

"Very funny."

"Wait," she said, "there it goes again."

"Alright, alright. I'd better finish up. What's Mama Teale gon'na say when you get home?"

"Prob'ly somethin' 'bout not makin' up my bed when I got up so early this mornin'."

"Huh?"

"Never mind," Hope said with a laugh, pointing her bike toward the edge of the road.

"You're crazy," Sandy called out as he watched her dip onto the path and disappear into the woods. He thought he heard her call out something to him, some kind of parting dig at Pam. He listened, heard nothing, then set off to finish his route.

 # Chapter 40

I t didn't feel right to Sandy, pulling on his sweatshirt the first week in August. It had rained, though, nearly every day for a week, and it was breezy and cool as he delivered his Sunday papers. Lawns that hadn't been cut grew unruly and wild. Rainwater pooled in an old hubcap someone left by the side of the road.

Sandy heard the high hum of a mosquito, and he slapped at the side of his ear. In the first hint of daylight, he saw something on the front page about Apollo, a recap of the week that was. And in the bottom-right corner of the page he saw the faint outlines of a photograph, a head and shoulders shot of a man wearing some kind of official looking cap, a policeman or fire chief, perhaps.

A dim light glowed from Pam's kitchen. Must be hard to sleep, Sandy concluded, what with the baby kicking and all. He was looking forward to seeing Hope at church.

"Pint of cold chocolate milk would go down good about now, but won't be seeing Whit Wheelan on Sunday," he said to himself.

Sandy thought about the bicycle man, the sadness and horror of losing his son. You could never tell what was going on inside another person, he thought, just by looking at his clothes or his bike. You never knew what was going on.

Something glimmered through the trees at the end of the road, seemed to glide just over the swamp. Strange, thought Sandy, peering toward the smooth water, where small ripples flowed from the edge. Straining in the dim light he saw it, crouched by the old cypress tree, a great blue heron, stately and still atop spindly legs. It had a body the size of a tomcat, a clutch of spiked feathers at its throat. The boy stared at the bird, following the line of its painted beak.

"Hey there, ol' fella," he whispered. "What you looking at in there?"

There was a flicker of light in the forest. A pair of headlights crested the hill, a car slowed, edged to the side of the road and pulled up alongside Sandy.

"You're out early today."

It was Lucky Pete in Winston's old Mustang, driver's window rolled down.

"Thought I'd catch you at the paper stop," he said. "Checked and saw all your papers were gone. Hoped I'd find you down here."

Sandy stood by the door of his district manager, awaiting the juke and jive he'd come to expect from Lucky Pete, the man ever on top of the world. Looking into the car, Sandy saw Pete's right hand gripping the gearshift knob, a stack of Sunday papers in the passenger seat. It wasn't a policeman, Sandy could make it out now, but a soldier in uniform.

"How you doin'?"

"Fine," Sandy replied, eyeing the Mustang. "You got this baby gleamin'."

"I was up half the night waxin' it in my old man's garage," said Pete. He shook his head. "Just couldn't get it off my mind."

He stared straight ahead into the forest.

"Lucky Pete," Sandy said, "everything alright?"

Pete looked up at Sandy and flashed a wan smile.

"You haven't looked at the paper?"

"Not really," said Sandy. "What's the deal?"

Pete jammed the shifter into first and shut off the engine. The headlights went dark and Sandy heard him set the parking brake.

"Put your bike down," Pete directed, getting out of the car, "and come with me."

"Pete," the boy said, suddenly worried. "What's going on?"

"Just come on," was all Pete would say, as he headed down the path and into the woods.

Sandy leaned his bike against a tree and scrambled to catch up. "Hey," he called out when he crossed over the creek, pressing past the dark hedge of bamboo. "Wait up." He followed Pete through the brush at the edge of the churchyard and over the rickety fence.

Little light filtered through the trees in the tiny cemetery where they stood. Pete looked around briefly, took a few steps, then bent down near a small marble marker. He reached in his pocket, struck a match near the stone, blew it out and then rubbed his palms.

"Over here," he said, sinking down to one knee, as Sandy followed him to a simple tombstone with a small American flag attached on a plastic bracket.

Pete took a deep breath. "I hadn't counted on bein' the one to bring you this news," he began, laying a hand on the stone. "Hadn't much counted on this at all."

Sandy had never heard the forest so quiet; not since he passed through it after the big snow last winter. Pete looked down at the gravesite and brushed away the dry stems of a fallen bouquet.

"Then again, maybe you already know. Maybe you're both together somehow. But Mose, my man, there's no other way for me to say this." Pete looked up at the sky, then turned his face back to the stone.

"You see, Winston . . ." he picked up the dead flowers, neatly laid them back down, and clawed up a handful of soil. "Winston's gone, Mose," Pete said slowly, his body beginning to heave. "Oh God," he said, looking at Sandy and dropping to both knees, "Winston's gone."

Sandy reached out to Pete, who raised his arm and signaled him off.

"I'm okay, man. I'm alright." Pete steadied himself on Mose Marable's tombstone.

"No. It's not that," thought Sandy. Just give Pete time to explain.

He looked off at the old church, felt a chill in the forest and a sinking, sick feeling inside. He suddenly wanted to be back at the paper stop. He wanted to be with Hope.

"What . . ." Sandy said at last. "What's happened?"

Pete sighed, seemed to collapse into himself, then sat at the edge of the grave. "Got shot down," he said, hands clasped in front of his face. "A week or so ago. Talked to his parents a few days back. They got word he'd gone missing. Nobody was sure. They thought, maybe . . . but then," Pete paused, opened his hands and pulled them back across his face. "They found his remains in the jungle, where his helicopter went down and burned. Just bones."

The words seemed to sail past Sandy as if Pete were firing off blanks. This isn't what really happened. It didn't even sound like Pete's voice.

"Bones? So, it might not be him. Maybe he got away."

Pete took a shallow breath.

"Identified him by his teeth."

Sandy absently bit down on the side of his hand — went suddenly light-headed, as if he might faint — sat down in the dirt and the leaves. His body felt like a statue. He couldn't turn his head.

He stared past the quiet graveyard, past Mose's stone. He couldn't smell the honeysuckle or hear the breeze off in the trees. He just sat there beside Pete and breathed.

"I'm sorry," Pete said, "to be the one to tell you."

This isn't happening, Sandy thought. The words, the story, the violence, this place, the dots just didn't connect. "I can't believe it. I don't believe it."

Pete looked him in the eye, and said nothing.

So that was him, the thought flared through Sandy, his picture on the front page. Pete must have known it the night before. Wanted to be there, at the paper stop, when Sandy arrived.

Sandy pictured Mary Kay. Would she wake up this morning to this? But, then, if Pete knew, of course she must have known. But when? Who told her?

Pete laid a strong hand on Sandy. The gearshift hand, Sandy thought to himself. Winston's burgundy car.

He thought of Pete waxing it through the night, working to make it shine. "He was your best friend, wasn't he?"

In the soft light in the forest, he saw Pete nod. "Yeah, my best friend."

They sat there a long time without speaking. They watched shadows creep through the woods.

A black Buick, faded and dented, pulled in beside the old church. Someone got out of the car. Moments later they heard a wooden door open and shut, then what sounded like a chair being dragged across the floor inside.

Soft and unsteady it started, like icicles melting in rain, notes that broke off unfinished, bars that drifted off without end. Then from the piano there rose a sound that gathered force and started to roll, the uncut hem of a familiar melody hand-stitched to graceful chords.

"Be Thou my vision, oh Lord of my heart," Pete whispered softly. "Nought be all else to me, save that Thou art. Thou my best thought, by day or by night. Waking or sleeping, my treasure Thou light."

The sky was a quilt of purples and blues; the forest dark shades of green.

"Stapleton Moses Marable," Sandy read on the tombstone before them. "December 14, 1949 – May 8, 1968."

He remembered the funeral service, the soft whir of the ceiling fans, Winston standing in the back of the church with the old man.

"Where's Gabriel?"

"Right over there," Pete motioned with a tilt of his head, looking across the small graveyard toward a flat grey stone marker the size of a pair of Bibles.

"Do you think they might be together somehow?"

Pete didn't answer right away, just looked off toward the swamp.

"Everybody's got their own ideas about heaven, I guess," Pete said at last.

"For lot of folks, it's bein' reunited with family and friends. Loved ones we've lost."

He ran a finger in the damp dirt alongside the gravesite.

"I've also heard it said that it's a journey, and when we leave this Earth, we travel in our own favorite way, walkin' along some green hillside, floatin' on a river downstream, maybe even flyin' like a bird through the air."

Sandy thought about the heron, gliding like a soul unleashed across the swamp.

"For me," Pete said, "heaven's the place we get to when we have people like Winston in our lives, even for a little while." He lifted an open hand to his heart.

Over and over again that day, Sandy tried to make sense of the details. A mission to bring out the wounded. Long range reconnaissance patrol. Shots from deep in the jungle, .51 caliber rounds. Somewhere along the Cambodian border. The young pilot fighting to rein in the shaking Huey, its screaming engine in flames. The page-one story beneath the black and white photo.

"Richmond pilot Winston C. Coleman," the caption read. "Warrant Officer, First Class, United States Army."

# Chapter 41

I've got to replace that spoke, Sandy told himself, as he rode toward the paper stop on a wobbly wheel, rolling off the wet pavement and onto the muddy lot. "It's just a light drizzle," he said to no one. Still, it hadn't let up in weeks.

Through the clouds and thin fog a faint grey light cast an eerie pall over the paper stop. Water ran down a crease in the tarp slumped over the vegetable stand, and Sandy heard the gurgling runoff wash over a large yellow squash left to spoil in a bin.

Maybe someone had made a mistake. Things get screwed up all the time. He stared off into the darkness, as if he might just somehow appear. That would be like Winston, Sandy thought to himself, just show up, like nothing ever happened, like nothing was wrong. Nothing unexpected or out of the ordinary. He stared off into the darkness, the mist and the fog.

He leaned his bike against the trash basket and, in the ghostly light, he probed for his papers, rummaging through heavy bundles in the sandy mud.

There was a soft jangling in the distance, like a child's tambourine, the lapping of rubber against the wet street and what sounded like the dull slap of a harp being plucked with soggy cardboard. Sandy peered deep into the mist, saw the dark outline of the old sewing store, then heard a low rattling symphony of motion and worn metal he recognized as the sound of the bicycle man approaching.

"Rain, rain, rain," he grumbled, as he coasted onto the lot.

"Wha'choo complainin' 'bout now?" Sandy called out. "Looks like you're pretty well covered to me."

Affixed to his handlebars with a large C-clamp was a black umbrella with one rusted strut poking out of a torn edge.

"If 'at thing don't keep you dry, I don't know what will," Sandy joked. "'If it don't put out an eye."

"Go on 'n laugh," the old man said, guiding his bike beneath the shelter of the vegetable stand. "But me 'n ol' Violet here, we've done a mile or two, 'n come rain 'r shine, I 'spect we just keep gettin' right on along."

Sandy hauled a bundle into his basket and walked his bike under the tarp alongside the old man.

"That what'cha call her?" Sandy asked.

"Well tha's her name. Her Christian name, that is."

Sandy leaned his bike against a watermelon bin and went back for his second bundle.

"Good 'n fat today," the old man called out, fingering the papers in Sandy's basket as the boy returned with the rest of his papers.

"Ah, now, damn it all," Sandy said, reaching back to an empty hip pocket.

"Don't fret, boy, I got mine right here."

"Thanks," said Sandy, taking the greasy wire cutters from the old man's wet hands. "You think it's ever go'n stop rainin'?"

"Don't say a word, son. I tolt' ya a damned month ago, we shouldn't 'a been messin' 'round up there on the Moon."

Sandy looked up at the old telephone pole, listing hard to the left. No one had bothered to replace the burned out light bulb still.

"Neil Armstrong says it's the beginning of a new age."

"Sheed," the old man mocked. "Man on the Moon. Ought'a try puttin' a man on the streets of Detroit, might do somebody some good."

Sandy looked at the old man and started to smile.

"But naw," the old man continued. "Now here we are, mid'la August, had three solid weeks 'a rain. We done messed up the weather, gon' up messin' roun' where we don' belong. Mark my words, they's gon' be hell to pay."

Sandy snipped the wire to open a bundle in his basket.

"You don' b'lieve me, do you?" the old man asked.

Sandy stood up straight, stretched out his back and put his hands on his hips.

"You know," the boy said, "I ain' really thought about it that way, 'bout the Moon and the weather 'n all."

"I told you when they went up there, didn't I? Had no damned business messin' 'round."

"Yeah, I 'member you sayin' that."

"Nobody'd listen."

"Come to think of it, though," Sandy joined in, "it's rained just about every day since then."

"Ain't no damn coincidence," the old man stressed. "I said so at the time."

But did anybody listen? Shee. Went right on 'n sent the man up there, carryin' on like a damned fool on the Moon where we shouldn'a gone. Now we done messed up the weather."

A pale yellow light fell across the man's face. He wore a faded poplin cap with a pair of golf clubs crossed on the bib.

"You a golfer?"

"Caddy," the old man said, tugging at a stained and tattered jacket. "Make myself a pretty penny, when I feel up to it."

The light grew brighter, Sandy turned and saw headlights rounding Ridgetop Road. He heard a truck engine gearing down, as it slowly rumbled onto Misty Hollow Road and then edged onto the vacant lot.

The old man turned his face from the bright lights and raised a hand to shield his eyes. Sandy squinted out of the side of the vegetable stand and recognized the familiar red script on the side of the River Bend Dairy truck.

"Mornin' Clayton," a voice rang out from the cab.

Sandy looked at the old man. So that was his name, the boy thought.

"Mornin', Whit."

The milkman left his truck idling, dimmed his headlights, and scrambled across the muddy lot and under the tarp.

"Mornin', sir."

"Mornin', son," Whit replied. "What're we gon'na do, you reckon, 'bout all this here rain?"

The old man climbed off his bicycle.

"Me 'n the boy here's just talkin' 'bout that."

Whit pulled out a pack of Camels, offered one to the old man, who declined, then lit up and took a long drag.

"Yes'sir, I's glad to see it at first," Whit said, laying out a smooth column of smoke in the heavy moist air. "My tomatoes grew big as grapefruits. Pulled the vines 'bout down to the ground."

"Mmhmm," the old man nodded, looking off toward the road. "Mine too, 'til the damned fungus took a hol't of 'em."

"Same damned thing happen'd to mine. Now it's nothin' but a swamp back there."

"Thas' right," the old man said, lifting up a hand to gesture, almost breaking into a smile, then quieting down again. "Yeah," he said, letting out a sigh. "Nothin' but a damned swamp."

"We don't get a few sunny days here soon," Whit added, "'ever' damned one of 'em's gon' go bad."

The old man nodded.

"Yes, sir," he said, "we need a few sunny days."

Sandy thought of Gabriel. He looked at the truck, wondered whether it was the same one Whit had been driving that morning. He drew a paper from his basket and held it sideways against the headlights.

"Considerable cloudiness, chance of showers," he read off the corner of the page. "Highs in the mid-80s."

"Whew," Whit chimed in. "Gon' be another steamer."

Sandy looked at the headline across five columns on the front.

"Nation Hails Men of Apollo 11." There was a picture of Neil Armstrong waving from atop a convertible, a huge crowd lining the streets of New York, ticker tape streaming down. "Manhattan Motorcade," the caption read.

"Big doin's in New York," Whit said.

"Big doin's my ass," the older man piped up. "Can't do nuthin' 'bout this damned rain."

Sandy smelled the fresh ink off the paper, the sweet scent of Whit's cigarette and the exhaust from the idling truck.

"Look here," Sandy read on, "says the astronauts were feted in three other cities besides — Houston, Chicago and Los Angeles."

"Four cities in one day? How'd they do that?" Whit wanted to know.

"Says here they flew across the country aboard Air Force One," said Sandy, skimming the article. "Had a big parade in Chicago, and a state dinner Nixon hosted in the Century Plaza Hotel in L.A. Nearly fifteen hundred governors, diplomats and congressmen, dined on poached salmon, filet of beef and a dessert named clair de lune — French for light of the moon."

"Ain't that sump'in," said Whit. "Hey son, you got an extra copy today?"

Sandy looked at the old man, saw raindrops gathered on the umbrella cocked sideways atop his handlebars, and handed him back his wire cutters.

"Naw," said Sandy. "I ain't got an extra, not today."

"Aw, c'mon," Whit chided. "It's good for a chocolate milk."

"Wish I could," said Sandy. "But then, there's two of us here."

"Don't drag me into it," the old man said. "I ain' messin' w' no choc-lit milk."

Whit glanced at the old man, then back at the boy.

"Thought you said you didn't have an extra."

"Don't," Sandy affirmed. "But, I might could get my hands on one if the price is right."

Whit cocked his head, looked out at the bundles lying in the rain, then looked back at Sandy.

"Alright then," he said. "Two pints."

Sandy nodded, headed toward the bundles, and the milkman walked back to his truck.

"I told ya', I ain' gettin' involved," the old man said. "I ain' messin' with it, now, I mean it."

F-15, Sandy read to himself, letting Catesby's papers fall back to the ground.

He picked up a bundle from another boy's route.

"He won't be missin' this one," he said, wriggling a paper out of the center. "Here you go," he said, presenting the purloined paper to Whit beneath the vegetable stand.

"Wait a minute," Whit said. "This'un here's torn. I ain't swappin' two pints a milk for a paper's torn."

"Alright, alright," said Sandy. He took a better copy from his own bundle, slipped the damaged one into his basket and took a cold carton of milk from Whit in exchange.

"Here you go Clayton," the milkman said, holding out his chocolate milk.

"Naw," the old man said with a dismissive wave. "Not for me."

He tossed his wire cutters into the old crate.

"Might as well take it," Whit said. "The boy here got it for you."

The old man looked down, raised his cap and scratched his head, folded his arms and looked off toward the road.

"C'mon," Whit urged. "I already done got it down off the truck. I ain' takin' it back."

He set it on the side of the vegetable stand.

Sandy opened his chocolate milk and took a drink, sweet and rich.

"Hell'u'va thing there 'bout Winston Coleman," Whit said.

"Yeah," the old man added. "That it is."

Sandy wanted to say something. He thought about Winston, then Gabriel, but didn't know what to say.

"He was a fine young man," said Whit. "I got to know him over the years."

Sandy remembered what the old man told him, how Winston helped the family after Gabriel was killed. He thought about Whit and Catesby, the morning his bike slid across Ridgetop Road.

"Yeah," the old man said, looking down at his bicycle. "I reckon we all got to know him some."

The engine stuttered, headlights flickered, then the old truck regained its footing.

"Well," said Whit, "I better be gettin'. Thanks for the paper, son."

Sandy stood there, by the old man, and watched the truck's red taillights fade. A long whistle pierced the distance. Sandy pictured a freight train down by the river, wet rails glistening in the grey light of dawn.

"Pete said Winston got the Distinguished Flying Cross," the old man said. "That's a high honor."

"Is that right," said Sandy, leaning over and squeezing the wooden frame of the vegetable stand. "Ain' no ticker tape parade waitin' on him, I don't expect, time his teeth get home."

He yanked at the weathered canvas, felt it give way and rip, as he turned to face the old man.

"How can the President have a celebration, big fancy dinner 'n all, with people like Winston gettin' killed?"

The old man stared off with a look worn and glazed. "The President don't make the world the way it is."

"Then what kind'a world is it, exactly, when a country can launch a rocket into space and can't keep its helicopters safe?"

The old man looked at Sandy but didn't respond.

"Kind a country, can put a man on the moon, but can't save its own men from a crowd of swamp shooters? Kind a people just pretend like it's normal?"

The old man rocked his bike back and forth in the mud.

"You know boy, all the money 'n might in the world can't make right from wrong. We ain' quite figured that out yet. But we learnin'. We learnin' the hard way, maybe, but we leanin' all the same."

Old Blue stirred from across the street. Sandy heard a jingle in his chain.

"They's all kinds of things this country can do," the old man said. "But just be'in able to do a thing don't make it right."

"Seems like I've heard something like that somewhere before."

"Could be."

"Yeah."

Sandy thought back on that morning an eternity ago, felt the muscles in his mouth start to tighten and twist.

"Pete says, it'll be a graveside service," the old man said. "Full military honors."

"Yeah," Sandy said, wiping a damp sleeve across his eyes. "Full military honors."

The fog was lifting. Sandy looked up and saw a lone star in a thin patch of sky.

The old man threw a leg over his bike. He picked up the small carton of milk Whit Wheelan left behind, pressed it to his cheek and closed his eyes. He held it cool and waxy against his face, then breathed in long and deep. He slipped it into his jacket pocket, as gently as a father might tuck a son into bed. Then he pushed his bike across the soggy lot and pedaled off into the mist.

 Chapter 42

Sandy didn't immediately grasp the connection between rock 'n roll and sewing machines. And yet, there it was on the Teale's new Magnavox, special Sunday night programming, "Singer Presents Elvis."

"Look at that color," Daddy Teale crowed. "Feels like you could almost reach out 'n touch him."

Over an earlier dinner of cold ham and hot biscuits, he'd extolled the virtues of automatic tint control, how the new space-age feature all but eliminated green lines and purple faces, with exciting new technology that coincided perfectly with the return of the King of Rock 'n Roll, resurfacing after years of seclusion in the hope of reclaiming his crown.

Sandy wasn't sure how he'd rated an invitation to the Gloucester place, whether the visit was meant to further initiate him into the family fold or to bid him a formal good riddance before Hope left for school. The Teales could draw someone in or cast them out with equal measures of hospitality. A person never quite knew whether they were coming or going.

Either way, the river house was far from the waterside cottage he'd envisioned. A two-story colonial of grey stone and white clapboard, it was well over a hundred years old, built on land that had been in Mama Teale's family since the first wave of Desmonds and Murdochs arrived from Ireland in the early 1800s. Glin, the place had been named from the start, after the castle town the family called home.

"The English crown had a particularly difficult time with the people of Glin," Daddy Teale explained, in one of his favorite riverside dinner tales. "After a rebellious son of the keep was hanged, drawn and quartered by agents loyal to the crown, his mother carried him in pieces through the town and personally delivered him to the family burial plot."

Daddy Teale shot a glance to his wife. "It wasn't only limericks, sonnets and four-leaf clovers, you see, those people brought over with them."

Daddy Teale's own roots, a bit more ambiguous, were seldom discussed. Rather than dwell on his hardscrabble upbringing by a single mother in southside Virginia, he'd embraced his wife's heritage. Over four decades of uneasy marriage, he'd more or less made her story his own, piggy-backing on her pedigree for the credentials that secured him entrance into the College of Richmond law school and the contacts that helped him to launch a fruitful career.

"The people of Glin came as manual laborers, peasants really, one rung up the ladder from slaves," he said. "They joined other Irish immigrants and Africans in digging Washington's canal alongside the river and building Jefferson's capitol overlooking Richmond."

Ensuing generations, though, scratched together the means to buy the family spread and the slaves they depended on to carve farmland out of the forests and tend the broad fields. They built a plantation by the river, Daddy Teale continued, on deep water where tall sailing ships could dock, offloading goods from England or sugar and spices from the Caribbean in exchange for half-ton hogsheads of tobacco.

On the strength of the wealth spun off by that trade, the family built the grand house at Glin, now a weekend retreat for a Richmond lobbyist who leased out a bit of acreage for feed corn and soybeans to keep the place on the tax books as a working farm.

The house had a spacious foyer with high ceilings and wide heart-pine floors. Soon enough, the thought occurred to Sandy, Hope would descend the ornate staircase in a taffeta gown, officially coming out for a society deliberately structured to winnow out the likes of him.

The entrance seemed surprisingly modest to Sandy, until Daddy Teale explained he'd come in the back door. The front of the old house didn't face the road, which wasn't there, after all, when Glin was built. The front faced the serpentine brick wall and terraced lawn falling off to the north shore of the York River, the watery highway long centuries before.

"Somewhere right around here is where Nathaniel Bacon's men buried him," Daddy Teale said on the walking tour of the grounds he'd given when Sandy arrived. "Well, not exactly buried. They filled his coffin with rocks and sank him in the river so the British couldn't find the body. They'd a hanged the corpse if they'd a found it. That's what Virginians did to rebels before they came to appreciate the virtues of rebellion."

Sandy stared out across the wide sunlit river and wiped a thin line of sweat from his brow.

"Just let it sink?"

"Right to the bottom," he responded. "Bones probably still moldering away somewhere out there in the mud and the marl."

Daddy Teale expressed a curious familiarity with historical figures, at times seeming to get along better with the musty forebears of the Old Dominion than with its contemporaries.

"Few miles 'round that bend," he went on, "is where our friends the French helped us trap the British at Yorktown, puttin' an end to King George's dream of British empire in America."

Sandy half expected to hear the phone ring with Lafayette on the other end.

"And just upstream a ways was Chief Powhatan's home."

"I thought he lived near Richmond."

"Was born there, but moved down here. That river was too dangerous."

"Our river?"

"Yeokanta, Powhatan's people called it. Bloodiest river in American history. Indian wars before the settlers arrived. Fights with them once they got here. Slave rebellions. Revolution. Civil War. No sir. Too damned dangerous for Powhatan. He moved his whole operation just upstream, to Werewocomoco, place of the great chief. And, of course, his favorite daughter, Pocohontas," he said, glancing at Hope.

If family pride at Glin knew no apparent bounds, neither, it seemed, did the expanse of hallways and rooms in the great house. It could amply accommodate at least two families and sundry kith and kin. Sandy, however, was assigned less regal quarters, a spare loft atop a run-down tobacco barn out back.

"Best place in the world for a boy," said Daddy Teale, as he led Sandy to his rustic roost. The boy set down his knapsack and unrolled a sleeping bag atop a bed of straw stuffed inside an old corncrib. "Many a night I'd soon sleep out here myself."

Daddy Teale wasn't sleeping there, though, and never had. He also wouldn't risk having this kind of riffraff spend the night in the same house with his teen-aged granddaughter. That much, to Sandy, was clear.

With Hope entering boarding school, though, the old man agreed to let Sandy come, as much a concession to Mama Teale, it seemed, as to Hope. It would be a stretch to suggest that Sandy had won the old woman's heart, but he'd been surprised at the interest she'd shown, or feigned, during the car drive down after church.

"How much longer," she'd asked, "you expect to be delivering newspapers?"

"Actually, I'm giving up my route in a few weeks," he replied, drawing a surprised look from Hope. "Lucky Pete, my district manager, is going off to college. My parents want me to have a little more time for school. And I got a friend says he can get me work as a caddy on weekends."

"At the club?"

Sandy was stumped, thought to improvise, then remembered the crossed golf clubs on the old man's cap.

"Yes ma'am," he replied confidently. "At the club."

"Who's gon'na take over your paper route," Hope asked.

"Got somebody coverin' for me tomorrow," he said. "If that works out, I 'spect they'll be takin' it over for me."

And so, out of good fortune or ill omen, there he sat, just after dark, on the plush crimson couch, a respectable distance from Hope, sharing an evening of Elvis with Daddy Teale.

"We're caught in a trap," the singer crooned. "I can't walk out . . . because I love you too much ba-by."

Where else, but in America, a program host asked at one point, could a man born in a two-room, dirt-floor, shotgun shack in Tupelo, Mississippi go on to become an international sensation?

Setting the story of Elvis aside, the news from the Delta that night wasn't good.

"Hurricane Camille slammed into Mississippi with hundred-and-fifty-mile-per-hour-winds early today," the commentator announced on the late news. "By this afternoon, two hundred thousand people had fled inland to escape tornadoes and torrential rain that turned day into night along the Gulf Coast and sent seas rising twenty feet above high tide."

"That's one whale of a storm," Daddy Teale interjected. "Guess we'll be gettin' the gutter wash next coupl'a days."

There was footage from some place in upstate New York, some kind of music festival on a farm.

"One man has died from drug overdose and two women have given birth during three days of unbridled bacchanalia at the Woodstock Music and Art Fair near Bethel, New York," a television correspondent intoned. "Heavy rains and traffic jams didn't deter crowds estimated at three hundred thousand from turning out to gulp down buckets of soft drinks and beer and to listen to the music of . . ."

"Bunch'a'damn hippies," Daddy Teale exclaimed.

A burst of color flared, then the screen went dark.

"Look a' that," the old man boasted, pointing to Sandy with a small hand-held device. "Turned it off without even havin' to get out'd my seat."

Daddy Teale proudly set the remote control down on a mahogany coffee table and pushed himself up from a heavy wing chair.

"Come on Hope," he said, taking her by the hand. "It's time for bed. Sandy, son, can you find your way out back all right? Think Mama Teale's got a flashlight if you need one."

"Grandaddy," Hope admonished. "He's a paperboy."

"Not for long," the old man shot back. "Well son," he said with an out-reached hand, "see ya' bright 'n early tomorrow."

It wasn't how Sandy had pictured things ending, but there it was, he thought to himself, making his way by the light of a quarter moon across the lawn sweeping away from the big river house and down the dirt path that wandered through a field of high corn.

The air was warm, the sky was clear. He'd never seen it so lit with stars. Following a bend in the path he walked up a slight rise and saw the sharp angular outline of the tobacco barn, framed by the broad boughs of a sturdy beech tree spreading out over the field.

A smooth wooden slat on thick worn ropes hung from a limb of the tree. Sandy grasped the ropes and leaned out over the plank. A barren patch beneath the swing testified to long hours of use, and he pictured a young Hope sailing through the shadows on long ago summer days, hair flying back from her sunburned face.

From the lone window in his upstairs loft, Sandy could see a row of dormer windows faintly lit in the big house. He slipped off his tennis shoes and shorts, stretched and looked once more. A light shone from just one window, white curtains drawn and closed.

Sandy walked across a threadbare rug toward a small lamp on a corner table. He picked up a yellowed paperback from a sagging bookcase and saw a waist-up drawing of a woman, her naked back exposed.

"Unchastened," Sandy read off the cover, "a story of burning desire."

He shrugged and turned out the corner lamp. Making a pillow of his backpack and shorts, he lay down in the corncrib and could see the moon, its silvery light sparkling through the great beech tree.

The room was alive with the low hum of crickets combing the summer corn, the trill of cicadas in the trees, the low and intermittent warble of some kind of swallow in the eaves of the barn.

Sandy stared outside. He imagined his sleeping bag a magic carpet that could transport him at will across the field to the big house, through the dormer window and into waiting arms.

"The moon was a ghostly galleon," he whispered, "tossed upon cloudy seas."

He raised his head and peered out toward the river. Through a break in the tree line he saw moonlight off the water. Bacon's bones, the thought occurred, then sudden sadness and terror. Bones. And teeth. A terrible fire. A mass of metal falling from the sky. He buried his face in his hands, shook his head, lay down and looked up at the Moon.

"The wind was a torrent of darkness, in the dusty trees."

He imagined himself on horseback, riding up to the old Glin door, riding, riding. He breathed in the scent of the ripening corn, the fertile tidewater beyond, closed his eyes and could almost smell her face on the pillow by the curtains, a ribbon of moonlight in her hair . . .

"Come on Sandy," she reached out to him. "Get up, Winston's here."

"What?"

Sandy looked up in the darkness, and rose from a bed of corn.

"John-ee Rivers," he heard him calling, "Get on out here."

"I'm coming," he said, "I'm coming."

"We're going down by the riverside."

"I'm coming."

He heard an old woman playing piano.

"Gon'na lay down my sword and shield."

There was a Bible, a cross, and a long white robe.

The stairs fell away beneath him. He glided out the barn door. A large wooden frame hung on thick ropes from the tree.

"Hope," he called out. "Winston?"

He grabbed onto the ropes, stepped into the frame and felt himself flying into the night . . .

"God help me," Sandy whispered, raising a sweat-soaked head and looking around the room. "God help me." He took a deep breath and looked out the window through bleary and puzzled eyes.

The pattern of stars had shifted. The light in her window was out. Moonlight swept the broad field before him. He heard a rustling in the corn. A small clutch of quail fluttered and flew low over the tops of the stalks. Nearby, along the path, something moved.

Still dreaming, Sandy told himself, as her figure moved into view, tall and sure in the silvery light, soundlessly through the corn. He felt the stairs beneath him this time, the splintered wood against his feet. He stepped outside and there she was, on the swing, holding on to the ropes.

"Nice night," she said, dangling her toes in the dirt.

Her brother's old cotton shirt fit her like a robe. The image of the woman on the tattered book cover flashed through Sandy's mind, as he walked up and laid his hands on her shoulders. "I would be worried about Daddy Teale," he said, "but I know this is only a dream."

"Oh, the threat of Daddy Teale's real enough all right. But let's don't worry 'bout that right now."

Hope stretched her legs out from beneath the long shirttail and pointed her dusty toes. Sandy took the ropes in his hands and clumsily pulled back the swing.

"Not like that," she laughed. "You want me to fall out?"

She took his hands in hers and lowered them to her waist.

"There," she said. "Right there."

Sandy drew her back slowly, then let her go.

"Look, I can almost touch the leaves."

Sandy watched her sail through the darkness, her head slung back, hair blowing free, the gentle creaking of ropes and wood.

"I can't remember a time without this old swing," she sang out. "I've seen pictures of daddy holding me in it just a few weeks after I was born."

Sandy pushed against the base of her hips.

"In the wintertime, when the trees go bare, you can see the water from here. I used to pretend I was sailing a big ship, down the river and out to sea."

Sandy watched the shirt flutter against her back, caught her in his hands and shoved.

"They cut the corn in October, and this field is jet black with crows."

"Caw," Sandy called out softly. "Caw, caw!"

"Pathetic. Sounds more like a cat. A cat's been run over by a truck."

There was a long, low sound from across the field.

"Horned owl," said Hope.

"Shh. Don't scare it away."

"You crazy boy," Hope said. "That thing can hear a mouse beneath snow a quarter mile away. It hears every breath you take."

"Oh really? Think he can hear this?"

Sandy leaned over and blew softly in her ear as Hope sailed quickly past.

"Hmm. Not sure about that."

"What about this one?"

"I really couldn't say," she replied, dragging her toes through the dirt. "Try again?"

He caught the swing from behind, reached his arms around her waist, shuffled his feet through the dirt as he slowed her, put his head against her shoulder and whispered.

"Do you think Mr. Horned-and-ever-hearing Owl hears this?"

Hope let go of the ropes, pulled his arms around her and leaned back against his chest.

"I know for certain he hears this," she said, feeling his heartbeat against her cheek. "Come here, I want to show you something."

She led him around the side of the tree, and knelt in the cool of the grass.

"Just lie here," she said, as Sandy stretched out at her side.

In the still air beneath the tree he could smell the breath of the leaves, heavy with the rich, green fullness of summer. He heard some insect's mad scraping against the emptiness of night and gazed into a strangely pulsing dance of light, an open box of shimmering jewels from the far side of eternity.

"They look like tiny planets," Sandy said. "Adrift and lost in the trees."

"Shh," Hope put a finger to his lips. "They're trying to tell us something."

"Let's see now. Somewhere very near this spot, there's a place where magical fairies dance. They're called . . . fireflies."

Sandy looked at her and smiled, her face like cream in the moonlight, her voice a whispering seance reaching out to some long slumbering place in his soul.

"The beating hearts of summer. That's what Daddy calls them. He says they light the way to our dreams."

She laid down in the grass beside him and lowered her face to his chest. He pulled her close and gazed into the sky.

"Is this our dream?"

"Of course it is. Daddy's always right. Well, least when it comes to dreams."

"What else does he say about dreams?"

"Well, pretty much what everybody knows."

She pulled herself up on one elbow and turned her face toward his.

"Some say dreams are really life, and this," she motioned with one hand, "is the real dream."

She lay her head back down and ran a finger along his chest.

"He told me a story about it once."

"Your father?"

"Mmhmm. Wanna hear it?"

"Sure."

"Okay then," she said, patting down the front of her shirt. "Long ago in China, there lived a very wise old man. His name was Master Cheng. He was a great philosopher. And, one night, he dreamed he was a butterfly, with gold and crimson wings."

She swept the air with her hand.

"He fluttered among the lilies, growing white by the edge of the pond, then rose high above his village, looking down on the rice fields below. He floated up into the mountains and cooled himself by a stream, then glided back down on the afternoon breeze and fell asleep in a mulberry tree."

Sandy stared into the darkness and felt the grass against his legs.

"Time the butterfly woke up, night had fallen. There was a moon, that very one, in the sky. And he flew to his own windowsill, where he watched himself in his bed."

Sandy looked at Hope and felt as safe as a child.

"When the sun came up the next morning, the old man woke from his dream, his arms tangled in a faded sheet. All that day, through the long afternoon, he puzzled over what it might mean. 'Am I a man who dreamed I was a butterfly,' he wondered. 'Or am I really a butterfly, dreaming I'm a man?'"

Sandy looked up at the fireflies.

"What did he decide?"

"He spent the rest of his life not knowing for sure."

She traced the side of his cheek with one finger.

"But it didn't really matter what he knew. All that mattered was what he believed."

"And what was that?"

"That, wherever he was, he knew, deep inside, he could fly whenever he pleased. And, for him, because he was a very wise man, just knowing that was enough."

Hope sat up against the tree. Her fingers roamed its weathered skin, the lines on the face of the bark.

"Sounds like a very wise man, indeed. Your dad, I mean."

Hope tilted her head and brushed her hair from her face. Sandy leaned up to take hold of her hands.

"I love you, Hope. For always."

She leaned into him and pressed a finger to his lips.

"For always," she replied.

They lingered in each other's arms, not speaking, not thinking, perfectly alone.

"I'm not going to boarding school," she whispered, her head weightless against his chest. "I'm going to stay in Richmond, move in with Mama Teale."

"When did you decide all this?"

"I didn't. The fireflies told me."

He held her closer, felt her run a hand along his neck and up the back of his head, until they fell back into a single moment swallowed up by the grass.

How long it lasted, he couldn't guess. He saw the Moon hanging low in the sky. He felt the length of her body against him, wondered if she'd fallen asleep, then lay there listening to her breathe. He imagined the world and all he knew before had faded away into the nothingness of the night.

"Hope?"

"Mhmm."

"Do you think I'm a boy in love with the most wonderful girl in the world, or am I really a butterfly, dreaming I'm a boy in love with the most wonderful girl in the world?"

He felt her smile against his neck, pulled her close and looked up at the leaves. Moonlight fell like a string of pearls across the glistening skirt of her throat.

"Sandy, I've got to get back."

He held her hand as they walked through the field, over the rise to the rim of the lawn.

"Okay," she whispered. "Thanks for the great swing."

"Drop by my tobacco shed anytime."

Hope smiled, kissed him quickly then turned and ran toward the house.

He watched her open the screen door, never heard it close, and remembered the wide staircase. He thought he saw a shadow drift past her window, though he couldn't tell for sure.

He walked back toward the barn, imagining her curled up beneath her bedspread, yellow bits of dried grass in her hair. He wondered whether she'd lie awake and remember, or fall asleep, and dream.

As he crested the rise he saw them twinkling in the trees, tiny green flares in the darkness, wandering the formless landscape of night at the far edge of the field.

# Chapter 43

Sandy smelled bacon and coffee as he walked barefoot across the sun-lit lawn and knocked on the kitchen door. In the driveway sat Mama Teale's Chevrolet, gleaming like freshly brushed teeth. Daddy Teale's aging Buick was gone.

"Come on in, gotch'a hot breakfast waitin'."

"Mm, mmm, that smells good," Sandy said, taking a seat at the kitchen table. "How'd you sleep Mrs. Teale?"

"Right well, thank you, Sandy, and yourself?"

"Like a bug in a corn crib."

Mama Teale let out a laugh.

"Hope's brothers always liked it out there," she said. "Used to call it the Tobacco Suite."

"I could still smell it," said Sandy. "How long since any was there?"

"Ages, I guess. But it gets in the wood."

"Smelled good to me. Like a kind of sweetness in the forest."

Mama Teale wiped her hands on her apron, and set a plate of bacon and pancakes in front of Sandy.

"Boy," he said, pouring himself a glass of milk. "This looks great."

"Well, I hope you like it."

Sandy glanced up from buttering his pancakes, toward the door to the living room.

"Have some hot maple syrup," Mrs. Teale said, pouring from a small copper pot.

Sandy watched the butter melt and listened for sounds overhead.

"Guess Hope's catchin' up on her sleep."

Mrs. Teale slipped off her apron, draped it over the side of a chair, sat down and looked him in the face. "Sandy," she said. "Hope's gone."

He felt a knot in his stomach, put his fork down and looked at her.

"She 'n her granddad left early this morning, got breakfast 'long the way, wanted to check in before lunch at All Saints, get her moved into her dorm 'n all."

Sandy looked out the back window, toward the open field and the barn. "But I thought . . ."

"She left this for you."

She handed him a small box wrapped in faded newsprint, a white envelope attached. Sandy pulled out a plain parchment card.

"My Dearest Sandy," he read to himself. "I've been up all night, unable to sleep. Or maybe I'm lost in a dream. I only know that if I had the wings of a butterfly, I'd sail from this room to you. Wherever I might find you. Wherever you might be. Please know, wherever I am, my heart stays with you, for always. Hope."

Sandy folded the card and set it down on the table. He looked off as if in a daze.

He turned toward the little box, picked it up and gave it a shake. He read the words on the newspaper wrapping, something about a small step for man. He slowly tugged at the paper, wondering what might be inside. It fell out hard and heavy in his hand, like a rock wrapped in thin white tissue.

"I found this that morning, after the moon walk, by the little creek along-side the bamboo," he read on the note she attached. "It must have washed up from the ground in the storm. I called out to tell you, but you'd already gone. So I saved it for you. I hope it reminds you of being with me."

It was an old pocketknife, rusted in places, with a brown and cream-colored handle, made from the antlers of deer. Sandy tried to open it, then noticed three small letters engraved in the grip.

"I'm sorry Sandy," Mama Teale said. "I told her to wait and tell you goodbye herself, but her grandfather thought this was best."

Sandy wasn't listening. He was lost beside a shaded stream, where a fright-ened child left something behind on a long ago evening by a place called Skinquarter. He clutched the pocketknife, held it up to the morning sunlight and read the three small letters once more.

# Chapter 44

The first Tuesday in September, by the warm spread of dawn, Sandy eased on his brakes at the first house on the left at Tempest Lane. He read the name on the mailbox, Hollis T. Smith, slipped a small box from his pocket and tucked it in with a copy of that morning's Richmond Times-Daily.

"Clifford," he called out, as he began rolling again, "you guys get the next two boxes on the left, skip the third, then hit the fourth."

"Listen up, Jenks," the boy hollered to his brother, "this is the last time we'll have him out here to show us."

"That's right," Sandy called back. "Startin' tomorrow, the route's all yours."

A few months shy of their eleventh birthday, the Marable twins weren't quite old enough to have a route of their own. Just before leaving for college, though, Lucky Pete found a way around that. "I think your nephews can handle it, since it's the two of them," he'd told their old "Uncle" Clayton. "Long as, technically at least, the route's in your name."

"I'll look aft'a 'em," the old man had promised, "and help 'em out on the heavy days."

Sandy stopped to hand off more papers to the boys, and saw the headline across the front page. "State Begins Slow Climb Back from Camille," he read to himself. "Recovery to Take Years, Governor Says."

It was no gutter wash that blew in on the back of Hurricane Camille, but torrential rains that wrought floodwaters of Biblical proportions the full length of the great, muddy river. It overflowed its banks through the heart of Virginia in one of the deadliest natural disasters in the state's history. By the end of August, more than a hundred deaths had been accounted for in a single mountain county alone, with officials certain the grim toll would rise as the water continued to recede.

Could it possibly have had anything to do with Armstrong's walk on the Moon? What if, Sandy wondered, the old man was right? Maybe, he found himself thinking, we had no business putting a man on the Moon after all.

"Wha'da we do here?" Jenks called out, straddling his bike in front of the box at a small Cape Cod with amber pebbles in the drive.

"Make sure this one gets a good paper," Sandy said. "Nice lady. Got a baby on the way."

There were further directives, some inside tips, and, by the time the three of them came to the end of the road, Sandy had little doubt the boys he'd first seen beside the casket of their cousin Mose would take good care of F-45.

"Okay guys, which one of you's gon'na be the treasurer?"

Jenks and Clifford looked at each other.

"Well," said Jenks, "he's always been better at math."

"You'll have to get good too," said Sandy. "You're a paperboy now."

He reached into his basket and pulled out his tattered canvas-covered collection book. He looked at it for a moment, thumbed its ink-stained pages, and then handed it over to Jenks.

"Here you go, Clifford," said Sandy, putting his rusted pair of wire clippers in the younger boy's hand. "Good luck. Now head on home and get ready for school."

He watched them disappear down the narrow path that led to Midsummer Night's Lane. He could still hear their excited chatter as they made their way past the bamboo grove, the little church graveyard, Gabriel, Winston and Mose.

There was one paper left in his basket. Sandy picked it up and caught a headline in bold black type just above the fold. "North Vietnamese President Ho Chi Minh," it read, "Dead at 79."

He glanced up to the door at old man Sullivan's place, half expected to see him come out one last time, in a sleeveless undershirt, to say thanks, maybe, or to wish him well.

There was a sound like a distant whisper from the honeysuckle swamp. Sandy turned and gazed past the thicket's edge to the sagging fence. Ensnared by the vines and foliage of another summer gone by, it looked oddly permanent there, as if it had somehow grown out of the earth, forever wedded to the land.

In the soft light Sandy caught the slow moving flight of a great blue heron, gliding on outstretched wings toward the old cypress tree, the hanging tree, he'd been told as a boy, where it took up a silent perch. Mirrored in the swamp's smooth surface, a single star shimmered above. Sandy looked up and saw the rose-tinted edge of a long grey cloud like a quilt with a hem of fire.

"It must always be morning in heaven," he said to himself. He stared at the regal bird, the unearthly grace of its elegant neck, the holy miracle of winged flight. "Are we in heaven?"

Maybe so, the thought slipped through his mind. Maybe the heron is young Martin, come back to fly, and this place his eternity, somewhere he can share his dreams with the fireflies in summer, watch the leaves change color each fall and huddle by winter in the bosom of an ancient cypress tree, looking out on the moon-swept snow. Maybe he found the crossing place after all. Maybe it was there all along.

Sandy turned to the rusting mailbox, leaning over a sagging post. He held his paper and narrowed his eyes. Silken threads spanned the open mouth of the box and fell like drapes to the wooden post. Backlit by a single, splendid shaft of dawn, dewdrops clung like diamonds onto silver filaments spreading out like the wintry breath of a child. Sandy swiped his paper through the stillness of morning and watched the web faintly sway in the air.

He slapped the spine of the Times-Daily against his basket, rolled it into a thin, taut tube, aimed it toward the cobweb-shrouded box, and then stopped. A spider, thin and brown, was working its way up the post. It seemed to tiptoe over the threads of the web on spindly legs, a daybreak ballerina across a gossamer stage.

"So you're the resident prima donna," Sandy mused, wondering at the fragile beauty she'd spun. "Pretty good architect, too. But why'd you spin it out here in the open where everyone can see?"

The spider vanished into what seemed to Sandy like a warm and salty fog. He wiped his eyes on his tee shirt, took a breath and shook his head. He leaned closer, cleared his vision and watched the spider fall from the web, trailing a single almost invisible strand that left it suspended above the ground.

"You're just dangling out there, aren't you," Sandy said, "somewhere between fear and faith."

He sat up straight, reached for the sky to stretch his back and saw a wall of cloud lit red. Long shadows spread from a row of pines. Sunlight fell warm on his face. He drew in the scent of honeysuckle, struck off across the damp lawn, tossed the Times-Daily between two wrought iron rails and watched it fall open on Sullivan's porch. Then he rose up on his pedals and crested the rise at the end of Tempest Lane.

 # Epilogue

When, Rivers wondered, had they gotten around to paving Midsummer Night's Lane? "In all this rain," he said to himself, "thank goodness someone did."

Through his windshield wipers the building came into view, fresh white paint on clapboard siding with a proud new steeple on a glistening tin roof atop the Skinquarter A.M.E. Church of God.

All the parking spaces were taken, mostly with late-model cars. Sandy edged his aging station wagon to the side of the road, got out in the rain and walked.

The benediction had been delivered, the final strains of the last hymn played out, as Sandy opened the door in the back to see people rising from their pews. Soft lights glowed from the ceiling. There was an electronic organ where the piano once sat. A large window opened up on the cemetery out back and a young preacher stood at an altar of polished oak.

Beneath him, face up in an open casket, lay the gaunt body of the white-haired old man.

Sandy scanned the crowded sanctuary. Curious faces turned toward him.

"Can we help you, my brother?" the preacher asked. "We're concluding funeral services here."

"I . . .," Rivers started, "I'm sorry to be late. I just learned . . ."

The preacher stared at him. "This is a house of worship, sir. These families are bereaved."

This was a mistake, Rivers thought to himself. What am I doing here?

"I didn't mean to interrupt," he stammered. "I'm sorry."

He turned to leave.

"Wait."

It was a fine-boned man in a charcoal grey suit, a Bible in his hand. A pallbearer, Rivers reasoned. Close family friend, perhaps. "Wait," he repeated. "I know this man. He was a friend of Clayton's. You worked with him at one time, I believe."

"Yes," Rivers replied, looking deep into the man's face. "Yes, Mr. Jeter, I did."

"Please," Jimmy Jeter responded, gesturing with an upturned palm toward the coffin. "Come join us. You are welcome here today."

Rivers stared at the outstretched hand as he walked down the aisle, drifting through a hushed sea of faces toward the casket. He stepped to the edge of the coffin and gazed into the wizened face.

"There you are," Rivers whispered, touching the curve of the old man's brow. "Hello there, old friend." He looked up beyond the altar, to a small, dark cross on the wall. He turned and faced the sanctuary.

"Is there," the puzzled preacher asked, "something you'd like to say?"

Yes, there was, Rivers felt, but what? He hadn't imagined it might unfold this way. He looked up at Jimmy Jeter, who nodded at the preacher.

"Please," the pastor said, looking out at the people standing in the pews and motioning to them with both hands, "be seated."

Rivers took a deep breath. Distant images rushed past, as if breaking through a cloud.

"Long ago, not far from here, I met Henry Clayton Woods," he began. "I never called him that before today. I never even knew his name. To me, he was just, the bicycle man."

He heard the din of muffled whispering, the uncertain sound of his voice. His throat was dry; his hands trembled. He searched for the words to press on.

"We met by a road on a dark night, I suppose. I'm not sure how to explain it."

He looked beyond the congregation and felt, for a moment, he could almost see the old man, standing in the back beside Winston that morning long ago.

"I guess, sometimes, there's nothing we need more than to know somebody, somewhere, believes in us. Maybe, sometimes, that's all we need. I want to thank this man for believing in me, and for having the grace to stand by me until, somehow, I came to believe it myself."

He pressed his hands against his face, closed his eyes and breathed in air suddenly rich with the scent of ink and paper, summer vegetables in the dust, of smoke and glowing embers, wet canvas in the rain.

"Someone once told me that heaven isn't a place we go to, so much as a journey we share. We take our first steps right here on Earth, and we spend eternity traveling the course we lay down."

He looked to the first row of pews and saw a middle-aged woman gently smiling at him.

"Maybe there's nothing to it. But, if there is, then I know Henry Clayton Woods, the bicycle man, is sailing through his own eternity right now, gliding without effort or struggle or pain, high above this haunted landscape, beyond our broken promises, beyond our buried dreams, beyond the wars and aching wounds we grieve within our souls. Gliding along a smooth and gently sloping road, into a green and sunlit valley by clear waters with no end."

"Tha's right," someone said softly.

"Mmhmm," another affirmed.

"And I believe he's going in his own special way," Rivers smiled. "On a creaking old bicycle held together somehow with rusty wire, a little tape and all the wonder and love one heart can hold."

Rain fell softly on the tin roof above. Heads nodded. People smiled.

"That's his heaven," Rivers said. "That's his eternity. That's what I believe."

Rivers dropped his hands to his sides and lowered his face toward the floor. He pictured himself turning to kiss the old man's forehead, but stood looking down instead.

"Amen," the preacher let out. "Thank you, brother, for those heartfelt words of affirmation and faith."

Rivers looked back at the pastor and nodded.

"At the family's request, we'll gather for burial out back in about . . . well, as soon as the Good Lord sees fit to lift this doggone rain!"

There was the easy laughter of welcomed relief. People rose and stretched. Rivers shook a few hands and made his way to his car.

Where the parking lot ended, at the edge of the road, he stopped and looked past the small graveyard. His eyes searched the once familiar terrain, but the path to Tempest Lane was gone, consumed by scrub pine and ragweed run wild. A new house stood where the forest once opened onto the road. A wooden fence backed up to bamboo.

He thought of the path as he drove all the way back to the newspaper building downtown. There was a stack of blank expense reports waiting for him upstairs, and a green desk mate to be mentored. Through the tall glass before him he watched the giant presses spin. Thick spools of newsprint rushed past. He shut off his engine and stared straight ahead through his windshield and into the rain.

# Author Q&A

Editors Note:
John Burbage, publisher of Evening Post Books, sat down to discuss The Bicycle Man with author Bob Deans. Their relationship reaches back four decades, when Burbage was metro editor for The Evening Post newspaper in Charleston, and Deans was a cub reporter there. Excerpts from their conversation follow.

Burbage: What, in a nutshell, is The Bicycle Man all about?
Deans: It's a story about promise and friendship and heartache and reckoning, both in the life of a boy and the life of the nation. One kind of mirrors the other. It's set on the outskirts of Richmond, Virginia. It begins in April, 1968, on the day the Rev. Dr. Martin Luther King Jr., was assassinated in Memphis. It ends in September, 1969, the day Ho Chi Minh died in Hanoi.

Burbage: Interesting bookends.
Deans: Those sixteen months are among the most momentous in American history. King's assassination sparked massive riots. Then Bobby Kennedy was assassinated. Richard Nixon was elected president. We put a man on the moon. Woodstock.
And, of course, we had half a million Americans fighting in Vietnam, where 1,400 GIs were being killed every month. We were losing, every three months, about as many troops as we've lost in 17 years in Iraq. That war touched everyone. It changed the country.

Burbage: Why did you write this book?
Deans: I wrote an essay in 1999, recalling what it was like to be riding a bicycle with a broken spoke and delivering papers with that epic headline, "Man Walks on Moon," three decades before. And it occurred to me there was a rich story to be told there, about boyhood in a simpler time, but also about the country itself, and that chapter in our national journey, which was, obviously, anything but simple.

Burbage: Who is Sandy Rivers, the main character?

Deans: Sandy is a paperboy. Thirteen years old when the story begins, he's very proud to have his first real job. He's thrilled to be entrusted with a paper route. And, while he doesn't really see it, delivering his papers each morning becomes a kind of hero's journey that takes him into the troubled heart of a country that's torn by social and political ferment.

All of this touches Sandy, through the papers he delivers and through snippets of conversation with others. And so he becomes, in the story, a kind of metaphor for a country going through its own adolescent struggles with a troubled past, blind spots and a kind of misplaced belief in its own might, political infallibility and delusions of righteous omnipotence.

We now know where, by the early 1970's, that all led. At the time, though, we're trying to figure it out, as a nation, without a script. So, too, very much, for Sandy.

Burbage: Who is the Bicycle Man, the title character?

Deans: Sandy has no idea at first, and neither does the reader. He's an older man who appears one morning in darkness on a bicycle he's pieced together from spare parts and makeshift components. He's resourceful and uses his imagination to make ends meet.

Without giving it away, he shocks Sandy by treating him very differently from what Sandy fears and even feels he deserves. That causes a shift in how Sandy might otherwise have experienced the man. It opens the door to a connection neither one of them expects.

That sets the table for the older man, over time, to offer Sandy a unique perspective. It's not always wise. It's not always welcome. But it challenges the boy and he grows from that.

Burbage: Where does the Bicycle Man come from?

Deans: He has a kind of elder status in Skinquarter, an African American community separated from Sandy's paper route by a thin forest of bamboo, intentionally planted, we learn early on, for that specific purpose. It's an artificial barrier meant to keep two worlds apart and unfamiliar with each other.

That separation, and the ignorance and misunderstanding it perpetuates, breaks down in the face of authentic human connection. That's really the only way it breaks down - then or now.

That's the story, really. It's about unexpected connections that can bend the arc of our lives and shape our very identity, the story we tell ourselves about who we are, what we do and why we matter.

Burbage: Tell us about Hope.
Deans: Hope is a girl Sandy meets at cotillion, on a night when things really don't go quite as planned - for anyone, really. They inhabit different worlds that somehow keep intersecting. When they do, Sandy finds himself way over his head.

Hope has two older brothers and she's a little bit tougher, as a person, than Sandy. A little bit more worldly. A little sharper edged. She knows things - about the river, the fields, the ways of animals - and she has her feet beneath her in a way that makes Sandy feel perpetually off balance. He tries hard to keep up with her, but she's ever a couple steps ahead of him. He's pretty much completely lost.

Burbage: The book includes several Sunday sermons and a pair of eulogies. Why?
Deans: The story is set in the South.

Burbage: No, seriously.
Deans: So much of our culture is grounded in the Bible, from stories we're told as children about the life of Jesus, to epic sagas rooted in Revelations. And a huge part of our national story is narrated from the pulpit. It's a literature of faith.

Those sermons we listen to, those eulogies we hear, are formative. They're foundational. They help to forge many of our deepest beliefs about where we come from, what's expected of us and how we fit into the larger world, the larger cosmos.

Remember, in 1968, the United States was pitted in what many viewed as an existential Cold War conflict with the Soviet Union - Godless Communists with nuclear arms. That played itself out in the space race and, oftentimes, in church.

Burbage: How does all that impact Sandy?
Deans: There are two preachers, black and white, who feature prominently in the book. Sandy takes their words onboard. If not entirely sacred, they're inspired, he believes, by something true and pure. He carries that with him.

He reflects on it. He finds strength in it when he's frightened.

Most of the story takes place outdoors, a lot of it in near darkness informed as much by sound as sight. Sandy's world is full of natural wonder, fleeting beauty and mystery unexplained. That's Biblical. To Sandy, it's holy.

And so, when words he hears from the pulpit, or hymns he sings in the sanctuary, connect with something he's experiencing or trying to figure out, the spiritual becomes substance. It sets his life in a larger context, a kind of moral order. And, it's like radio. There has to be some moral field of force in order for that field to be disturbed in a way that can carry a signal. We can't tune in to what's troubling to Sandy, or understand exactly why, without some glimpse of that order and its origins.

Burbage: The story takes place in the late 1960s, long before cell phones and the internet. And it's clearly a very different time for the country, which, today, seems to be more and more divided, in part by social media.

Deans: The Bicycle Man recalls an era when the daily paper was a kind of cultural totem we all touched each morning. It started us out more or less on the same page. The nightly news put us to bed with a common story. And top-40 radio had us singing, as a nation, from the same sheet of music.

Those were powerful forces for unity. They pulled us together, as a nation. They reminded us how much we shared in common.

In some ways, though, that unity was an illusion. It was a media narrative dominated by white men, some great editors and reporters, no doubt, producing a lot of great journalism.

The problem was that minority groups, African Americans and others, were largely missing from the story. Their voices, their perspectives, were just beginning to be heard, most often in times of conflict and trauma. We weren't as united as it may have appeared. In the story, the cracks are beginning to show.

Burbage: How does that present itself in the book?

Deans: For Sandy, those voices that seldom surface in the pages of his newspaper break through in ordinary places that take on extraordinary meaning. The vacant lot where he picked up his newspapers before dawn. The narrow footpath through a bamboo thicket along a honeysuckle swamp. The old graveyard behind the Skinquarter A.M.E. Church of God. Crossing places, as

Sandy sees them at one point, where chance encounters can bring different worlds together. The Bicycle Man, himself, is the embodiment of all that. Sandy also encounters people who are embracing change, and others who are rejecting it. What he's experiencing, one-to-one you might say, echoes, on a personal level, what was happening across the country and what, in many ways, is happening today.

Burbage: And yet, reading this story, there does seem to be something about trusted sources of news - the morning paper, Walter Cronkite. That feels very different from where we are today, with everybody throwing out opinions, conspiracy theories, invective and even falsehood. Is there something here that's been lost?

Deans: We're at risk, in some ways, of losing the idea of trusted sources of news. We're looking, instead, to reliable sources of agreement, sources that reinforce our world view, rather than inform it in the way that enables our thinking to evolve. That stunts us, as a society. It impedes progress. It's one reason we're so divided as a nation.

Disagreement doesn't have to mean division. In a functioning democracy, people find ways to disagree and still get along, to compromise and make progress, to vest faith, not in an outcome, but in a process, even when we don't get everything we want, because we know we'll get to come back and try again next time.

All that gets poisoned when the only way we know to disagree with someone is to demonize and disparage and delegitimize them. It puts every conversation on contested footing in an all-or-nothing fight. That leaves no room for common ground. And common ground - those interests, aspirations and values we share - is where real unity takes root.

Burbage: What does The Bicycle Man show us about the difference between where we were, just a generation ago, and where we are now?

Deans: It's about accountability. That's basic, and its essential in a democracy. What we see in Sandy's world, right from the start, is an emphasis on accountability. Sandy gets held to account. He experiences forgiveness. He gets a second chance. But he's made to experience shame because he's hurt other people, he's disappointed other people. He sees other paperboys get held to account. Leaders get called out - from the pulpit, no less.

And the newspaper is held to account. Care is taken. Corrections are made. Credibility is the coin of the realm because readers won't tolerate being lied to and the newspaper is a pillar of the community, on par with our independent courts, our elected leaders and lawmakers. That's what it means to be the fourth estate.

Sandy is reminded of all that, not only when he delivers his papers, but when he sneaks off into the pressroom and sees the massive machinery, a city block long, that produces the paper each day. That's capital. That's real. People's jobs are at stake. You don't put all that at risk by reporting falsehood that undermines your authority, misleads readers and opens you up to a libel suit. Sandy feels the weight of that, what he calls the weight of truth, when he hoists a bundle of papers into his basket and when he tosses a paper and watches it land on a porch.

Burbage: What's the lesson for us today?

Deans: That democracy without accountability is farce.

We're living in a moment when some online sites, social media and cable news outlets have blurred the distinction between opinion and fact. With people unsure where to go for the truth, our leaders can traffic in falsehood, distort the real impact of their actions and leave the rest of us in the dark, cowering in our partisan corners.

That won't work. It will break our democracy. In some ways, it's breaking now. Government by the consent of the governed means we, as citizens, must hold our leaders to account - for what they do, or fail to do, on our behalf. Reward them when they do the right thing and make them pay a price when they don't, confident in our ability to know the difference between the two.

That's why we can't separate the quality of our democracy from the quality of the information we take in. In the book, we see Sandy learning that for himself, one story, one conversation, one headline at a time.

Burbage: Is he trying to tell us we were better off before?

Deans: My generation thought the internet would deliver us from falsehood and free our minds in a great open air market where only the best ideas would flourish. Instead, it has destroyed hundreds of newspapers without replacing them with anything remotely comparable to what they once provided.

Papers in small towns and rural America, especially, have been gutted, leaving behind vast news deserts where people struggle to find out what's going on in their own communities. I think Sandy's telling us we haven't begun to grasp, as a nation, the magnitude of what we're losing.

Burbage: How do we turn it around?

Deans: We have to be more discerning as consumers of news. Support news sources that tell us the truth, and stop squandering our civic inheritance on those that don't.

I'm optimistic we'll get this right. What gives me hope is the great journalism that's being published, in print and online, by national papers like The New York Times, The Washington Post and a few others, as well as committed local papers, like The Post & Courier in Charleston and The Times-Dispatch in Richmond.

The printing press had five good centuries. The internet's, what, thirty years old? There's time to fix this. But we can't afford to keep losing ground.

Burbage: What do you hope readers will take away from this story?

Deans: Fiction gives us all the chance to participate in a part of the human experience we might otherwise miss.

I hope younger readers, who know of this period from their history books, will experience it through the eyes of someone going through the same growing pains every teenager knows firsthand.

And I hope readers of my generation, those who grew up in the '60s, the '70s, will reflect back on the ways this period played itself out in our own lives and how it shaped the people, and the nation, we've become.

Burbage: What did you take away from writing this book?

Deans: It had me asking questions about how I processed the events of that period. How did those events influence me? What lessons did I take from them at the time? What mistakes did I make? What did I do that might have hurt someone else? How might I do things differently, if only in my heart, the second time around?

Burbage: What was your biggest surprise, in writing the story?

Deans: I thought I was writing about community. I assumed the characters would get along with each other. That's not always how it turned out.